P9-CEI-666

FOLLY COVE

HOLLY ROBINSON

BERKLEY
NEW YORK

BERKLEY
An imprint of Penguin Random House LLC
375 Hudson Street, New York, New York 10014

Copyright © 2016 by Holly Robinson
Readers Guide copyright © 2016 by Penguin Random House LLC

The author acknowledges permission to use the following: "The Quarry at Folly Cove" by
Emily Ferrara

BERKLEY is a registered trademark and the B colophon is a trademark of
Penguin Random House LLC.

Library of Congress Cataloging-in-Publication Data

Names: Robinson, Holly, 1955– author.
Title: Folly Cove / Holly Robinson.
Description: Berkley trade paperback edition. | New York: Berkley Books, 2016.
Identifiers: LCCN 2016018826 (print) | LCCN 2016026354 (ebook) | ISBN
9781101991534 (paperback) | ISBN 9781101991541 (ebook)
Subjects: LCSH: Domestic fiction. | BISAC: FICTION / Contemporary Women. |
FICTION / Family Life. | FICTION / Coming of Age.
Classification: LCC PS3618.O3258 F65 2016 (print) | LCC PS3618.O3258 (ebook)
| DDC 813/.6—dc23
LC record available at https://lccn.loc.gov/2016018826

First Edition: October 2016

Printed in the United States of America
1   3   5   7   9   10   8   6   4   2

Cover art: Photo of woman on beach by Joseph Devenney / Getty Images; photo of woman
on horse by Jo Bradford / Green Island Art Studios / Moment Select / Getty Images
Cover design by Rita Frangie

For Tracy,
whose heart, courage, and intelligence always shine bright.

And for Dan and my children:
You are the reason my heart is so full of love.

THE QUARRY AT FOLLY COVE

A deep spring slakes the quarry in me.
Gulls preen in calm resolve. My cries
haunt the brindled ledges of lacquered
weeping. Time succumbs sumac and seep.

I navigate by what is seen: fog cowering
in the Twin Lights of Thacher Island.
Fields of feldspar and mica, the folly of sky.

How to trust what is not trustworthy,
the imperfect armament of hindsight,
the archipelago, the arc of unknowing.
It is braver to navigate by surrender here.

Braver still to stand on the promontory,
listening. For unseen shoals at high tide.
The wreckage and the sheer. To hear
the quarry speak: Repeat after me. *After me.*

BY EMILY FERRARA,
AUTHOR OF *THE ALCHEMY OF GRIEF*

FOLLY COVE

CHAPTER ONE

Anne shivered as the taxi's red taillights winked down the gravel drive. Her feet refused to move. The baby, motionless in her arms, seemed stunned by the sudden cold of a New England night.

Now that she was here, she wanted nothing more than to escape again.

Everything looked the same as it had when she'd last visited two years ago. Her father's great-grandparents had built the Folly Cove Inn as a grand resort for wealthy Bostonians, erecting it on a rocky point above a small, horseshoe-shaped beach. The inn had fifty-two rooms, with a wraparound porch between its turreted towers.

Anne couldn't see the water from where she stood, but she smelled the Atlantic's sharp brine. How odd that this was the same ocean she'd seen below the deck of her house in Puerto Rico only yesterday.

To banish the mental images of Colin in their bed and of Luquillo Beach, with its soft white sand and turquoise water, she pictured the opposite side of the inn: a broad porch with a pale blue ceiling and a row of white rocking chairs. Sitting on that porch as a child used to make her feel as though she were gazing straight across the ocean to Europe.

Finally she was too cold to stand outside any longer. She slid Lucy into the backpack and pulled the blanket up around her. Now the baby was barely visible. Anne was rewarded with a drooling smile.

Anne grinned back and kissed her daughter's warm cheek. She hoped Laura wouldn't be here. She couldn't handle the idea of facing her eldest sister. Not tonight. Maybe not ever again.

A bellhop in a navy blazer and red plaid tie hurried outside to help her as she reached the front door, dragging her suitcases and the car seat behind her. "Sorry to keep you waiting, ma'am," he said. "Big wedding party tonight—all hands on deck." He was a young guy with jug ears and acne scars. Not anyone she recognized, thank God. His name tag read TOMMY.

"No worries," Anne said.

She tipped him for helping her carry the luggage into the reception area and was about to approach the front desk when her mother rounded the corner. Sarah was deep in conversation with Betty, who had managed the housekeeping staff forever.

Tonight her mother was dressed in tan slacks and a black wool blazer. The outfit was accented by an antique silver brooch set with rubies. Sarah had inherited the Bradford family jewels and was never shy about wearing them.

Anne crossed her arms over the stains on her sweatshirt. She deliberately didn't look down at her feet, still in sandals. She couldn't remember the last time she'd had a pedicure. There wasn't much point when you spent hours a day on a surfboard.

Betty was leaving now, taking notes on a clipboard. She either hadn't noticed Anne or hadn't recognized her. No surprise—the last time they'd seen each other, Anne was wearing a cocktail gown.

The DJ in the ballroom was playing a Van Morrison song, "Have I Told You Lately." Anne remembered dancing with Colin to this song in a San Juan hotel and had to swallow hard to speak. "Hey, Mom. I'm here."

Her mother frowned and checked her watch. "You're later than I'd thought. Was the flight delayed?" Her tone was polite yet cool; she might have been addressing a guest. Sarah hated public displays of emotion.

Anne instinctively adopted the same measured tone. "No. But I had to wait nearly an hour for the train at North Station."

Her mother bristled. "I'm sorry you were forced to rely on public transportation. I was sure you'd ask a friend to give you a ride."

Anne thought of Hattie, her best friend from high school. She would have been more confident about the whole trip if Hattie had been able to greet her at the airport. Unfortunately, Hattie had left Boston yesterday for her sister's wedding in Colorado.

She had never been an anxious traveler, but Anne was terrified during the flight from Puerto Rico. Since becoming a mother, she'd felt as if every dangerous thing in the world was aimed straight at her baby: speeding cars, stinging insects, viruses, terrorists, the sun's toxic rays. As they'd landed at Logan International Airport, she'd been convinced the plane would continue taxiing into the glittering sea.

"Hattie's out of town this week," Anne said.

"Laura couldn't pick you up?"

"I didn't ask Laura."

Her mother sighed. "I hope you two have gotten over whatever you were fighting about."

"We're fine," Anne lied. "Laura's so busy. I didn't want to bother her."

"I see. Well, I would have driven to Boston myself, but you know what it's like around here on weekends. It would have been much more convenient if you'd arrived during the week."

This was one reason why Anne had moved away in the first place: the inn always came first. There had never been much room in Sarah's life for anything else. Certainly not after her father disappeared.

"Mom, it's fine. I made it here."

"And I couldn't be more delighted!" Sarah cocked her head, openly appraising Anne.

This, too, was a reminder: their mother had been appraising Anne and her sisters every day of their lives, making sure they were well turned out and behaving. She liked to remind them that they were Folly Cove's "ambassadors" and that the Bradford family name could be traced back to William Bradford, who'd helped found the original Plymouth Colony of Massachusetts.

"Is that a tattoo?" her mother asked now. Her tone was conversational, but her eyes were narrowed.

Anne touched the outline of the small bird, a Puerto Rican night-jar, on her wrist, then pulled down her sleeve to cover it. "Yes."

"I see. Well, that will certainly give people in the nursing home something to gossip about when you're my age."

Anne was about to say that her tattoo wasn't any of her mother's business, but then the doors to the grand ballroom swung open behind Sarah. Three couples emerged. The men wore tuxes and were arguing about the Patriots. Behind them, the women walked with heads held high on slim necks, their bridesmaids' dresses frothing around their legs like sugary peach concoctions.

Her mother waited until the couples disappeared up the wide car-peted staircase with its oak railing, then said, "Your skin looks divine, Anne. Puerto Rico's climate must agree with you. And I'm sure we can schedule a haircut for you next week. David often has openings on Tuesdays. Would that suit your schedule?"

"Sure. Whatever." Anne's shoulders were beginning to ache with the weight of the backpack and the tension of wondering when her mother would spot what was in it.

Sarah smiled. "Well, let's not stand here. You must be exhausted. I'm sure you'll want to bathe and change before dinner. I'll ask Tommy to help carry your things to my apartment. How does that sound?"

"Fine."

"Good." Sarah finally crossed the wide, deep green ocean of the Oriental carpet separating them in the reception area to kiss Anne's cheek. Her eyes widened when she saw the backpack over Anne's shoulder. "Goodness. Is that a *baby* in there?"

Anne had to laugh. "Yes."

Sarah pressed her lips into a thin line, then said, "Is it yours?"

"*She.* And yes. Her name is Lucy."

"Well, at least you didn't choose one of those awful modern names. Where is Lucy's father?" Her mother's gaze flicked about the reception area, as if Anne might have hidden a man behind one of the brocade Victorian sofas.

"New York City."

"Will he be joining you?"

"No. Things didn't work out. That's one reason I'm here."

Sarah let her eyes drop to Anne's left ring finger. "And you never married him, I assume."

"No." Anne waited for the inevitable "I told you so." She didn't have to wait long.

"I see." Sarah sighed heavily. "So this is what came of your grand adventure in the tropics: a baby and no husband. My God. How could you let yourself get into this mess?" Her mother clasped her hands and rocked slightly on her heels. "Turn around."

"What?"

"You heard me. Turn around! I want to see my new granddaughter."

Anne obeyed. She waited while her mother fiddled with the baby blanket and examined Lucy, who must either be asleep or too terrified to make any noise. Most children were terrified of Sarah. Anne had seen her mother silence an entire birthday party of elementary school children with a look.

Finally Sarah instructed Anne to face her again and said, "She isn't a bad-looking baby despite the red hair. Still, we should present this carefully. I don't want any unnecessary talk." She tapped a scarlet fingernail against her pursed mouth.

Anne's scalp prickled. "It's the twenty-first century, Mom! Nobody's going to care if I had a baby on my own. And how is this any worse than Grandfather gambling away the family fortune? Or Dad being a drunk and then disappearing? You tell people those things often enough."

"Sex is different." Sarah lowered her voice as an older woman in khakis and a blue Fair Isle sweater entered the reception area carrying an ice bucket. "Wait here, please, Anne."

Sarah walked over to the woman, greeted her warmly, and pointed her toward the ice dispenser in the hallway, all while answering questions about a whale-watching tour and the best place to buy lobster. Her mother confided in the other woman as if they'd grown up together. Once Sarah spoke to a guest, that guest felt completely at home.

Too bad Sarah's own daughters had never been granted that same magical guest treatment. Anne's knees and back still ached whenever she thought about how many bathrooms she'd scrubbed and how many loads of linens she'd washed in the industrial machines downstairs.

Her mother returned and said, "I know this may be difficult for you to understand, given your age and lifestyle, Anne, but sex is always a scandal in New England. This is not the Caribbean. And people expect an inn like Folly Cove to uphold certain family values."

Her mother's hair, always a sign of her mood, was starting to unravel from the coil piled on her head, long white strands rising like cobwebs. "We'll have to tell people you're newly separated from the baby's father and it's too painful for you to talk about it," she went on. "We'll imply that you're getting divorced."

"You're kidding."

"I most certainly am not." Her mother's voice was patient but determined. "If you're staying here at the inn, that's exactly what we're going to say. And my apartment isn't suitable for a child, I'm afraid."

Beyond the double doors, the band began playing Pink's "Raise Your Glass" in the ballroom, and the crowd sang along. Anne nearly had to shout above the music. "Why not?"

"I don't have room for a baby. Or the patience. As you know."

Anne remembered how, as a child, she'd once kicked her mother in the shins out of frustration. She felt exactly the same way now. "Lucy won't be any trouble. She can't even crawl yet."

"How long are you planning to stay?"

"A couple of months? Just until I find a job and get back on my feet. It would be nice to spend Christmas together, right?"

"Naturally, I would be delighted if you stayed through the holidays." Her mother brightened. "I have the perfect solution. I'll put you in the east wing. I have a room available on the third floor. That way none of the guests will hear the baby fussing and be disturbed."

Anne's face felt hot; she knew a flush was probably spreading across her neck, face, and torso. As a redhead, she'd never been able to hide her emotions. Her skin might as well have been a neon sign.

"Mom, I can't do all those stairs multiple times a day with the baby! Please. Let me stay with you." Anne hated having to beg.

To make matters worse, she could feel Lucy wiggling in the backpack. She was probably hungry; at four months, Lucy was accustomed to nursing every few hours.

Anne imagined breastfeeding right here in the inn's reception area. She could plop down on the couch and whip up her shirt. What would her mother do if she flashed her boobs at the guests? A bubble of hysterical laughter escaped before Anne could swallow it.

"I'm glad you find this situation so amusing," Sarah said. "I'm afraid I don't see the humor in the fact that you, with all of your fine education and opportunities, are reduced to being a single mother, tattooed and without a job, like half the teenage girls in Gloucester—girls without your advantages." Sarah turned away and gestured to Tommy to retrieve Anne's luggage. "Room 307," she said, then turned back to Anne. "Come with me and I'll show you to your room."

I was an idiot, thinking I could come here, Anne thought as she followed her mother down the hall to the back staircase, still carrying Lucy and the diaper bag.

Anne kept her eyes on the floor as they passed the couples returning to the grand ballroom, avoiding the sight of these women in their peach dresses and pearls. Women who were doing exactly what was expected of them instead of what she had done, which was to burn every bridge behind her.

It should have been an easy shoot. As sweet and sunny as the pop singer Tia.

Unfortunately, like so many things about life in L.A., this music video went belly-up fast. And it was Elly's fault.

To pinch pennies for the producer, Elly hadn't called her usual location scout. Instead, she'd booked a house in Laurel Canyon. The property belonged to the friend of a friend—a mostly out-of-work, stoned actor.

Elly had hung up after securing the house and pumped a fist in the air. The location fit their budget. The backyard was made private by a row of stately cypress trees, and one end of the infinity pool had a waterfall tumbling over shiny black rocks. It was perfect.

Perfect, until the day of the shoot.

The pool was the first thing to go wrong. The water should have been bathwater toasty; most pools in Southern California felt piss warm to Elly, making her long for the biting cold of the ocean at Folly Cove, where she'd grown up. Water so icy even in August that it sucked the air out of your lungs and numbed your limbs in seconds.

But this pool heater must have gone on the fritz last night, which resulted in Tia, who had been sitting on a pink inflatable flamingo in the water while they were fiddling with cameras and lighting, passing out from the cold.

Even worse, nobody noticed right away. Elly was the production designer; she was occupied arranging shrubbery with her assistant. The director, Paul, was busy yelling at *his* assistant to tell the neighbor to please shut his mower the hell off while they were filming.

"Silence on the set!" Paul finally bellowed over both the mower and the constantly repeating track of Tia's next hit song.

That was when someone shouted to forget the shoot, because the singer was unconscious. Everyone assumed drugs. That's what you always assumed in L.A. Tia's agent immediately went into damage-control mode, demanding that everyone pocket their cell phones so no photos could be taken and issuing statements for publicity purposes about how the singer had taken vows of chastity and sobriety at eighteen.

Elly jumped into the pool to pull the girl out, since everyone else seemed momentarily paralyzed by the sight of the bony teenager in a sparkling silver mermaid costume lolling unconscious across an inflatable flamingo amid a herd of grinning inflatable dolphins. The girl's lips were Gatorade blue, a shade darker than the dolphins.

Hypothermia, Elly thought as Ryder Argenziano, the cameraman and Elly's occasional hookup, helped carry the singer through the glass doors into the house. He started to call 911; Tia's agent immediately snatched the phone from his hand.

"She's coming around," the agent snarled. "No ambulance. We don't want the press."

Paul was useless—still hopping around on his little black leather sneakers, wringing his hands in distress—so Ryder took over. He instructed Elly to hold up a furniture blanket to protect the singer's privacy while the wardrobe stylist stripped off the mermaid costume and wrestled her into a dry sweatshirt and a pair of yoga pants so brightly spiraled in red and white that Tia's skinny legs looked like twin barbershop poles.

Tia was awake now, but her teeth were still chattering. The agent and stylist helped her into a sitting position and wrapped Tia in a blanket, urging her to drink coffee and eat a granola bar. She nibbled it between her hands like a hamster; she probably lived on Vitaminwater and lettuce.

Then Tia phoned her mother. "Mama! I almost drowned! I saw my life flash before my eyes!"

Ryder, who was standing next to Elly, leaned closer to her and grinned. "It probably lasted five seconds," he whispered. "What could she have stored in her memory banks? The day she got her braces off? Her high school prom?"

Elly made a face at him. She had actually hesitated before taking this job because of Tia's high IMDb rating. Tia possessed star power no matter how young she was. That spelled headaches for everyone.

"Doesn't matter," she said. "We're in for it now. Tia's been in the business since preschool. She knows the value of playing up a crisis to ramp up her demands on set."

Just then the morning took another downward turn. The animal handler's portable electric fence had apparently been unplugged—probably by one of the production assistants—and now the bear contained within it came lumbering past the patio doors. Elly caught a strong musky whiff of its scent. She started for the doors, trying to move slowly to avoid catching Paul's eye.

Elly had wanted live animals for the shoot because she'd designed the set around the only decent lyric in the song, which referred to freeing the caged beast within every woman's heart. She'd contacted every affordable animal wrangler in Hollywood to see what beasts she could get to their location on a limited budget. She'd pushed Paul for the animals, convincing him that it was worth taking money from the camera package and putting it toward the set. She'd haggled with the trainer over his price, and this morning he'd arrived with only a boa, a lethargic molting parrot with a cancer-victim vibe, and a black bear the size of a dog.

If Mr. Smokey the Bear here did any damage to the set or the equipment, it would all be on her. Before Elly could make it through the patio doors to yell at the handler, a neighbor's cat streaked across the lawn. The bear charged after it with surprising speed, crashing through the wall of flowering bushes that Elly had rented from a prop shop early this morning. The bushes were in tatters within seconds. Leaf confetti was scattered all over the patio and dirt clods were dissolving in the pool.

Damn it. What a nightmare mess to clean up. Plus she'd have to pay extra to replace the shrubbery.

"Okay, people, that's a wrap," the director announced. Fortunately, Paul was standing with his back to the patio doors as the trainer rocketed down the driveway after the bear.

Paul was a short man who successfully practiced intimidation tactics. Elly had worked with him on several projects over the past two years. He wore leather no matter what the season in Hollywood: black leather pants and jacket, black leather shoes. Even his notebook was black leather.

"That's it for the day, huh?" Ryder said. He never seemed bothered by Paul or by anyone else, maybe because he'd grown up in northern California. His West Coast chill was partly what had attracted Elly to him, despite the fact that Ryder never wore anything but blue jeans and crap T-shirts, like somebody's basement-dwelling teenage son.

"Yup," Paul said. "We're done here. You'll all get a full day's wages." He knelt beside the singer. "Is your mom on her way to pick you up, Tia sweetheart?" He said "sweetheart" like other people said "toe fungus."

When Tia nodded, he said, "Good. Fantastic. Really, really great. Now, make sure and let me know how you feel this afternoon, okay? Anything you need, anything at all, tell me and it's yours. Right, Michelle?"

"Of course. I'm on it. Whatever you need." Michelle, Paul's assistant, a sleek Japanese woman wearing a vintage floral dress with bright purple high-tops, was taking notes at his elbow.

"Elly, call me after you get this place cleaned up," Paul barked as he stood up again. "Later, people." He zipped out the front door, walking so fast he was nearly on his toes.

"That's it for me," Elly said. "I'm dead to him."

"Probably," Ryder said.

She jabbed him in the ribs. "You're not supposed to agree!"

Ryder shrugged. "I'm no sugarcoater. That's why you like me."

"That's why I *used* to like you," Elly said.

"Oh, chill out. If you have lunch with me, I'll help you clean up."

"Deal."

When Elly called Paul on her cell phone an hour later while inching along the highway, the director cut straight to the point: he wouldn't be using her for this video when they resumed shooting tomorrow, nor for the commercial they'd talked about scheduling the following week.

"But I've done good work for you, Paul," Elly protested.

"Not my call, sweetheart. It's the producer's. And you know how many fucks the producer doesn't give about whatever you did yesterday. This guy's all about tomorrow."

"Come on, Paul. Go to bat for me. Who can you get to step in for me on such short notice?"

"That's the thing, babe. The stars aligned. I found this young guy— maybe you know him. Jay Goodwin? Anyway, I ran into him at my juice bar on Sunset. The guy's got a wall lined with VMAs, but he's got two days free. Producer's thrilled. Look, don't take it to heart. You've been around the block enough to know it ain't personal."

Elly repeated this conversation to Ryder as they bought tacos at a food truck and walked over to Silver Lake Meadow by the reservoir. Ryder had stopped for a six-pack of beer, too.

"He's right," Ryder said. "Hollywood is Tomorrowland and we're past our sell-by dates. Know how old Paul is?"

"Thirty?" Elly guessed.

"Twenty-six."

"Crap."

"Right. And you're on the wrong side of thirty-five. I'll be forty next year." Ryder finished his first beer and uncapped another. "Paul's probably wondering how we still get around without wheelchairs."

"Gee, thanks. I feel so much better." Elly bit into the taco, savoring the sudden shout of spicy meat and salsa on her tongue. Beneath this note of pleasure, however, was humiliation: Ryder had accurately guessed her age. That stung, especially since she was wearing lash extensions and that new under-foundation primer her stylist promised "fills in your cracks and holes, like spackling your face."

She said, "I'm thirty-eight. Guess I'd better invest in more maintenance."

"Stop. You look fine." Ryder waved a hand toward the park, where a pair of Latina women in platform sandals pushed strollers, a well-oiled guy in a Speedo was sunbathing, and a kid was riding a skateboard with a Chihuahua tucked under one arm. "Look at this cross section of humanity. There's always a way to make it in L.A., right? Walt Disney knew that. That's why he built his first studio right here in Silver Lake."

Elly finished her beer. "Wasn't Disney only twenty-five when he built that studio?"

"Twenty-two."

"Shoot me now."

Ryder laughed. "You can always do something else if you get sick of production design. Why did you move here, anyway?"

Elly finished her taco and wondered what version of her past life she should share. She'd slept with Ryder a few times—he was the first since the affair with Hans, which had left her in zombie mode for two bleak years when it crashed and burned—but she'd sidestepped any personal conversation. Their hookups were fun and nothing more. She always had Ryder come to her house, but never allowed him to spend the night. She preferred to sleep alone. Besides, it would be a long time before she would trust a man again, after everything Hans had put her through.

"I moved here to be a singer," she said finally. "I got a few gigs at first. You know: cable TV commercials, voice-overs for minor characters in cartoons. Never enough to keep me going. After ten years of scrambling, I finally started helping a friend who was a production designer. She trained me."

"You could still sing on the side and work your way into something."

Elly shook her head. "No. These days, anyone who makes it in music does it by having a YouTube channel and suffering constant sacrifices. As in: no fun, no food, and definitely no sleep. I'm not willing to chase a rabbit down that hole. And I'm happy designing sets. I'm thrilled just to be living someplace warm and far from the hospitality business."

"When did you do that?"

"All my life. My family owns an inn north of Boston," she said. "Folly Cove is the kind of old-school place where people have been coming for generations to marry off their daughters, or to celebrate milestone birthdays and anniversaries. You know: a pile of wood on a cliff above the ocean where people sit on Adirondack chairs on the lawn, swilling gin and tonics until it's time to stagger off to their prime-rib dinners."

"Sounds good to me."

"Sure, if you're a guest," she said. "But for us, life at the Folly Cove Inn was one deadly chore after another. Having an inn is like keeping house for a family of two hundred strangers."

"Do your parents still have it?"

"Just my mom now."

"What happened to the better half?"

She socked him lightly on the arm. "Dad was a drunk. Took off when I was eight. Haven't seen him since."

"Ouch. Must have been hard on your mom."

"You'd think, but no. She runs Folly Cove with an iron fist encased in a velvet evening glove. She's a Boston blue blood and never lets anyone forget it." Elly finished her beer and set the empty bottle back in the cooler. "I wouldn't have minded my childhood so much if Mom hadn't made indentured servants out of my sisters and me. We were the cleaners, kitchen help, models, and entertainment, all in one."

"How many sisters?" Ryder had finished eating; he rolled his napkin and taco papers into tidy balls and made a game of tossing them into a nearby trash bin. He made every shot.

"Two," Elly said. "Laura's the oldest, I'm the middle, and Anne's the youngest." She told him about the inn's TV commercials and brochures that she and her sisters had posed for through the years. "Photographers loved us because Laura's a brunette, I'm blond, and Anne's a redhead. One magazine writer even called us 'Sarah's Singing Angels.'"

"I don't get it."

"After the TV show *Charlie's Angels*? Sarah's my mom's name."

He laughed. "Fun."

"Not exactly. Once, I had to pose in the garden in a green dress with a white pinafore. That dress had so many layers, I looked like a cabbage."

Ryder grinned and stretched out on the grass, toeing off his sneakers. "I'd pay good money to see that photo. And you worked at the inn when? In high school?"

"And elementary school. College, too, even though I was going to school in Boston. But probably the thing we Bradford girls were most famous for was singing."

"*All* of you? Like, together?"

Elly nodded. "Mom was a jazz singer. That's how Dad met her, when she performed at the inn one summer. After Dad ran off, Mom struggled financially to keep the inn afloat. God knows why she didn't sell up. Anyway, she realized we could provide free entertainment and save money. I was about ten when we started performing. She made us wear matching outfits and the guests ate it up."

"Like the von Trapp family in *The Sound of Music*! Were you any good?"

"We were, actually. No matter how much we fought, my sisters and I could always sing in perfect harmony." Elly watched a group of Frisbee players for a few minutes—a ragged bunch of shirtless guys in board shorts—then glanced down at Ryder.

He'd closed his eyes. He had freckles across the bridge of his nose. His brown hair hung nearly to his shoulders and was streaked with gold highlights from the sun. Or did he bleach it? You never knew in L.A. Elly was surprised by her urge to run her fingers through it. She clasped her hands in her lap.

"Are your sisters still in Massachusetts?"

She leaned back on her elbows beside him. "Only Laura. Anne's in Puerto Rico, living the dream, surfing and all that. Laura always planned to leave Massachusetts, too. She's an equestrienne, worked really hard at it. She was on her drill team in college and talked about training for the Olympics before she decided to get married and be a mom."

"You must miss them."

"Not really. Our mother's not exactly the warm and fuzzy type. I call on her birthday and Christmas, visit every couple of years. Laura and I still talk once a week. I used to be closest to Anne, but this past year we've been too busy to stay in touch. You know how it goes in families: once you move out, you have to wonder if you'd be friends with your siblings if you weren't related."

"Sure."

Ryder had agreed so easily that Elly at once felt defensive. "What about your family? Are you guys close?"

"Not so much. I'm an only child. My parents always preferred each other's company to anyone else's. They're both teachers and raised me in a semipagan cohousing community in northern California, in a town time forgot," he said. "Where the hippies still sell homemade bread out of baskets on the streets and live in their vans if they can't afford tents. I had lots of kids to run around with, but not all that much contact with my own mother and father. I think they were relieved when I moved away, truthfully."

"See? People move on," Elly said.

"I guess. But I always felt pretty envious of people like you."

"People like me?"

"People with real families: a mother and father, siblings. Presents around the Christmas tree. You know."

Elly felt him roll toward her and opened her eyes when he began kissing her neck. "Stop!" She pushed him away, laughing.

"Why?" He kissed her again.

"We're not exactly alone here." She moved away as a Frisbee whizzed by overhead.

Ryder's hand shot up and grabbed it. He tossed it back to one of the players. "We don't have to be here." He gestured with his chin in the direction of his truck. "I live only three miles from here."

Elly insisted on following him in her car. A little frolic would be a welcome distraction from this morning's travesty of a shoot, but she wasn't about to get trapped at Ryder's place.

She expected Ryder's apartment to be something like her own: an overpriced studio in a nondescript building. Instead, he surprised her by pulling into the driveway of a shingled gold bungalow with a teal door and a fence covered in scarlet bougainvillea.

"Nice place." Elly felt suddenly shy. She was sweaty from setting up and breaking down the shoot, then picnicking in the sun, and her mouth tasted like a pub floor. "Mind if I shower?"

"Not a bit." He led her through a gate into an enclosed courtyard and handed her a towel, then pointed to an outdoor shower concealed by a latticework fence. "Is this when I'm supposed to leave you alone to do your secret lady rituals?"

She laughed. "Or you could scrub my back."

"Thought you'd never ask." Ryder tugged off his T-shirt in one fluid motion.

It was Sunday, but Laura was up at sunrise, replaying last night's conversation with Jake in her mind as she dressed in the bathroom to avoid waking him.

"We're going to have to ask your mother for Kennedy's tuition money," Jake had said. "I don't see any way around it."

"I can't," she'd protested. "Not again."

"Laura, I don't see what the big deal is," he'd argued, running a hand through his hair. "Your mom is the one who insists Kennedy should go to that school. What's the solution? Send her to public school? Fine by me, but you and your mother would hate it."

Laura pulled on her jacket and hiked down to the barn to feed the horses and turn them out so she could muck the stalls. Lately, the barn was the only place she felt like she had any control in her life.

She took deep gulps of the cold air. Their property was only half a mile from the Folly Cove Inn, but on the opposite side of the street from the ocean. Trails led from the back of the property into the woods and trails of Dogtown. There was no water view, even when the leaves were down for the winter, but at least there was always the suggestion of salt on the breeze.

This morning, the indigo sky was washed with peach along the horizon. A few oaks were already tinged yellow and the maples were scarlet despite its being only the last week of September. The pasture was still green beneath the low-lying morning mist.

Laura turned all of the horses out except one of the boarder mares, a bay Morgan. The horse had injured her leg on a jump and the owner wanted her kept in for another week.

She crosstied the mare in the stable aisle and felt some of the tension seep out of her shoulders as she curried the horse and picked its hooves clean. The smooth texture of a horse's coat beneath her hands, the smell of leather, the velvet muzzle searching for carrot nubs in her palm were all familiar touchstones, things she'd loved since childhood.

Her father, Neil, had encouraged her to take riding lessons. He'd attended every one of her horse shows until the night he disappeared. Laura was ten years old by then—old enough to know he probably wasn't ever coming back. Even so, she had continued picturing her father in the stands at every horse show, his face ruddy and cheerful beneath the floppy-brimmed hats he wore against the sun, standing and whooping whenever she took a ribbon.

So ironic that she was the only sister who'd stayed on Cape Ann, when she had once dreamed of the Olympics. She usually blamed her failure on meeting Jake, on getting pregnant and dropping out of college, or on her mother's needing her.

But sometimes Laura wondered whether she was here simply because she was still waiting for her father to return. More than anyone, he had always made her believe in herself.

Unfortunately, the fact that Laura owed her mother money meant that she was the only Bradford daughter still expected to drop everything if Sarah needed help at the inn. But what would they do without her mother's financial support?

Laura sighed and walked the mare back to the stall, her mind going in its usual circles. Her husband's dental practice seemed to be thriving. The riding stables had started turning a profit a few years ago. Yet their debts kept climbing.

Her friends paid for luxury cars, vacations, and new clothes without having to calculate how many glasses of wine they could afford at a restaurant—or whether they could even eat out. Laura socialized with these people. She dressed like them, talked like them, and helped them raise money for the less fortunate. But she was *not* like them.

Even with her mother's help, Laura had to pinch pennies just to pay basic bills. She shopped at consignment stores, even Goodwill. They'd had the same furniture for twenty years. She used coupons at the grocery store.

Whenever she considered what else they could do without, she was flummoxed. Kennedy loved school. How could she deny her daughter the same education Laura and her sisters had?

Her mother also paid their Annisquam Country Club fees, and Jake claimed that being a member of the club was good for business— for his practice and her riding stables, too, since most of her students and the horses she boarded came from families they socialized with there.

Laura pushed the wheelbarrow into the first empty stall and began forking manure into it. *You're here because you want to be,* she reminded herself.

Besides, what problems did anyone ever solve by running away? Elly and Anne had escaped Folly Cove, but neither had a home or a family, or even a steady career.

Still, Laura wouldn't mind having a little more freedom.

She threw herself into cleaning stalls—eight for her own horses, plus a dozen for boarders—and pushed loads of manure out to the cart and tractor. Eventually she shucked her jacket, but her shirt was soaked with sweat by the time she finished.

She was spreading fresh sawdust in each stall when her mother phoned. "I need your help with the flowers for this afternoon's wedding," Sarah said. "Mindy called in sick and there isn't anyone else. Can you come this morning?"

"Of course," Laura said. "I'm nearly done in the barn. I'll bring Kennedy with me."

An hour later, she was in the Folly Cove kitchen, trimming and arranging flowers. Kennedy had helped Laura collect them from the garden; now, as Laura glanced up, she saw her daughter hovering in front of the inn's enormous stainless-steel refrigerator, the door open.

"For God's sake, Kennedy," Laura said. "Shut the refrigerator! Don't stand there mooning. You're wasting electricity."

"Sorry, Mom."

Laura watched Kennedy slink into a corner of the inn's kitchen, an éclair in each hand. At only thirteen, she already had a muffin top blooming above the waistband of her jeans. Laura worried about her daughter's tendency to binge, especially because she didn't like sports.

Kennedy didn't even ride the expensive mountain bike they'd given her last Christmas. That bike had cost three months' worth of groceries. Lately, Laura had been tempted to sell it. She and Jake could use the money.

Thinking of money made her remember that she still had to ask her mother for help paying Kennedy's tuition. The prospect made Laura's throat feel clogged, as if a web had been spun at the base of her throat.

She glanced at Sarah again, assessing her mood. Not good: her mother had stopped trimming flowers to watch Kennedy wolf down the éclairs like a starving refugee in some desert camp.

Don't say anything, Mom, Laura silently begged.

Seconds later, Sarah said, "Kennedy, darling, should you really be eating that junk for breakfast? You're in seventh grade now. Fat girls don't have fun in junior high."

Kennedy ran out of the kitchen, weeping.

"Mom!" Laura said, longing to follow her daughter and offer comfort, despite knowing all too well that Kennedy cried the way other people sneezed: suddenly, loudly, and often without provocation.

"Yes, dear?" Sarah said over a trio of blooms in her hand.

"What were you *thinking*?" Laura said. "You can't say things like that to her!"

Sarah arched a penciled brow. "Why not? Someone has to tell it like it is. Do you really want her to keep piling on the pounds? She should be having yogurt for breakfast, not ice cream. What are you now, Laura, a size fourteen? Kennedy looks even larger than you do and she hasn't hit puberty. Or has she? Has Kennedy gotten her period yet? I've read that puberty starts earlier in girls these days."

Her mother often couched her opinions in research, or even in pseudo research picked up from morning talk shows. That way nobody had the nerve to question her.

The worst part was that Sarah was right: Laura was an undeniably solid size fourteen. And she could hardly blame this on baby weight anymore, since she was forty and her child was a teenager. "No, Kennedy hasn't started her period," she said.

"But soon, do you think?" Her mother plucked another dahlia out of the flowers heaped on the counter.

"Yes. And her doctor thinks she'll probably experience a growth spurt then and slim down naturally. Meanwhile, we shouldn't fuss over what Kennedy eats. The doctor says lecturing her could backfire and turn her into an anorexic."

"Oh, well. A little anorexia never hurt anyone." Sarah tucked one last scarlet dahlia into a crystal vase already bursting with bold scarlet, orange, and white blossoms. "These days everybody wants to pathologize a woman's responsibility to maintain her figure. In my day it was expected."

"Yes, and before that, women wore whalebone corsets," Laura joked through gritted teeth.

Her mother smiled. "I still miss my girdles. Spanx just don't measure up. I know what! How about if you and Kennedy join a mother-daughter Weight Watchers group? I'd be happy to fund that. Or any other healthful activity."

For a single thrilling moment, Laura imagined taking the vases they'd filled with flowers and hurling them, one by one, against the kitchen's tiled floor. But she reined herself in: she still needed a favor. "Maybe I *will* look into Weight Watchers," she said. "Good idea, Mom."

Sarah smiled and smoothed her hair. Her blond hair had gone

white, but it was still long and thick. She typically wore it coiled into a neat French twist at the nape of her slender neck. Somehow, even while arranging flowers or doing the inn's accounts, Sarah managed to look like an actress in a French film—the sort who would take two lovers at a time, one of them much younger.

"At least Kennedy's smart," Sarah said. "That's a comfort. Her looks won't matter if she can get into a decent college and earn her own living. Researchers say more women are happy living alone these days, fulfilled by their careers and such."

"Mother, will you please stop!" Laura said. "Kennedy's fine. She's a late bloomer, that's all." God, she hoped that was true.

"I'm sorry, but I do worry. You girls were never hefty at that age. Of course, you were all so active, I could hardly keep up with you. Maybe Kennedy needs to help you more around the house. Doing chores can be wonderful exercise."

Sarah picked up three of the vases and swept toward the door leading to the dining room, her stockings rustling beneath her tweed wool skirt, her red jacket snug around her waist. Watching her made Laura remember something her father's sister, Aunt Flossie, had said once: "Your mother walks like the *Queen Mary* parting the waves."

Laura was all too aware of her filthy jeans and sneakers as she forced herself to follow her mother into the dining room, desperate to get the words out and go home. "Mom, I hate to ask, but since we're talking about Kennedy, I need a huge favor," she said in a rush. "Her tuition's overdue and we can't swing it. Can you help us out?"

Sarah deposited her vases on tables. "How much?"

When Laura told her, Sarah simply nodded. "I'll have a check ready for you tomorrow morning. You can pick it up from Rhonda in the office."

"Thanks," she said. "I don't know what we'd do without you."

Sarah smiled. "What are families for?" She headed back toward the kitchen. "By the way, Anne's here. She arrived last night."

"What? Why?" Laura felt such a jolt of anger at hearing her sister's name that she dug her nails into her palms.

"You didn't know? I thought you girls kept in touch online these days and I was the only one out of the loop." Sarah waved a hand, dismissing all of social media with a flutter of her fingers. This was an act: she was an aggressive and savvy online marketing whiz.

"No. How long is she staying?" Laura's stomach churned. Two blissful years Anne had been away.

"At least until Christmas, she says."

The swinging door closed behind her mother before Laura could respond. She remained frozen in place. Not Anne, on top of everything else! She couldn't bear the idea of seeing her.

Laura pushed the door open and followed her mother into the kitchen. "Where is she now?"

"Upstairs. Still sleeping, I imagine."

Laura's vision blurred with rage. "Why is she staying so long? Did she lose her job or something?"

Her mother seemed about to answer, but then shook her head. "It's probably best if you ask Anne directly. You know I don't like to get in the middle between you girls. Now, let's see. I was going to put those tall Oriental vases on the buffet tables. What do you think?"

"Sure. I'll bring in the rest of the smaller vases while you do that," Laura said, forcing her shoulders down from her ears. Her body was tense, holding in a scream that was building.

She hurried out to the dining room with two more vases of flowers. Better finish her work here fast if she wanted to avoid her sister.

Still, she stopped to gaze through the windows at the lawn, a rolling hill that dropped toward the sea, seeking comfort in the familiar view. The garden was a series of shallow stone terraces built to create a staircase effect down to the shoreline. There was a patio in the middle terrace with a white trellis; for most of the summer, the trellis was a bower of pink Eden roses. Now that it was September, the famous Folly Cove Inn roses were fading, but late perennials in the gardens still bloomed in a tapestry of rich velvety golds and oranges, reds and purples.

Below the garden was a rocky bathing beach. The ocean sprayed against the rocks as Laura watched. Today's wedding reception was scheduled for three o'clock. The tide would be out by then, revealing the golden horseshoe of sand, gulls wheeling above it and flashing white as they turned in the air. The wedding guests would carry their drinks down to the shore and take photographs.

Laura knew that drill by heart. Twenty years ago, she had been the bride standing beneath that rose trellis. The bride who had followed the footpath through the perennial gardens afterward, holding her train high as she led the way, laughing, to the beach.

There on the sand, she and Jake had posed for wedding photographs that were now safely entombed in a white silk album tucked on the top shelf of her bedroom closet. Anne's return was one more reminder that Laura hardly had the heart to look at them anymore.

CHAPTER TWO

Elly watched movies, music videos, and television shows online nonstop after leaving Ryder on Friday afternoon, bringing her laptop into the kitchen and alternating between swilling coffee and sipping wine. Well, more than sipping: she'd polished off two bottles of wine today already, and it was only six o'clock on Sunday evening.

She had dutifully noted the credits on everything she watched and made phone calls, first trying people she'd worked with in the past, then resorting to cold calls. She hated every minute of it, even as she made her pitches: "Hey, do you have anything new in the works? I've got a free window."

Elly gave herself pep talks along the way, reminding herself that the only way to succeed in Hollywood was to keep putting herself out there, wearing her skin like some bulletproof shell, slick and impermeable.

By now, however, the confidence she'd felt driving home from Ryder's house on Friday had evaporated. Meanwhile, Ryder kept texting, asking if she wanted to meet up. For dinner yet! Or a movie! A date. Like they were sixteen!

All right, yes. She was tempted to see him after that glorious, head-spinning sex. But the last thing she needed was a relationship to derail her job search. Especially with Ryder, who was like one of those big friendly dogs that keeps jumping up to greet you no matter how many times you tell it to stay down.

Her face was still chafed from Ryder's stubble. She rubbed a hand over it, remembering the way his legs had entwined with hers after they'd made love, how sweetly pleasant it was to doze in his arms. She had awakened Saturday morning to find Ryder smiling down at her, his eyes surprisingly tender.

Definitely a mistake to see him anytime soon. Why get attached and ruin a good thing?

The sun was starting its descent, the usual L.A. ball of fire fizzing orange behind the palm trees swaying outside her wrought-iron balcony. She might as well give up until Monday.

Elly sighed, shut down her laptop, and went into the living room, carrying the last dregs of the wine with her. Her phone rang just as she flopped down onto the cheap leatherette couch and reached for the TV's remote control.

It was Laura. "Elly! You're home! Thank God."

"What's up, Lorelai?" Elly continued flicking through channels with the television on mute.

"You've got to help me."

Elly sat up. "What's wrong? You okay?"

"No, of course I'm not okay! That's why I'm calling! You should *know* that!"

"You always call me at this time of day," Elly pointed out. "While you're washing dishes," she couldn't help adding.

Laura was the diva of multitasking; she couldn't even make a phone call without simultaneously doing some chore. Tonight it sounded as though she was throwing plates into the stainless-steel sink in her kitchen.

"Well, this time I'm calling you because things are definitely not okay, *okay*?" Laura's voice was high and tight above the clatter.

"So spill," Elly said.

"Anne's here!"

"At your house?"

"No! At Folly Cove with Mom."

There was another crash in the background. Elly frowned, trying to picture Laura. Her sister's straight dark hair, cut in a chin-length bob since college, was now laced with gray; she was probably wearing her usual barn clothes: jeans and a sweater.

Elly's entire apartment could fit inside Laura's kitchen. Sometimes Elly envied this, but mostly not. Her sister was moody, and she often wore her unhappiness like a shawl, scratchy but pulled close to her chin anyway.

"Say something," Laura demanded.

"So Anne's there. So what?"

"Did you know she was coming home?"

"Nope. I haven't talked to her in a while." Elly shut off the television to focus better on her sister's tense, disembodied voice. "I'm surprised she's home, but I don't get why it's such a big crisis."

"You *know* why! I can't have Anne around Jake."

"Come on. Don't be stupid. That was a million years ago."

According to Laura, Anne had once stayed at Laura's house to look after the horses while Laura and Kennedy were away, and she'd put the moves on Jake. Truthfully, Elly found this story tough to swallow. Jake was a nice guy, sweet and handsome in the regular way of a blandly appealing Ken doll, but he was definitely not Anne's type. Anne went for bookish, bearded men usually recovering from substance abuse or a tragedy. The sort of men who were appealing because they were dangerous, and dangerous because you couldn't fix them, but you got hooked on trying.

"Wrong! Remember when Anne was here just two years ago?" Laura was saying. "How I caught them during Mom's big Christmas party at the inn?"

"I'm sorry, sweetie," Elly said. "I know that hurt, too, but I still say it was a drunken party kiss. I really don't think Anne and Jake were ever involved. Maybe having Anne come back is a good thing. You guys can try talking about things more rationally now. You can't hang on to this forever."

"I don't *want* to be rational!" Laura shouted. "I don't trust Anne. I never will again."

Elly sighed. She understood Laura's feelings, but at the same time, she'd always been close to Anne, and Anne had denied everything. Most of all, Elly hated not being able to be with her sisters at the same time. So awful and awkward. "I doubt you have anything to worry about now, anyway," she said. "Last time I talked to Anne, she was living with some guy in Puerto Rico. She sounded madly in love."

"Not anymore." Laura's voice was grim. "Mom thinks they broke up."

"But you don't know that for sure."

"Anne's planning to stay here until Christmas! What does that tell you?"

Elly had to admit that sounded potentially bad. "Why did they break up?"

"Mom didn't say, and frankly, I don't care. But I can't stand it," Laura said. "*Hell* no. I'm going to tell Mom that Anne has to leave."

Elly laughed. "Be serious. You can't do that. It's not like you own Folly Cove."

"I'm the only one who stuck around. That should give me some leverage, right? I'll be the one pushing Mom's wheelchair when it's time."

"Don't bet on it. Mom will probably outlive us all."

"Maybe," Laura said. More plates crashed in the background. "But what am I supposed to do while Anne's here? You've got to help me!"

"How? I'm in California."

"Come home," Laura said. "You haven't been here in ages, and I need backup."

Elly started to say that she couldn't possibly fly to Massachusetts right now because of work. But she didn't have any work.

And as she glanced around her apartment, Elly saw that the philodendron hanging in the window was already dead, a scattering of brown leaves curling on the windowsill beneath it. Not even her plant would miss her if she left.

Why not fly home for a visit and catch her breath, and maybe help her sisters mend fences? She could job hunt from there. Maybe she'd sublet her apartment for a month. That would bring in some cash.

And Ryder would have to take no for an answer if she was three thousand miles away.

"I'll think on it," Elly promised. "Besides, isn't Mom about to turn sixty-five? Seems like we should give her a party."

"Somebody should," Laura agreed glumly. "And that means us."

Despite her exhaustion and the crisp white sheets, Anne wasn't sleeping well at the inn. Being awake wasn't much better: the minute she opened her eyes, her evil monkey mind started replaying that last horrible day with Colin.

She'd gotten up early to take Lucy outside so Colin could sleep. He was a writer who kept late hours as he worked on his second book. His first novel had made him "practically famous," he'd told her, "at least in Ireland, where they're not afraid of a dark story."

When his first book's sales didn't warrant a U.S. deal, Colin, who was originally from Dublin, had married Barbara, a wealthy American woman, and moved to New York City. He'd returned to school for a degree in computer science. When the marriage unraveled, he'd wanted to follow in Hemingway's footsteps and live in Cuba, but since that was still politically dicey, he'd chosen Puerto Rico instead.

Now Colin worked as a consultant for a U.S. telecommunications company and wrote during his free hours, he'd explained the first night they met in the Surf Riders Bar and Grill, where Anne was working. Colin had shown up at the bar in a pin-striped suit, a lone older man swanning through a crowd of board shorts and bikinis "like a heron among pigeons," as her friend Josefina had observed from behind the bar.

Anne was impressed by Colin's dedication to his writing. He had rebooted his life after his marriage ended, just as she had started her life over when she left Massachusetts, after earning her bachelor's and master's degrees in education. She'd taught elementary school for a decade. Then, once she'd struggled to pay off her student loans and save some money, she'd moved to Puerto Rico—both to escape Jake and to experience the adventures she'd never been able to have while studying and working so hard. His openness to make such a drastic change, just as she had done, was partly why Anne had fallen hard for Colin despite their fifteen-year age gap and the fact that his divorce wasn't quite final.

When she got pregnant a few months into their relationship, Colin hadn't wanted the baby. Anne was thrilled. She was thirty-six and had always wanted a child. Finally Colin capitulated once she promised to take on all the child care responsibilities.

After Lucy was born, Colin called the baby his "happy little accident." Anne was sure that he would love his daughter in time. When his divorce came through, they might even marry, but she cared less about that.

Colin insisted that they rent a house after Lucy was born so he could have an office. Anne had put up the money—first and last months' rent, plus a security deposit—because Colin said he had to send most of his monthly paycheck to Barbara, his ex. Their rental house was in El Yunque rain forest, nestled on a hillside among towering tabanuco trees laced with vines. Below the deck off their bedroom, the flor de maga trees flamed bright red and there were thick stands of orange bird-of-paradise flowers. Lizards sunned themselves on the railings.

They lived only five miles above the tourist bars and food kiosks of Luquillo Beach, yet El Yunque was so cool and misty that it felt like a different world. She and Colin hiked the trails at off times. Their favorite path led to a small waterfall. Before Lucy was born, they used to make love behind the silver curtain of water, their skin hot and stinging in the icy water. Anne wrapped her legs around Colin's waist as they balanced on the slippery rocks, breathless with love, with desire, with trusting each other not to let the other one fall.

Puerto Rico was, quite simply, paradise.

The day before she left the island, Anne had put Lucy down for a morning nap while she showered and dressed for work. Colin didn't stir as she was leaving. His habit was to stay home and write while the baby napped; he'd bring Lucy down to the restaurant when she woke. Then Clara, the owner's sister, would watch her while Anne finished her shift.

Anne had worked at Surf Riders Bar and Grill for two years by then. The tips were good and the owner, Mateo, was flexible about giving her time off. He also let her cook once he realized that Anne knew her way around a kitchen. She made the more innovative dishes and desserts. They talked excitedly about transforming Surf Riders from a casual beach bar into a destination for tourists, especially the moneyed people from Miami and New York who kept yachts in the Fajardo marinas.

"You class up the joint," Mateo announced when Anne produced her first chocolate flourless torte for him, a staple recipe at the Folly Cove Inn. She'd given the dessert Puerto Rican flair by topping cake slices with guava ice cream.

Whether she was classy or not, Mateo still insisted on Anne wearing her bikini—the standard outfit of all Surf Rider waitresses—when she was waiting tables or bartending, even after the baby, despite her new breast size and the added layer of padding around her waist and hips.

"This is Puerto Rico, not Manhattan or L.A.," Mateo had declared when she'd protested and said she felt self-conscious about her figure since motherhood. "Guys around here dig a real woman's curves." His only compromise was that if Anne was cooking, she could pull on a tunic over her suit.

That last day at the restaurant, she was wearing her red bikini and mixing cocktails. Patrons were already lined up when Anne arrived, crowding around high-tops made of surfboards. She soon lost track of time as she chatted with people and poured drinks.

Anne was in her groove, adding fresh mint leaves to a trio of frosted mojito glasses, when Colin came striding into the restaurant. His mouth was set in a tense line, and he carried Lucy under one arm like a football. The baby didn't seem to mind. She was drooling and grinned at Anne as if she could fly straight into her mother's arms.

"What's up?" Anne came out from behind the bar and reached for Lucy.

"I'm leaving." Colin ran a hand through his hair, causing it to crest at his forehead like the feathers of an exotic parrot.

She frowned, confused. "That's fine. I told you to bring Lucy down when she woke up. I know you need to write."

"It's not that."

"What, then?"

"Colin, you need to get out here. *Now*." A woman's voice, sharp and nasal.

Colin took Anne's face between his hands and kissed her forehead, a quick benediction. "You will always be special to me, Anne. I hope you know that."

By now everyone in the bar was staring and Lucy was squirming, causing the bottom of Anne's bikini to slide lower on her hip. Anne hitched it up with her free hand. "What's going on?"

"Colin? What are you doing?" The owner of the voice entered the bar then, a stocky woman in a white blouse, denim skirt, and sneakers. Her short hair was gunmetal gray and cut to the same length as Colin's, and her jaw was just as square as his. She looked enough like Colin to be his sister. For a few seconds Anne allowed herself to hope this was true.

She knew it was not. This woman had to be Barbara. His wife.

"Is this her?" Barbara demanded, pointing at Anne. "You said you weren't going to see her. You were just going to drop the baby off at the door," she said, as if Lucy were a UPS package. No signature required, apparently.

"I'm Anne. The mother of Colin's child." Anne shifted Lucy a little higher on her hip, proof of her claim.

Barbara dismissed her with an impatient flick of her fingers. "We don't have time for your usual theatrics, Colin. We have a flight to catch. I'm giving you five more minutes." She left without a backward glance.

"Colin, please. Talk to me," Anne begged. "What's going on?"

"That was Barbara," he said, then sputtered to a stop.

It didn't matter. In a single sentence, Colin had unveiled the truth: his lies to his wife, his lies to her.

"You're going back to her," Anne said.

"Yes," Colin said with the ghost of a smile. "Sorry."

"But *why*?"

"You know why." Colin reached over and gently tucked a loose strand of hair behind Anne's ear. It was such a familiar, intimate gesture that she closed her eyes briefly to fight the pleasure of it. "I'm married, as you bloody well know," he said softly. "I never wanted to do this whole parenting gig. I tried. I really did. But I can't abandon my art for diapers. Writing feeds my soul."

In a flash Anne understood: Barbara must have threatened him financially. She was probably supporting Colin, not the other way around.

Anne lost her temper then. "You can abandon your child but not your *art*? Or your wife's *money*?"

A flicker of impatience flared in Colin's eyes. "Look, you can't say I didn't warn you. I promised we'd have fun, and we did. But I'm not cut out to be a family man."

With one last rueful glance at the baby, who had stuffed a fist into her mouth and was watching him with round blue eyes, Colin walked out of the bar.

Anne followed but was stopped by the sight of Barbara leaning against a shiny blue sedan. Some of the bar patrons had followed them outside, too. Anne wished desperately that she'd grabbed her tunic off the hook behind the bar to cover up. Everything was on display here: her body, her new stretch marks, her tear-streaked face, the baby.

"I'm sorry, Barbara," Anne managed. "Colin told me he was leaving you. Otherwise I never would have gotten involved with him."

"Oh, please. Don't feel sorry for *me*," Barbara said. "I feel sorry for *you*. You're not his first, you know." She went around to the driver's side. Colin was already seated in the car.

Anne had wished, for one second, that she could close her eyes and become invisible, the way her own father had let her believe was possible when she was a child: *if you can't see me, I can't see you.*

Instead, she had to stand alone with her baby on a hot sidewalk, burning with shame as the car drove away, while everyone who had stepped out of the bar to watch the drama unfold discovered what kind of woman she was: a woman who would sleep with a married man.

Mateo had fired her on the spot. "I never thought you were this sort of woman," he said.

"I never thought I was, either," Anne said, and left with the baby. She hadn't even gone back to the restaurant for her final paycheck.

Now, in their overheated little room on the third floor of the Folly Cove Inn, Lucy was waking up, cheerful and babbling. Anne nursed her, then put her in the crib while she showered and dressed before carrying Lucy down the three narrow flights of stairs to breakfast.

Fortunately, it was early on Monday morning and none of the inn's guests were up yet. Rodrigo, the Brazilian cook who had been preparing meals at the inn for thirty years, was happy to see her. He made a fuss over Lucy and took her for a few minutes so Anne could eat in peace.

She heaped scrambled eggs, sausages, and pancakes onto her plate from the chafing dishes and began to feel restored as she ate in the elegant dining room, with its embroidered white linens and vases of fresh flowers.

She and her sisters used to love playing in here on the rare days when the inn was empty, the three of them arguing over who would be the queen and who was the prettiest princess. Sometimes, if their mother was busy in the office, they'd even sneak china teacups off the shelves.

Anne used to love helping out in the kitchen, too. She'd peel potatoes, whisk dry ingredients, crack and separate eggs, arrange the dinner salads. Rodrigo got a special stool for her and folded one of his aprons in half.

She had loved the tall, shiny pots and the shelves laden with tools and appliances: pasta makers, espresso machines, electric blenders, chocolate shavers, pepper mills. Most of all, Anne had loved the soothing symphony of clattering lids on pots, spoons ticking on bowls, hissing steam, whirring electric mixers, and Rodrigo's low voice conducting them all. It was the complete opposite of her mother's tense silences or barked commands.

"Well, look what the cat dragged in."

Anne hadn't heard Aunt Flossie enter the room. Now she jumped up to throw her arms around the other woman's bony shoulders. "I'm so glad to see you!" she said.

"Likewise," Flossie said, "but there's no need to break my ribs. Down, girl, before you puncture this old bat's lungs."

Anne laughed and released her. "How are you? You look great."

"Better than you, by the looks of it. I could pack a week's laundry into the bags under your eyes."

Flossie was her father's older sister. Past seventy now, but still fit. She had always practiced yoga and hiked with her dog every morning through the trails of Halibut Point, even in bitter weather, her only concession to the winter a pair of ice cleats strapped to her boots. Her short glossy cap of brown hair was woven through with gray, but her skin had the healthy burnish of someone who spent more time outside than in. Flossie wore a uniform of cotton yoga pants and sweatshirts with sneakers, except in summer, when she preferred Birkenstock sandals.

"Your aunt looks like a homeless hippie," Sarah often groaned. "I hate letting her wander loose among the guests."

The guests, however, seemed universally charmed by Flossie. She lectured the adults about local history and delighted their children with tide pool explorations and wild stories about talking foxes and magical snowy owls.

Now her aunt poured a cup of coffee and sat down at the table. She was perfectly capable of making breakfast in her own house just down-hill from the inn, but came here for meals because it bugged Sarah. She'd been away at a yoga retreat for the weekend, she told Anne now. "I couldn't believe it when your mother told me you were back."

"I can't believe I'm here, either."

Flossie lifted her chin toward the porch, where Rodrigo was bouncing Lucy in his arms. "Cute baby. New grandkid?"

It took Anne a moment to understand that Flossie thought Lucy was a member of Rodrigo's vast extended family; they all lived in Gloucester, and Sarah was surprisingly tolerant of the cook's children and grandchildren. She even gave the kitchen staff a huge party every Christmas and made sure all of their children had presents under the inn's enormous Christmas tree.

Her mother must have chosen not to tell Flossie about her situa-tion, Anne realized. "Um, no," she said. "That one's mine."

Aunt Flossie picked up her coffee cup, eyeing Anne over its rim and taking a noisy sip before nodding. (Another thing that irked Sarah: Flossie's complete disregard for table manners.) "Well. You cer-tainly know how to shock an old woman's heart into beating faster. Congratulations. Or my sympathies, whichever you prefer."

"Congratulations. Thank you."

"You're welcome. I always knew you'd make a wonderful mother."

"You don't know that," Anne said. "I don't even know that."

"Oh, but I do. You will, too, in time." Flossie set down her cup. "Did it ever occur to you to send us a little birth announcement?"

"I was planning to surprise everyone at Christmas." Anne fiddled with her fork. "I didn't write, because I wasn't sure how Mom would react to a second grandchild, especially since I'm not married. I thought it might be better to present Lucy in person."

"Ah. The old fait accompli. And? How did Sarah react?"

"Well, she hasn't set the hounds on me yet."

"Decent of her."

They finished eating while Flossie shared news about her yoga retreat, the inn's recent summer season, the various classes she was teaching out of her home studio, Laura's riding stable, and Jake's dental practice.

"What about Kennedy? Didn't she turn thirteen last month?" Anne felt a whisper of guilt: she'd sent no gift. Not even a card. Laura had forbidden Anne from having any contact with her family. "How's she doing?"

"Oh, she's morose, like all girls that age," Flossie said. "What about you?"

Anne wanted to tell her aunt everything, but Rodrigo was returning now that guests were beginning to filter into the dining room. He handed her the baby. Lucy settled on Anne's lap, her solid body instantly comforting.

"I'm okay," she said. "Just needed a little break from my life."

"Are you going back to your mother's apartment after breakfast?" Flossie reached over to wiggle one of Lucy's feet, making the baby grin. "I could bring you some toys for the baby. I still have a box in one of my closets from when you used to stay with me."

"Thanks, but please don't. Mom put us on the third floor of the east wing. I don't have room for toys. I'll bring Lucy to your house to play with them."

Flossie scowled. "Your mother put you and the baby on the third floor, with that awful twisty back staircase? That's ridiculous! What on earth was she thinking? You can't stay there. Come to my house. I'll find someone to clean the Houseboat by midweek. You and Lucy can stay there as long as you need."

"I couldn't do that," Anne said, though she immediately pictured Flossie's small cottage on the ledge above the beach, with its bedroom windows overlooking the ocean and a narrow porch with its own pair of rocking chairs. "The Houseboat," as Aunt Flossie had always called her little caretaker's cottage, would be the perfect place to hole up and lick her wounds.

"Nonsense. It's settled." Flossie pushed away from the table and stood up. "You can tell me everything over a bottle of wine when you're moved in."

Maybe not everything, Anne thought, but she stood up, too, and embraced her aunt.

Sarah couldn't believe it when Anne showed up in the reception area to announce that she and her child were moving to Flossie's, and then to that horrid little cottage of hers. Or maybe she did believe it: her sister-in-law had always been a meddler, especially where Anne was concerned. She coddled that girl. That's why Anne had never learned any discipline. It was Flossie's fault Anne was in this predicament, as far as Sarah could see.

You had to take a firm hand with children. Yet too many adults these days—sadly, she included her own daughter Laura among them—continually gave their children anything they asked for, rendering them helpless whenever they finally stumbled out of their nests and into the harsh sunlight of real life. Sarah didn't have to look any farther than her own waitstaff to see this. Some were in their thirties, yet still had no car, no mortgage payments, and no direction in life. She had disciplined Anne the same way she'd disciplined Laura and Elly, yet she'd turned out no better than these drifters. Such a travesty.

Well, it was a fact that daughters were tougher to raise than boys. Some said boys were the devil to raise, but Sarah would argue that point. Boys—and men, for that matter—were simple creatures with simple needs. They were either angry or happy, with not much in between.

"Uncle Gil is here," Rhonda announced, poking her head into Sarah's office. She sounded suspiciously gleeful, despite knowing Sarah was going on this date with her uncle only as a favor.

"Thank you. Please tell him I'll be out in a few minutes."

"All right. I'll offer him coffee, shall I?"

"Of course," Sarah said with a brisk nod.

She always made a point of keeping her office door open so she could track whatever was going on at the front desk. She trained her employees thoroughly, especially those answering the phones and taking bookings, because they were the faces and voices of the Folly Cove Inn. Still, she liked to be on hand, especially for morning check-outs and afternoon check-ins, and greeted guests personally whenever possible. People remembered that sort of thing.

Rhonda was her favorite staff member. Sarah had hired her for the front desk two decades ago because the girl—well, she must be fifty now, with children in college—was tall enough to be imposing and had such a luxurious mass of dark hair that Sarah had been sure at first that it was a wig. It was not. Rhonda's mother had grown up in England, so she used proper diction and even had a slight British accent. Hers was the perfect voice to advertise the inn's growing reputation as "a place to celebrate life's shining moments," Sarah's latest advertising tagline. Not original. She knew that, but still, sometimes people responded better to language that felt familiar.

Rhonda appeared in the office doorway again and folded her arms, looking over her blue eyeglasses at Sarah. "I brought him the coffee," she said. "He said take all the time you need. I told him five minutes." She tapped her foot for emphasis.

"Five minutes," Sarah agreed, but she couldn't help sighing after Rhonda left. She wouldn't have agreed to this foolhardy outing if anyone but Rhonda had asked her for this favor, saying her uncle was lonely.

About five years after Neil left, when it became clear that he was never coming back, Sarah had started seeing other men. There had been several businessmen and an architect, a banker, and even an ex-senator over the years. Eventually she'd stopped bothering. Men were too much work. And, after a time, the ones who were interested in her were so old that she knew she'd end up playing nursemaid. No, thank you.

She had never bothered divorcing Neil and continued wearing her wedding ring. By now most people thought she was widowed. Sarah was comfortable financially, physically, emotionally. Besides the inn, she had civic duties, memberships in the art association and the concert hall. Friends. Daughters. (Though, except for Laura, they scarcely seemed to give her the time of day. And sometimes she suspected Laura came around only because of the money.)

Plus, she'd mostly lost her appetite for social intercourse beyond making her guests feel welcome. Her own company and the sanctuary of her tidy apartment at the inn were all she needed to be content.

Then, about a month ago, Rhonda had mentioned her uncle Gil, a widower who had recently moved to Rockport. "I wish you could meet him," she said. "My uncle Gil doesn't know a soul here, and you could tell him so much about the area. Just lunch at the inn, maybe? I know you'd like him."

Sarah doubted that very much. She liked few people. However, Rhonda was like another daughter to her, and as Rhonda kept pressing her, she'd realized she'd have to relent to keep the peace.

Lunch at the inn it was, then: she wouldn't even have to put on a coat.

"Mrs. Bradford?"

Sarah looked up and saw Betty, her head housekeeper, standing in the doorway of her office. "Yes?"

"The occupants of room 212 haven't checked out," Betty said. "I wanted to make certain there wasn't a special arrangement for a late departure before I have the maids knock on their door."

Sarah shook her head. "Only the honeymoon suite requested a late checkout today. Ask Rhonda, but I don't think we have anyone else coming into that room tonight. We can offer them a half-day rate if they're staying through lunch."

"All right." Betty gave her a curious look. "Are you feeling all right? You look pale."

"Of course. I just need a cup of tea."

"I'll bring that to you straightaway, Mrs. Bradford."

"Thank you, Betty, but there's no need. I'm going to have lunch in the dining room."

Betty expressed surprise—Sarah usually ate lunch in her apartment—but Sarah would bet her best pearls that Betty had known about the date within seconds of her agreeing to it: Folly Cove, like most well-run inns, operated as a single organism. "Have a lovely time, Mrs. Bradford," she said, and retreated.

Sarah dropped her eyes to her desk, to the stack of brochures waiting to be mailed to people who somehow still couldn't manage to download the pdf from the Web site. She had been mindlessly stuffing them into envelopes for the past hour while she thought about Laura and the awful scene with Kennedy, and about whether she should have told Laura about Anne's baby.

She hadn't done so because something was wrong between those two, and Laura already seemed to be carrying the weight of the world. After they had finished with the flowers on Saturday morning, Sarah had watched Laura and Kennedy trudging up the driveway, their bodies solid and their heads bowed as if they were peasant milkmaids bearing buckets on yokes across their shoulders.

The sight had infuriated her. Sarah wanted to call them back inside at once. To tell them that they, too, had backbones, despite everything they clearly believed about themselves.

She'd felt such confidence in Laura once. Lately, though, Sarah had felt concerned about her eldest daughter's marriage and mental state. She hoped it wasn't depression reducing her most reliable child to this careworn woman who never wore a stitch of makeup and mysteriously never managed to make ends meet. She suspected Jake was up to something, but what?

Impatient now—wallowing in speculation and emotions was never productive—Sarah slipped a cream-colored cashmere cardigan on over her navy blue wool dress, picked up her handbag, then locked the office door behind her. It was time to get this date over with, so she could get back to work.

"You can't possibly be working today," Laura said when Jake announced that he was going into the office on Sunday.

They had been reading the newspaper at the kitchen table after breakfast. This was one of Laura's favorite rituals. Kennedy slept late most weekend mornings, so this gave her time alone with Jake.

Every Sunday, she went down to the stables early to feed the horses and turn them out. Then she made a special breakfast. Something celebratory: waffles and sausages, maybe, or eggs Benedict, the way she'd always done, since they first were married, hoping to remind them of that precious time when they were young and so in love that they had chosen to change their lives for each other.

This morning, mindful of Anne's arrival last weekend, Laura had started a diet to recover her waistline. She'd made poached eggs served on a bed of spinach. No muffins. No hollandaise. Only a guilt-free melon slice on the side.

Jake hadn't complained about the scaled-back meal. Watching her husband wolf it down, Laura doubted he'd even tasted it. Then he'd slipped away from the table while she was nursing a second cup of coffee.

Now Jake was leaning down to kiss her forehead. He smelled of mint mouthwash. His hair, dark and buzzed short on the sides but long in front, was slicked back from his forehead. "This isn't the first time I've gone in on a Sunday, Laura. You know that as well as I do. And it's an emergency extraction. Would you really want this poor woman to suffer until tomorrow?"

Laura set down her coffee cup. He was right: several weekends a year, Jake was called in for emergency procedures.

She tightened the belt of her plaid flannel robe as her husband opened his briefcase and checked its contents. It was the sort of briefcase that doubled as a backpack; Jake rode his bicycle the six miles to his office in Gloucester every day, even in the rain, and typically carried his laptop and lunch in the backpack. Another reason he still looked thirty.

She, on the other hand, could easily pass for someone's grandmother. How was it possible that they'd aged so differently?

"You promised you'd cut back your hours," she said.

"If I do that, we'll have even less money than we do now, and I already feel bad enough about asking your mom for help with Kennedy's tuition." He glanced at his watch.

"I know. And I appreciate how hard you're working," she said. "But we never do anything as a family anymore."

Jake shifted his feet. "We took Kennedy to the mall last Sunday. And she's older now, Laura. She doesn't want to spend time with us."

"That's exactly why we should! She'll be off to college in the blink of an eye! When was the last time you had a real conversation with her? Or invited her on a bike ride?"

Or acted like you wanted to spend time with me, Laura added silently.

Jake laid a hand on her shoulder, gave her a friendly squeeze. "I promise to reserve next weekend. Maybe the three of us can hike in Ravenswood Park or something. Listen, I'm sorry, but I've got to go." He leaned forward and kissed her again, this time on the top of her head, then closed the door gently on his way out.

Laura knew she should be grateful to have this peaceful Sunday morning to herself, with her daughter sleeping upstairs. She had nothing to do at the stables until tonight, when she'd bring the horses in again, toss them some grain and check their water. No lessons until tomorrow. It was a blessing to have these leisurely hours wide open before her.

The thing was, she didn't *want* to be left alone. She wanted them to be a *family*. Not three separate people peeling off in different directions. She'd grown up with a single mother who was too busy to spend time with her children, and Laura was determined to give Kennedy the stability that she and her sisters had lacked.

And, P.S., why couldn't Jake understand that not everyone in this family would leap at the chance to take another *hike*?

But the real thing gnawing at her was this: Laura didn't believe Jake was really going into the office. Wouldn't he have taken his laptop with him? His computer sat on the kitchen counter, silver and sleek. Mocking her.

Jake hadn't mentioned Anne this morning, even when Laura had vaguely said over breakfast that her little sister "might be visiting." Yet now Laura felt anxious, her caffeine-fueled imagination shifting into overdrive. What if Anne had secretly been texting Jake? What if they'd been in communication all along?

It was possible. In the past few months, Laura had learned it was easy to deceive your spouse. Just this morning, she'd answered three texts from Tom while she was down at the barn, then deleted them all, even though they'd arrived on the burner phone she'd bought so the bill couldn't possibly appear on their family plan.

Laura quickly cleared the breakfast dishes, forcing her mind away from Tom. He wasn't a problem, she reminded herself. It was an online friendship. A virtual flirtation, at most. She could stop anytime she wanted.

At least Elly would be here tomorrow. She was the only person Laura had ever confided in about Jake and Anne. As she rinsed the dishes and moved like a robot through the kitchen, clearing and cleaning, Laura replayed that horrible day, exactly as she'd described it to Elly.

Three years ago, she'd taken Kennedy to visit friends in Maine for a weekend while Jake was at a conference. Anne had a teaching job with summers off, so Laura had asked her to stay at the house and look after the horses. She'd even offered to pay her, but Anne had refused the money.

"It's a vacation for me, too, getting out of my hot little apartment," Anne had said. "And you deserve time off."

Anne had always been generous. But she was also a man magnet: a combination of fierce and vulnerable, a tomboy with movie-star curves and dusky skin. Her eyes could go from blue to silver depending on her mood, and she had red hair—not that horrible ginger-carrot color, but a rich auburn. Laura had often been jealous of her, growing up. Much more so than of Elly, even though her middle sister was the traditional beauty, with her long legs, sharp cheekbones, and straight blond hair.

Still, Laura had never imagined that Anne would try to poach her own husband.

Anne had taken off surprisingly early on the morning that Laura and Kennedy returned from Maine. Laura had felt a sting of disappointment; she'd been looking forward to a sisterly night out to thank Anne for house-sitting.

When Laura asked Jake why Anne had left so soon, he'd shrugged. "No idea," he said.

Laura sensed something was up from his potent silence and continued to press him. Finally her husband became agitated and said they needed to have "a serious talk" after dinner.

Despite that warning, Laura was blindsided. Money was usually the subject of Jake's "serious" talks: how they needed to tighten their belts, cut back on restaurants and clothes, et cetera. She knew the drill.

Laura put Kennedy to bed early, then poured herself a generous glass of wine before joining Jake in the living room. Too generous: the wine sloshed over the rim of the glass. It was impossible to scrub the red stain out of their white Berber carpet.

Later, she would pull up the rug in a fury, hacking away at it with kitchen shears. She wouldn't have been able to stand looking at the stain and knowing what it represented.

Once Laura was seated on the living room couch, Jake pulled the hassock over and perched on it in front of her, hands dangling between his knees. "Look, I'm sorry about this, but I need to be honest," he began. "First of all, you should know that I would never do anything to deliberately hurt you and Kennedy."

Laura's stomach had immediately started roiling. She drank the cheap wine anyway, finishing it in a rapid series of swallows that made her throat burn. "Wow. That's a rough merlot," she'd said, not wanting him to continue.

He did anyway, clasping his hands and rubbing his thumb over his plain gold wedding ring. Jake's bangs were too long. She wanted to yell at him to stop hiding behind his hair, the way she often scolded Kennedy.

But Laura had remained silent despite instinctively knowing that the conversation was headed straight off the cliff of domesticity and into the frigid black waters of troubled marriages. She had also known that she would forgive Jake for whatever he'd done. Laura couldn't imagine life without him. She had loved him since college. They'd helped raise each other into adulthood.

Jake told her that when he'd returned from the airport at two o'clock in the morning, the lights were off downstairs, but there was a light on in the guest room. "I didn't want to scare Anne, so I called her name as soon as I went upstairs."

Laura had to stop herself from bolting from the room. She didn't want to hear any more. "I'm sure she was expecting you. Anne knew when you were coming home. I even sent her an e-mail with your flight information."

"I know. You're always so thoughtful." Jake's voice broke. "That's why this is so hard."

"Jesus, Jake," Laura said. "Just tell me! Did you sleep with my sister? Is that it?" She had to tuck her hands beneath her thighs; they were trembling. She was trembling all over, as if she had the flu.

"No," Jake said, "but almost."

"What do you mean?" Laura cried out. "*Almost?* What is this, *high school?* Are you talking first base here? Second? *Third?* With my own *sister?*"

He began to reach out to touch her knee, but her expression must have stopped him. Jake folded his hands in his lap instead. "The door to the guest room was open a little," he said, "so I poked my head in to say good night. Anne told me to come in and tell her about the trip."

"All right," Laura said, staring at Jake's hands now. "Then what?"

"Anne said she was glad I was home, because she'd been thinking about me. Fantasizing, she said."

"She *said* that?" Laura's gaze flew up to his face.

Jake nodded. "I thought I'd misheard her. But that's what she said. So I asked why, and she got out of bed and came over to me." His voice trailed off. "Oh, God, Laura. This is rough. I'm so *ashamed*. And I don't want you to hate your sister."

"Tell me," she said, but she could guess. She'd seen Anne in action. Whatever her little sister wanted, she usually got.

Especially if what she wanted was a man. Even in high school, Anne had managed to sleep with Sebastian Martinson, who was already at Yale when Anne was only a junior. Laura had caught Anne with Sebastian at a party one night, a tangle of limbs in a car, her sister's burnished hair on fire beneath a streetlamp, her legs milky white around Sebastian's waist.

"Tell me," Laura repeated, though she wanted to cover her ears.

"There's no easy way to say this, honey," Jake said. "Anne was naked, but she got out of bed anyway. I was too shocked to move. She put her arms around my neck and started kissing me, pressing herself against me. I think she must have been drinking." He winced. "I swear that's all that happened. I got out of there as fast as I could. Your own sister! I am so, so sorry."

Laura had stroked her husband's bowed head, shushing him, relieved that his confession had ended here and not where her own mind had gone. "You didn't do anything wrong," she said. "It's okay. *We're* okay. Anne has always been wild. Any other man would have gone to bed with her. You didn't give in. That's what matters."

"Because I love you too much," Jake said, pressing her hand to his lips. "I would never do that to you."

"I know," she said, and kissed him.

Afterward, Laura had driven to her sister's apartment, breaking the speed limit even before leaving the driveway.

Anne had denied everything. She told a completely different version of events that Laura didn't buy for a minute. And catching them together two Christmases ago proved to Laura beyond a doubt that Anne couldn't be trusted with her husband.

Now Laura rose from the breakfast table and began methodically tidying the newspapers. Jake wouldn't just go off and see Anne, would he?

He might, if Anne was having some sort of crisis and that's what had brought her back to Folly Cove.

Laura loaded the dishwasher, wiped the counters, and ran upstairs to get dressed. Fifteen minutes later, she was in the car and driving toward Jake's office in Gloucester. She needed to see for herself that his bicycle was actually there.

Laura drove the way she usually did, one hand on the wheel, the radio on loud, with no regard for speed. She knew these roads well enough to drive them blindfolded.

In less than fifteen minutes, she arrived at Jake's office building. It must have rained here last night; there were puddles as bright as mirrors all over the tarmac.

She pulled into the lot and sat there with the engine idling. Jake's bicycle was there, padlocked to the bike rack. He had been telling the truth! Her relief was colored by shame. She shouldn't have doubted him.

Her prepaid phone buzzed. She knew it was that phone because the other one was set to a jungle ringtone that Kennedy had chosen. This one sounded like a wasp trapped in a jar.

Laura removed it from her purse, her fingers trembling. Tom, of course. Nobody else had this number.

She glanced up quickly, absurdly fearful that Jake might be able to see her and would somehow know what she was doing. But that was ridiculous. Besides, she wasn't doing anything wrong. Not really.

She looked down at the phone's screen, smiling when she saw that Tom had texted her a picture of a sign advertising a horse show in Hamilton. *The universe is working hard to make sure I see u everywhere,* he'd texted. *Are you competing in this show? I could come cheer u on.*

Laura leaned her head back against the seat. She should stop this now. Text him to say it was over, then throw this phone into a Dumpster. This had been a fun, harmless, virtual flirtation over the past months, but she wasn't about to cheat on Jake.

Another text. *You there?*

Laura dropped the phone into her bag and pulled out of the parking lot, panicked.

CHAPTER THREE

Their second lunch—Sarah refused to call it a "date," no matter how excited Rhonda looked as she waved them off—was an even bigger mistake. She knew that as soon as Gil Mandel walked her out to his blue car, a stocky man wearing carefully pressed khakis and a navy blue polo shirt. He must have pressed those pants himself, since his wife had been dead a year, according to Rhonda.

But what choice did she have? Here was Gil in his neatly creased trousers, gallantly opening the door of his Subaru, so Sarah swept her camel's wool coat beneath her legs and settled herself on the passenger seat. At least there were no crumbs or cans rolling around on the floor: she couldn't abide by any evidence of people eating in their cars.

They drove half an hour north to a restaurant on the water in Newburyport. Sarah had selected the place; she didn't want to meet anyone she knew. She loved a good Manhattan and felt immediately calmer when the drink was between her hands, despite noticing the water glasses were cloudy. Perhaps she'd have a quiet word with the waitress and suggest that they use a rinsing agent in the dishwasher.

They ordered their food from a waitress who called them "my little friends" and cheerily said, "I'll be taking good care of you," making Gil roll his eyes at Sarah.

Sarah minded the waitress's words less than she minded the look the girl gave them. She imagined the waitress, who was all of thirty years old, going back to the kitchen and gushing about "that cute old couple at table five."

She'd heard her own waitstaff cooing over elderly couples, as if a man and woman keeping company past age sixty-five was something to be either pitied or marveled over. Nobody young could imagine ever reaching this age or picture any sort of passion that might lead people with wrinkled flesh to press their bodies together in a moment of abandonment. Passion and abandonment were for the young. Sarah almost wanted to lean over and kiss Gil just to shock the damn waitress. She wouldn't think they were so cute then.

She focused instead on the menu. Sarah settled on grilled scallops on a bed of spinach. Gil ordered the baked stuffed haddock. The waitress gave them another approving look before bustling back to the kitchen with a hiss of panty hose and polyester.

Fine. The sooner they ate, the sooner Sarah could get back to the inn. The only reason she'd agreed to this second meeting with Gil was out of guilt: their first lunch in the Folly Cove dining room had been cut short when the smell of smoke caused a guest to call the fire department. There was no fire, only an overloaded and smoking surge protector, but the inn had been evacuated for two hours. Sarah had sent Gil on his way while she smoothed the feathers of the few guests checked in for a weeknight stay.

The view of the Merrimack River was spectacular, the grasses a burnished copper in the late-afternoon sun and the river a vivid blue. The weather was warm enough that there were still some boats in the water.

"I appreciate you taking time out of another of your busy days to see me," Gil said. He had Rhonda's careful diction and thick head of curly black hair, though his was dusted white. He was her mother's younger brother, Rhonda had said, married forty years until his wife died suddenly of pancreatic cancer last year, and had two grown sons.

"Yes, well, Rhonda seemed to think you needed a tour guide, since you're new to the area, and she's very dear to me," Sarah said. "I'm happy to fill you in on everything there is to do around here."

Gil laughed. "My niece has been worried about me since Marjory—

that's my wife—passed away. I'm getting along just fine, but it's true that I don't enjoy going out to lunch alone."

"I've never minded eating alone," Sarah said truthfully.

"Ah. I can see that. You're probably one of those efficient multi-taskers," Gil teased. "The sort who does the accounts while making toast and pays for advertising online while running on the treadmill. Rhonda says you work around the clock."

"Treadmill? Please," Sarah said, eyeing him suspiciously. What else did Rhonda say about her? "I do the tasks at hand in the order that makes sense. My goal is to stay ahead of my responsibilities."

"Sounds exhausting," Gil said cheerfully, spreading his napkin on his lap as the waitress delivered their plates. He waved a hand. "Me, I like a good sit-down with the morning paper, then a walk before lunch. I spent my whole life pleasing other people. Now it's time to please myself." He picked up his knife and fork. "If I want to see a movie in the middle of the day, I go right ahead and take myself off to the cinema."

Sarah tried to imagine life with so many empty hours and couldn't do it. Nor could she see its appeal. But she had the good manners not to say so. She speared a scallop with her fork. "You told me last time that you were a chemist before you retired. Why did you choose chemistry?"

"I always loved science as a kid. My father became a doctor, and his father was a doctor before him. Me, I couldn't seem to get out from behind the lab bench."

A scientist: that explained the precise way Gil was carving up the fish on his plate, Sarah decided, and the facts he'd delivered on their way to Newburyport. He'd seemed to know about everything from the salt hay mounded in the marshes along Route 1 to world politics. "You really don't miss working now that you're retired?"

"Not at all."

She studied him for a moment as they both chewed. Gil was a rough-looking bulldog of a man, balding in the middle of those black-and-white curls, with a thick neck and a wrestler's shoulders. Nothing like her tall, slim, elegant, mannerly Neil.

Sarah and Neil were a matched set. Everyone said so. Even the elder Mrs. Bradford, Neil's impossible-to-please grandmother. Yet

Sarah admired Gil's hungry, untamed look. You didn't see that in most men her age, who often appeared diminished and bewildered, even vacant around the eyes and mouth as their wives directed them around the grocery store or through the too-precious shops along Bearskin Neck in Rockport.

"Still, perhaps you should have kept working part-time," Sarah said. "Research shows that retirement can be detrimental to your health."

Gil hunched his thick shoulders upward, unimpressed. "Yeah? I've known plenty of guys who dropped dead because they didn't know when to call it quits. They stayed on the hamster wheel, and for what? One more Caribbean cruise? No, thanks. I'll take my freedom. Besides, now I've got plenty of time for my pet project."

A man eager to talk about his hobby. Please, God, let this lunch be over and done with soon. "Oh? And what's that?"

He leaned forward, a gleam in his eye. "I'm restoring a boat. She's a real beauty. A classic 1912 Fay and Bowen, a twenty-six-foot, extra-wide launch. I'm restoring it to saltwater standards, using all triple-plated brass hardware, even the strut, rudder, skeg, and prop. I've got fifteen coats of varnish on her already, and I'm planning to replace the engine and launch her this spring." He nodded toward the river. "You get out on the water much?"

Sarah shook her head. "Owning an inn doesn't leave much time for boating."

"Married to your work. I see. Not enough hours in the day and all that." He smiled, taking some of the sting out of his words, but by the way he sat back in his chair again, she knew she'd disappointed him.

She smiled back, but it irked her that he was somehow implying she lacked outside interests. Still, when she struggled to think of something else she enjoyed, she came up empty. "Innkeeping is a very consuming business."

"Sure it is. And if you're happy, that's what matters." Gil's tone was magnanimous, which irritated Sarah even more. "So, what about you? You told me you were a singer with a jazz group in Boston. How'd you end up way out here at the tip of Cape Ann?"

"The Folly Cove Inn hired us for a weekend."

"Why jazz and not classical? What appealed to you about the style?"

These questions surprised her. Most people wanted to hear about where she'd toured, what celebrities she knew, and whether she'd made any albums.

"I trained as a classical singer." Sarah had been telling this lie for so long that it seemed true. In reality, she had never made it beyond high school, and there had been no formal musical training—something even her husband never knew.

"Is that right?" Gil asked.

"Yes, but eventually I realized how much more I enjoyed loosening the rhythms of a song. Once I tried jazz, I embraced its spontaneity."

"Not sure I get what the difference is in how you sing the two styles," Gil said. He was eating his dinner methodically, one item at a time, working his way around the plate: he'd finished his fish and now turned the plate to start forking up the mixed vegetables.

"In classical music, the aim is to sustain your notes, because you're typically singing in front of a large audience," Sarah said. "When you sing jazz, you have more freedom of expression with the music. You can play around a little, even stress the offbeats and swing if you want."

"Uh-huh. I think I get it. How old were you when you started singing professionally?"

"Oh, very young. Sixteen." Sarah sipped her wine, remembering those first gigs: lying about her age and sneaking into Boston clubs, begging bands to let her sing with them. Eventually one of them did. That band, the Sweet Tones, was made up mostly of older musicians.

Rupert, who played the trumpet with the Sweet Tones, making it sound like anything from a foghorn to a weeping woman, fronted the band. He talked the rest of the guys into letting Sarah sing with them. She was all of eighteen by then.

"Man, what are you guys afraid of?" Rupert had asked them. "What harm can this skinny-ass chick do us? She's got some sweet pipes. That's what matters. And having a pretty girl might get us into some new clubs."

He was right about that. Sarah was ambitious. She was struggling to escape her mother's house and live independently. Contrary to what she'd told everyone, even Neil and his family, she did not grow up in a Back Bay brownstone, but in a cold-water apartment in Everett near the airport. She'd never told her daughters, either, wanting them to emulate the woman she'd become rather than the girl she'd been.

Sarah had no idea where her father was; he'd left them when she was an infant. Her mother's sole occupation was to entertain men. Not for money, her mother insisted, but it amounted to the same thing: men brought food and booze to the apartment. Many stayed the night, or sometimes an entire weekend.

Occasionally a man turned his attention to Sarah and made a pest of himself. She started sleeping with a kitchen knife under her pillow and had used it on more than one occasion. Eventually she found an abandoned car in the neighborhood and began keeping blankets she'd found stashed in Dumpsters around the city in it for the nights when certain men came around the apartment. The car had locks.

So, when Sarah joined the Sweet Tones, she was determined to make the band a success. She took over booking their gigs as well as becoming the lead singer, walking into clubs personally to introduce herself and talk up the band.

She told Gil how the Sweet Tones had played city clubs for years, mostly Boston and Providence at first, then New Haven and New York as their following grew. Musicians came and went, but she and Rupert—who by then had become like a father to her, offering Sarah advice on everything from music and clothing to the men she dated sporadically—stayed.

"I loved everything about touring," she said. This, too, was a lie, but only a white one: she'd loved being in the spotlight but hated the cheap hotels and long trips in the van with men who could never seem to stop smelling like animals.

Gil nodded. "Must have been hard to give up."

"Yes, well. We do what we must for love."

She explained to him how, ten years after joining the band, which by then was called Sarah and the Sweet Tones, she began scouting resorts, hoping for steadier bookings that would come with accommodations. "We played the Catskills, the Berkshires, New Hampshire ski resorts," she said.

And then, one day, they got a call from Neil Bradford's mother, saying the band they'd booked for a wedding event had canceled.

When Sarah cagily said they were already booked for that weekend—it was true, though it was only in a VFW—Mrs. Bradford said, "We're in a bit of a jam here," in a voice that made it sound as if she were chewing mashed potatoes while speaking. "I've heard your band is marvelous. Two of my friends have seen you perform at the Chelsea Club. We would be happy to pay more than your usual fee, given our predicament, if you'll cancel your engagement and come to us."

Sarah had doubled their fee and booked the gig.

"Huh. What a thing. You came here to perform at the inn and it changed your whole life," Gil said. "Do you ever think of what might have happened if you'd said no?"

"Sometimes."

"Why did you decide to stay at Folly Cove, and not any of the other places you'd been singing?" He'd polished off the vegetables and moved on to his potatoes.

Sarah poked at her lunch, still mostly untouched. "I met my husband. Neil saw me sing and booked the band for the rest of the summer. I didn't know until later that he did it without consulting his parents." She laughed. "All I cared about was that he paid the band up front for the next six weeks and gave us a place to stay."

Gil smiled. "The guy must have been head over heels."

"I was, too." Sarah smiled and took another sip of wine. "He was the nicest, most glamorous man I'd ever met."

She fell silent and pretended to focus on her food, not wanting to share the rest. She and Neil couldn't have been more opposite in background and temperament. Sarah was ten years older than he was when they met, but she didn't dare tell Neil. That wouldn't be such a scandal now, but back then it would have been unthinkable.

She was careful, so careful, with Neil. She refused to sleep with him right away. Didn't even let him kiss her until their third date. Flossie was still in France, so Mrs. Bradford had put the band up in what was now Flossie's house—a house they used to rent out by the week—while Sarah stayed in the dreadful caretaker's cottage. The Houseboat.

But, oh, how romantic the Houseboat was, when Neil began coming to her in the evenings. This man—with his energy for life and his passion for her—made Sarah feel, finally, as though happiness wasn't meant only for other people.

She knew she had to tread carefully if she was going to keep Neil interested in her and be accepted by his family. She offered various elements of her life story, some real, some not. Her goal was to demonstrate pathos without inspiring pity.

She told Neil that her mother was an alcoholic (true) and that she had grown up an only child in a Back Bay brownstone (false). She said her father traveled for work and she didn't see him much. (True. He was a milkman, back in the days when that was a thing, and had left the family when Sarah was a baby.)

Not that it mattered. Neil only ever half listened to her; he had graduated from Harvard that spring and was floundering, he told her, until he heard Sarah sing. "You've given me a direction in life," he pronounced. "You're like a Siren, daughter of the river god Achelous. I'm hopelessly drawn to you. You could lead me anywhere."

Neil wanted to travel with the band. Rupert rolled his eyes at this. "That boy's got about as much sense as a string bean," he grumbled. "Your fancy man would last about ten minutes on the road, grand as he is."

Rupert helped Sarah weigh her options. They agreed that her best choice was to become the wife of sweet, lovely, cultured, idealistic Neil Bradford. Neil was an optimist and an enthusiastic dreamer. He was darkly handsome and boyish, always ready to dash down to Folly Cove and throw himself into the numbing sea, to ride a bicycle with no hands, to entertain people with card tricks and limericks.

Neil hadn't yet grown into a man, but Sarah could see the potential there. She could make something of him, she told Rupert.

The Sweet Tones were never going to make it big, Rupert assured her. "You're doing the right thing." There wasn't going to be any recording contract. Rupert, a longtime smoker, was having breathing problems, and Tony, their drummer, was planning to quit after the summer season to work in his brother's garage.

"Tony needs a regular paycheck, I need a rest, and you need a husband," Rupert said. "This guy's so sweet on you, I expect you'll manage him all right."

Sarah had every reason to believe this was true. Neil was in her thrall, and she was in thrall of everything that the Bradford family represented: a grand hotel, a family with historic ties, breeding, and money.

Too bad all of that was nearly as much of an illusion as the story Sarah had spun for Neil.

"How long were you married?" Gil asked after a silence that had lingered too long to be polite.

Sarah finished her wine and set the glass down gently, smiling at him. "We still are," she said. "I'm afraid Rhonda may have misled you. My husband, Neil, has left the family, but he still writes to me now and then. We're not divorced. I don't expect we ever will be."

"Because that's what you want, or because it's easy?" Gil signaled to the waitress.

Good. He'd gotten the message that Sarah wasn't available. They could get the check and leave.

"I beg your pardon," Sarah said. "I am not, nor have I ever been, the sort of woman who takes the easy way out. I am married simply because I do not believe in divorce."

"Huh," Gil said. "The old-fashioned type, eh?" He smiled but narrowed his eyes in a way that suggested he was assessing her statement, determining just how seriously to take it.

Clearly, she'd sparked his attention. Gil saw her as a challenge and, like most men, probably longed to conquer it.

A part of Sarah was thrilled to see Gil look at her with undisguised interest. It had been a long time since any man had demonstrated an interest in her.

She was about to protest the idea of herself being old-fashioned—wasn't she an independent businesswoman?—when the waitress appeared at their table. Gil surprised Sarah by asking for two more drinks instead of the check.

Gil went on after the waitress had gone again. "I admire loyalty," he said. "It's a fine trait. I was loyal to my wife. Faithful, and not because I didn't have opportunities." When Sarah laughed at this, he held up a hand. "I'm not blowing my own horn. Just telling you like it is. I was married forty years to the same woman. We had our ups and downs, but we kept our promises to each other. I always knew I'd wake up and find her smiling at me in the morning, no matter how bad things got. I consider that one of the biggest blessings of my life. We all have opportunities to sneak around. But some of us actually manage to stay the course after we're married. If we do, our lives are richer for it."

"I can think of some exceptions to that," Sarah said, wondering how she and Neil would have gotten along if he'd stuck around. "But, in general, I agree. Congratulations to you and your wife."

"Yeah, well. It was all her doing," Gils said. "The woman was a saint, the way she put up with me." He waited until the waitress, who had appeared again with their second round of drinks, disappeared again. "There are too many liars and cheaters in the world. I'm happy to meet you, Sarah." He raised his glass. "Here's to you, for knowing your own mind and living by your principles."

Sarah raised her glass, but didn't touch it to Gil's, because that would be like telling one more lie.

Anne shook the cocktail shaker hard, trying to block out the too-cheerful wedding band DJ and the babble of guests hopped up on hope. She couldn't believe she was back at the inn, tending bar the way she had every summer since her twenty-first birthday, until the summer things went so wrong with Laura.

The pub room looked exactly the same. This was one of the inn's main attractions and her mother had never redecorated it. "We can't improve on perfection," Sarah always told guests who were seeing the pub for the first time.

Anne thought she was probably right. She loved the pub. The wooden ceiling had heavy beams, and the ornate silver-lined mirrors hung on the linen walls were imported from Spain. The wainscoting, too, was from Spain, hand-carved mahogany panels beneath a gold chair rail. Shreve,

Crump & Low had crafted the original light fixtures, which were inlaid with semiprecious stone. The bar was a narrow but elegant slab of Italian marble that encouraged customers to order cold martinis or hot whiskey.

Sarah had phoned late this afternoon in a panic because the bartender originally scheduled to work tonight called in sick at the last minute. The guy who would otherwise fill in was away at his father's funeral.

"Anne, please. I need you to help me tonight," Sarah had said. "I'll ask one of the maids to look after the baby. And I'll pay you twice the usual rate. It's a wedding reception for one of the Martinson girls. The youngest, Paige. You know her, don't you? We can't let down the family. They've been so loyal to the inn!"

Paige, two years ahead of Anne at school, had been one of Elly's best friends and less hateful than most of that crowd of leggy ponytailed jocks. Still, Anne had toyed with the idea of refusing her mother in retaliation for the way Sarah had relegated her to a third-floor room. Her back still ached from carrying Lucy up and down those stairs seemingly countless times before moving to the Houseboat.

But Anne needed money, and Aunt Flossie said she'd be delighted to look after Lucy. She'd left the baby and two feedings' worth of frozen breast milk with her aunt, then hiked up to the pub.

As she mixed a cosmopolitan for one of the bridesmaids—a woman in her thirties with a rodent's small dark eyes and a stocky body encased in a pink taffeta bridesmaid dress—Anne noticed a man standing by the far corner of the bar. He was nursing a beer; he must have brought the bottle into the pub from the dining room, because she hadn't served him.

The man seemed to be alone, unlike most of the people who entered the pub room in knots of partygoers, and he was attractive in the dark, aloof, slightly worn way of a famous actor down on his luck. Tall and lean, a long nose with a slight bump keeping it from being perfect, thick black brows. His hair was the color of an old penny and curled around the collar of his tux. He must be in the wedding party.

It wasn't until she'd finished carving a lemon peel for the bridesmaid's drink—making the woman shriek, "Oh my God, so pretty! Like a flower!"—and walked the length of the bar to serve another patron close to the man that she recognized him: Sebastian Martinson. The bride's older brother. Sebastian looked more like his father now than the boy she remembered.

Her face flamed as she thought about the last time she'd seen him. She and Sebastian had hooked up at his sister Paige's high school graduation party twenty years ago. That night, Anne had gotten drunk and declared to Hattie that it was time to lose her virginity. "I can't have sex hanging over my head going into senior year."

"You're one sick chick," Hattie said admiringly. She'd had the same boyfriend since freshman year, and had lost her virginity that summer. "You should wait for L-O-V-E!"

"Love is like unicorns: we can fantasize about owning one, but in the end it's just a horse with a fake horn," Anne replied, making Hattie snort vodka through her nose.

Hattie helped her scout the party for likely candidates. Somebody from out of town would be optimal, they agreed.

Sebastian would be a safe bet, Anne decided after surveying the crowd. He had come solo to his sister's party and was home for only a week before leaving on some South American college mission trip. Plus, Sebastian was four years older, a classmate of her sister Laura at the same private school they all attended. Twenty years old! Definitely had to be experienced.

When Sebastian left the graduation party, Anne followed him down the long driveway to the street. She couldn't remember now what she'd said by way of introduction, but she'd pretty much accosted the guy while he was unlocking his car. She'd pushed him against the hood of his Volvo and kissed him when he turned around in surprise at her greeting.

So reckless. And rude! She'd used him, plain and simple. At sixteen, Anne had believed she was invincible. In charge of her own destiny. How naive could you get?

Even worse, Laura saw them together. Her sister had mistakenly opened the car door, thinking it was someone else's Volvo, and caught Anne lying beneath Sebastian on the backseat. She'd teased Anne mercilessly the next day, saying, "You are *such* a slut! No wonder Mom's in despair about you."

Anne's shameful reverie was interrupted by one of the waitresses, Clarkie, who set her tray down on the bar near Anne and glanced at Sebastian. He was sitting straight up on his barstool with his eyes closed. Anne couldn't tell if he was unconscious or rapturously listening to the music.

"Ooh, look at the lone wolf," Clarkie said. "I'd like to make that one howl."

"What do you need?" Anne said, hoping Sebastian hadn't heard.

"Two more martinis for a couple of guys who think they're dancing but look like they're having seizures." Clarkie glanced at Sebastian again. "Wait. That's what's-his-name. The bride's brother, right? I heard he's got a serious screw loose."

"What do you mean?" Anne focused on mixing the drinks.

Clarkie shrugged her doughy shoulders. "He went batshit crazy after his wife drove herself off a cliff or something." She circled her temple with one forefinger.

Anne stared at her in horror. "God. That's awful."

"Yeah, well. We live in a world of hurt, baby." Clarkie left the bar, balancing the silver drinks tray on her fingers above the crowd.

By the time Anne looked at Sebastian again, he had disappeared. Maybe he'd gone back to the wedding. Or fallen off his stool. Fine. If he wanted to pass out on the floor, she'd leave him in peace until closing time.

Thankfully, the crowd was beginning to thin out. Anne's back ached and her breasts were too full. Her mother had been right about the tips, though, so that was something. A few pub shifts like these might give her enough to put down a deposit on a studio apartment.

She was polishing the glasses that had come out of the dishwasher when Jake appeared in the doorway and started scanning the room. She had to fight her first impulse to hide behind the bar.

"Go the hell away," Anne muttered under her breath, turning her back to the room and hoping Jake wouldn't recognize her.

"I'm sorry?"

Anne whipped her body around. Sebastian Martinson was back at the bar, in front of her this time. His face looked haggard even in this dim light, but the recognition in his eyes was immediate.

"Oh," he said. "It's you."

"Yes," she said. "Me."

Sebastian glanced away from her, then back again, as if making sure she wasn't a hallucination. "I heard you moved away." He had another beer on the bar in front of him and spoke with great deliberation; she wondered how much he'd had to drink.

"I did."

"Where were you?"

"Puerto Rico."

"Why?"

"I was surfing."

He frowned. "The Web?"

"The waves."

Sebastian gave her a glum, unfocused look. "Good for you."

"Yeah," she said. "So good. I can't even tell you how good."

One corner of his mouth turned up. Anne felt herself smiling back. She suddenly wanted to make this man laugh. To erase some of the pain creating deep furrows between his eyebrows.

Unfortunately, Jake spotted her then. He moved toward the bar, grinning, his perfect square white teeth gleaming in the dim light like Chiclets. "Anne! There you are! Laura told me you were back. I've been looking all over for you." He hopped up on the stool next to Sebastian's, giving him a quick nod in greeting.

Sebastian arched an eyebrow in return. Sebastian's tux was so wrinkled that it looked like he'd dug it out of a bread box. His shoulders were hunched and his eyes were dark. Misery came off him almost visibly, a sort of indigo fog. Anne's eyes stung when she looked at him.

Jake, by contrast, was pressed and polished, jittery and amped-up. Except for a long forelock that he swept out of his eyes with one hand, his dark hair was buzzed short. The close haircut revealed a thin face with small, neat features. He'd played lacrosse in college and had always been a poster boy for fitness; his body was as lean and muscular now as ever. He was dressed in his standard khakis and polo shirt. The shirt was a bright salmon color and tucked neatly into his trousers. Anne wondered if Laura bought his clothes.

Looking at her brother-in-law evoked a smoky swirl of bleak memories. Anne desperately wanted to get rid of him.

"What can I get you, Jake?" she asked. "I'm about to close up here."

"Oh, I don't drink anymore," Jake said, patting his flat belly. "Too many empty calories. But a seltzer and lime would hit the sweet spot."

"No problem." Anne poured the drink and handed it to him, careful to slip her hand away before their fingertips touched.

"I'm not interrupting anything, am I?" Jake looked from Sebastian to Anne, smiling broadly.

"No," Sebastian answered.

At the same time, Anne nodded and said, "You are, actually, Jake. So if you don't mind?" She pointed toward the tables at the back of the bar. "Plenty of open seats."

"I'm comfortable here, actually." Jake smiled and turned to Sebastian, who was staring at Anne in confusion. Jake offered him a hand and the two men shook. "I don't think we've met. I'm Jake Williams. Anne's brother-in-law. Married to Laura, Anne's older sister." He gestured at the tuxedo. "You must be in the wedding party."

"I am. Sebastian Martinson, brother of the bride." Sebastian was gripping his glass with his free hand as if it might fly off the table.

"Shouldn't you join the party?" Jake pointed toward the door, through which they could hear the DJ cranking up "Last Dance" by Donna Summer. "See your sister off on her happy day?"

Why, Anne wondered, did everything Jake say sound so stiff, as if he were reciting lines in a play for the first time?

"No. Paige already left," Sebastian said. "She and her groom have an early flight to Italy." He jerked a thumb over one shoulder. "Those are just stragglers. Friends of hers. Nobody I know."

Jake cocked his head to one side. "You're not driving home, are you, buddy? Because you're in no condition. Just saying. You might want to start mainlining the coffee."

Sebastian shook his head. "I'm walking. I don't live far." He turned to Anne, surprising her by adding, "I went to Italy on my honeymoon, too."

"Sounds romantic," Anne said, then winced at her own thoughtlessness. Clarkie had said that Sebastian's wife was dead. She wondered how long they'd been married before she died.

She turned a shoulder to them and went back to drying glasses, hoping Jake would leave now that he'd seen she wasn't alone. The last thing she wanted was for Laura to show up, too, and see them together. All hell would break loose then.

But Jake leaned over the bar and said, "Look, Anne, I need to talk to you. Alone," he added pointedly. "Before Laura comes gunning for me."

She looked up from the glass in her hand, heart pounding. "Why would she do that?"

"Yeah, why?" Sebastian said. "What have you been doing?"

Jake kept his eyes trained on Anne. "Nothing! But you know how Laura worries. She wasn't home when I stopped by the house after work, so I came here. She'll be wondering where I am." Jake reached across the bar and grabbed Anne by one wrist. "I need to talk to you."

Anne snatched her hand away. "I'm working." She moved out of reach.

"I don't think Anne wants to talk to you, *buddy*," Sebastian observed, resting his chin on one hand.

"Anne, look. I'm not trying to be a jerk, but we need to have a conversation. You don't get it." Jake's voice was pitched high. Desperate.

"No. *You're* the one who doesn't get it." Anne crossed her arms. "Until you tell my sister the truth about what happened, you and I have nothing to say to each other."

"I can't do that. Not yet," Jake said. "Look, you have no idea how difficult this has been for me."

"How difficult this has been for *you*?" Anne asked. "Are you *kidding*? You made it impossible for my own sister to trust me!"

"I know. But my marriage is falling apart. You need to help me fix it."

"I don't need to help you do anything, Jake. You have no right to ask me for favors! My sister hardly speaks to me anymore. She hates me. Because of *you*."

"I know. I know. But if you hear me out, you'll understand why I had to do what I did. Trust me, Anne."

"*Trust* you?" The bar was empty now, except for the three of them; Anne decided her best course of action was to close early. She opened the gate separating the bar area from the pub and passed through it. "That's a laugh, after everything you've done. Look, we're done here. I'm asking you to leave and then I'm locking the pub doors. You, too, Sebastian. Out!"

She made it halfway across the room before Jake caught up with her and grabbed her arm. "Wait!"

"Let go of me." Anne was vaguely aware that Sebastian had followed Jake; he stood within arm's reach of the other man, swaying a little.

"You heard her," Sebastian said. "She wants you to leave her alone."

Oh, great, Anne thought. Caught between an adulterer and a sad drunk. "It's fine, Sebastian," she said. "Go back to your sister's party. Jake, let me go," she ordered. "Or I swear I'll scream."

"Hello? Are you still serving?" a woman's voice called from the doorway. It was the bridesmaid who'd been in the pub earlier. "I'd love, love, *love* another cosmo," she said. "Lord, you make the prettiest, sweetest drinks. And then they knock you on your *ass*!" She giggled and put a hand over her mouth. Her pink nails matched her dress.

The wedding reception was clearly over; the music had stopped and the lights were on in the dining room, which meant the servers were clearing the last things away.

"Sorry," Anne said. "The bar's closed for the night."

The bridesmaid turned away with a mew of disappointment.

"Anne, please, let's go someplace quiet and talk," Jake pleaded.

"She's not going anywhere with you," Sebastian said.

Just then Laura stalked into the bar. When she was angry, Laura walked in a way that made floors shake and dishes shatter. Tonight her powerful stride was accentuated by knee-high riding boots pulled over jeans. Jake dropped Anne's arm at the sight of his wife.

Laura must have arrived home, realized he wasn't there, and gone out again, pulling her boots on because they were always next to the door. Even so many years after not being allowed inside her sister's house, Anne could picture the mudroom with its wooden cubicles, its neat rows of boots and sneakers.

Laura clomped over to them. "Jake, what the hell? I thought you were coming home from the office for dinner. I was worried sick when I got back and didn't see you."

"Laura." Jake's smile was brittle. "I did go home. You were out. I assumed you had book club or something, so I went to the gym and then stopped by here for a drink."

Liar, Anne thought, but she was too afraid of Laura to say anything.

"I took Kennedy to the mall for new sneakers," Laura said. "Which you would have known if you'd read the note I left on the whiteboard in the kitchen, where we're *always* supposed to leave family communications." She turned to Anne. "So this is where you've been hiding out. Mom said you were back."

"I'm not hiding," Anne said. "I'm only working here tonight because Mom had an emergency."

Laura rolled her eyes. "And you were the only one available to fill in?"

"That's what Mom said."

"And now it's closing time, so you're looking for someone to take you home." Laura looked from Jake to Sebastian. It took her a minute to recognize Sebastian—Anne could see the wheels turning before the confusion on her sister's face cleared.

"Ah," Laura said then, smiling. "Sebastian. It's been a while. Last time I saw you, my sister was screwing you in a car. Back for more?"

Sebastian didn't flinch. "Hello, Laura."

"Hello," Laura said sweetly. "History repeats itself. You must be as drunk now as you were then."

"His sister's wedding was tonight," Anne said. "He's entitled to be drinking." She nearly added, *because his sister's wedding reminds him of his dead wife,* but caught herself.

"Of course he's entitled," Laura said. "Aren't we all? Maybe I'll get trashed tonight and join the club." She raked Anne up and down with her gaze. "So why are you here? What happened in Puerto Rico?"

"Haven't you talked to Mom?" Anne asked.

"Of course. I see her every day," Laura said pointedly.

"Then you must know why I'm here." Anne watched her sister's face and felt a small shiver of satisfaction when Laura frowned, then quickly tried to make her expression blank. Her mother must not have told Laura anything about the baby. Good. Let her sister wonder what was going on.

"Laura, let's go home," Jake interrupted. "You look tired."

There was a silence, then Laura said, "That's wonderful to know. Thank you."

"Rule number one: never tell a woman she looks tired," Sebastian said. "They don't like it."

Jake tried to slip an arm around Laura's waist, but she shrugged away. Her sister was close enough that Anne could smell coffee on her breath, overlaid with mint toothpaste. Laura had been married to Jake long enough that she took dental hygiene seriously.

Laura said, "What are you really doing here, Anne?"

"I came home for a visit. That's all. No big agenda."

"Really? Last I heard, you weren't ever coming back to Folly Cove. What changed your mind?"

"Look, it's late. Let's talk tomorrow." Anne's knees felt leaden, but she managed to walk past her sister and the men toward the door.

"Fine," Laura called after her. "Just remember that I'm keeping an eye on you."

Anne wheeled around. "Maybe you should keep an eye on your *husband* for a change! He came here looking for me tonight. Ask him!"

"That's a lie!" Jake said.

"He did come in here looking for Anne," Sebastian said. "I think."

Jake gave him a pitying look. "And I think you're going to have some headache in the morning, buddy." He turned back to Anne. "Please, Anne. You'll just stir things up if you insist on fabricating stories again." His face had drained of color; he ran a hand through his hair so that it stood up in brown tufts around his ears.

Anne curled her hands into fists. "You're the only one fabricating anything here. *Tell* her, Jake."

"Oh, will you please shut *up!*" Laura said. "I've seen you in action, Anne. Once a slut, always a slut!" She lurched forward and slapped Anne across the face.

The sound reverberated off the marble bar. Anne held her face for a moment, then lunged to slap Laura back.

"You bitch!" Laura shrieked. She reached out to grab Anne by the hair, but Anne ducked sideways so fast that Laura nearly fell over.

Jake caught Laura around the waist and held on to her as Anne went back to the freezer, grabbed a handful of ice, and pressed it to her face, staring at Jake, willing him to defend her. He dropped his eyes and led Laura, who was crying now, out of the bar by one arm.

"Wow. You okay?" Sebastian said.

"What do you think?" Anne said. "Look, go home and have some coffee. Can't you see it's closing time?"

CHAPTER FOUR

Outside the terminal, Elly spotted Laura parked by the curb despite a red-faced state trooper gesturing at her to move. Laura's expression was stoic as she sat with both hands precisely placed on the steering wheel and pretended to be deaf and blind to the cop. Kennedy, in the backseat, was almost unrecognizable. When did her niece get so big and round?

"Hey, you're early!" Laura leaned over to give Elly a one-armed hug after she'd climbed into the car, then pulled away from the curb with a queen's wave at the cop.

"Yeah. The trip was still stupid long, though," Elly said. "You'd think we'd have faster planes by now, right? Or at least flying cars. How did the Jetsons get things so wrong?"

"Who were the Jetsons?" Kennedy asked.

Elly pulled down the visor mirror and rolled her eyes at her niece. "Just the best cartoon *ever*. What's your mom making you watch on TV these days, huh? CNN?" She slipped off her shoes and propped her feet up on the dashboard.

Behind her, Kennedy giggled.

"What's so funny?" Elly asked.

"Mom doesn't let us do that," Kennedy said.

"Do what?"

"Put our feet up there! It wrecks the car. And she hates looking at dirty bare feet."

Laura was silent, staring ahead at the traffic on Route 1 as they headed north from Logan airport. The cars appeared sluggish and benign to Elly after surviving Los Angeles freeways, where people thought nothing of driving eighty in bumper-to-bumper traffic, but her sister was squinting in concentration.

"Your mom doesn't like it, huh? That's too bad." Elly pushed her feet higher on the dash toward Laura and wiggled her toes. Her toenails were a satisfying, shocking orange. "My feet are clean as a whistle. Oh, except for the piss I stepped in when I went barefoot into the airplane bathroom. Some men can't aim for shit."

"Ew!" Kennedy said, laughing.

"Language!" Laura said, though to Elly's satisfaction, she was grinning.

"Watch yourself, miss, or you will be the ruin of this family," Elly said, pitching her voice high to imitate their mother.

This made Laura snort. Kennedy fell all over herself howling. Elly laughed, too, and leaned over the seat to high-five her niece. She'd been right to come home. Her girls needed her to lighten things up in gray old New England.

Laura wanted Elly to stay at her house, not at the inn. Elly was happy to oblige. "I'm glad I'm staying here," she said after Laura had sent Kennedy to the den with a handful of cookies and a book. "I wasn't too enthused about having Mom hover over me and quiz me about my singing career. Or about men. God, she's probably going to ask me about boyfriends, isn't she?"

"Probably," Laura said. "I think the older Mom gets, the fewer filters she has."

"I suppose we'll be like that."

"I already am," Laura said. "It's like my thoughts roll straight out of my head onto my tongue and fall out of my mouth. I want to slap myself sometimes."

They were sitting at the kitchen table with cups of coffee. Jake wouldn't be home from work for at least another few hours, Laura said. "We never eat dinner before nine or ten," she warned.

"That's fine. It's three hours earlier my time, remember." Elly glanced out the window at the yard and the stables beyond it. Behind the stables was the pasture, hemmed by the thick woods of Dogtown. Their father used to take them hiking in Dogtown as children when the inn was busy, "to keep you out of your mother's hair."

Dad loved Dogtown, an area of about thirty-six hundred acres between Gloucester and the far edge of Rockport. In the mid-1600s, these woods had been the site of the original Commons Settlement, the most prosperous area of Gloucester until after the Revolutionary War.

After that people began moving out to the coastal areas, but some war widows and other loners remained, using guard dogs to protect them and earning this place its name. She and her sisters used to come here as children, terrifying each other with tales of what corpses might have been tossed into the icy depths of the reservoirs.

Elly's favorite hike in Dogtown was what her father called the "blueberry highway," a narrow path through gnarled blueberry bushes. They'd pick berries until their mouths and hands were stained purple. Elly had loved seeing the old stone walls and cellar holes, and pretending with her sisters that it was still Colonial times.

She wondered where her father was now, and shivered despite having added a sweater and socks. A few of the trees were already turning orange and gold and red, the leaves trembling against the pewter sky. She'd forgotten about autumn in New England, when everything looked like a high school yearbook page and the temperature fell twenty degrees the minute the sun started going down.

"Is your heat broken or something?" she asked. "It's freezing in here."

"We never put the heat on before October thirty-first," Laura said. "Do you know how much a tank of oil costs?"

"Oh, come on. You're married to a friggin' *dentist*. I bet he makes bank."

"Jake has dental school loans coming out his ears. You don't even want to know how much debt we're carrying."

"Fine. Bring me a blanket, then. I'll pretend I'm homeless."

"You've got to be kidding," Laura said. "It's sixty-five degrees in here."

Elly wrapped her arms around her shoulders. "Do I *look* like I'm kidding? When it's this cold in Los Angeles, people break out fur coats and down parkas."

Laura shook her head, but went into the living room and returned with an afghan crocheted in tan and cream. She wrapped the blanket around Elly's shoulders with exaggerated care, tucking it high around her chin.

For a minute, their eyes met. This close, Elly could see the sadness there, flecks of gray in Laura's pale blue eyes, like stones below a river of sorrow.

"Oh, honey," Elly whispered. "Things are really that bad, huh? I'm so sorry." She reached out to hold her for a minute before Laura pulled away. "What's going on?"

"I saw Anne last night." Laura sat down again.

Her grim expression did nothing to enhance Laura's looks, though she was still attractive in the way certain women are appealing, Elly thought. Women who are generous and practical. Dependable. The sort of women you'd want in your Conestoga wagon if horses were pulling you across the prairie, because they'd know the right herbal remedies for ailments and could fire a shotgun, too, hunting for food along the trail.

Laura had obviously made an effort to put on makeup this morning. Her skin was smooth, tan but not dried out like the skin you saw on the bronzed women of Southern California. She'd taken the time to add mascara and eye shadow and had slicked on a rosy lip gloss.

Unfortunately, she was dressed in clothes that she'd probably ordered from one of those catalogs aimed at suburban women who longed to be thought of as on the go: jeans, white Oxford cloth shirt, a navy cardigan. And sneakers. *White* sneakers, for the love of God, Elly thought. Her sister had always been athletic, but did she have to look so *old Yankee mannish*?

"And?" Elly asked, tearing her attention away from her sister's appearance when she realized Laura wouldn't say more without prodding. "How does Anne seem?"

"She's fine. But it was a complete disaster. I acted like a total a-hole."

This was so unexpected coming from prim Laura that Elly choked on her coffee. "What do you mean? What kind of disaster? Like high school level or nuclear war?"

"World War Whatever." Laura sighed. "I got home last night and Jake wasn't here, so I went out looking for him. I found him with Anne at the pub and kind of went ballistic."

"*Kind* of?" Elly held up a hand. "Wait. Back up. Are you saying Jake was at *work* on a Sunday?"

"Yes. Sometimes emergencies crop up," Laura said, sounding defensive. "Jake has a solo practice, and he tries not to use on-call dentists because he's afraid he might lose patients to them. Believe it or not, dentistry is a dog-eat-dog world."

"Okay, got it," Elly said, though she couldn't imagine a situation where she would go looking for a husband, unless maybe she was afraid he was *dead*. "Where was Anne?"

"Bartending."

Elly was still having trouble following this. "Wait. Sorry. Still catching up here. Why was Anne behind the bar?"

"Apparently Mom had a big party and a staff emergency. Whatever," Laura said. "The point is, I caught them together in the pub!"

"I'm sorry, but do you realize how insane you sound?" Elly said. "What do you mean, you 'caught' them? They weren't actually fornicating on the marble bar, were they? Maybe Jake really did just stop by the pub for a drink. He probably didn't even know Anne was working."

"Maybe not. But he had his hand on Anne's arm when I showed up." Laura's eyes were bleak. "I saw them touching and went mental. I called her *names*."

Elly had to put down her coffee before she choked on it again. "Like, what names?"

"'Slut.' And then I slapped her."

Elly was astonished enough to laugh. When Laura didn't join her, she stopped. "So what was going on? Did you ask him?"

"Of course. Jake said he was telling Anne that she needed to stay away from him, but she didn't want to take no for an answer."

"And you believe him?"

"Yes! You and I both know Flossie spoiled Anne silly, and Mom never disciplined her the way she did us. Anne wants what she wants, and there's no stopping her until she gets it." Laura stood up and went to the sink, filled a glass with water and drank it, then refilled her glass and did it again. "Weight Watchers tip," she said when Elly raised an eyebrow. "Drink a glass of water before and after every meal."

"But we're not eating."

"Yeah, but I forgot to drink water after breakfast."

Obviously, Anne's arrival had triggered Laura's determination to diet. "You look fine, you know," Elly said.

"You're sweet. But if you'd seen the way Anne looks, you'd be guzzling water, too."

"Why? How does she look?"

Laura shrugged. "Gorgeous, as usual."

Elly considered this. "You know, I never really thought Anne was beautiful when we were growing up. Not with that red hair and those skinny legs and freckles."

"You're right. Anne's not that pretty, if you take her apart feature by feature," Laura said. "Which, believe me, I have. But she's a man magnet. I don't know why. Maybe it's her voice. That husky alto thing? Guys get hard just hearing it."

"Hey. I thought I was the one with the voice," Elly teased. "Mom gave *me* all the solos. You hated that."

"I know," Laura admitted. "I was jealous of everything you and Anne did when we were kids. So stupid." She sipped at a third glass of water, made a face. "The problem with drinking so much water is that it makes me have to pee every twenty minutes."

"In L.A. they call that 'cleansing.' Really, Laura. Let's be serious here. Are you *actually* worried about Anne and Jake? Because to me it seems over the top. Just saying."

Laura shrugged. "I don't know. Maybe I'm being super paranoid because this isn't a great time for Jake and me. I mean, we're not fighting outright about anything—other than about money and the usual domestic stuff—but something definitely feels off. We aren't happy."

"Something's off, like what?"

"It seems like Jake's always avoiding me."

"Even in bed?"

Laura turned her face away, confirming Elly's suspicions. "Stop right there. I'm not going to talk to you about our sex life."

"That bad, huh?"

"Drop it, Elly!"

"Okay, okay," Elly said. She'd always known something was up with Jake. Or *not* up, rather: she'd never seen Jake touch her sister in a way that wasn't, well, *fraternal*. She still couldn't understand why Laura had been in such a panicky rush to marry the guy. Or why she stayed married to him, for that matter, if she was so unhappy. She supposed it must change everything when there was a kid involved, but still, she hated to see her sister this miserable. "Tell me what I can do to support you."

Laura peered into her empty water glass. "Talk to Anne. Find out what's really going on with her. Then tell me what she says."

"You do realize that whatever Anne tells me might be very different from what Jake has told you, right? And that neither one might be telling the whole truth?"

"I know. But I need to hear what's going on in Anne's head. *Her* version of the truth. Promise me!"

"Okay," Elly said. She rinsed out her cup, hugged Laura, and walked out of the kitchen, hoping that whatever Anne told her wouldn't be something that could destroy what was left of Laura's marriage.

"So how did it go with Uncle Gil? He's a doll, right?" Rhonda said, cornering Sarah in her office late on Monday afternoon.

Sarah had returned from lunch yesterday and ducked into her office until Rhonda left, knowing she'd be asked exactly this question. How could she tell Rhonda that she wasn't interested in her dear uncle without hurting her feelings? That even if she were interested in dating someone, which she certainly wasn't, her uncle wouldn't make the cut, with his bearish build and boatbuilding? She'd gone out with him twice. She'd done her part.

"He certainly knows his own mind," Sarah said.

Rhonda laughed. "Oh, yes. My mom calls him the Truth Teller. Then Gil always quotes some writer—Orwell, I think—and says, 'In a time of universal deceit, telling the truth is a revolutionary act.'"

"Very profound," Sarah said agreeably, thinking, *So annoying.*

"Did he tell you about the boat he's working on?" Rhonda crossed her arms and leaned on Sarah's doorway, beaming. "It's really something."

"Oh, yes. He told me all about it. Rhonda, darling, you know that I'm still married to Neil," Sarah said gently. "I went out with your uncle as a favor to you, but I'm in no position to be seriously dating anyone."

"Your husband has been gone for thirty years!" Rhonda said. "Aren't you divorced by default?"

"No, dear. Nor would I want to be," Sarah said. "I explained this to Gil."

"Oh." Rhonda's face fell. "Well. That's too bad." She wandered away again, her normally tall, slim figure slightly hunched with disappointment.

Well, it couldn't be helped, Sarah thought. Her life was nobody's business but her own.

An hour later, she met with a couple about their golden wedding anniversary party. Fifty years! Sarah marveled at this, wondering how on earth people managed to stay together that long. Perhaps it was lucky Neil had disappeared; maybe that was the only reason *she* was still married.

This evening's celebratory pair had dined in the inn's restaurant at five o'clock, taking advantage of the early-bird special—prime rib for the man, salmon for his wife—and now Sarah sat with them over dessert and coffee (on the house, of course) to discuss party arrangements. About fifty people, they said, holding hands across the table.

"A delightful size for an anniversary party," she said when the woman expressed doubts about the guest list. "Big enough to be festive, but small enough to feel intimate. Besides, not everyone will come," she added reassuringly, when the woman still looked panicky around the eyes.

The husband, Rick, was gray-haired, and so was his plump little wife. They looked like a pair of pigeons mated for life: he wore gray knit pants with a light gray sweater, and she had on a deep gray knit dress that made her look round as a tick. The wife kept tugging the tunic down over stocky thighs encased in black leggings.

Maybe some people fit together so naturally that they could never imagine being anything but a pair, like these two. Sarah wondered what Neil looked like now. He'd once been so handsome that women would turn around to watch him walk down a street.

Neil had completely disappeared after she kicked him out of the house. Bad enough that he'd been drinking, but the drinking wasn't what had done them in. She could have lived with that. But not with his belief that she'd betrayed him.

Over the past thirty years—a time frame she still couldn't wrap her mind around, despite the arthritis in her fingers and the vague aches plaguing her knees—she'd received intermittent letters from him. There was never a return address, so she had never written him back.

The postmarks were from different cities, most of them in Florida, where she supposed it was possible to live on the street. His letters were never maudlin or angry, as hers to him might have been, but simply truthful and occasionally nostalgic. She had never told the girls about this correspondence because she didn't want to get their hopes up for any sort of reunion. She'd learned the hard way that their father was unreliable.

Then, a year ago, Neil had sent a letter she'd reread so often that she'd memorized most of it:

There are such wide spaces between us, dear Sarah, both of geography and of the heart. Yet I find myself wanting to leap the miles, to swim the rivers and fly across the canyons that separate us. You have always held my heart in your hand. I know now that you were telling the truth about some things, but not others. Trust me when I say that things are different for me now, yet my love for you and our daughters remains an unbroken river, flowing as strongly as ever and always in the direction of Folly Cove.

Sarah would have answered him if she'd known where to write. She might have even told him to come home, despite her doubts that Neil had truly made a recovery and was no longer drinking. But that was the last letter she'd ever received from him. Now she was glad she hadn't told the girls anything.

The woman across the table had stopped talking and was looking expectantly at Sarah, who realized she'd dropped out of the conversation entirely.

"I'm sorry, I'm going to have to ask you to repeat that," Sarah said. "I was deep in thought about flowers."

"Oh." The woman looked confused. "I thought we were discussing the menu." She was petulant now. Her mouth, already small, pursed into a tiny red berry.

"I really am sorry," Sarah said. "Your anniversary is of the utmost importance. I want to give every detail of your party the attention it deserves."

Just then she noticed a young woman hovering in the dining room doorway. A tall blonde, very striking despite her casual clothing. It took a moment for Sarah to recognize her.

"Elizabeth!" Sarah said, and leaped from her seat, startling the older woman out of her pout and causing the man to stand up and turn around to stare. But of course he would. Her daughter was beautiful.

Sarah had heard from Laura that Elizabeth—who now called herself "Elly," such a dreadful nickname, like something out of a children's book—was planning to visit. Laura had made it clear that she had invited Elizabeth to stay with her. It had cost Sarah to agree gracefully, because of course she'd prefer to have Elizabeth stay in her apartment. But Laura had been struggling—Sarah had been afraid to delve too deeply into why—so naturally she'd want her sister's support.

Sarah smiled at her daughter now, proud to claim this elegant creature as her own. In her view, every family had one child that stood out as superior to the rest, and this was hers. Elizabeth was her most beautiful, talented daughter.

This wasn't only Sarah's opinion. It was fact: Elizabeth was the one with the golden hair and the golden voice, the girl whose legs were shapely and whose height made her look regal even in jeans.

Elizabeth had an easy personality, too. She was never stubbornly methodical like Laura (which, admittedly, made her competent at many things, and reliable) or furiously, cheerfully defiant like Anne. No, Elizabeth always listened to her mother, and because of that, she'd won nearly every singing contest in the region and earned roles in some of the North Shore's top theater productions before moving to Los Angeles.

Sarah hadn't wanted to let her go west. Or, if she were truthful, what Sarah had really wanted was to go *with* Elizabeth and help manage her career. Of course that was unthinkable. She couldn't leave the inn. Still, she thought of Elizabeth every day, usually when she first woke up, imagining her daughter going to auditions and singing on stages all over Los Angeles, just as Sarah would have done, given that chance at her age.

She went to Elizabeth and embraced her, then released her to have a better look. Elizabeth looked well, very tan and as slim as ever. She was dressed in stylishly snug jeans and knee-high boots, a short black leather jacket and scarf. Her blond hair fell in soft waves around her shoulders. Sarah's own Hollywood girl!

"You look absolutely wonderful," Sarah said, then turned to the couple. "Rick and Jean, I'd like to introduce you to my daughter, Elizabeth Bradford. She's visiting from Hollywood, where she's a singer."

"I'm a production designer, mostly," Elizabeth said.

Sarah waved this off. "My girl has talent dripping from her fingertips."

"Work with movie stars, do ya now?" Rick asked. Red-faced and jovial, he looked like he enjoyed a good Scotch. "Gonna get your name up there in lights?"

Elizabeth smiled at him. "Someday, I hope."

"Oh, she will," Sarah promised. "Elizabeth sings like an angel. Why, I bet she'd be happy to do a little song for you right now."

"Mom," Elizabeth said. "No. Please, let's not do that. I know you're busy. We can visit later. I'm looking for Anne, actually."

"Anne? Oh, honey, I'm sorry. She's not here." Sarah felt a flush of irritation creep up her neck. She didn't want there to be any talk about her daughter choosing to stay in that mossy little cabin by the water instead of the inn. "She's living in Aunt Flossie's cottage for now. She wanted a kitchen of her own."

"Oh," Elizabeth said, frowning. "All right. I'll walk down there."

"You will come back and visit me tomorrow, though, won't you?"

"Of course." Elizabeth leaned down to kiss her mother's cheek before leaving.

Sarah turned back to the couple and flashed a smile. "All right. My apologies for the interruption. Let's talk about flowers for your big day," she said. "Have you thought about a color scheme?"

Things would be all right now, she thought, as she paged through a photo album of floral arrangements. Elizabeth was home. She would cheer up Laura and bring some excitement into their lives.

Elly hiked down through the gardens toward the shore. There was still enough light for her to admire the tall white birches, their green leaves already turning a warm gold. She'd forgotten how New England autumns carried such a sense of possibility. She inhaled deeply and hoped she was clearing her lungs of toxic Los Angeles smog.

She reached the beach and followed the crescent of hard-packed buttery sand to her aunt's house and the little cottage on the ledge beside it. As kids, she and her sisters had always called this tiny cottage "the Houseboat." Against their mother's wishes, Flossie had stocked the Houseboat with snacks and drinks and encouraged them to use the place as teenagers, free from parental supervision.

"Every girl needs a room of her own," Flossie had declared.

Once, during a discussion about virginity at the Thanksgiving table, Flossie had blown up at their mother. "For heaven's sake, Sarah!" she'd cried. "You keep telling your girls to save themselves, but for what? Your daughters should sample what's out there and learn what pleases them before they decide who to love and how to live."

"What do *you* know?" Sarah had responded, tossing her napkin onto the table like a gauntlet. "You were a *nun*! Pretty flawed reasoning coming from a woman married to *God*!"

Flossie had rolled her eyes at that. "For the millionth time, get it straight. I was a *Buddhist* nun. I never believed in any authoritarian creator God, thank you very much."

Laura was the only one who hadn't taken Flossie's advice. She had met Jake in college, gotten pregnant, and married him within a year despite losing the baby.

"You don't have to get married now!" Elly had said when Laura told her about the miscarriage.

But Laura had shaken her head. The invitations had gone out, she told Elly. Most important, their mother approved of Jake. And Jake loved her.

"I can't back out now," Laura had said. "It would break Jake's heart. And Mom's. This is her wedding as much as mine."

"Even more reason to cancel it!" Elly had shrieked at her sister.

Now she was ashamed of herself for not being more supportive. The only thing Laura had ever been guilty of was trying too hard to make other people happy.

She continued up the rocky ledge along a natural staircase of boulders and paused to catch her breath just below the scrap of lawn surrounding the Houseboat. The grass was tall and yellow around the little house and made a sound like a crowd whispering, audible over the surf because the sea was calm and flat today.

Anne was seated cross-legged on the porch with her back to Elly. What was she doing out here in the near-dark? Yoga?

After a moment, Elly realized that her sister was singing. She moved closer and recognized the song as an old sea chantey: "What shall we do with the drunken sailor?" She and her sisters used to make up verses to entertain the guests at the inn, inviting them to sing along. People loved it.

Elly had always loved that song, too. As silly as they could get singing it, a haunting melody lay beneath the song, which had originally been sung on whaling boats. It was easy to imagine those ships just off Jeffrey's Ledge here, as she stood below the cottage listening to Anne's sweet alto drift out to sea.

She was tempted to surprise her sister by joining in. Then Anne abruptly stood and bent over to pick something up off the porch and wrap it in a blanket. What was that thing?

A baby! A tiny foot came loose from the blanket. Anne had a baby! Elly clasped a hand to her mouth to keep from crying out in shock.

Elly had imagined countless different scenarios for her little sister. From their most recent flurry of Skype calls a few months ago, she knew that Anne was excited about some guy. A writer. She'd moved in with him. They'd stopped communicating soon after that, but Elly hadn't thought much of it; she'd been busy and assumed Anne was, too.

During that span of silence between them, whenever Elly did spend a few minutes wondering what Anne was doing, she'd imagined many things. Maybe Anne would move with her writer to a Brooklyn brownstone. Or to Paris, where she and her lover would scribble in journals and drink cheap red wine.

These were far-fetched fantasies, but Elly could sooner imagine Anne living either of those lives than being a mother way out here on a lonely cliff overlooking the gray Atlantic.

Elly felt bereft and angry, despite knowing these emotions meant she was some petty kind of *idiot.*

Still, she couldn't help but wonder what she had in common with Anne and Laura anymore, if they were both mothers and she was childless. It was as if a ravine had opened between them. They'd found love and moved on without her. Gone on to the next level of adulthood. Put their biological stamp on the next generation.

By now Anne had carried the baby inside. The sun was sinking fast. Elly continued up the path to the cottage and rapped on the door.

"Hey, you," she said when Anne opened the door.

"Elly!" Anne's rich auburn hair was cut to her chin and curly. It was the same haircut she'd had as a kid, when she was in perpetual motion on a bicycle or a skateboard. She wore jeans and a flannel shirt. Her grin was broad and genuine. "I didn't know you were coming!"

"But I texted you!"

"You said you 'might' be coming," Anne said. "I figured that was California-speak for 'maybe.'"

"Well, here I am. You going to let me in?"

"Oh! Sorry!" Anne opened the door. "Sorry about the mess, too. I just moved in here because Flossie wanted to have the place cleaned first. I haven't finished unpacking. Of course, now you can't even tell it was ever cleaned, I've got so much crap." She bit her bottom lip. "The thing is, I didn't come alone."

"I know."

"How? Did Mom tell you?"

"No. I saw you on the porch a minute ago," Elly said. "I nearly had a stroke. Why didn't you tell me you had a *baby*? Or Laura? She doesn't know, either, right?"

Anne made a face. "Laura and I aren't exactly on speaking terms. Anyway, I thought Mom would tell her."

"She didn't. Who knows why not? Mom's mind works in mysterious ways." Elly peered over her sister's shoulder at the baby. It was lying in a portable crib, wearing a sleeper—yellow, an unhelpful color, if you wanted to determine gender—that snapped up the front. The baby had hair a shade redder than Anne's and was waving its arms and legs at a handmade mobile of string and driftwood and shells.

"He or she?" Elly said.

"She."

"How old?"

"Four months."

"What's her name?"

"Lucy. Isn't she beautiful?" Anne said, then began to cry.

Elly wrapped her arms around Anne. Her sister was several inches shorter, the perfect height for leaning her coconut-scented head on Elly's shoulder.

Anne had never been a pretty crier. Not like their mother, who Elly had always suspected of manufacturing convenient tears when things weren't going her way. No, Anne was heaving and snorting and rooting around in the pockets of her jeans for tissues.

"Sit down before you fall down," Elly said. "What's wrong?"

"Everything!" Anne said.

"Okay, okay. Take a breath. Come on." Elly led Anne over to the couch facing the windows. Below them, the gray-green waves were fanning toward the shore, trimmed in white lace as the surf sprayed against the rocks.

Elly wanted to kill Writer Guy. She didn't need details to know that he'd stomped on her little sister's heart. Evil bastard.

The couch was the same one that she remembered lying on with countless boys in high school: bamboo with removable cushions covered in brown burlap cloth. The cushions could fly out from under you at awkward moments, like that time Billy Oswald—her bad boy in leather jacket and torn jeans, senior year—was lying on top of her and trying to talk dirty. Elly finally shoved him off because she couldn't breathe, she was trying so hard not to laugh.

The colorful print had faded on the old feedbags Flossie had used to cover the cushions in a creative act that infuriated their mother. "Your aunt decorates like she lives in a barn." Sarah had scowled.

But Elly thought the rough burlap cloth suited this narrow living room with its honeyed pine paneling. The two chairs, also bamboo, had cushions covered in cream-colored muslin and blue plaid pillows, but the windows were bare. Flossie had never bothered making curtains. Why would she? There was nothing beyond the windows but the sea.

The baby was starting to fuss. Elly didn't think Anne would hear the mewling noise above her own sobs, but some mothering instinct kicked in. Anne wiped her face on her flannel shirt and scooped the baby into her arms. The baby stopped grizzling for a minute, then screwed up its face in a howl.

Elly grinned. "You sure produced an ugly little troll. Look at that face."

"Be nice." Anne dropped into one of the chairs across from Elly.

Now that Anne's back was to the window, her curly hair rose in a burnished halo around her face. She lifted up her shirt to feed the baby. Her breasts were engorged and creamy white, with rosy nipples.

Elly turned away for a moment, pain and jealousy making her eyes burn. "I still can't believe you kept this a secret. What the hell?"

"I know. I'm a horrible sister. I'm sorry." Anne leaned her head back and closed her eyes. Her face relaxed.

The act of nursing seemed to calm her. Hormones, Elly supposed. The baby had grabbed on to Anne's shirt. Her hands were pink and tiny. Starfish hands.

Again, Elly had to look away. "So what happened in Puerto Rico?"

"Everyone keeps asking me that, but I never know what to say. It's so complicated," Anne said.

"Start with the basics. Who knocked you up and where is he now?"

Anne opened her eyes. "Colin. New York."

"Has he left you and the baby for good?"

Anne nodded. Her face was blotchy from crying. Elly thought, for a brief absurd moment, of Snapchatting a picture of Anne to Laura. If Laura could see how Anne looked right now, she would realize she had nothing to worry about. It was obvious that Anne hadn't come home for Jake. She was simply hiding out after her own train wreck.

"Were you in love?" Elly pressed. "Was this guy Colin on board with the whole baby thing but backed out? Or was this unplanned? Just another cosmic joke?"

Anne made a face at her. "What is this? Twenty questions?"

"Oh, honey, I'm just getting started." Elly crossed her arms and waited.

Her sister glanced down at the baby, stroking her curls with her free hand while she told Elly about surfing and living with friends in a beach house. Working as a waitress. Her dream life.

"Really? Waitressing is your dream life?" Elly asked. "You have a master's degree in education."

"I'd started cooking, too," Anne said. "I was thinking about going to culinary school."

"I thought you hated working at the inn."

"I hated working with *Mom*," Anne corrected. "Anyway, I wouldn't ever want to run an inn. I just want to cook. To bake, actually."

"Fair enough. And when did Mr. Asshole arrive on the scene?"

"Don't call him that. He's still Lucy's father." Anne switched the baby to the other breast. Lucy fussed a little, but Anne soothed her quickly. "He's a writer. I met him in the restaurant."

Her sister managed the baby so naturally that again Elly felt her own black heart contract with envy, raw and terrible.

"What kind of writer?" she prodded when Anne leaned her head back against the chair. Anne's throat was tan and slender; her lashes were as lush and dark as a doll's against her freckled cheeks.

"A successful one," Anne said, sounding dreamy now as she told Elly about Colin.

She was reliving that first flush of love, Elly thought as she listened: that wild, sweet emotion you feel when you're entering the danger zone of passion and feel certain everything will turn out fine, despite all evidence to the contrary.

"Colin's Irish," Anne went on. "He published a novel in Ireland about ten years ago that was made into a TV movie over there. He came to Puerto Rico to write a sequel."

Elly was begrudgingly impressed. She didn't have enough fingers to count the number of her Hollywood friends who would kill to have a book or script made into a movie. "Okay, enough about him. So then you got pregnant. Too bad they never taught you about birth control when you were getting your master's degree."

"I know, right? I was stupid. Colin told me right up front he'd never wanted kids." Anne's eyes were dark with misery, nearly slate. She started crying again, which led to hiccups. The baby didn't seem at all bothered by this; she continued to nurse with little grunts of satisfaction.

Jesus, Elly thought. Babies are total parasites. "So the guy's a bastard. Don't give him another thought. He doesn't deserve you."

"No. Colin never made me any promises. Then his wife came to Puerto Rico and got him!"

For an absurd moment, Elly pictured a woman with a lasso, roping her wandering man. "Oh, honey," she said, because now Anne was doing more than crying: she was collapsing, folding in around the baby as if protecting her child from falling shrapnel.

Which, in a way, she was. Elly could see it all now: Anne's delusions, then her fantasy life being shattered as suddenly and completely as if someone had fired a missile into it.

Elly crossed the room to kneel on the braided rug in front of her sister to comfort her. Laura was going to have another hissy fit when she found out Anne's baby daddy was *married*.

Had Anne known Colin had a wife? Maybe he'd lied to her all along. For the sake of a truce between Anne and Laura, Elly hoped so. She rapped on her sister's knee sharply with her knuckles. "Look at me!"

Anne snapped her head up. "What? Why are you hitting me?"

"Did you know this guy was *married*? I mean, from the beginning?"

"Yes, but Colin told me he'd been separated for two years. He said he was *this close* to getting a divorce." Anne held her thumb and forefinger up an inch apart.

Elly sat back on her heels. Colin was probably thrilled to be playing Papa Hemingway and screwing his pretty island girl. Then the baby arrived and he was off like a shot, back to the bed his wife had been keeping warm for him. "What a total dick."

"Don't *say* things like that. I don't want Lucy to think her father meant nothing to me." Anne gave the baby a worried glance, as if the little slug could actually understand the conversation.

Elly shrugged. "Fine. But if your kid's lucky, she'll never meet that jerk. Remember: we all got along just fine without Dad."

Though the minute she said this Elly knew it was a lie. She had missed her father from the moment he left.

The morning after Dad disappeared—he'd taken off at night while they were all asleep, the coward—Elly had sneaked into his bedroom closet and stolen one of his neckties, her favorite one with the black Scottie dogs on a green background. She still had that tie in a dresser drawer.

She'd ridden her bike to Gloucester the next day, trying to find him. The police had to take her home. She was eight years old. Now she wondered what her mother had been doing that she hadn't even noticed Elly was gone. It was Flossie who'd called the cops.

In her early teens, Elly kept asking her mother about her father's whereabouts. One Saturday night, while the two of them were alone in the kitchen at Folly Cove and polishing silverware, Sarah had thrown her hands up in exasperation as Elly grilled her.

"Look," Sarah said. "Your father was an alcoholic. He went out of his mind and accused me of terrible things," she'd said. "That's the truth! I have no idea where he is now and no reason to think he'll ever come back."

"But, Mom! Didn't you even try *looking* for him?" Elly had yelled. "What kind of woman doesn't look for her own husband? Alcoholism is a *disease*, you know. An addiction! Like heroin! We learned that at *school!*"

"For heaven's sake! I can't believe I'm paying tens of thousands of dollars to that prep school of yours so some nitwit teacher in wrinkled *khakis* can make you believe that getting bombed and abandoning your family is normal." Her mother's glare was incredulous.

Elly got up now and went to the refrigerator—all of ten steps from the living room—in search of wine. There wasn't any. She filled a glass of water and sat down on the couch again. "What about Mom? She must have totally freaked when she saw the baby."

"She wants me to say I'm divorced." Anne's voice was bitter. "Oh, and she also made it clear that Lucy and I aren't welcome at her apartment."

"Well, I guess one good thing about Mom is that you always know where you stand with her." Elly reached across the narrow living room to touch the baby's hair. A red ringlet curled around her finger. Elly smiled. "I can guess why you named her Lucy. Narnia, right?"

"Yes," Anne said, smiling back. "Because of Dad reading us those Narnia stories."

It came to Elly then, another memory: her father, his whiskey-sweet breath and the scratchy feel of his face as he gave them "super kisses," blowing air out on their arms or bellies and making them giggle after reading to them from the C. S. Lewis books.

"God," she said. "I haven't thought about those books in ages. Remember how Dad used to sit with us on that big window seat upstairs while he read to us? And how he used different voices for the Narnia characters?"

Anne laughed. "I loved it when he was the faun, Mr. Tumnus."

"Me, too. But we were terrified when Dad acted out Jadis. Remember her? The White Witch who froze Narnia for a hundred years?"

"Of course. I used to hide under the covers!" Anne said. "I was petrified. Then you and Laura started calling Mom 'the White Witch' because you said she could freeze us with a look. We all thought that was hysterical even though it was true."

"Anyway, Lucy's a perfect name," Elly said as she considered how to pose the question Laura wanted her to ask Anne. "Look, I need to ask you something else."

"Sure," Anne said. "Whatever."

"Is there something going on with you and Jake?"

"Oh, Christ," Anne said. "No! I've been trying to avoid him, but Jake came into the pub while I was working. Laura saw us and turned into a screaming witch herself." Anne narrowed her eyes at Elly. "Wait. Did you come here because Laura asked you to?"

"Don't be an idiot. I would have come anyway. I've missed you." Elly kept her eyes steady on Anne's face despite the complicated, shifting emotions there. Anne was angry now and Elly couldn't blame her.

"I can't believe she asked you to spy on me! Or that you'd do that for her!" Anne dislodged the baby from her breast, put Lucy up to her shoulder, and patted her back.

"I'm not spying," Elly said. "I'm only running interference because Laura's hurting and freaking the hell out. She doesn't know about Lucy, so she's still imagining that you're hot after her man. She still hasn't gotten over what happened with you and Jake."

"That's ridiculous." Anne rose and paced, the baby curled against her shoulder. "You know there's never been anything between Jake and me!"

"Tell me again what happened that summer, *exactly*." Elly felt disoriented as she tried to follow Anne's agitated movements. There wasn't much space to walk inside the cottage: her sister followed a short,

U-shaped path from the living room into the galley kitchen, then back through the living room.

The baby's round cheek was turned to one side. Lucy's skin was pink and soft-looking, her lashes like moth wings, dark against that pale skin. Elly felt another sharp constriction beneath her rib cage.

Anne was standing on the braided rug in front of the windows. Behind her, the sky had darkened to violet, nearly the same color as the ocean. It was difficult to tell where the sea ended and the sky began.

"Fine." Anne took a deep breath, then said, "I was staying at their house and taking care of the horses while Laura and Kennedy were away. Jake was at a conference and came home really late the day before I was supposed to leave. I was sleeping in the guest room upstairs. It was hot, so I wasn't wearing a nightgown. I woke up because I felt cold all of a sudden."

Anne stopped talking and put a hand over her eyes.

"And Jake came into your room?" Bits and pieces of the story were coming back to Elly now; she was remembering the tearful call Anne had made to her in Los Angeles after it happened. Laura had already called Elly that same evening to describe a very different version. Back then Elly hadn't known who to believe.

Anne said, "Jake was standing next to the bed. He'd pulled the sheet down to look at me. He'd unzipped his pants. He was touching himself." Her voice was stilted.

"My God." Hearing her sister's flat tone erased any lingering doubts Elly might have had about Anne telling the truth. "Then what?"

"I yelled at him to get out of my room. Jake ran away like he was being chased by a rabid dog."

"I bet. What happened after that?"

"Nothing." Anne shrugged. "I got dressed and took off."

"You didn't talk to Jake?"

Anne shook her head. "Not that day. He tried talking to me about it a few days later, and apologized. I thought I could forgive him until that Christmas party two years ago."

Elly nodded. "When Laura saw the two of you."

"Right. I had tried to avoid seeing both of them anytime I came home, but the inn was having that big anniversary Christmas party and we were all here." Anne frowned. "Everyone but you. Why was that?"

"I had a singing job." Elly didn't say that it was only for an advertising jingle, or that she'd spent that particular Christmas Eve heartbroken and drunk and singing karaoke in a bar with a bunch of strangers, because Hans, the man she'd been in love with, had left her.

Anne didn't ask more about it, thankfully. She said, "Anyway, Jake cornered me in the back hallway during that party, said we needed to talk. Then he pulled me against him and started kissing me."

"You're kidding."

"No!" Anne said. She made a face. "Well, he didn't really *kiss* me. It was more like he mashed his mouth on mine like you see actors do in the movies. Like they're sucking each other's lips off. Don't you ever wonder who really kisses like that? Well, Jake does."

"Did you scream or anything?" Elly already knew from Laura that Anne had not.

"No. I thought about it," Anne said. "But I didn't want Kennedy and Laura to be upset, so I just tried to shove him off me. Then Laura walked in and saw us." Anne frowned. "That was bizarre, too. It was almost like Jake wanted her to catch him."

"What do you mean?"

"Well, for instance, why didn't Jake wait and try to corner me upstairs in my room? Or even outside? Why do it with his wife in the next room?"

"Maybe he didn't have a chance to think things through," Elly said. "Or he'd had too much to drink."

"He didn't seem drunk." Anne went into the bedroom to lay the baby down.

Elly stood up and followed her. "Wow. She's out like a light."

"Yeah, Lucy turns into a drunken sailor after she eats. That's why I always sing her that song." Anne sighed. "I'm pissed off at Laura for not believing me, but I feel bad for her, too. If Jake did these things to me, what's he doing to other women?"

"I never thought of that," Elly said. "Maybe you and I should do some detective work."

"No way! I'm staying away from him. From Laura, too."

"All right. I'll do it," Elly said. "If I can find some other women Jake has approached, Laura will have to believe you."

"Don't bother, Elly. Really. I'm done with Laura."

Elly raised her eyes to meet Anne's furious gaze and smiled. "No, you're not," she said. "We're sisters. We won't ever be done with each other."

CHAPTER FIVE

The riding lesson seemed to last forever. Laura glanced around, looking for her daughter.

She'd forced Kennedy to come out to the barn with her after school. Laura had tacked up the horses herself because she was afraid the ornery bay mare, Zelda, might blow up her belly if Kennedy saddled her. The clever animal would then expel her breath after her rider was seated, causing the saddle to slip upside down and dump the rider unceremoniously onto the ground. Laura had found this out the hard way: once, a student had gotten dragged across the ring when the saddle slipped and her boot was caught in the stirrup. Fortunately it was one of her tougher riders, a girl with a good sense of humor. One lawsuit could shut down the stables.

Today she'd put Kennedy to work cleaning stalls. Now her daughter looked pickle-faced with misery as she pushed a wheelbarrow of manure out onto the pile behind the barn.

It was good for children to do chores after school, Laura reminded herself, trying to tame the anxiety that so often flared up where her daughter was concerned.

Lately Kennedy seemed to have lost interest in everything, dragging through the days like a daydreaming geriatric. Was that really due to impending puberty and the roller coaster of heavy hormones?

Or was something going on at school? Maybe Laura should see the guidance counselor, check in with the teachers.

Or—and this was Laura's worst fear—maybe Kennedy was being affected by the fact that her parents weren't getting along, or by Laura's own stupid guilty secret.

Guilty or not, to cheer herself up, Laura allowed herself to dwell on Tom for a few minutes. Each time she did this felt like a welcome reprieve from her own life where, no matter how hard she worked or how determined she was to be cheerful, everything felt like a slog. Sometimes it felt as if her family were living on top of a sinkhole that only she could feel caving in, yet Laura didn't know how to warn them. And maybe warning them would be worse, anyway, because that would mean acknowledging that the problems between herself and Jake were too numerous to overcome.

She'd met Tom in high school, back when he was the skinny kid who sat next to her in algebra class. Glasses, braces, acne, a stutter: Tom was every jock's punching bag. He was so miserable at their private school that by the end of sophomore year he'd transferred.

Laura, on the other hand, was a high school standout. Top grades, involved in school council and various clubs, a popular girl who managed to dodge most of the bitchy infighting among the alpha girls because she spent most of her free time at a riding stable in Gloucester.

You were the only one at that school who ever had a kind word for me, Tom had messaged Laura a few months ago on Facebook. *After my wife died last year, I vowed to reconnect with people I cared about. I wanted to tell you how grateful I am to you for making my time in school a little less hellish.*

Laura had been touched but surprised by his message. She'd had to dig out her high school yearbook to even remember who Tom was.

It wasn't altruism, she'd messaged back. *You're the one who got me through chemistry. Did you stay in science? You were good at it.*

He had. They quickly graduated from Facebook to e-mailing, exchanging updates about their families and work lives. Tom had started an environmental company; one of their products was a cost-effective water-treatment system that removed mercury, lead, arsenic, and other harmful chemicals.

Wow! You're saving the world, she'd told him.

One drop of water at a time, he'd agreed. *I'd feel prouder, except my work is so fun it doesn't feel like a job.*

By then she had trolled through his Facebook photos. Most were postings of gadgets his company had patented. Among the few personal photos were some of his two children, both boys in high school. There were no photographs of Tom's deceased wife, but Laura had Googled the obituary and discovered she died of a brain aneurysm at age thirty-nine.

The only two pictures of himself that Tom had posted showed him astride a mountain bike against a woodsy backdrop. It was difficult to tell what he looked like, because he was wearing a helmet and sunglasses. When Laura clicked on a link to his company, there were glossy pictures of the company's products and high-tech labs. Nothing personal.

There was a lull in their communication in June and July. Not because Laura felt guilty about their correspondence—not then, not yet—but because she was busy. Then, last month, Tom had e-mailed her to ask how her summer was going, and Laura e-mailed him to ask advice because she needed a new laptop. At least that was the reason she gave him: in truth, she had begun to realize how much she missed their correspondence. How much she needed a friend who had nothing to do with her life.

Laura loved hearing Tom's thoughts on everything from robots to politics. He was curious about everything; recently, he'd inspired her to buy an astronomy map for her phone and had texted her once before a meteor storm. *I'll watch the sky show with you.*

Laura still hadn't felt guilty. She had even mentioned Tom in an offhand way to Jake, who said he was pleased that she'd reconnected with a childhood friend.

The turning point came a few weeks ago, when Tom sent her an innocuous photo of a red bicycle with a message more personal than any of the others: *We rode bikes at my house one day after school. You borrowed my sister's bike. You didn't know it, but that day was my birthday. You were my best present.*

One warm spring afternoon at the end of sophomore year, Tom had offered to help Laura with geometry. It all came back to her: she'd gone to his house after school, where they'd studied at the kitchen table. Tom was a patient tutor.

They'd ridden bikes to the park after finishing their homework. By then she'd stopped noticing the braces, the acne, Tom's occasional stutter. Instead, Laura saw him as someone who made her feel so comfortable in her own skin that she didn't care what her hair looked like or whether her laugh sounded like a "dying crow's," as one particularly vicious girl in her class had told her. Being with Tom was as easy as being with herself.

Tom transferred schools soon afterward and she never saw him again. But seeing the photo of the red bicycle, Laura experienced a sudden pang of nostalgia for the girl she had been. For how free and hopeful she'd felt back then, and how convinced she was that the best years of her life were still ahead of her.

Communicating with Tom wasn't just about catching up with a high school friend. It was a way to travel back in time, to recapture that rapturous sense of possibility.

Laura had texted him back after seeing the photo: *Now it's your turn to keep me going. Things aren't so great in my life right now.*

And so it had begun: her confessions to him and his support of her, no matter what dumb things she wrote. She poured out her worries: money, Kennedy, the stables. Funny anecdotes interspersed with fears about aging. Her concern that she'd taken on too much and wouldn't ever make her family happy.

The only topic Laura considered off-limits was Jake. She did not want to be unfaithful to her husband in any way.

Still, her conscience bothered her. She couldn't go a day without some communication with Tom. She had bought the prepaid phone a month ago and had come to think of it as her lifeline.

Tom had suggested meeting in person, but she'd refused. *I'm not interested in an affair,* she had texted back.

Sorry if I gave you the wrong idea. Just coffee, he replied. *I respect your marriage, but I want to look at you while we talk. To hear your wild laugh again.*

She'd smiled at that but had refused him anyway. *I'm not in a good place right now. And anyway, I don't laugh like that anymore.*

What she hadn't said, even to Tom, was that there were many days when she didn't laugh at all. That, lately, depression had set in, and she'd been going back to bed after Jake was at work and Kennedy was at school, once the breakfast dishes and barn chores were done. She slept for hours and woke only when her alarm went off in the early afternoon, feeling drugged and heavy.

But Laura couldn't stop thinking about him. She sneaked in phone time, hiding in the bedroom or bathroom to text Tom even while Kennedy was watching television or doing God knows what on her computer.

Last night she'd done something that made her face go hot with shame even now, as she stood in the center of the riding ring watching her students: on a whim, she had texted Tom a picture of herself with her shirt unbuttoned. She'd taken the picture with her hand caressing the curve of one breast, because she had been thinking of his hand on her skin.

Tom's reply was instant: *I want to kiss you there. And everywhere.*

Laura shivered now, thinking of these words, and folded her arms over her breasts. Her husband made love to her only when she initiated things; they hadn't touched each other in months. How wonderful, and how terrible, that as a result, she had gotten herself into this strange position of longing for a man she hadn't seen since they were children. How wrong was that? She didn't want to think about that. She only knew that she had to stop feeling this way if she was ever going to fix her marriage and find some measure of contentment in her life, which at the moment felt like all drudgery, all the time.

She began barking orders at the riders, the same commands over and over: "Heels down, everyone! Straight backs! No, Melanie, post on the *diagonal.* Watch your horse's shoulder! Cara, up out of the saddle! Up, up, up! Heels down! Back straight! Tully, don't ride the reins. No, don't let the horse crowd you against the rail, Jennifer. Use your legs to guide your horses, people! *Legs!*"

This was a full class—six riders, all middle school girls. Laura felt like she was getting whiplash trying to watch them trot around the ring. Finally she put Blizzard, an obedient palomino gelding, up in front. Melanie was riding him; she picked things up faster than the others. She and Blizzard would help pace the other horses.

The afternoon had turned damp and gray. Fog was blurring the woods of Dogtown beyond the riding ring in a way that reminded Laura of the "end of the world" game she'd played with her sisters: one of them would claim that the end of the world lay beyond the fog, and they would dare each other to run down the lawn below the inn toward the cliff.

Sometimes, if you ran fast enough with your eyes squinted shut against the damp, it did feel like you could tumble off the edge of the earth and plunge into nothingness. This was especially true if they ran toward Aunt Flossie's house and cottage, where there was the real danger of hurling themselves off the rocky cliff.

The cottage: Anne was there! "She's got a baby. Did you know Anne had a baby?" Elly had demanded when she returned to Laura's last night after visiting their little sister.

At first Laura didn't believe it. Why hadn't their mother told her? Surely she must have seen the baby when Anne arrived!

Finally, when Elly convinced her, Laura was so shocked that she had to pour herself a second glass of wine. She'd opened the bottle before dinner. Always a mistake. If she opened a bottle while she cooked, then poured two or three glasses for each of them at dinner, the bottle was gone in an evening. As if the calories weren't bad enough, there was the expense that didn't bear thinking about. Laura bought only the cheapest wine tolerable. But even at ten dollars a bottle, a bottle of wine a night translated into $310 a month. She and Jake couldn't afford that. Not if they wanted to buy groceries.

Though some nights Laura would rather have had wine than food.

To Elly she'd said, "I never even knew Anne wanted kids."

"I'm not sure even Anne knew that," Elly said, and told Laura about the writer dumping Anne and leaving her to go back to New York.

Laura was sympathetic at first. Then the wary look in Elly's eyes caused her to suspect her sister was holding something back. Finally it hit her. "He's married, right?"

Yes, Elly had admitted, adding that the guy had gone back to his wife, which was why Anne had left Puerto Rico.

"Anne really did believe he was getting divorced," Elly said. "He told her he was separated from his wife and working on it. I guess we all believe what we want when it comes to love."

By then Elly was on her second glass of wine, too, and dinner wasn't even on the table. Luckily, Jake had called to say he'd be later than usual.

"What a fool," Laura had said to Elly. "How could Anne let herself get pregnant? Especially when he was *married*?"

"She was in love," Elly said simply. "Really, you should see her. Anne's a hot mess."

"She should have been smart enough not to get involved with a married man in the first place," Laura snapped, though inwardly she had flinched, thinking of herself and Tom. But no: she was not involved with him. Just acting stupid because she was lonely. All of that was about to stop.

"Maybe. My point is, you have nothing to worry about," Elly had said. "Anne isn't after Jake."

"You could have fooled me," Laura said.

Elly had argued with her then, had told Laura that same old horror story from Anne's point of view. Lies about Jake leering at her and touching himself while Anne was sleeping! As if Jake would do something that perverted! Jake would barely do anything beyond the missionary position. With his own wife. In the *dark*.

"I don't trust Anne. I never will," Laura had reminded Elly.

Elly had shrugged. "Whatever. I'm just saying that Anne might not be the only one at fault."

So the sides were drawn. And Laura, as usual, was standing alone on hers.

She didn't blame Elly. Anne could be extremely persuasive. Laura patted the pocket of her jeans, reassuring herself that the phone was still there. At least she had Tom.

For now.

By the end of the lesson, three of the six students had nearly mastered the posting trot. The others were still as floppy as rag dolls on the backs of their horses; Laura didn't hold out much hope that they'd improve, either. She'd been teaching these girls since summer camp.

But at least they were doing **something** active after school. Her own daughter was sitting on a hay bale, oblivious to everyone, her nose in a book.

"Kennedy, put that book away and come help with the horses," Laura yelled, more sharply than she'd intended, making her daughter jump.

She crosstied two of the horses inside the barn for Kennedy to groom, then asked Melanie and Cara to lead the other four out front and hitch them to the rail. The girls offered to help her untack and curry the horses, chatting while they worked.

Melanie reminded Laura of herself: driven, competitive. A perfectionist. Laura had competed in the top horse shows for years and even made an equestrienne drill team in college. She would have gone further if it hadn't been for Jake.

When she'd gotten pregnant in college, Jake had proposed marriage and said he'd go to dental school. "I want to provide for you," he'd declared. "You should stay home with our kids." Both of them were shaky but brave, determined to do the right thing. Then she'd lost the baby.

Only Jake shared the depth of her grief over that loss. How could she *not* have married him?

Melanie's mother, Sandra, arrived to pick up her daughter. Laura knew Sandra from the club. Her husband was a doctor of some kind, the kind that kept regular hours and drove a car with heavily tinted windows that looked bulletproof. The license plate read WINNING.

Sandra didn't work outside the home, but when she saw Laura, she often made a point of ticking off the tasks crammed into her harried days: getting the boys to soccer and Melanie to dance or riding lessons, plus fitting in her massage / hair appointment / tennis lesson / pedicure / yoga class / church work / charity benefits for the hospital. Sandra was a trustee at the school where their girls went, too, and effective at corralling everyone into voting for things like improvements to the field house.

Every town needed a Sandra. She was a model citizen and could hold a nut-free bake sale like nobody else.

Sandra was what Laura had imagined she'd become after she stopped riding competitively. Instead, Laura had transformed into a woman she didn't recognize: an unhappy wife and uncertain mother. A woman on the edge.

Like her daughter, Sandra was whippet slim and blond. Today she was dressed for yoga in electric blue leggings and a fitted yellow hoodie with purple piping. Her outfit probably cost two weeks' worth of groceries. That's how Laura measured everything these days.

Sandra was smiling at her daughter. "How'd it go, honey?" she asked Melanie.

Melanie scowled. "*Fine.* Can I have the keys? And did you bring me a snack?" She stomped off, car keys in hand, after her mother assured her there was a nonfat yogurt and fruit smoothie waiting for her in the car.

Sandra shot Laura an apologetic look. "Sorry."

"Don't worry about it," Laura said. "Melanie's always perfectly pleasant with me."

"I think she's being bullied at school," Sandra said.

Laura was startled. "Really? Why? She's so smart and pretty. A talented rider, too."

"Riding is saving her life," Sandra said. "I have you to thank for that. The thing is, Melanie's *too* pretty. If she were less so, she could just be ordinary instead of competitive. Happy, you know? Nobody would bother her if she was just average."

Like your own invisible lumpy daughter. Was that what Sandra meant?

"Well, they all grow up eventually," Laura said. "There's no point in worrying too much." As the words came out, Laura realized how lame they sounded. It wasn't even how she felt: it was how she *wanted* to feel. She worried every minute about Kennedy.

"I know," Sandra agreed. "Anyway, listen: I've been meaning to invite you and Jake to join Wayne and me for dinner at the club. How about next Friday night? We don't get to see enough of you!"

"Oh, I don't know. Things are kind of crazy at the moment."

"I know, right? Life is insane!" Sandra said. "But when isn't it?

Especially for working moms like you? Gosh, I admire you for working. But you need a break, girlfriend! This would be perfect! Melanie babysits on Fridays, and Hunter and Tyler both have hockey, so we use Friday nights as date night. I'm sure you and Jake must need to schedule romance, too?"

Laura cast around for an excuse. Dinners at the club weren't cheap. Just one cocktail each and they'd be out a hundred bucks, even without dessert.

"Just say yes!" Sandra said. "When was the last time you had *fun* with your husband?"

When, indeed? Laura thought. And shouldn't they be having fun now, since Anne was home? "All right," she said.

"Great! Seven o'clock okay?"

When Laura nodded, Sandra waggled her fingers over one shoulder as she walked to the car, ponytail bouncing. In the passenger seat, Melanie's blond head was bent forward over her phone, her thumbs jabbing at the keypad.

Watching Melanie on her phone led Laura back to the barn, where she glanced furtively over her shoulder before taking her own phone out of her pocket. She was ending things now before it was too late. *We need to stop,* she texted Tom.

Then, almost immediately, she sent another: *But I don't know how. You are my joy.*

Laura leaned against the windowsill, willing herself to go inside and make dinner. But she felt paralyzed, waiting for Tom's response.

She smiled when it came: *And you are mine. Please don't leave me. Not yet. Even if we never meet, we have so much more to say.*

Still, she replied, *I'm not kidding. We need to stop. Soon. I hope you understand.* Then she pocketed the phone and walked back to the house.

Jake balked at the idea of dinner at the club, of course. "We hardly know those people," he said when she presented the idea to him after Kennedy went upstairs. "And with what money? We can barely pay the electric bill and it's not even November. I swear those horses are taking showers."

"I have to run the lights in the barn now. It gets dark before I finish teaching," Laura said. "Look, I know the club's expensive. But aren't you the one who says we should socialize more because it's good for business?"

"Yeah, sure, but only when we can afford it. Have you looked at the latest credit card bill? No, of course you haven't," he said.

"I always offer to do the bills," Laura said. "You won't let me!"

Jake sighed. "I know. I'm sorry. Look, it's fine, honey. Let's go out. Lord knows you deserve it." He kissed her forehead and went upstairs.

Laura folded laundry in the utility room off the kitchen before following, heaving the third load of the day onto the counter and sorting it, then folding shirts and pants and balling socks into pairs. She was glad Jake had come around to the idea of dinner. So why was she upset? Why did she wish Jake had kept fighting?

Because at least when they were fighting, they were talking.

Tom texted her again just as she was finishing in the laundry room: *Urgent.*

What? she responded, breathless with fear. What if something had happened to him?

A photo. A field thick with bluebells, the color vibrant even on her phone. And a message: *I want to lie with you here in the sun. I want to breathe in your smell and touch your hair. And hear that crazy laugh. I've thought about this. J. doesn't make you happy. I know what misery feels like. I got past it. You can, too. Let me help you do that. See me. Five minutes. No strings. Just coffee and a kiss.*

"Honey? What are you doing down there?" Jake called from the top of the stairs.

"Be right up," Laura said. "Just getting the laundry."

Lies upon lies. She studied the photo again before deleting it. *No. This has to stop now,* she wrote. *Tonight is IT.* Then she dropped the phone into her pocket.

Upstairs, Laura stopped in Kennedy's room to say good night and leave her a pile of clean clothes. "Hey," she asked as she bent to kiss her daughter's forehead, "why don't you ever invite Melanie over after school?"

"I don't even know her. We're on different teams at school." Kennedy was playing a game on her phone, scowling at the tiny brightly colored shapes.

"You do know her. You see her at the barn every week," Laura pointed out.

"Yeah, but she's a bitch. Why would I talk to her?"

"Language, sweetie!" Laura said, taken aback. "Her mom says Melanie's being bullied. Maybe she could use a friend like you."

Kennedy rolled her eyes. "Yeah, right. Like Melanie would *want* me as a friend. I can't even!"

"You can't even what?"

"Never mind, Mom. *God.* I'm literally dying here with you preaching at me."

Anxiety rose, thick and sour in Laura's throat. If Melanie—with her limber athlete's body and magazine hair—was getting bullied, where did that leave poor Kennedy, with her menopausal waist and stocky legs?

"Well, at least be kind to her," Laura said. "Everyone deserves kindness in this world."

"Sure, Mom. Tell that to the world, and maybe everyone will put down their guns." Kennedy jammed her headphones on then, effectively cutting off the conversation.

Laura stepped out into the hallway just as Jake was coming up the stairs. "Coming to bed?" she said.

"Soon. I've got to check my schedule and catch up on a few e-mails first," he said, turning into the guest bedroom that doubled as his office. "You go ahead and shower first."

In the shower, Laura washed her hair and rinsed it twice, hoping the hot water would dissolve her sticky, weighty feeling of despair. She thought about the tiny bathroom in the first apartment she and Jake had rented after they were married. They'd shower together because the hot water ran out so fast. Sometimes they'd even make love with the water running, Laura with her back to Jake, hands pressed against the white tiles.

Now their master bath was the size of their old bedroom, with a double showerhead system and a bench inside the vast blue-tiled space.

Big as it was, Laura couldn't remember the last time they'd been in this bathroom together, never mind sharing the shower.

Once, when she'd asked Jake why that was, he'd said, "I hate intruding on your precious private time."

Laura stepped out of the shower and toweled off. She picked up her clothes with a sigh, intending to toss them into the hamper, and felt the burner phone in the pocket of her jeans. Usually she stored it beneath the files in her bottom desk drawer at night. She glanced up at the door. It wasn't locked, but Jake wouldn't come into the bathroom while she was in here.

She pulled the phone out, not daring to hope that Tom had texted back after her last message.

But he had. He had! *I respect your choice to be faithful within your marriage,* he'd written. *I just want you to know that you deserve to be happy. You should stop communicating with me if it makes you uncomfortable, but please know that I'm here when you need me. As a friend you can trust.*

Laura raised her eyes to the bathroom mirror and wiped the steam off with her hand. She was thicker-waisted than she wanted to be, yes, but now that she was nude and free of constraints, she felt thinner. Almost sexy. Would a man want her?

Tom would. She didn't know why she was so sure of that, but she was.

Before Laura could reconsider, she raised the phone and took a picture of herself from the neck down and sent it to him with a message: *In the shower and thinking of you. Can't think of you without smiling. Thank you for always being there.*

Then she shut off the phone, tucked it back into the pocket of her jeans, and shoved the jeans into the hamper beneath the rest of the dirty clothes. What the hell. Jake hadn't done laundry in twenty years.

Immediately she felt ashamed of her own recklessness. Guilty.

Well, that was the last of it. A keepsake for Tom. And maybe for the Internet, if he turned out to be a creep, but at least she'd had the sense not to send him a picture of her face.

Laura felt a little shiver of pleasure as she imagined Tom opening up that photo. Maybe he would feel the same desire seeing it that she'd felt taking the picture. Rare moments of joy for both of them before she ended their communication for good.

Meanwhile, she had to find her way back to Jake. She would be kinder. More loving. And firmer about the two of them spending time alone and really communicating. She had reached out to Tom because she so often felt like she was howling alone in the wilderness, overwhelmed by worries that she knew Jake must share in some way. Maybe she could even admit to Jake that she'd been tempted to see Tom. If nothing else, that could serve as a wake-up call in their marriage. She had invested far too many years in building her family to just throw her life away.

The sad thing was, her parents had argued constantly about money, just as she and Jake did. The inn, like everything else, was an infinite dark well that had required her parents to keep pouring money into it. Laura had sworn that she would never, ever have a marriage like theirs. And she wouldn't!

Her father had wanted to sell the inn and use the money to move somewhere warm. Mexico, maybe, to a small white stucco house with a jacaranda tree dripping purple blossoms. Neil had described this imaginary home so vividly that, as a child, Laura believed this house actually existed.

She'd fallen in love with Jake because he was the polar opposite of her father. Neil Bradford was the son of once-wealthy parents who grew up to be an impractical, irresponsible dreamer. Laura had known that about her father even as a young child: Daddy played with them, took them hiking in Dogtown and fishing and sailing while Mom worked. That's how it was.

"Your father's allergic to chores," her mother told them, if the girls asked why Neil didn't have to make up any beds or wash any bathrooms.

Jake was a hard worker from a modest home in central Massachusetts. He was driven to succeed in college and as an athlete, too. He'd played varsity lacrosse in college and morphed on the field from a sweet guy who'd hold doors open for you into a beast, growling and waving his stick, charging at opponents on the field as if he had superhero strength.

Laura ran a comb through her hair, applied moisturizer, and slipped into a nightgown before entering the bedroom. Her best nightgown, the white one. She'd been careful not to put this nightie in the dryer the way she had all the others. Tonight she would make love with her husband and clear her mind of everything—and everyone—else.

She was reading, her eyes threatening to close, when Jake joined her half an hour later. "Sorry. Hope I didn't keep you up," he said. "I'll just grab a quick shower."

"Whatever," she said under her breath, suddenly irritated with him.

Sometimes Laura imagined her husband hiding in his office or even in the bathroom until she fell asleep. Well, she'd force herself to stay awake this time. Maybe they wouldn't make love after all. She wasn't in the mood anymore. They really needed to talk about Anne. Laura sat up straighter, yanked the pillow out from behind her, and propped it high against the headboard.

Twenty minutes later, Jake emerged from the bathroom, dressed as he usually was in his fitted gray boxer briefs that showed off his body in a way that would have put Representative Anthony Weiner's scandalous sext to shame. Laura set aside her book. To hell with talking. She was filled with desire for him. What could she say to induce him to make love with her?

Then she noticed that he was carrying a phone in his hand. *Her* phone!

Jake showed it to her. "Honey, whose phone is this? And what's it doing in the hamper?"

Laura felt her face flood with heat so fast that she thought she might pass out. How had Jake found her phone? She'd made sure to bury it deep in the hamper. And what if he'd seen her texts to Tom? Or—worst of all—that last photo she'd sent?

"Laura? You okay?" Jake stepped closer to the bed, still holding the damning phone.

"I'm fine. Why?"

"Your color doesn't look right. And you're sweating." He reached out with his free hand to touch her forehead.

Laura forced herself to smile and nod, though her head felt like an anchor attached to her neck and her tongue was thick in her mouth.

"I'm just feeling stupid. That's one of my student's phones. I forgot all about it. I can't believe I nearly washed it!"

He frowned, the phone still lying faceup in his palm. "Why do you even have it?"

Laura resisted the urge to snatch the phone away. "I took it because she was trying to text during the riding lesson. Can you imagine?"

Jake laughed. "Sure. We have a daughter, remember?" He started to hand the phone over, then hesitated, studying the screen. "It's a funny phone for a kid, huh? Looks really cheap. I thought all the kids had iPhones."

"I know. I thought it was strange, too," Laura said, reaching out for it again.

This time Jake relinquished the phone and came around to his side of the bed. "Whose is it?"

"Melanie's," Laura said, then hastily said, "No, wait. I mean Georgina's. Yes, that's right." Georgina's family didn't belong to the club; Jake would be less apt to run into her. "Anyway, who knows why the kid has this phone. Maybe this is the new thing, right? Throwaway phones?"

Jake snorted, sliding beneath the covers beside her. "Yeah, soon they'll be printing their own. Every kid will have his own 3-D printer in a few years, along with a drone to deliver his homework."

She managed a weak laugh. She couldn't believe she was lying to him like this, and yet she couldn't imagine telling him the truth about Tom. Not with her sext possibly still on this phone. "I know what you mean. Our grandkids will be microchipped at birth so their parents won't lose them."

"And they'll be using iPads in their cribs." Jake reached over for his own phone, which he'd left on his nightstand during his shower, and started scrolling through it.

Laura waited a beat, then said, "Jake, how did you find the phone? Why were you looking in the hamper?"

"What?" Jake turned to look at her, frowning again. "Oh. I thought I left something in my pants pocket," he said vaguely.

"Hold me," she said impulsively. "I missed you today."

Jake looked surprised but complied, after first plugging his phone into its charger, then removing his glasses and folding them to put on the table beside the phone. This all took longer than Laura would have expected.

She rested her head on his shoulder when he'd finished. "I'm sorry about arranging that stupid dinner with Sandra," she said. "I just didn't know how to get out of it."

"I know. I'm sorry I upset you. Let's just go and have fun." He stroked her hair.

Jake smelled as he always did: of mint mouthwash and deodorant. In her fantasies, men smelled of sweat and leather and horses.

What would Tom smell like?

Thinking of Tom led her to think about Anne, of Anne brazenly making love with a married man. *Choosing* to have his baby! Anne should have stopped things before they got that far. All it took was willpower, which was what Laura was summoning now: she had to end all communication with Tom before it led to an affair. Or to Jake catching her in a lie. Otherwise, what kind of hypocrite would she be?

"Better now?" Jake asked, and released her after a quick squeeze.

Laura sat up. If Jake would kiss her—*really* kiss her—maybe that would be a sign that she had nothing to worry about. That her marriage was going through a rough patch but was as solid as ever.

She turned to Jake and smiled, then immediately pressed her lips together again. The last thing she wanted her husband to be thinking about was her teeth and whether they needed another cleaning. He made her go three times a year as a matter of course; his hygienists were lovely girls, but so relentless when it came to scraping off plaque, Laura was often left with a headache afterward from the vibrations. A wonder she had any enamel left.

Jake did not kiss her. Instead, he reached for his glasses and phone.

"Elly saw Anne today," Laura said before he could start reading again. "She's staying down at Flossie's cottage."

"Oh? How's she doing?"

"She has a baby now. Did you know that?"

Jake's face froze. "Hell no. She never said anything to me about it."

Laura watched him out of the corner of her eye while pretending to adjust her nightgown strap. "She didn't?"

"I just said that, didn't I? Of course not."

Laura gave up pretending not to look at him. "Why 'of course not'?"

"I only saw her once, Laura, at the pub that night. I swear! Other than that, Anne and I haven't communicated in two years."

"Okay. Sorry." Laura touched her husband's hand where it rested on the sheet between them, the fingers tapping nervously, as if there were a keyboard beneath the covers.

"Why isn't Anne staying with your mom?" he asked, fingers still twitching.

"Elly says Mom didn't want a baby in her apartment. Mom's also insisting on telling everyone that Anne is divorced. I guess she doesn't want everyone to know that her daughter forgot to keep her legs closed."

"Don't be nasty," Jake said gently. "We got pregnant by accident, too, remember. That's how we ended up here. We're just lucky it worked out for us."

Laura opened her mouth to protest, to say it was different when they got pregnant because they were in love and neither of them was married to someone else. It had made sense for them to get married.

But it didn't. Not really. Two weeks before their wedding day, she'd ridden her horse over a jumps course. The horse had refused a stone wall and pitched her over the saddle. She had miscarried.

Briefly, Laura closed her eyes. So much blood. She'd never known a body could bleed that much. She shouldn't have been riding, though the doctor had told her it was fine. She was fourteen weeks along.

Jake had gone with her for the D & C. The doctors told her it would be easier to get pregnant again if she had the procedure. Laura had curled up in bed for days afterward, weeping. Jake stayed with her. Fed her. Even bathed her. It wasn't her fault, he said. The doctors had told her it was fine for her to keep riding and that they'd have more chances to be parents.

What Laura had never admitted to anyone was that as she was riding that day, she had been fantasizing about falling, about an accident that could cause her to miscarry. She was only twenty years old, and Jake was the only man she'd ever slept with, yet she'd known something was wrong between them even then.

When her wish came true, the guilt had nearly crushed her. Jake had cried over the loss as much as she had. Laura couldn't bring herself to break up with him.

"That cottage seems like a chilly place to be stuck alone with a baby," Jake said now.

"I know." Then, partly because she'd promised Elly that she'd clear this up for good, Laura added, "You know, when Elly saw Anne, Anne kept saying those same terrible things about that time she was house-sitting for us."

"What things?" Jake was clenching his jaw.

"You know! About how you went into her room. And, you know. *Exposed* yourself." Laura felt sick, saying this.

Jake rubbed a hand over his face. "I have no idea what Anne's talking about. I've told you. There's nothing between us. There never has been."

"I know," Laura said. "But it bothers me that Elly believes her."

"Come on. You know me." Jake took her hand. "Have I ever given you any reason to think I'd do something like that? Or to doubt how much I love you?"

You don't desire me. Isn't that reason enough? Laura wished she could say this, but she was suddenly tired of picking at the same old scab. What good would it do?

"I don't care about what happened between you and Anne. Or about what Elly thinks, okay?" Laura stroked Jake's cheek, wishing she could erase the tension from his face as effectively as she smoothed out the wrinkles of the quilt on their bed each morning. "That's all in the past. I'm letting it go. All we have is the present and the future, right? And what matters is that we're okay. We *are* okay, aren't we?"

Jake's smile was tender. "Of course we are." He drew Laura into his arms, just as she'd wanted him to, and held her tightly against him, stroking her hair. "I love you so much."

It was almost enough, when he said that, for her to feel content.

CHAPTER SIX

I t was raining lightly when Anne woke at six to feed Lucy, but now the sun was out. Through the window she could see gray clouds parting to make way for brilliant blue sky. Jagged splashes of light reflected on the honeyed wooden walls.

She could hear the tide rolling in and out of the cove below the house, as steady and rhythmic as her own breathing. The bouncing watery light, the soundtrack of the gulls overhead, and the cottage's tidy built-in bookshelves and drawers made her feel as if she really were floating in a houseboat at sea.

Anne switched Lucy to the other breast, wondering about Colin. Was he still in New York, writing? Did he miss their old life, or even think about it?

The steady sound of the sea made her remember one of the first trips she'd taken with him. Colin had convinced her to skip the usual group kayak tour of Puerto Rico's Bioluminescent Bay. Instead, he'd borrowed a kayak from a friend and they'd set out on their own. It was close to midnight; even the touristy street stalls in Fajardo were shuttered.

It was a cloudy night. Anne had worried about rain and about how they'd navigate the kayak through the mangrove swamp in the dark. But her desire to be with him had surpassed her fears.

That night was so inky black that Colin's muscular shape in front of her was barely visible as they'd maneuvered the kayak along the winding river through the swamp. The sound of the coqui frogs was deafening. She'd been scared of having snakes drop onto her from the trees, knowing boas might be wrapped around the limbs.

Anne forgot her fears once they'd paddled deep enough into the trees and the water began lighting up around the boats, brilliant jeweled sparks beneath the water's glossy black surface.

"Put your hand in the water," Colin had urged.

Anne did it despite her fear of jellyfish and snakes, laughing as she cupped water in her hand and saw a miniature fireworks display in her palm. The bright flashes in the water were caused by plankton called dinoflagellates, Colin explained. Even the jellyfish were glowing, odd geometric shapes pulsing with light.

"Did you like your adventure?" Colin asked as they carried the kayak back up onto the beach afterward.

She'd kissed him in answer. Then they'd made love on the sugary white sand.

Anne forced herself to sit up. She tossed the covers aside and put Lucy on the bed to change her diaper, making faces and nonsense sounds to distract her. Colin had promised to give her adventures. He'd delivered. She couldn't deny that. But right now she had to *think*. To *act*. To learn how to be on her own again.

Well, not really on her own: here was Lucy. Smiling at her. Depending on her for everything. That's why Anne felt so anxious. What if she didn't live up to her own daughter's expectations?

She carried the baby into the main room of the cottage. One wall was painted a light apple green, a pop of color against the warm brown paneling, and Flossie had filled the chipped white enamel pitcher on the table with scarlet dahlias. Anne smiled, knowing her mother would have a fit if she knew Flossie had wasted dahlias on her, especially in the Houseboat.

It was amazing, really, that Sarah and Flossie were both still here on the same property, when neither had much good to say about the other. Flossie had always been a rebel; when she inherited a bit of money from a spinster aunt, she'd dropped out of her all-women's Ivy League college to travel and eventually joined a Buddhist convent in France. She'd come home for her brother's wedding, and her parents had pushed her toward the son of a family friend, a man from Essex who was eager to marry her. Flossie had refused him. She was far from celibate—Anne had seen men coming and going from her house through the years she was growing up—but Flossie had never married.

"I prefer my own company," she always told Anne. "Gives me time to think my own thoughts. The thing about men is that they take up an awful lot of space, and I don't mean just physically."

Sarah, who had always been about following the rules and upholding tradition and the Bradford family name, couldn't believe Flossie had turned down her parents' choice of partner. "A man with shoreline property in Gloucester and plenty of money? That would have solved all the Bradford family's money problems," she declared. "The Bradfords wouldn't have needed me to save their inn if she'd married him. Flossie was selfish to turn him down, if you ask me."

Anne, who was in her twenties by the time she heard this story and studying literature in college, had been appalled. "But that's terrible, Mom! It sounds like an arranged marriage out of Jane Austen's time. Why should Flossie have agreed to marry a man she didn't love?"

"Because at least then she wouldn't be poor and alone," Sarah snapped. "It's not like Flossie had some great career to keep her busy. Remember, Anne: you can work for money all your life, or marry it in five minutes."

Not that their mother had been so successful at following her own advice. Sarah had probably thought she was marrying into money when she chose their father. Instead, she'd had to work around the clock to keep the inn out of bankruptcy.

Anne got dressed and spent the next hour surfing job sites online, applying for any teaching or restaurant positions open within an hour's drive of Folly Cove. Between applications, she made herself coffee and ate yogurt with sliced banana, then nursed Lucy again and bathed her in the tiny sink.

The phone rang as she was dressing the baby. "You need to get out of that house," Flossie commanded.

Startled, Anne glanced over her shoulder toward the windows, half expecting to see Flossie striding across the sand toward the cottage from her own house. The beach was empty. "What? Why?"

"Because you'll get depressed, cooped up in that dank old shed."

Anne laughed. "I like this old shed. But you're probably right. I am feeling a little down. I've been looking for jobs online and there isn't much."

"I'm pleased to hear that you've been productive. However, as your landlady, I demand that you leave the house. And bring that baby over here. I need to pinch those cheeks."

Anne bundled Lucy up and carried her in the backpack across the beach. The sun was warm and the tide was in; she had to pick her way across the rocks before climbing up the wooden stairs to Flossie's porch.

The house and her aunt were opposites. Flossie's house was a tall, formal Victorian painted a solemn gray with white trim. Her aunt was delicate, birdlike, and never formal. She was dressed this morning, as always, in workout clothes: black yoga pants and a black fleece. She greeted Anne on the front porch, shading her narrow face against the sun with one hand, and took the baby at once, lifting her deftly out of the backpack. Lucy gave her a toothless grin.

"There," Flossie announced, smiling back at the baby. "Now, that's what I call the sun coming out." She looked at Anne. "What about you? Where's your sunshine? Your face is all clouded over."

"I do feel a little gray," Anne admitted. "It's a lot to do, starting my life over with a baby. I didn't realize how tired I'd feel." She followed Flossie into the living room, where her aunt sat on the couch and balanced Lucy on her lap. Anne chose the floral armchair across from them.

"You don't need to do everything at once," Flossie chided. "Why don't you go riding? It'll clear your head."

Fresh air was Flossie's prescribed cure for everything. Anne's mother had told her once that, when Anne was a baby, if Flossie was watching her she'd put Anne outside for a nap on the porch in nearly every season. Flossie would stretch out on the bamboo sofa beside her.

"It could be fifty degrees, and that woman would still think it was a grand idea to sleep outside," Sarah had grumbled. "I swear your father's sister was raised by wolves."

"How can I go riding?" Anne asked.

Flossie scowled. "How can you *not*? You rode every day of your life when you lived here. Walk down to the stables. I haven't ridden General all week and I bet he's raring to go, on a day this fine. There won't be many more days like it."

"I can't," Anne said, gesturing toward the baby, though her thigh muscles tightened, anticipating the feel of a horse beneath her.

"You can." Flossie gave her a sharp look. "Lucy and I are old friends by now, aren't we, darling?" She made a comically wide-eyed face. Lucy grinned obligingly. "I'll watch her. Or don't you trust this old bat?"

Anne shifted her weight on the porch. "Of course I do. But Laura wouldn't like seeing me at the stables. We're not exactly on speaking terms." *More like screaming terms,* she added silently.

Flossie swept her gray bangs out of her eyes. "Oh, for crying in your beer. You two are going to have to get over that. Husbands come and go, but sisters are forever. I know you're not after Jake, and pretty soon your sister will have to realize that *you* are not the source of her marital problems."

"You heard what happened with Jake and me?" Anne felt her neck itch with embarrassment. She had never told Flossie any of it. "I mean, what Laura thinks happened but definitely did *not*?"

Her aunt nodded. "The walls have ears. And, for the record, I'm on your side."

Anne was touched. "Thanks. That means a lot." She stood up and went to the mantel, where among the framed photographs was one of her parents' wedding day. They looked happy, leaning into each other. Her mother's hair was like Elly's, honey blond and straight, like a sleek gold shawl around her shoulders. She wore a simple white strapless gown and veil.

Her father was barely out of college and boyish looking, a skinny guy with a shock of hair that looked dark in the photograph but was auburn like her own. He wore a tux but somehow gave off an indie-rocker vibe. Flossie wore a white blouse and black pants and scowled off to one side of the group photo. Her head was shaved.

"I forget," Anne said. "Was the wedding right after you came back from the convent in France?"

"Yes. I only came back for your father."

"You've never really told me anything about why you joined that convent."

Flossie's tone was brisk. "I studied abroad my sophomore year of college and spent a semester in Paris. While I was there, I took a meditation course taught by Buddhist monks from Nepal. That changed my life."

Anne sat down again on the chair. Lucy lay on her back across her great-aunt's knees, apparently fascinated by the ornate brass light ceiling fixture. "How?"

Flossie swayed her legs a little beneath the baby, smiling when Lucy waved her arms and babbled at the overhead light. "My parents weren't much for talking. They certainly weren't ever going to answer my questions. As a child, I'd sit with them in church and wonder how they could believe in a God that would allow things like war to happen, and what our purpose should be as protectors of the planet."

Anne laughed. "Life's little questions, you mean."

"Exactly. Meditating with the monks made me realize how angry and alone I felt, and how much I needed a community that would help me find a path for living that made more sense to me than what my parents had always stood for: keeping the status quo no matter how nonsensical it was. You have to remember that this was in 1971, just before the mess in Vietnam ended. A turbulent time. I felt ignorant and overly attached to my life. To all these worldly goods the Bradford family was so hell-bent on protecting."

She smiled as Anne glanced around the room. "Okay, I'm a bit of a hypocrite. A hoarder of antiquities and memories. But I like to think I learned something about acceptance and patience, anyway, while I was in Europe." She nodded to the table next to Anne's chair. "Take a look in there."

Anne gently pulled open the drawer of the Queen Anne table. The table was old and wobbly, covered with a lace cloth. In the drawer lay a photograph of her aunt in a simple pine frame. Flossie looked young and happy, smiling against a backdrop of jagged snowcapped mountains. She wore orange robes and her head was shaved. Her smile was brilliant, as white as the snow behind her.

"You look so happy. Where is this?" Anne asked.

"Nepal. That's Annapurna in the background. A gorgeous mountain. My favorite in the Himalayan range. Annapurna often looks pink, the way it catches the light, and the snow comes off it in these long, filmy white scarves."

"It's beautiful. So are you."

"Ha! I looked like a molting robin," Flossie said. "But it was a wonderful time. I went to Nepal to study Buddhism before entering the convent in France. I keep that photograph to remind me of who I was and what real contentment feels like."

Anne studied her aunt's plain face, the deep lines around her eyes and mouth. "And do you still feel content?" she said. "Sometimes I worry that you're lonely."

"Lonely? Me?" Flossie stared at her for a moment, then tipped her head back to laugh. Lucy startled and screwed up her face, but Flossie quickly put the baby against her shoulder and stood up, walking to the window to show Lucy the view of the water. Lucy stopped fussing at once.

"Yes, you," Anne said. "I mean, I'm lonely here, and I've only been here a little while. Plus I've got Lucy for company."

"You don't know anything about my life." Flossie's tone was calm rather than accusatory. "This is the life I've chosen, dear girl. I've had one great love, and I've felt affection toward many men since that first one. In the end, though, I prefer to be on my own. To be at one with the rhythms of nature rather than dependent on the whims of others. The few times I've felt at loose ends, I have found that meditating— especially when I do it with others in my meditation group here in Rockport—lets me think of loneliness as a background landscape I'm moving through temporarily. So, yes. I am generally content."

"That's amazing," Anne said.

"It isn't really. We think of our emotions as being the result of something happening to us, but happiness is a choice. It's a choice I've made. You can make it, too, no matter what happens in your life," Flossie added. "People think they have to physically die before going to heaven or starting new lives, depending on their religions. The truth is that you can start a new life anytime you choose, as easily as waking from a dream."

Anne tried to imagine this. Could she wake up and choose to start a newer, happier life under any circumstances? She had her doubts. But she could try. And maybe that was a choice, too: making the effort to be positive rather than negative. That would have to be enough for her right now.

Flossie jiggled Lucy a little in front of the window, then turned to look at Anne over her shoulder. "You'd better go get a ride in before this child decides she's hungry for something I can't provide."

Anne stood up, then hesitated. "Are you sure?"

"I am. And if that bossy sister of yours gives you any grief, tell her I asked you to exercise General in exchange for staying in my cottage. He's still my horse, after all."

"What if Lucy cries while I'm gone?" Anne asked anxiously, zipping up her vest.

"Tell you what. If Lucy starts screaming, I promise to hold her out a window. You'll hear her down in the woods. You can come galloping up the beach in time to catch her when I throw her out."

Thankfully, the barn was empty when Anne arrived, and Laura's car wasn't parked in the driveway by the house. Anne tacked up the horse and left a note on the stall door.

The sun was stronger now. Anne lifted her face to it and relaxed in the saddle. General was a stately black gelding, nearly seventeen hands high, with a white nose and two white socks. Now fourteen years old, the horse plodded at a gentlemanly pace despite his slender thoroughbred build.

Anne followed a cart road along the pasture to one of the trails entering Dogtown. Soon she was in deep woods. She headed for the area with the Babson boulders, which had been carved with inspirational sayings during the Depression by out-of-work laborers. She reached the "Truth" boulder and urged the horse into an easy trot through the thick stands of pines interspersed with birches and maples. It was only the first week of October, but the autumn leaves were almost peaking.

The early-morning rain had rinsed the air of pollen, and the light alternated between buttery gold, where it filtered through the oaks, and fiery red around the sugar maples. Anne took deep breaths, content to be alone with the sound of a horse's hooves on the pine-padded trail. She'd forgotten what a gift it was to be left in peace to hear her own thoughts, especially given the remarkable beauty of Massachusetts in autumn.

Of course, by late November, the leaves here would be gone. Only the pine needles would remain, dark green, almost black against the gray tree trunks. In winter, New England's coast had more shades of gray than anything else: dark gray storm clouds and slate gray sea, pale gray tree trunks and chilly gray rain. Sometimes the ocean looked like a thick layer of smoke against the horizon in November.

Maybe she wouldn't be here then. She hoped not.

Especially not if Laura continued holding this senseless grudge.

Her sister probably had no idea that Jake had stalked her in Gloucester a week after his bizarre behavior in their guest bedroom. He'd waited outside the elementary school where Anne had taught third grade until she was sitting in the driver's seat of her car, preparing to drive back to her apartment. She was searching for her phone in her purse when the passenger door opened and Jake slipped into the car.

Anne didn't scream for help. Even after everything, she wasn't afraid of him. Jake had always seemed like a man who was uncertain of his own power. His own identity, even.

When Laura married him, Anne had the odd thought, while standing near the altar in her itchy blue bridesmaid's dress as her sister and Jake exchanged vows, that Laura must have been looking for an unfinished man to mold. That must be why she'd chosen this one.

"Get out of my car!" Anne had shouted at Jake that afternoon. "I don't want you anywhere near me."

"Please," he'd begged. "Hear me out."

Anne sighed. "Five minutes. And it better be good."

He'd rubbed his palms along his jeans, ironed with a crease in them. Pressed by her sister, no doubt, Anne thought with a queasy shudder. "Look, I'm sorry I came into your room the way I did," Jake said.

"You *should* be! That was wrong on so many levels that I don't even know where to start."

"I know," he said. "I feel terrible about scaring you that way."

She crossed her arms. "So why did you do it?"

Jake started talking fast; he told her he'd been about to break up with Laura before they got married, but then she'd gotten pregnant. "I know your sister's a good person. I wanted to do the right thing."

But their marriage had always been more of a business partnership than a passionate connection, he went on. "I'm unhappy, but what can I do?" Jake pleaded. "I'm trapped, Anne! I could never leave Laura and Kennedy. They make me a better man. Leaving my family would destroy me. And them! But Laura's unhappy and so am I. What should I do? Tell me! You always seem to know what you want."

Anne had felt herself softening. Jake sounded so miserable. And he was right: Laura was a good person. The best of the three Bradford sisters in many ways: intelligent, reliable, honest, helpful.

"I can't tell you what to do," she said finally. "Only you and Laura can decide that. Have you tried counseling?"

Jake shook his head. "I asked her, but Laura says there's no point. She wants to stay with me and I want to stay with her. She says that's all we need to know." He lifted his hands, dropped them. "I wanted to be an architect, you know. But when Laura got pregnant, I knew I had to provide for a family, and my uncle's a dentist. He helped me get into dental school." He shook his head. "It was a mistake. I hate my life."

"Being unhappy still doesn't excuse what you did to me," Anne said.

"I know. Can you please forgive me? I feel stuck, but I don't want my daughter growing up without a father in her life." He'd started crying.

Anne didn't want that for Kennedy, either. She knew what it was like to grow up without a father. It would break her heart if Kennedy lost hers. Especially if it was her fault in some way.

So she had forgiven Jake, even hugged him as he got out of the car. But then there was that awful Christmas party two years ago, when he'd betrayed her again by acting like some drunk jerk of a frat boy, cornering her against the wall and kissing her.

"Screw you, Jake," Anne said aloud now, tipping her head up to watch a blue jay scold her from its perch high in a pine tree. "You hear me? I'm done with you!"

It was always a mistake to let your guard down on horseback. She had let the reins drop, so now, when an animal streaked across the path so fast that Anne barely caught sight of its bushy brown tail—a dog? a fox?—she had no hope of staying on when the horse bolted.

The gelding veered off the path and scraped Anne off against a tree before galloping away. For a second the landscape pinwheeled around her, a blur of green and red and yellow. Then Anne hit the ground and everything went black.

Witnessing Laura's life up close and personal was driving Elly crazy. Why was her sister such a doormat?

Laura ran errands, cooked meals, and did laundry for everyone, despite the fact that she was getting up before sunrise to shovel horseshit every day, then teaching lessons until dinner. She cleaned the house and even ironed Jake's shirts like the guy didn't have two good hands of his own. Elly got tired just watching her.

Kennedy was useless, too, hiding out in her bedroom unless she was skulking through the kitchen, where it never seemed to occur to her that someone had to put dishes in the dishwasher after she left them on the counter.

Last night Laura had stayed up until eleven to bake cookies, even though Jake wouldn't touch them. Kennedy, though, was a little hoarder, sneaking off with handfuls of cookies anytime she thought people weren't watching. Her bedroom smelled like a cross between a gym and a pastry shop.

Her niece spent most of her time in that purple bedroom, a color that made Elly's teeth ache. In the five days Elly had been here, Kennedy hadn't had any friends come over to shriek and play loud music after school, or to loll around watching brainless TV shows. Certainly no boys were sniffing around.

Also, there was zero evidence—Elly knew this because she'd been bored enough to snoop through Kennedy's bedroom while the kid was at school—of her niece doing drugs or even sneaking an occasional beer. She lived like a nun.

Whenever Kennedy *did* venture beyond her bedroom, she moped so silently around the house that Elly was often startled by her presence. Her niece would suddenly appear at Elly's elbow, reading or eating, occasionally peering up at Elly in a spooky way from beneath her raggedy bangs.

Like now: for the past half hour, Elly had been sitting in the living room with her laptop and answering e-mails. When she looked up, she realized Kennedy was lying on the couch across the room, as if she'd been tossed there like an extra pillow.

Her nose was buried in a book. Judging from the blond girl wearing a leather combat suit and carrying a futuristic weapon on the cover, it was probably one of those apocalyptic YA novels about a teenage girl saving the world, probably while choosing between two hot love interests.

Maybe that's what Kennedy secretly wanted to do: blow everyone away. Elly had certainly wanted to do that when she was thirteen. Especially her sisters, because Laura was too bossy and Anne was a whiny pain.

Elly closed her laptop. It wouldn't kill her to be nice. It was Saturday; Laura was teaching lessons all day and the poor kid must be bored witless.

"Good book?" Elly asked.

Kennedy shrugged. "It's okay, I guess."

"It's great that you like to read."

"Mom says I read too much."

"Impossible!" Elly tried to channel a supportive aunt. "Reading can open doors to new worlds."

Her niece rolled her eyes. "Where'd you hear that? A fortune cookie?"

Elly was startled enough to laugh. She loved a kid with a smart attitude and a quick mouth. "Probably. Want to know the truth? I hate reading. I always feel like I'm not really doing anything."

Kennedy finally closed the book. "You're a singer, right?"

"Not anymore. That didn't pan out, so now I'm a production designer."

"What's that?"

"Here. It's easier if I show you." Elly crossed the room and perched on the edge of the couch, holding her laptop open in front of Kennedy while she Googled her own Web site. She clicked on the montage of projects showcased on her home page: ad spots and music videos, a couple of Internet pilots, and a snippet from the animated movie where she'd voiced a singing penguin. She was pleased to see Kennedy's big blue eyes—the girl could be a mascara model with lashes like that—get even bigger.

"So you make, like, videos and ads and stuff?" Kennedy said when the three-minute clip had finished playing.

"I design the sets for them," Elly said. "Other people put together the music and costumes, and there are tech geeks who do things like lighting and cameras. But I'm in charge of the overall look and the props. Like, I might have to decide how to build a stone wall, or how to make a puppet that looks like an alien."

"That's so cool." Kennedy was sitting up straight now. "I wouldn't mind trying that."

Elly smiled. "Great, because I need your help. Your mom and I are designing a birthday party for your grandmother. Her favorite movie was made the year she was born, a musical called *An American in Paris*, so our mission is to turn the inn's dining room into a French bistro and find costumes we can wear. We need tablecloths, fake flowers, vintage clothing, and maybe stuff to build a statue of the Eiffel Tower."

"You're going to make the Eiffel Tower? For real?"

"Well, a replica of it, yeah."

"No way!"

"Way," Elly said. "I'd go shopping with you right now, except I don't have a car."

"Dad would totally let us use his! He always rides his bike to work. I'll call him!"

Jake agreed to let them borrow his brand-new Lexus. Must be nice to have a dentist dad, Elly thought as they headed into Gloucester to check out the consignment stores there.

Being home made Elly miss her own father in a way she hadn't in ages. She kept having oddball memories. As they were leaving the garage, for instance, Elly spotted Kennedy's bike in a corner and remembered how her father had taught her to ride a bike by attaching a broom pole to the rear fender, so he could run alongside her without bending over.

"You got this," Dad kept repeating. "You're built for speed, Elizabeth. Let's put the pedal to the metal!"

She'd pedaled her heart out for him, so fast that she'd forgotten to brake. She had crashed into the front steps of the inn as her mother was serving drinks to a pair of elderly couples. Elly wasn't hurt, but she was scared when her mother's face darkened with disapproval.

She could tell her mother was gearing up to yell at her about taking better care of the bike and the importance of not disturbing the guests. Then Dad had rushed up the steps and swept Sarah off her feet, dipping her like they were dancing and making her giggle. The old people on the porch had clapped.

He'd kissed her mother, then dashed down the steps again, picked up Elly, and tossed her over his shoulder, cantering like a horse across the lawn to take her into the apartment through their back door.

"Close one, but we dodged that bullet," he'd said as he cleaned up Elly's bloody knee and tenderly bandaged the scrape. "There's nothing like the element of surprise when you're sweet-talking your way out of a bad situation."

Elly wondered when, exactly, her father had run out of surprises and sweet talk.

After hitting up the Gloucester shops, she and Kennedy wound along Route 133 into Essex, passing antique Colonials and Capes shouldering up to the road. So funny how in Los Angeles everyone was all about big front yards, while here the houses were built practically on the street to eliminate the need to shovel snow great distances to the front door.

The river gleamed silvery blue behind the cattails and tall marsh grass, and the white churches had classic lines and narrow steeples. Churches and antique stores everywhere: it was like some quaint-to-death New England movie set. She wished Ryder could see this place. It would blow his mind.

Elly had first discovered consignment shops when she was a teenager; she and her theater friends relied on them to find clothes as different as possible from the boring mall rags the other kids bought. Even her dress for senior prom was a consignment-store find: a vintage cocktail dress in emerald green with a net skirt. She still had that dress and had worn it once to dinner with Ryder.

"I can't get this dress off you fast enough," he'd murmured against her neck as they'd ordered appetizers.

She missed him, Elly realized. She blamed this on reverse culture shock: it was freaky being back in New England.

On impulse, she texted Ryder a picture of the little Mexican place where she and Kennedy stopped for tacos with one word: *Picante!* Even Mexican food made her miss him. So stupid.

Elly dropped her phone back into her purse. She didn't let herself look to see if he replied. If Ryder didn't text back, it would serve her right, after the way she'd shut him down cold before leaving.

"Mom's favorite consignment store is in Ipswich," Kennedy was saying. "We could go there."

So far they'd scored bunches of silk flowers, checked tablecloths, and a white sweater—Elly had snagged these items thinking of the "I Got Rhythm" scene in the movie with Gene Kelly dancing on the Parisian street. When she explained this to Kennedy and her niece looked confused, Elly realized she'd never seen the movie.

They were still parked in front of the restaurant. Elly took Kennedy's phone and downloaded a YouTube clip of Gene Kelly's "I Got Rhythm" scene.

Kennedy's eyes bugged out. "Wish I could dance like that."

"You totally could!" Elly said. "I know what: let's dress you up like Gene Kelly for the party. That sweater we bought should fit you. You can dance and sing this song for your grandmother. She'd love that. Best present you could give her!"

"No way!" Kennedy looked panicked.

"Why not?" Elly said. "I can show you how."

She loved this idea. Her mind raced, imagining other scenes from the movie they could act out for their mother and her guests. "Or we'll ask Anne to do the Gene Kelly part and you can back her up. She's an even better dancer than I am. She and I used to sing with your mom and grandmother at the inn. We performed every weekend for years."

"Wait. What? Mom doesn't sing."

"Sure she does. She has a great voice."

"Well, I've never heard her," Kennedy said.

Elly stared at her. "Your mom hasn't ever sung to you? Not even a lullaby?"

"Are you kidding?" Kennedy rolled her eyes. "Mom's *way* too serious. I've never even heard her sing in the car."

How was it possible that her sister had succeeded in hiding this part of herself from her daughter? "Well, we'll have to change that," Elly said. "We'll get your mom to sing. Now let's go to Ipswich and see this store you keep talking about."

She'd forgotten how intense a New England autumn could be, like traveling inside a kaleidoscope. The landscape was starting to fire up for fall, the marshes already a dark red and brightened by bushes heavy with orange berries. The fields and oak trees blazed gold and yellow. Occasional birch trees glimmered white against a sky so blue and free of smog, it looked artificial.

"So is this your favorite shop?" Elly asked as Kennedy directed her to park in front of a small storefront with classic clothing displayed in the front window: a tweed blazer, a red cable-knit sweater, a stack of jeans.

"Not mine. Mom's," Kennedy said. "She buys most of our clothes here."

Elly was surprised. She'd pegged her sister as a total catalog shopper. "That's cool."

"Not really. She does it to save money. Mom says we can't afford the mall."

Another shock, given the size of Laura's house, the stables, the new Lexus. "Why are you guys so broke?" Elly knew it was wrong to ask, so she acted nonchalant, examining a canary yellow cardigan on one of the racks.

Kennedy shrugged. "Life's expensive. And money doesn't grow on trees, you know."

Her niece sounded like she was fifty years old. She must have absorbed that classic line at the dinner table, Elly decided, fingering a gold shirtwaist evening dress that looked like one of the dresses Leslie Caron had worn in the movie. It was too small for her, a size six. Maybe it would fit Anne.

She plucked it off the rack. "Good prices. Your mom's smart to shop here," Elly said, wondering what in hell Laura and Jake were doing with all their money.

CHAPTER SEVEN

"I put yesterday's mail on your desk," Rhonda said as Sarah came in from the dining room after her morning coffee and toast. "Oh, and I had two e-mails asking about winter weekend specials for couples. Are we running another promotion this year?"

"Yes," Sarah said. "I haven't written it up yet, but I was thinking of offering a ten percent discount on a two-night stay, plus a pass to the Cape Ann Museum."

"Not very romantic," Rhonda said. "But of course it's up to you."

Something was off. Rhonda's voice wasn't as warm as it usually was, and she had an unusually severe expression. Even her hair looked severe, pinned up like that instead of falling in its usual glossy curls. Sarah wondered if she should ask the girl what was wrong. Something was clearly bothering her.

We aren't friends, she reminded herself. It was always iffy to be friends with your employees. It was a fine line between professional and personal when you ran an inn, especially with employees who'd been with her as long as Rhonda had, but Sarah had always been careful not to overstep it.

She removed her wool coat, studying Rhonda as she moved with her usual efficiency behind the desk, checking out a middle-aged couple with enough bags for a European tour. Rhonda was all smiles with them.

Maybe Rhonda was sulky with Sarah because things hadn't worked out with that uncle of hers. She'd been so hopeful when she'd fixed them up.

"Tell you what," Sarah said after the couple had left the reception area, Tommy burdened with suitcases and hobbling behind them. "Why don't you write up the copy for the winter special, Rhonda. You always have such wonderful ideas. Yours put mine to shame."

This, at least, earned a small smile. "As you like," Rhonda said. "I'll have it to you after I've checked everyone out."

"Wonderful. Well, I'd better get to my desk, then, and see what mysteries await me in yesterday's mail." Sarah slipped into her office. Rhonda was a hard worker. And, in Sarah's experience, nothing could lift your mood like a job well done.

She turned on her computer and flipped idly through the pile of letters and circulars stacked on her desk. A thick manila envelope caught her eye. It was from an attorney's office in Venice, Florida. Sarah set the other mail aside and slit the envelope open.

At first she couldn't make sense of it. Phrases jumped out at her, but the sentences ran together, then seemed to fragment into pieces, as her brain struggled to process what her eyes were seeing.

Dear Mrs. Bradford . . . I regret to inform you about the death . . . I have been asked . . . your husband, Neil Bradford, being of sound mind and body . . .

He was dead. The lawyer had sent her a will, saying Folly Cove was hers. Neil was gone.

Her Neil.

"Rhonda," Sarah called. "Could you come in here, please?"

"Can you give me five more minutes, Mrs. Bradford? I'm just finishing up with that copy."

"No," Sarah said. She cleared her throat, then added, "I need you now, Rhonda. Please."

Her own voice, though it seemed disembodied, sounded coolly normal. No sign of the disintegration taking place in her vision, the buzzing in her brain, or the escalation of her heartbeat knocking against her ribs as Rhonda appeared at her door, knuckles to the wood, her mouth open and making sounds Sarah couldn't hear.

Rhonda's quizzical look quickly altered into something else, something Sarah couldn't recognize or interpret because her own vision was going completely dark now, her brain shutting down, her heart the only part of her still working.

But even that trusty heart of hers was about to stop, to crack into a thousand smaller beating pieces that would never be put together again.

Anne opened her eyes. She had no idea how long she'd been unconscious.

She was shivering from lying on the damp ground but was afraid to sit up. Every time she tried, there was a sharp stab of pain between her ribs.

She fiercely blinked away tears and tried to take progressively deeper breaths as she lay flat on her back and stared up at the mockingly cheerful sky. Finally she tried to sit up again. The pain in her left side was still too intense to bear. At least it wasn't her spine.

Anne gently lowered herself down to the ground with a gasp. She hoped General had made it back to the barn. Surely someone would see the horse and her note, then come looking for her.

Or maybe she could limp back on her own? Obviously nothing was broken. She could move her arms and legs and neck just fine.

She'd feel like a total idiot dialing 911. But who else could she call for help?

No sense in phoning Flossie. Her aunt was fit, but she'd have to carry the baby over to the cottage to get the car seat. And even then, how would she find Anne? Anne had no idea where she was, much less the closest access point to this trail from the road.

Who else?

Definitely not Laura. Calling her would only give her sister more reason to be pissed off, since Laura hated to be interrupted when she was busy. And Laura was always busy. Her sister was *born* busy.

Anne didn't dare call Sarah, either. Her mother would be useless. She would never consent to driving her car on dirt roads.

That left Elly. Elly didn't have a car, but maybe she could borrow Laura's or Jake's. Anne hoped her phone's GPS could get Elly to her. She wriggled the phone out of her jeans pocket, breathing through the pain, and pressed Elly's number.

No answer. Damn it. Anne left a message, then clicked on Google maps to see if the app could find her location.

It did: she was about three miles from the inn. Two from the stables. A long walk in this kind of pain. But the thought of Lucy made Anne push herself upright with her hands, an inch at a time, wincing.

"Ow," she moaned as the pain knifed between her ribs.

At least she'd had the sense to wear a riding helmet. She pulled the helmet off and felt along the base of her skull. Good news: no blood. A slight concussion, probably, given her nausea, and maybe a fractured or broken rib, but she'd live.

Maybe she should call 911 after all. The thought of a stretcher carrying her to Lucy made her decide to reach for the phone again.

Then she heard something crashing through the bushes. A very large something: a person, it must be. A deer or a coyote would probably be quieter.

Anne was about to call out, then clamped her lips shut. She'd read in one of the local newspapers about teenagers with paintball guns making trouble in Dogtown. Did she really want to deal with that?

She waited as the footsteps approached, her pulse so loud in her ears that she imagined whoever it was could follow the sound straight to her.

A dog broke noisily through the underbrush next to her, nose to the ground. It lifted its head when it saw her and started barking like a maniac. The dog was brown, shaggy, of no identifiable breed. Definitely the same animal that had spooked the horse.

"You dumb dog," Anne said. "Be quiet! You're the reason I'm in this fix!"

"Mack! Here, boy! Mack, where are you?"

Anne recognized the voice as Sebastian's before he pushed aside low branches near the dog and ducked beneath them. He bent to pat the mutt on the head, quieting the animal, then peered at Anne from beneath the brim of a cap in a vibrant shade of orange.

Hunters, Anne remembered, seeing the hat. God, had she been riding during deer-hunting season without realizing it? Another classic idiot move!

No, wait. Deer season was later. This was pheasant season, right up until November. Still, she should have been wearing bright colors, not her forest-colored green jacket.

"Oh," Sebastian said, looking confused at the sight of her on the ground. "You're why my dog is barking. Sorry."

"He spooked my horse," Anne said, pointing an accusing finger at Mack.

This gesture only caused the dog to trot in her direction—bravely, now that Sebastian was here—and start lapping at her face, making her laugh and then wince when pain shot up her side again. "Ow!"

"Mack! Stop that! Come here!" Sebastian stepped forward to collar the dog again and stood looking down at Anne. "Are you badly hurt?"

"No. But I'm in too much pain to walk back to the stables. I don't suppose you have a car?"

He nodded and jerked a thumb over one shoulder. "A Jeep. I came by the fire road."

"They let you do that in Dogtown?"

"I have a special research permit." He squatted beside her. Sebastian's eyes were more green than brown beneath the cap, and his russet bangs were flattened along his forehead above his nose. He wore a gold plaid flannel shirt and black jeans, like some Cambridge poet except for the hiking boots, clearly well worn. A canvas mailbag was slung over one shoulder. Branches protruded from the pouch. He must have been collecting specimens.

"Where's the pain?" he asked.

"My side, mostly. It's probably a broken rib. I'm okay as long as I don't take a deep breath."

"I don't think you should stand up if you're not sure."

"I'm sure!"

"Look, just take it slowly, all right?" he said.

"How much slower can I take it?" Anne complained. "I've been lying on the ground forever."

"Do an inventory," Sebastian suggested. "Let's make sure your back is all right. Lie down again and test your muscles head to foot, a little at a time. Here. I'll lie down with you. We'll do it together."

"What? That's stupid!" Anne said.

And yet, when Sebastian was lying on the ground next to her, talking her through it—"Wiggle your toes first; okay, good, now let's do our ankles"—she was suddenly less afraid. More relaxed. It was as if they were lying on a bed of pine needles, the sky a warm blue duvet pulled over them.

When they'd finished—he even suggested that they wiggle their ears, making them both laugh—Sebastian seemed assured that her spine was intact and asked if she was ready to stand up.

"Maybe." Anne was feeling sleepy now, too comfortable to move.

"Try. Let's see if we can get you to the car." Sebastian held out a hand, which made the dog leap to its feet and start wagging its tail. "No, Mack," he said, but the corners of his mouth were twitching. "He wants to help," he said. "Mack is everyone's best friend."

"Except my horse's."

"Yeah, look, I really am sorry," Sebastian said. "I'll pay any medical bills, all right? Yours or the horse's. But for now let's focus on getting you to an ER."

Anne shook her head. "Thanks, but I need to check on the horse and then go home."

"You really ought to get an X-ray."

"After," she said, breathing through the pain as she folded her legs beneath her and prepared to stand.

She wouldn't have made it upright without Sebastian's help. Then it took all of her willpower not to cry out when she took her first step.

Sebastian put an arm around her shoulders, half carrying her through the trees to the Jeep. Anne had to bite her lip to keep from swearing, she was in such agony.

Finally they were in the car, where she held her breath as Sebastian gently tugged the seat belt into place and buckled it for her because she couldn't twist to the side. The dog, meanwhile, had jumped into the back of the Jeep. She could smell its foul panting breath.

"Your dog stinks like a dying buffalo," she managed.

"I know. That's what makes him so lovable. Look, please let me take you to the ER. I'll drop you there and go find the horse."

She shook her head. "Stables first. Then home. I promise to go to the ER if I'm not feeling better in a couple of hours. Really, what would they do for a broken rib? They don't even give you a compression bandage these days. And there's something I have to do at home first."

The truth: Lucy was the reason she was desperate to get home. Not just to see her baby, but to nurse her. Anne's breasts ached, engorged and hard, adding to her misery.

Plus, what would Flossie do if Lucy was hungry? There wasn't any more frozen breast milk.

As she pictured Lucy wailing and her aunt frantically pacing, it was all Anne could do not to shout at Sebastian to go faster. He was driving like a centurion, no doubt trying to spare her more pain.

Laura was standing outside the barn with a cell phone pressed to one ear when they pulled up in front of the stables. A half dozen horses, tacked up and waiting, were tied to the fence.

Laura was dressed smartly in yellow jodhpurs, tall black boots, and white quilted vest. She narrowed her eyes at them.

"For heaven's sake. There you are," Laura said after she'd hung up the phone. She marched over to Anne's door and opened it. Her eyes flicked to Sebastian behind the wheel, then dismissed him. "I was just on the phone with Flossie. She's worried sick. Where the hell have you been, Anne? Having a little *date* while Flossie watches your screaming kid?"

"No! Jesus, Laura. I couldn't get home because I fell off General," Anne said. "Sebastian found me. Is Lucy all right?" She ignored Sebastian's startled glance in her direction. He obviously hadn't heard about her child, then.

"How did you fall off *General*?" Laura asked. "That horse is like riding a sofa!" Her eyes raked over Anne's appearance, taking in her torn jeans, the bloodied knee Anne hadn't noticed until now. "Why didn't you call me?"

"Because I didn't think you'd come. Is General here? Did he make it back?"

"Yes. But come on, Anne. I would've picked you up if I'd known you were in *pain*."

"And if I weren't?" Anne shot back.

"Look, this whole thing was my fault entirely, not your sister's," Sebastian cut in. He pointed to Mack, now lying obediently in the back of the Jeep, pretending to be the best-behaved dog in the world. "My mutt apparently spooked the horse."

"That horse doesn't spook." Laura crossed her arms.

"Right. Tell that to General." Anne closed her eyes, feeling suddenly nauseated. "Is he all right?"

"He's fine. But imagine my shock, seeing him tacked up and wandering loose in the barn, munching hay in the aisle with nobody around."

"I left a note so you'd know I took him." Anne's head felt boulder-heavy, her neck barely strong enough to hold it upright. She was exhausted, suddenly, and having trouble forming words.

"I never saw it," Laura said. "Really, Anne, you must have been in a coma if General got out from under you. You're a better rider than that!"

"Apparently not." Anne wished people would stop telling her she should be better than she was; she felt like a huge disappointment to everyone. "Look, I need to get back to Flossie's house now." She turned to Sebastian despite the knifing pain coming up her left side in little bursts of sensation. "Can you drive me?"

"Of course." Sebastian apologized to Laura again for his dog's behavior, then rolled up the windows and pulled out of the driveway. "I really think you ought to get an X-ray first."

Anne shook her head. "No. I need to get back."

"For God's sake. Don't be so stubborn."

"I *have* to go back," she snapped finally. "I'm nursing. My baby needs to be fed."

Sebastian glanced at her. She felt his eyes on her breasts before he yanked off his cap and tossed it into the back of the Jeep. As he pulled out of the stable driveway, they could hear the dog happily scrabbling after the hat.

"Mack will chew your cap," Anne said.

"I have other hats."

Sebastian didn't speak again until they'd driven back to Flossie's house. "Need me to help you to the door?" he said then.

"I'll be fine, thanks." Anne managed to wrestle the Jeep door open, then had to stop to catch her breath. Sebastian hurried around the car to help her.

Before they'd even made it up the path, she glanced up and saw a note on the door. "I don't think they're here," she said, suddenly panicked. What if something had happened to Lucy, too, while they were apart? "Please. Read the note. I'll wait here."

She managed to hold herself upright by pressing one hand to her throbbing side while Sebastian took long strides up the porch steps and snatched the note off its thumbtack.

"They're at the Houseboat," he said, waving the note at her. "Where's that?"

Anne told him. He helped her back into the car and drove to the other side of Folly Cove.

Once he'd parked in front of the cottage, Sebastian came around to her door again. Flossie appeared on the porch as he helped Anne out of the car. Lucy was in Flossie's arms, wailing; she reached for Anne and nearly wiggled out of Flossie's arms.

"Well, you're a sight for somebody's sore eyes," Flossie said. "This child is destined for the opera with her lung power." She raised an eyebrow at Anne's bloody knee. "What on earth happened?"

"I fell off General," Anne said. "I'm banged up, but I'm okay."

Sebastian nodded in her aunt's direction. "Hello, Flossie," he said. "Good to see you again."

"And you," Flossie murmured, watching him help Anne hobble up the porch steps.

Anne tried not to wince, knowing that would worry her aunt, but she shook her head when Flossie came toward her with Lucy. "Wait. I can't hold her until I'm sitting down," she said.

"Yet she wouldn't let me drive her to the ER," Sebastian said.

"Because I'm *fine*," Anne said.

"Sure you are," Flossie said. "Right as rain. Never seen you look better."

Flossie followed them into the house, still carrying the screeching baby, and waited for Sebastian to lower Anne to the couch before settling Lucy on her lap. Anne lifted her shirt and unhooked her bra, too intent on quieting the baby to care who saw what.

Flossie gathered her sweater and keys. "I'll be off," she said.

"So soon?" Anne asked in alarm.

"I've got things to do. Call if you need me, but I think she'll go down for a nap after she eats. The little bugger didn't sleep a wink at my house. I'll bring dinner around later." Then Flossie was out the door.

Sebastian hovered with his hands in his pockets, looking everywhere but at Anne. "I've never been in here," he said.

"Why would you have been?" Anne leaned her head back on the sofa, watching him through half-closed eyes, finally relaxing now that Lucy was in her arms.

"My grandmother and your aunt were good friends until Nan died last year."

"Oh. I didn't realize."

"I don't think many people knew. They were women from very different circles."

Anne was curious now. "I would think they'd be from the same circles, actually. Your family and mine go way back, right? The Bradfords used to have money, too."

"My grandfather never approved of Flossie." Sebastian hesitated, then added, "Flossie is a woman who knows her own mind and doesn't care what people think. A free spirit and a feminist. My grandmother was the sort who ironed her husband's shirts and made sure dinner was on the table at six. Old-school in every way. But she admired Flossie."

"There's a lot to admire," Anne said.

The pain seemed more manageable now; maybe it was the effect of the hormones coursing through her body. Lucy nursed so noisily that it was embarrassing. Still, Anne wanted to laugh with relief at the sensation of holding her baby and with the knowledge that she wasn't going to die in the woods, after all, or be paralyzed or suffer any of the other awful things that could have happened to her. What a responsibility, being a mother and having to keep your body intact so your child would survive.

All at once, Anne felt an unexpected pang of sympathy for her own mother. Sarah had coped with raising three children while running a business on her own. How had she done it without falling apart?

She shifted Lucy to the other breast and remembered to tug down her shirt, though probably not in time to spare Sebastian the sight of her bare breast. He had finally looked at her, and now he couldn't seem to look away. She was startled by the depth of longing in his eyes.

"Sit down," she said gently. Then, remembering, "Is your dog all right in the car? You can bring him inside. He can't hurt anything in here."

Sebastian went out, then returned with the dog. Mack bounded into the house and went around the corners of its small, tidy spaces, sniffing loudly, making them both smile when he nosed at Lucy, then finally circled at Sebastian's feet and threw himself down with a groan.

"I really am sorry about him," Sebastian said, gesturing toward the dog. He sat down in one of the chairs across from her, crossing his long legs at the ankle. He was tall. Anne hadn't realized how tall until now.

"It wasn't the dog's fault. Mack was just doing what dogs do." Anne put Lucy up against her shoulder and patted her back. The baby's head felt hot beneath her chin, bowling ball hard. Her hair was damp and curly, her body heavy and still. She was already drifting off to sleep.

"Of course it was his fault," Sebastian said. "Mine, too. If I'd had him on a leash, you wouldn't have fallen off. Your sister seems to think you're a great rider."

"No. *She's* the great rider. I'm the family daydreamer," Anne said. "That's why I lost my seat. I'd dropped the reins and slipped my feet out of the stirrups. Anything could have caused the horse to spook and I would have gone right off. So dumb. I don't know what I was thinking." She smiled down at Lucy, who'd fallen asleep, head lolling on Anne's arm, her lips pursed and red.

Sebastian smiled, too. "She's a beautiful baby. How old?"

"Four months."

He didn't ask about the father, but Anne saw his eyes drop to her ring finger. "Is she the reason you came back from Puerto Rico?" he asked.

Anne shook her head. "No. Lucy's father and I split up. I came home to lick my wounds and get back on my feet."

"I'm sorry."

"Don't be. That was my fault, too. Even dumber than what happened with the horse. Again, I should have seen it coming."

"We can never see everything coming our way," Sebastian said, his expression dark.

His hair was uncombed and he needed to shave. Looking at him across the room, at his wild hair, long legs in jeans, and broad shoulders beneath his flannel shirt, Anne thought Sebastian belonged outdoors, like some feral cat. Even now, his eyes scanned the room, taking in details she'd probably never noticed.

Anne remembered his wife, then, and wondered if it was true that she'd killed herself. What a tragedy, however she'd died. So young.

"What were you doing in the woods?" she asked, hoping Sebastian hadn't guessed what she was thinking.

"A university botany project on invasive species."

"What kind?"

"Garlic mustard."

She couldn't help laughing, this sounded so absurd. "Ouch." She put a hand to her side.

"What?" Sebastian scowled. "It's an important project. The first of its kind to show that an invasive plant can harm native hardwoods like maple and ash trees."

She was trying to stop laughing—not to spare his feelings, but because laughing hurt—yet couldn't get ahold of herself.

Then, as if someone had flipped a switch, Anne was weeping: from the pain, from the relief she felt at being reunited with Lucy, from exhaustion most of all. She'd never felt so incapable of coping with something as simple as standing up and putting her baby down for a nap.

Sebastian got to his feet and crossed the room in a single long stride, plucked the baby from her shoulder, and said softly, "Where?"

Anne gestured with her chin toward the bedroom, where Lucy's portable crib was just visible beyond the doorway. He carried her daughter—who looked absurdly small tucked against his broad chest—into the bedroom, lay her down, and gently covered her with a blanket. Then he closed the door partway and came back.

"You're tired and hurting," he said. "Let me get you some ibuprofen, at least. Where is it? Bathroom?"

She nodded. "Cabinet. Top shelf."

He fetched her two tablets and a glass of water, waited for her to swallow the medication, and returned to the kitchen with the glass. "There. Now I should go and let you rest. Sounds like your aunt has dinner covered."

"You don't have to leave. I'm fine. Really I am."

Sebastian smiled at her, the first real smile. His face was transformed. He was handsome. Perhaps even better-looking than he'd been in high school, and that was saying something. "You're not. But you're too thick-headed to let me help you, so I should leave before I make you crazy by trying to talk you into doing something you don't want to do."

"You wouldn't," she said.

"Which? Make you crazy, or talk you into something?"

"Neither."

"You don't know that." He shook his head. "My wife," he began, then stopped.

"Your wife, what?" she said.

"Never mind. It doesn't matter." Sebastian picked up his keys from the table and called the dog unnecessarily: Mack was already on his feet, feathery tail wagging. "Call me if you need help with anything. It's the least I can do." He reached out and Anne handed him her cell phone. He put in his number and gave the phone back to her. "I mean it. Call me."

"I'll be fine. But thank you."

"I'll check on you tomorrow anyway, if that's all right," he insisted, and bent down to kiss her cheek.

Anne tipped her face up toward his and saw the shock of recognition in his eyes as she felt the brief touch of his warm lips on her skin. It was as if they'd already made love, which they had, so long ago.

But that was before either of them knew what love was, or how it could tear you apart.

CHAPTER EIGHT

When Laura's last afternoon lesson on Friday canceled, she decided to escape for a ride alone and do what she should have done months ago.

She hurriedly tacked up Star, the newest horse in the barn, before she could change her mind. She had bought the four-year-old gelding at auction last month despite knowing his upstart reputation: a veterinarian friend who had examined the horse said, "This one's rock solid, but watch yourself. He's an ornery cuss."

Laura was intrigued. She had a soft spot for difficult animals and appreciated Thoroughbreds. They could be high-strung, but were usually intelligent and made good show jumpers because of their speed, agility, and height. She had a couple of advanced students who might perform well with Star in the spring shows once she got him settled down. Besides, Star was a beauty, a rich chestnut color with a white mark below his forelock that had earned him his name.

Star stood at seventeen hands, so Laura used a mounting block to get her foot into the stirrup and swing her leg over his back. The horse tossed his head nervously and sidestepped in a half circle. She gentled him with her voice and patted his neck before setting off toward the road along the driveway.

So far she'd ridden him only in the ring, where Star relaxed if she kept him on the fence. He was used to being on the rail because of the track. Now, without the security of a fence, the horse was startled by every fluttering leaf or snapped branch. It was like riding a four-legged pogo stick.

That was fine with her. Having to keep her seat on a nervy horse forced her to sweep all unnecessary thoughts out of her mind and focus on her mission: she was headed for Halibut Point, determined to end all communication with Tom by destroying her burner phone. She couldn't chance Jake finding it again. Now the phone was tucked into her bra, where the solid weight of it was like a bruise on her skin.

It took twenty minutes to trot along the soft shoulder of the two-lane road to the park, where she turned Star onto a narrow footpath beneath a tunnel of trees, the overhanging branches so low that she had to lean across the horse's neck. The land gradually sloped downhill toward a web of rocky trails leading to the sea. The wind had picked up and the tall yellowing grasses shushed in the breeze, a harsh whispering sound that caused Star to prance with excitement, ears pricking back and forth.

Several times Laura halted the horse, letting Star eyeball his surroundings. The first couple of times, the thoroughbred snorted and tossed his head, angling to get the bit between his teeth, but she kept him firmly in hand.

When Star relaxed, she used her calves to urge him into a trot. Finally they reached the straightaway and she signaled him to canter. Laura leaned low against the horse's neck as the animal flattened into a smooth gallop. The wind made her eyes tear as the landscape blurred by in yellows and reds and golds. The speed let her empty her mind. There was nothing but this moment, this animal beneath her, the landscape whipping by, the sharp sting of salty air on her face. She was blissfully free.

They reached the end of the trail in minutes. Below, the sea was a brooding slate, frothing cream against the rocks. The sun was a red haze to the west, its reflection made up of sparkling gold and pink lights on the water.

Laura reached into her bra and, without letting herself hesitate, hurled the phone into the water. She was done with Tom. With secrets. She was married. A mother. The sort of person who believed in doing the right thing—even if it was the hard thing.

Tears slid down her face as she stared out at the empty horizon. Not even a boat broke the flat gray line delineating sea and sky. Never had she felt so alone.

Laura held Star to a slow jog as they returned through the field. She didn't want the horse to be lathered up at the end of the ride; tonight she and Jake were meeting Melanie and her husband for dinner. She wouldn't have much time to cool Star down.

At least now she could look Jake in the eye across the dinner table with a clear conscience. She had not cheated on him. She *would* not. She was back on track and so was her marriage.

Or it would be, once she saw Anne. Laura intended to apologize for her behavior in the pub. She meant what she'd said to Jake: she was letting the past go. At the same time, she would make sure her sister got the message that she needed to steer clear of Jake if things were going to remain civil.

Anne wisely hadn't shown her face around Laura's house since that stupid stunt the other day, when she'd fallen off General. Laura still couldn't figure out how Flossie's reliable old horse had thrown a rider as experienced as Anne. A baby could probably ride that animal and be perfectly safe.

A baby.

Anne has a baby. Anne has a baby. Anne has a baby. Laura found herself repeating this chant as she rode back through the state park, where Star shied as a trio of wild turkeys crossed the path in front of them, running through the grass like homely long-necked children.

Did Anne *look* like she'd had a baby? Laura frowned as sweat prickled beneath her velvet riding helmet, trying to remember how Anne had looked the night they'd fought at the pub.

Laura's own body had been completely transformed by pregnancy, and not just by the extra weight. She'd erupted in varicose veins and cellulite, and her breasts had never recovered from nursing. But Anne's waist and hips seemed as slim as ever.

Motherhood wore you down. Exhausted and debilitated you. Laura knew that firsthand. She loved her daughter, but having Kennedy was the start of the troubles in her marriage. Of Jake's lack of desire and of her own feelings of inadequacy.

"Well, it was a mistake to let your husband watch the birth," her mother said when Laura, in a fit of weakness, confessed that Jake seemed less interested in making love after Kennedy was born.

"Understandable," Sarah had pronounced. "No man wants to see that. They don't have strong stomachs like we do. He'll get over it. Jake needs time to forget that awful spectacle."

It was true that Kennedy's birth wasn't easy. When Laura's water broke, Jake had insisted that they go straight to the hospital even though her labor hadn't started.

The labor hadn't progressed. Finally, the doctor suggested inducing it. Laura had resisted, remembering one friend describing her induced labor as a "bullet train straight to hell." But Jake sided with the obstetrician, saying they couldn't chance an infection now that her water had broken.

Laura finally agreed. Minutes after she was on the IV, the contractions were slamming her body. They'd given her an epidural to help manage the pain. An hour later, with the baby still not coming, the obstetrician made the call: the baby was in distress. Laura needed an emergency C-section.

When Kennedy was born, Laura was in a surgical theater with bright lights, numb from a second epidural, weeping from anxiety, a sheet drawn up so she couldn't see what was happening to her own body. Jake stood on her side of the sheet, but could see what was happening over the top. When he'd suddenly gasped in distress, Laura cried out, "What's wrong?"

The baby was fine, Jake had assured her quickly. "I just didn't expect so much blood."

Maybe her mother was right, and that experience had robbed Jake of his desire for her. He had hardly initiated lovemaking since.

Yet Laura was certain Jake loved her. After the baby, he had treated her tenderly, taking over the housework and cooking until she was back on her feet. He'd even encouraged her to take a spa weekend once Kennedy was weaned, and told her to color her hair despite the expense.

She had reached the two-lane road. Laura halted the horse to look for traffic, patting his neck absently, and glanced toward the inn, then at her watch. It was four o'clock. They weren't going to the club until seven.

Plenty of time to ride to the cottage and see Anne. Laura would show up and surprise her.

She'd be civil, Laura decided, turning the horse in that direction. Elly was right: the three of them were going to be sisters forever. They didn't have to like each other, but they could get along if Anne behaved herself. There was Mom's party to get through next month. Then the holidays. Plus, with Anne so unsettled, that poor baby would need her aunts.

A few minutes later, she turned the horse down the gravel drive leading to Aunt Flossie's house and its caretaker's cottage. Lights were on in both; the sun was setting earlier now.

It was the witching hour, that terrible time of day when nothing calmed babies. Kennedy always chose that last hour of daylight to go ballistic, usually when Laura was struggling to make dinner before Jake came home.

Now Laura imagined Anne with a furious wailing infant in her arms, looking pale and distraught as she tried to make the piercing cries stop. She was inexperienced and wouldn't know what to do.

Laura would take over. She would rock Anne's baby across her knees, soothing her. She smiled, picturing this scenario, her sister's eyes ringed in dark circles from lack of sleep. The look of gratitude on Anne's face when Laura quieted the baby with her magic touch.

Then Laura rounded the hedge of beach roses delineating the tiny yard around the cottage—a few pink flowers still bloomed, pink and papery looking—and was startled by the sight of not just one, but two unfamiliar cars. Had Anne bought a car? Who else was here?

Laura rode Star a little closer to the house, squinting in the rapidly diminishing light.

She stopped the horse when she recognized the blue Jeep as the same one Sebastian Martinson had been driving on the day he'd found Anne in the woods and brought her home, like some knight in shining four-wheel-drive. She sat astride the horse, biting her lip and staring at the cottage.

After a few minutes, someone stood up from the couch by the front windows. It was a woman, but not anyone Laura recognized. Next there was a burst of laughter as the front door opened and people began spilling onto the porch: Sebastian—she recognized his tall, lean frame even at this distance—along with a woman, another man, and several children, followed by Anne holding a baby in her arms.

More laughter, clearly audible over the distant surf. Laura felt ill. A crowd of laughter and love surrounded Anne. She didn't deserve it. Not after stealing another woman's husband to make a baby of her own!

A family. That's what Anne had created, after being here for only a short time: an entire family made up of Aunt Flossie, Sebastian, Elly, and that couple, plus all those children and her own baby, too.

Laura instinctively felt for her extra phone, her lifeline to Tom, and suffered a sharp stab of loss when her fingers encountered nothing but her own chilled skin through the thin fabric of her clothes.

"Come on, Star," she said, wheeling the horse around so sharply that there was a spray of gravel.

Back at the house, Elly was cooking—amazing, to see her glamorous Californian sister at the stove, her thick honey-colored hair slicked into a ponytail—with Kennedy chatting at her elbow and stirring something in a pot. Laura had calmed down on the ride home, telling herself, *So what if Anne has friends? Every new mom needs them.*

Now, however, she felt a fresh stab of despair, like a sudden wood splinter under her skin. She'd had lots of friends in college, and early on with Jake, too. Where had they all gone? She'd been so busy between the barn, helping out at the inn, and raising Kennedy practically on her own that she'd lost track of them.

She listened in wonder, sometimes, to the mothers who came to the barn to collect their daughters, some of whom she'd known in high school, as they talked about their tennis meets and club lunches, their movie nights or weekends at the spa with girlfriends. Even if she had the money for those activities, where would she find the time?

Laura sat on the mudroom bench and tugged off her black leather boots. Watching the brightly lit scene through the kitchen doorway made her feel like a voyeur spying on another, happier woman's life through a window.

Kennedy was adding salt to whatever was in the tall pot on the stove, giggling at something Elly said. It was a sweet moment, but there might as well have been a glass window between Laura and the kitchen. She could see the light but felt none of the room's warmth.

Elly joked with Kennedy and did her hair in new styles, took her shopping. Kennedy was carrying herself differently, lighter on her feet; she even looked a little thinner. Maybe that was because Elly was helping her choose different clothes. They'd been to dozens of consignment shops, preparing for Mom's birthday bash.

Laura felt pained, thinking that Kennedy was happier shopping or cooking with Elly than doing anything with her own mother. But why wouldn't she be? Her own mother had turned into a scold.

She reached again for her missing phone, then remembered it was gone and had to bite her lip to keep herself from crying out at the unfairness of having to give up the one thing in her life that had been making her feel happy.

Which is why you had to stop, Laura reminded herself, forcing herself to step into the brightly lit kitchen. "Hey, girls, what's cooking?" she chirped, her words sounding false even to her own ears.

Elly looked up and smiled. "We're making spaghetti *alla puttanesca,*" she said, then frowned. "What's wrong? You look like shit."

"Language," Laura said.

"Spaghetti *alla puttanesca* means 'whore's pasta,' Mom! It's the real name, look! It's in the cookbook. So you can't talk to *me* about language!" Kennedy said, and doubled over, laughing.

"Nice. Thanks, Elly." Laura stomped upstairs.

She showered, fiercely washing her hair, massaging her head until it burned and then giving in to odious self-pity, letting herself weep. She raised her face to the showerhead so the tears would wash away instantly as they fell. She was *useless, useless, useless.*

At last Laura stepped out of the shower to apply moisturizer and comb her hair. She wrapped a towel around her torso and opened the bathroom door to find Elly sitting on the end of her bed, paging through a magazine.

Elly looked up. "What's going on, Laura?"

"Don't ask."

To Laura's surprise, Elly shrugged. "Fine. Want help getting dressed? I know you're dreading this dinner."

"No need to help me. It doesn't matter what I wear," Laura said dully, sitting down beside Elly. "I'll look the same. And I hate how I look."

"So look different, then."

"Yeah, right." Laura gestured down at her towel. "Maybe I'll wear this."

"That would certainly get their attention." Elly grinned. "But I have a better idea."

Twenty minutes later, Elly had tucked Laura into a pair of black wide-legged trousers she dug out from the back of the closet—pants bought for a holiday party ages ago—and a gold silk blouse left partly unbuttoned over a black camisole with a lace edge. Elly added a wide black belt and a pair of high-heeled boots from her own clothing, spilling out of the giant suitcase in the guest room.

Then Elly made her sit on a stool in the bathroom, back to the mirror, while she painted Laura's nails with bright red polish and blew her hair dry, tugging it smooth with a rounded brush. Finally Elly did her makeup.

Laura closed her eyes and felt the tension drain out of her shoulders as she tilted her face up and surrendered to her sister. Elly's fingers fluttered like moths on her face and eyelids, and she kept up a constant, entertaining patter about Hollywood celebrities that demanded no response from Laura.

"So, what are you worked up about?" Elly finally asked as she applied what felt like a bucket of mascara to Laura's lashes.

By that time Laura was feeling so relaxed that she confessed the whole sorry mess: how Tom had started contacting her on Facebook, their e-mails and texts increasing in intimacy and frequency, the phone she'd just tossed, her guilt over deceiving Jake when, simultaneously, she had been harping on him about Anne.

She was afraid to look at Elly after that. But when Elly turned the chair toward the mirror and told her to open her eyes, Laura glanced at her sister's face and was shocked to see an expression of surprised admiration.

"Wow," Elly said. "And here I thought you were the family saint! Thank God you have *some* secrets."

"You don't think I'm awful?"

"Hell no," Elly said. "I think you've been lonely because Jake has pulled away and you're scrambling to save your marriage. But what about this other guy, Tom? Do you *want* to see him?"

"No," Laura said, then corrected herself. "Well. Maybe a little. But what we have isn't real. I know that. We haven't seen each other since high school! But Tom made me feel like I matter, you know? Like I'm an actual person instead of a cog in the family wheel." She laughed. "A rusty cog in a broken wheel covered in mud."

"Oh, get off the pity pot," Elly said. "You're essential. Jake and Kennedy depend on you. Mom does, too. It's no wonder you feel swallowed up. What you need is more time for yourself. You need to make yourself as much of a priority as you do everyone else."

"That sounds like dreary advice out of a woman's magazine." *Or from a woman who doesn't have to juggle work, a marriage, and children,* Laura thought, but she didn't want to insult her sister by saying that.

Elly shook her head. "I'm not talking spa getaways or even therapy, though both of those things might help. What I meant is that you need to be the real *you* with Jake and Kennedy. Ever since I got here, you've been faking things."

"What's that supposed to mean?" Laura demanded.

"You act happy when you're not," Elly said. "Remember how controlled Mom was when we were kids? Even that time Dad got so drunk that he mowed down the new rosebushes she'd spent all day planting?"

"She's still the Ice Queen," Laura said. "I can't remember the last time I saw her yell. Or cry."

"Right. She's a victim of her highborn Boston family. A stuffed-shirt, stoic New Englander to the nth degree." Elly smiled. "I can see that more clearly now that I've been living in California, where even the waitresses share their life stories within five minutes. But, look, think about what you're teaching Kennedy. Right now she's watching you and learning that it's not okay to ask for help. You need to let your flaws hang out more. Ask for what you want. What you *need*. You deserve to be happy as much as anybody."

"Thank you." Laura moved to cover her face, ashamed to have Elly know what a fool she'd been with Tom, yet relieved, too, that someone knew what she'd done.

Elly stopped her with both hands on her wrists. "Not the face! Don't touch the face!" she barked. "At least stand up and admire my artistry before you smudge yourself." She stepped away from the mirror.

Laura stood up and saw a wonderfully distorted reflection. The woman in the mirror looked taller and slimmer than Laura. Her eyes were dark blue and shining and long-lashed; her hair was a smooth, sexy bob of lustrous brown streaked with silver.

This woman was elegant. Beautiful. Not like Laura at all.

"I can't believe you did this," Laura said. "You're a magician."

Elly waved a hand. "Just think what I could do if I had my makeup artist with me." She began tucking the brushes and tubes back into her travel bag. "Now your job is to show off. Head high and shoulders back, okay? Strut into that club like you own it. Beauty is all about attitude. Mom taught us that, if nothing else."

Jake joined Elly in the kitchen while Laura lingered upstairs, helping Kennedy with some homework. He'd dressed up for the evening, too, opting for old-school preppy: a tweed jacket over slim-fitting brown wool pants and a white shirt with a red bow tie. Comb tracks were still visible in his dark hair, which he'd slicked back from his forehead to emphasize the widow's peak, his cleft chin, and his warm brown eyes. Even she had to admit he looked good.

Elly pretended to read the newspaper on the table as Jake went to the refrigerator and pulled out a bottle of white wine. Being alone with him had always made her uneasy. Not only because of what Laura and Anne had told her, but because Jake was a charmer.

For instance, he never failed to make coffee for her if Elly happened to get up early. Breakfast, too. He held open doors, complimented her clothes and hair, and poured her wine. He was solicitous about how well Elly had slept and whether she'd eaten enough for dinner. No man had ever made such a fuss over her. Jake did these things for every woman; Flossie used to call him "Jeeves" behind his back.

Lately Jake had made a point of asking Elly about work. He remarked on how interesting her career was, praising her as a "true artist." He said encouraging things whenever he saw her surfing job sites on her laptop in the kitchen: "Something always turns up when you least expect it." "Keep knocking on doors and one will open." "Opportunities are made, not given."

Everything Jake said amounted to fortune-cookie platitudes, but Elly found herself falling for them anyway. She was comforted by his belief in her.

"Earth to Elly! Want this?" Jake was standing directly in front of her, offering a glass of wine.

"Sure," she said. "Thank you."

To her surprise, he'd poured seltzer water for himself. "I'm driving," Jake explained, then grinned. "Hey, what did you do with my wife, and who's that gorgeous stranger upstairs?"

Elly smiled to be polite. "Your wife is always gorgeous."

"I know." Jake was immediately contrite. "Inside and out. I don't deserve her."

No, you don't, Elly thought. *You don't make her happy. And you came on to my little sister.*

Just then Laura breezed in. "All set, honey?" she said.

"I don't know," he murmured. "It's tempting to take you right back upstairs, the way you look tonight."

"Ew, gross!" Kennedy said. She had followed Laura downstairs. "Get a room!"

"Have fun, you two, and call me if you need a ride home," Elly said, noting the sudden stiffening of Jake's shoulders as he escorted Laura out the door. Why was he so nervous?

Elly and Kennedy slurped up the spaghetti from plates on their laps in the home theater downstairs, where Jake had installed a projector and massive TV screen that made Elly want to move the couch back another ten feet. They watched *Singin' in the Rain* again, pausing it to study the French posters on the wall behind Gene Kelly during the song "'S Wonderful."

"I bet we can get posters like that online," Elly said.

"And we can totally make those French straw brooms," Kennedy said.

"So who do you want to be? Henri—that's the guy whistling during "S Wonderful'—or Jerry, the one tapping?" Elly asked. She demonstrated some of the easier steps and was astonished by how easily Kennedy picked them up. "You go, girl!" she said as they carried the dishes upstairs. "You'll be the star of Grandma's party, dancing like that."

"Except I am *so* not dancing," Kennedy said. "Not in front of people!"

"So I'm not people?" Elly teased.

"Nope. You're some kind of, I don't know. A clone! My real aunt is still in California, hanging with Miley Cyrus."

"Please. Miley is so last decade."

Kennedy cracked up as Elly started singing "Wrecking Ball" while they rinsed plates and loaded the dishwasher. When they were finished, Kennedy said, "There's one thing I don't get."

"Yeah? What's that?" Elly was tucking plastic containers of leftovers into the fridge, marveling at how much food a refrigerator was meant to hold. She'd never stored much more than eggs, wine, and yogurt in hers.

"So, you said we're doing this movie because it's Grandma's favorite and was made the year she was born, right?"

"Uh-huh." Elly was wiping the counters, only half listening.

"Yeah, well. I Googled *An American in Paris*," Kennedy said. "It was made, like, in 1951, but that's not when Grandma was born."

"What are you talking about?" Elly rinsed out the sponge. "She's turning sixty-five. Of course that's when she was born. I'm bad at math, but even I can add and subtract."

Kennedy shook her head. "No. Grandma told me she was born in 1941. She says her birthday, December 8, 1941, was easy to remember because it's when President Roosevelt made his Day of Infamy speech after Pearl Harbor was bombed."

Elly froze in the middle of the kitchen, staring at Kennedy. "Why on earth would she tell you that?"

"We were studying World War II in school. Grandma thought it was cool that I was learning about ancient history, I guess."

Elly laughed. "First of all, that's hardly 'ancient' history. And Grandma must have been making up that story so you'd do your homework. My mother was born right here in Boston in 1951. Hers was one of the original families in Boston, just like Grandpa Bradford's family. They're both old-school blue bloods, which is what you call rich old families that started out in Back Bay. And she was definitely born in November, not December. I should know my own mom's birthday, right? We always gave her a party just before Thanksgiving."

"No," Kennedy said. "Grandma was born in 1941. Ask her if you don't believe me."

"I'm not going to do that! She'd never speak to me again! If Grandma was born then, she'd be turning seventy-five! Does she look seventy-five to you?"

"No. But that could be because she had, you know. *Surgery.*" Kennedy pulled her skin tight around her eyes with both hands.

"What surgery? You mean a face-lift?"

"Yeah. That's why her face looks young, but her neck still looks old. She came home last year wearing bandages like a mummy. Just her eyes and nose and mouth showing."

"Huh." Elly rinsed her hands at the sink. It was possible her mother had work done. She did look good. And Laura might not have mentioned it if there were no complications. Or if Sarah had ordered Laura to keep her surgery a secret.

Still, Kennedy had to be wrong about her mother's birthday. Why would her mother lie about her age?

Because she can, a small voice in Elly's mind chirped. Because Sarah would hate getting old. Still, wouldn't she have slipped up at some point and mentioned her real birthday?

Elly tried to remember whether she'd ever seen her mother's driver's license or birth certificate. Oh, what did it matter? Who cared? They could still celebrate her mother's birthday this November. Surely Sarah

deserved to have her daughters make a fuss over her and uphold whatever precious illusion she might have created about her age. Who cared?

Oddly, Elly did. She hated being lied to, even by her own mother.
Maybe *especially* by her own mother.

"Hey, I know what we can do tonight," Kennedy said, shattering
Elly's concentration. "We should totally go see Aunt Anne's baby!"

Elly was about to ask Kennedy how she even knew about the baby,
since her niece hadn't seen Anne. But of *course* Kennedy would know
about the baby. Teenagers were like bats, seeing three times better than
humans and using their big ears to echolocate sound waves bouncing
off objects.

She'd learned those fun factoids from Ryder, whose last text had
included a photograph of him in the outdoor shower, just his head and
shoulders showing over the wooden door. Grinning over his shoulder
at the camera. *Wish you were here,* he'd texted.

Elly wished she could be there, too, enjoying him. Feeling his hands
on her sun-warmed skin.

Now Kennedy was grinning like a demented clown in a horror
flick. She'd probably been planning to spring this outing on Elly the
minute she heard Laura and Jake were going out tonight.

Elly folded her arms. "Are you actually suggesting that I take you
over to see Anne while your parents are out, even though your mom
would absolutely, positively hate me for doing that?"

"Mom doesn't have to know." Kennedy widened her blue eyes in an
attempt to look innocent. "Besides, how else am I going to see my new
cousin? My *only* cousin! Don't you think I should meet her, even if my
mom's mad at Anne for whatever stupid reason?"

"I do." Elly grinned. What the hell. She was this kid's aunt. Who
else was going to teach Kennedy that some rules were made to be broken? "But you can't tell your parents I took you."

"No duh."

"Okay. Get your coat."

A few minutes later, they were parked in front of the Houseboat.
Elly knocked on the door. Kennedy was hopping up and down on the
porch.

"Will you please stop?" Elly grumbled as Anne opened the door.

Her sister was dressed as casually as she'd been the last time Elly was here, in jeans and a soft gray sweater. Yet she looked different. Maybe it was her hair: Anne had slicked her auburn curls back with a tortoiseshell headband, making her look younger than ever, and she wore long turquoise earrings. Somehow, Anne in jeans and a hairband still looked classier than ninety percent of all other women gowned for the red carpet.

Anne's smile was wide and warm. "Wow! Kennedy! You're here!" She hugged her niece, then stepped back. "Look at you, girl. So tall and gorgeous! Come meet Lucy!"

Kennedy practically fell over her own feet rushing through the door. Anne put a hand on Elly's arm as she followed and whispered, "Is this okay? Did you ask Laura?"

"No, but Kennedy won't say anything." Elly hoped she was right.

She followed Anne into the living room. She could hear Kennedy in the bedroom, talking a mile a minute to Lucy: introducing herself, commenting on the seashell mobile above the portable crib, picking up various toys and jiggling them.

"I hope Lucy wasn't sleeping," Elly said. "I'm sorry. This was an impulse thing. I should have called."

"Don't apologize! I wanted to see Kennedy." Anne lowered her voice. "But where's Laura? Seriously, how did you get away?"

"She and Jake went to dinner at the club and won't be back until late. You know how it goes there." Elly rolled her eyes. "Food from the fifties and giant cocktails."

Anne sighed. "This is so hard, having Laura hate me. I don't even know what's happening in her life anymore."

"She doesn't hate you."

"Well, she doesn't exactly love me," Anne said glumly.

"Give her time." Elly flopped down on the couch. "Anyway, I'm *staying* with Laura, and I don't know what's going on with her."

"What do you mean?"

"Let's just say that Laura's not the saint we thought she was."

"Really?" Anne sat beside her and tugged off the headband. Her curls sprang in all directions. Elly felt a twinge of guilt. She didn't want to betray Laura's confidence. "Look, I can't give you details. Laura really would kill me then." She leaned forward and dropped her voice to a whisper. "But a classmate from high school contacted her out of the blue. A guy! I think Laura came this close to having an affair." She held up her thumb and forefinger, an inch apart.

"Oh. My. God. Well, I almost wish she *would* cheat on Jake," Anne whispered back. "He doesn't deserve her. Plus, then she'd have to stop thinking of me as a trashy skank."

"Actually, you might want to hang on to that image." Elly grinned. "Trashy skanks have all the fun in L.A."

Anne laughed. "Speaking of L.A., how's the job search?"

"Nada." Elly shrugged. "I'll probably have to go back to really network. Hollywood is all about being in the right place at the right time if you want to work. How about you?"

"I'm not making much progress, either. I have a job interview at a Catholic school in Danvers next week, but I don't know what I'll do with Lucy if I have to work full-time."

"Hello? Day care?"

"I hate that idea. She's so little. I can barely stand having Flossie watch her."

Elly patted Anne's knee. "Don't worry. Something will turn up, and it'll get easier to leave Lucy when she's a little older." She knew this sounded lame, but it was a reality that she and Anne both had to work. They didn't have rich dentist husbands paying the bills.

Or who *should* be paying the bills: Elly was still trying to puzzle out why Laura and Jake were as broke as Laura said.

"What about your love life? Anything new there?" Anne asked. Elly must have reddened, because her sister laughed. "Spill!"

"I will if you will," Elly said.

Anne rolled her eyes. "Like anybody's going to want me now."

They were interrupted by Kennedy calling from the other room. "Hey, Aunt Anne, can I pick her up? Lucy's awake."

Anne and Elly exchanged a grin. "I bet she is," Anne said. "She's probably all excited about meeting you. Sure, you can hold her. Let me show you how to pick her up." She stood up and went into the bedroom.

From where she was sitting, Elly could see Anne bend over—just her hips showing through the doorway—and then Kennedy emerged with Lucy in her arms. Wide-eyed at the sight of this new face, the baby babbled, making them all laugh.

"I think she likes me," Kennedy said, gazing down at her cousin.

Kennedy's round face was softened by a sweep of long bangs. Elly had cut her hair in a shoulder-length blunt cut that emphasized Kennedy's high cheekbones. The girl looked pretty tonight, maybe because she was smiling. How could she not, with a baby grinning at her like she was a rock star?

Elly felt a twist of envy in her gut and had to turn away.

"Want to give her a bottle?" Anne asked. "She's probably hungry again. Lucy eats like a lumberjack."

Kennedy started to hop up and down, then remembered the baby and stopped. "Can I?"

"Sure. Come on."

The two of them went into the galley kitchen. Anne took a plastic bag of milk out of the refrigerator, dipped it in a bowl of warm water for a few minutes, then transferred it to a bottle while Kennedy chatted about some class she'd taken in junior high that had required them to carry eggs around.

"The teacher was showing us how much work it is to take care of a baby, so we'd be like all abstinent and stuff, but I *liked* taking care of my egg," Kennedy said. "I even drew a face on it and made it a little bed out of a Kleenex box."

"You'll be a great mom," Anne said. "But you should probably wait a while to have sex. Or at least use birth control, so you don't end up like me."

Kennedy looked shocked, then laughed. "Yeah, don't worry. The boys in my school are gross anyway. And so boring! All they talk about is farting, video games, and sports."

"Some boys don't ever grow out of that, sadly." Anne handed Kennedy the bottle, then glanced at Elly.

Elly had been working hard to keep her expression neutral despite the knot in her throat, but whatever Anne saw on her face caused her to say, "Kennedy, why don't you feed Lucy in the bedroom? She'll prob-ably fall asleep while you rock her. That would be a huge help to me."

"Okay," Kennedy said.

Anne got her and the baby settled, then closed the bedroom door before returning to the couch. "Tell me."

"Tell you what?" Elly said woodenly, but of course she knew. It was time to tell someone. Besides, she'd never been able to hide anything from Anne, the little sister who had adored her and tried to copy her every move growing up.

Anne the pest. Anne the whiner.

Anne, her sister, who was touching Elly's face gently with one fin-ger now, saying, "Sweetie, please tell me. What's wrong? Why are you crying?"

"I'm not," Elly said, but then she touched her own face, and damn it. She was.

"Did Laura do something to upset you?"

"No."

"Jake didn't try anything with you, did he?"

Elly wiped her face on her sleeve. "God, no. He wouldn't dare."

"What about me? Did I say or do something that upset you?" Anne looked worried, but she kept her hand on Elly's face, her palm warm-ing Elly's skin like a small sun.

"No!" Elly pulled away and stood up. "Do you have any wine around? I could murder for a glass of wine."

"As it happens, I do. I had some people here for lunch today."

"Here in the Houseboat?" Elly laughed and wiped her face on one sleeve.

"Sure. Plenty of room, if half the people don't mind standing. As in, half of eight people." Anne went to the kitchen and poured a glass of red wine for Elly and another for herself. "Maybe if I drink a little more wine, it'll sedate the baby when I nurse her."

Elly laughed again. This was what she needed: to laugh. Maybe then she could watch Anne holding Lucy without falling apart.

"Now talk to me." Anne sat down beside her and handed her the wine.

"So there was this guy," Elly said. "I wanted to forget about him, but I couldn't. Still can't." She took a few restorative sips of wine.

In the other room, Kennedy was singing "Rockaby, Baby." She had a sweet voice, nearly as low as Laura's rich alto, with a natural vibrato. Elly slowly started to feel at peace.

Finally she began telling Anne about Hans. "He was the reason I skipped the big Christmas party at the inn two years ago," she said. "I wanted to spend the holidays with him. I thought I'd met the love of my life. That sounds so stupid now."

"No, it doesn't. But why didn't you bring Hans here with you? Or at least tell us that's why you stayed?"

"Hans didn't want to come east. And I didn't tell you because I was ashamed to be choosing a man over seeing all of you," Elly said. "God! So lame. But it's like I was under some kind of spell and couldn't bring myself to leave him. I wanted to be with Hans every second of every day."

She closed her eyes briefly, picturing Hans so vividly that she could imagine reaching out to touch him even now, in this tiny cottage three thousand miles away.

Hans was a Swedish producer and had the square, top-heavy build of a pugilist. Elly met him on a movie they were doing together. Within a week she'd started spending most nights at his stucco ranch house in the Hollywood Hills, a place with floor-to-ceiling windows overlooking a canyon where they could hear the coyotes howling at night and where you had to be careful on the back patio because rattle-snakes occasionally sunned themselves around the pool.

Elly was certain she'd met the man she was meant to spend her life with, because Hans was fun and funny, dramatic and sexy, intelligent and inquisitive. Everything she did with him was exciting, whether they were skiing in Tahoe or lying on his living room floor and playing chess. She especially loved the way he placed his palm at the small of her back when they kissed.

"Kissing Hans felt like dancing," she told Anne.

"Sounds like you were in deep," Anne said.

"'Insane' might be a better description," Elly said, remembering how sometimes she'd show up at Hans's place in the middle of the night. Even in the rain. Even during wildfire alerts, mudslides, and once during a storm that left her car pockmarked from the hail.

"Was it the sex?" Anne asked. "Was that why it was so intense?"

"Everything was intense with Hans."

Elly told Anne about their Sunday mornings on Venice Beach and their dinners in Koreatown, and about Hans's love of good cigars and whiskey, his sandy hair, and his eyes that could be the solemn gray of a winter sky or the warm pewter of liquid metal. "I was sure I couldn't live without him," Elly said, her tears still ridiculously, shamelessly flowing. "Sometimes I still feel that way."

It was a relief to say this. Anne was the only person she'd ever told about Hans. Not about the beginning of her time with him—all her friends and colleagues in Los Angeles had heard about that, because Elly was so dizzy with excitement that she couldn't keep silent about the start of their affair—but about the horrible, sad, sudden, bitter end of her fairy tale.

"So what happened?" Anne asked.

"I chose to spend Christmas with him two years ago instead of coming home partly because I thought Hans might propose, or at least ask me to live with him. But then he just left."

"He left you on *Christmas*?" Anne said.

"Christmas Eve, actually," Elly said.

Hans had called her that morning, saying he needed to go back to Sweden. No explanation.

"Was it a visa issue or something?" Anne asked. "Was he deported?"

"No."

"Then what? Was he married?"

"No," Elly said, adding that later, much later, she had been told by a criminal investigator that Hans was embezzling money. A lot of money. "He had raised funds from investors for an independent documentary, then spent it on himself. He'd skipped the country to avoid any lawsuits. Pretty soon he left Sweden, too. Nobody knew where he went. I never heard from him again."

She could tell by her sister's expression—her eyes deep blue and very still on Elly's face, like two cooling chips of ice—that Anne understood the rest without Elly having to say it: how she had spent that Christmas alone, drunk in her darkened apartment, the shades drawn. She'd stayed inside for nearly a week despite the warm December sunshine, until the booze ran out and her food, too.

Elly had told everyone who called from Massachusetts that she couldn't possibly get away for Christmas, but that she'd come later in the spring.

She hadn't done that, either, though, because she was sick. A fever first and dull cramping. It was painful to urinate. A bladder infection, Elly thought. She drank gallons of cranberry juice and ate yogurt at every meal. She didn't want to go on antibiotics unless it was absolutely necessary.

The pain worsened from mild to an intense burning sensation. Then there were sharp, stabbing cramps in her upper abdomen. She would have seen a doctor sooner, but she'd landed a union job, a music video with a major artist on a tight schedule. Elly took ibuprofen by day and drank tequila at night to help her sleep.

"Sounds like hell on earth," Anne said.

Elly nodded. "It was bad. And I was stupid not to get checked out sooner. Finally, when the shoot finished, I went to my gynecologist. The doctor did a pelvic exam and ordered blood tests and an ultrasound. The diagnosis was chlamydia, which had apparently traveled to my internal organs."

Anne reached over and took Elly's hand in hers. "Why didn't you call me?"

"I don't know. The whole thing with Hans left me feeling ashamed, I guess. As if I'd somehow helped him steal that money." Elly told her then about the surgery to remove an abscess caused by the infection. "The doctor said there was some scarring. Enough that I might be infertile."

"But you don't know for sure," Anne said quickly.

"Right." Elly closed her eyes and rested her head on Anne's shoulder. "But it's possible that I can't have kids."

Anne squeezed her hand. "Oh, Elly. I'm so sorry."

"I'm the one who needs to apologize."

"What do you mean? For what?"

"For being less than cheerful around you and Lucy. It's just hard, looking at you with a baby and knowing I might not ever be a mom."

"You don't *know* that," Anne said. "If you ever decide you want kids, there are lots of ways to make that happen."

Elly sat up and rubbed her face with both hands. "Look, let's not talk about me anymore, okay?" She turned to face her sister, leaning on the arm of the couch and tucking her feet beneath her. "You look great. Something must be going your way. Or someone? You said you had people over. Anyone special?"

By the way Anne blushed, she knew she'd guessed right. "Who is he?" Elly said, grinning.

"Nobody! God!" Anne said, but she was smiling, too.

Kennedy materialized in her strangely silent way and stood in front of them, a triumphant look on her face. "I put the baby to sleep," she said, then narrowed her eyes at them. "What's going on?"

"Nothing!" Anne and Elly chorused, then laughed and pressed their feet together the way they used to do as children, warm sisterly soles connected, their strong legs like part of one creature, a current of energy running between them.

CHAPTER NINE

They had redecorated the country club since the last time Laura was here. Everything was hunter green and gold now, even the plaid carpet. Vintage framed golf cartoons marched in neat rows above the fireplace. Silk flowers in tall vases stood on the tables, which were covered in cream tablecloths edged in gold embroidery. It was the sort of setting that made you worry about getting lipstick on your teeth.

Laura chose the cheapest chicken dish on the menu and a single glass of cava, the only wine under twelve dollars a glass, and smiled at the elderly waiter to show that she appreciated his efforts. Jake ordered soup and salad, no wine at all.

Sandra and her husband, Wayne, must not have eaten all day: they ordered appetizers and prime rib entrées with three sides, accompanied by a bread basket and two bottles of expensive Bordeaux. Now they were having dessert and VSOP cognac. When Laura did the math in her head, she could hardly breathe: five hundred dollars on dinner, at least. She hoped they wouldn't suggest splitting the bill.

"You two eat like birds!" Sandra exclaimed when Laura and Jake passed on dessert. "I exercise like a madwoman all week so I can have dessert on Friday nights. I love the club's molten lava cake, don't I, hon?"

She patted her flat belly, wrapped tightly into an emerald green dress. Both the aging waiter and Jake seemed to be having a tough time keeping their eyes averted from the snowy pillows of Sandra's breasts plumped above the dress's deep neckline.

"My sweetie loves her sweets," Wayne agreed, leaning back in his chair to swirl the amber liquid in his balloon snifter.

Wayne wasn't nearly as handsome as Jake. His face was cratered with acne scars and he was overweight, his stomach visibly distending his shirt beneath the blue blazer. He had a heavy South Boston accent and the manners of a ten-year-old boy on a camping trip. He had slurped his soup; eaten his salad with his large fork; and carved his steak like he was butchering the cow, sawing in the wrong direction with his knife until Laura had to look away.

Yet he was a likable man. Wayne seemed to know everyone's name. He had warmly greeted the host, the servers, even the water boy. The wine steward seemed to be a particularly close personal friend. Wayne asked about the man's wife and recommended a mechanic when the steward mentioned his Volkswagen was giving him trouble.

During dinner, Sandra raved about the magical effects of horseback riding on Melanie's confidence, then asked about Kennedy's favorite teachers and hobbies. There were also Sandra's sons to discuss in detail: sports every season, nothing but trouble in school; they'd have to get into college on hockey or football rather than grades.

Wayne, who'd earned a football scholarship to Boston College, shrugged this off. "What are you gonna do? Boys should be raised on the streets and in the woods. The actual real world! That's where you get yourself a real education! Ain't that right, Jake, my man?"

Jake cleared his throat. "Absolutely. Nothing like the great outdoors. I keep trying to convince my girls to camp with me, but they'll have none of it."

"Yeah, well. They don't get to bring their blow-dryers and mascara, it ain't a real vacation," Wayne said, patting Sandra's thigh with obvious affection.

Sandra giggled. Laura smiled with her lips pressed shut.

When Wayne steered the conversation toward work, Laura was pleased to have something to contribute. She talked about the riding stables and her decision to build an indoor riding arena last year while Sandra chewed silently. Then Laura was annoyed with herself for being petty and competitive.

She was relieved when Sandra chimed in about her volunteer work, clearly proud of her efforts to make the school a better place. Sandra told them she'd written a grant to fund a new science lab, "possibly the only middle school science lab in our area," she added.

Throughout dinner, Wayne expressed his adoration for his wife verbally and physically. At one point, he draped a beefy arm around Sandra's shoulders to give her a proprietary squeeze. Another time, he leaned over to nuzzle her neck like they were teenagers on a hot date that would end in the backseat of a car. Laura was amused, if a little repulsed, by these ridiculous, lusty public displays.

Still, as they left the restaurant, Sandra giggling and leaning on Wayne, Laura found herself wishing that Jake would at least hold her hand. They'd had a date. It was Friday night. They were out on the town.

Jake was silent beside her, probably calculating the damage this dinner had cost them. (Wayne had suggested splitting the five-hundred-and-twenty-dollar bill in half and Jake had complied without argument. Yet another charge on the credit card they never seemed to pay off.)

Laura sighed. She didn't want to think about money. It was a beautiful fall night, the moon nearly full and very bright above the meticulously groomed golf course, Venus a bright sequin beneath it. She wanted to make the most of their rare time alone together.

The parking lot was nearly deserted after Wayne drove away, waving from the window of his Range Rover. Laura became aware of the wind humming through the tall pines lining the club's long driveway. The stars were out, a full display of constellations that reminded Laura of the app Tom had encouraged her to download for her phone. She took her phone out and aimed it at the sky as Jake unlocked the car.

"Trying to get a signal?" Jake asked.

"No. I'm using a sky map," she said. "Come look."

Jake moved around the hood of the car to peer at her phone. "Pretty neat. Who showed you that? Kennedy?"

"I think so," she lied. "Can't remember. Look, we're facing south. Here's Capricornus and Sagittarius."

"Nice," Jake said. "Let's go, honey. I'm beat and you're shivering."

She *was* shivering, but not from the cold. She was upset, now that she didn't have to smile and pretend she was enjoying herself. Low moods always made her feel like she was coming down with the flu.

Loss. That's what she was feeling: Laura wanted to take a picture of the night sky and Snapchat it to Tom, but of course she couldn't. That was all over now.

As it should be.

"Did you notice how Wayne couldn't keep his hands off Sandra?" Laura said. She glanced at Jake, wondering if he'd felt any of the same envy she had. "Though I guess any guy would want to grope her. Sandra's dress didn't leave much to the imagination."

"Right. Kind of a cheap display." Jake started the engine and backed carefully out of the parking space despite the empty lot. "She seems nice, though. I hope our girls will be friends."

Jake's response was predictable. He'd never been the sort of man who approved of women in revealing clothing. He had once told Laura to blame his prudishness on his "inner Puritan" when she surprised him at his office for their tenth wedding anniversary wearing a skintight red strapless cocktail dress over nothing at all. He'd actually laughed when she took off her coat and crossed the office to rub against him in her red dress. She had cried then, which of course made him feel terrible.

"It isn't that you don't look good," he had explained earnestly. "You look amazing. But I would feel awkard, taking you to dinner looking like this. Like I'd have to defend your honor because every man would undress you with his eyes."

"But you're the only one I *want* to have undress me!" she'd wailed.

At that, Jake had closed the office door and locked it. Then he'd slowly, tenderly peeled the dress off Laura's shoulders and made love to her on his desk, leaving her breathless and satisfied, yet ashamed, too, because she'd manipulated him into making love.

"Honey? What do you think?" Jake glanced at her.

"About what?"

"About Melanie and Kennedy being friends. That would be nice. Kennedy doesn't seem to bring anyone to the house anymore."

"I doubt that's going to happen," she said. "Kennedy thinks Melanie's a bitch."

"She actually called her that?"

"Uh-huh."

"Wow." Jake laughed. "Our little girl's growing up."

"Faster than I'd like. I hope she and Elly found enough to do tonight."

"I'm sure they did."

He sounded distracted; Laura could tell from his tone that he'd lost interest in the conversation. "Jake, are we okay? You seemed really distant tonight."

"You mean because I wasn't pawing at you, like Wayne was all over Sandra?" Jake sounded irritated now. "Of course we're okay. I mean, I'm tired tonight. It's the end of a long week. But I had fun until Wayne suggested splitting the bill down the middle. That hardly seemed fair."

"Can we for once forget about money? Stop trying to derail the conversation."

"Am I? Sorry."

Laura sighed. "You are. But never mind. I'm too tired to deal with it anyway."

"To deal with what?"

"With trying to examine our lives!" she said. "With asking myself where we're going. Whether we're happy. Maybe it's because I'm forty, but I've been asking myself those questions a lot lately. Haven't you?"

"No. I've been too busy worrying about other things. You know, like how the hell we're going to pay down the credit card and make our bills next month." He glanced at her. "Sorry. Money again, I know. Off-limits." Jake sighed, ran a hand through his hair. "Look, I feel bad that our date didn't cheer you up. At least we tried. We should definitely socialize more often."

Laura smiled. "Because we're having so much fun, you mean?"

He laughed. They had reached the house. Jake parked the car and reached over to pat her knee. "Because you're wonderful and deserve to have fun every day. By the way, have I told you how lovely you look tonight?"

"Yes. Several times. You can stop now. Anyway, Sandra was the gorgeous one."

"Okay, it's my turn to tell *you* to stop," Jake said. "You look classy and beautiful. I would never want you to dress like Sandra. She tries too hard. Anyway, what I'm trying to say is that I'd be lost without you. You're my guiding light, Laura. You make me always want to be a better man. I hope you know how much I love you."

"I do. But thanks for saying it."

Jake came around to her side of the car and opened the door for her as he always did, offering his hand. Laura took it. They held hands up the brick walkway leading to the house.

She glanced up at Jake's handsome profile and smiled. It had been a good night. At least they were talking openly now. That was more than they usually had time and energy for at the end of every busy day.

And Jake loved her. She knew he did.

Anne was drifting off to sleep when there was another knock on her door. She squinted at the clock. Elly and Kennedy had left more than half an hour ago. Who would want to visit her at nine o'clock?

Laura! She probably came home and found out that Elly had brought Kennedy over here. Anne pulled a pillow over her head. Maybe if she didn't turn on a light, Laura would give up and leave.

The knocking continued. Finally, Anne sighed and sat up to peer out the bedroom window.

She was shocked to see her mother standing beneath the porch light, a slight figure hunched into the shawl collar of a long coat. Her gray hair gleamed silver in the bright light.

Her mother had stopped by the cottage only once so far, to hand Anne an envelope of money for tending bar. On that visit, Sarah had stayed for just a few minutes and stared at the furniture as if it might be covered in thorns. Then she'd surprised Anne by scooping Lucy into her arms when the baby started fussing.

Sarah had rocked in place from side to side, shifting her weight from one foot to the other while holding Lucy and whispering about what they could see out the window: a pair of cormorants, a distant fishing vessel gleaming bright red against the blue sky. The baby had calmed down at once.

As soon as Lucy was quiet, Sarah had handed her back to Anne and left the cottage.

What could her mother possibly want now?

Anne climbed out of bed, anxiety making her forehead feel covered in spiderwebs. Her rib was better now—she hadn't broken it, as an X-ray proved when Sebastian had insisted on driving her to the hospital the day after her fall to be checked—but she moved carefully out of habit as she pulled on a flannel shirt over her T-shirt and slipped into a pair of black yoga pants borrowed from Flossie.

She silently felt her way out of the bedroom and closed the door behind her before turning on the living room table lamp. The last thing she needed was for her mother to wake Lucy.

Anne opened the door and shivered in the rush of damp salty air. Sarah was wrapped in a calf-length mink coat. She'd never paid any attention to animal rights campaigns. Once, when Anne was in college and going through a vegan phase, she'd complained about her mother's furs.

"Aren't I an animal, too?" Sarah had demanded in response. "If a lion could eat me or wear my skin and stay warm in a New England winter, I'm sure he would do it. I'm just lucky to be the real queen of the jungle."

"Goodness," Sarah said now. "You look like you were asleep. Were you?"

"Yes."

"It's not even ten o'clock!" She peered around Elly's shoulder. "Where's that baby?"

"She's sleeping, too, Mom."

"Well." Sarah looked distressed, her face cratered in shadows. "I thought I should come by with her baby gift. I meant to bring it sooner, you know. But I suppose Lucy can open it tomorrow. Just make sure she knows it's from me."

Like Lucy would know the difference, Anne thought as her mother thrust a heavy box wrapped in flowered paper into her hands. Like she'd even be able to open this. Besides, the baby would probably be more interested in the wrapping paper than in whatever was inside the box. But she smiled and nodded. At least her mother was making a token gesture of acceptance.

"Thanks, Mom. Do you want to come in for a minute?" she added with a yawn.

"No, no. I don't want to bother you," Sarah said, but stood there until Anne repeated the invitation.

Her mother nodded then. "Well, if you insist." She stepped into the room, shrugging the mink coat off her shoulders as if a butler were waiting to take it from her.

Anne scooped up the coat before it hit the floor and draped it over a chair. She wasn't a vegan anymore, or even a vegetarian—pregnancy had caused her to crave meat—but she still hated the idea of fur coats. Even so, she had to admit this one was beautiful, a velvety buff color with darker stripes.

"It feels heavy. What is it?" Anne set the gift down on the narrow kitchen counter.

Her mother waved a hand. "A silver cup, bowl, and spoon. Every baby should have an heirloom set. You had one. I still have it in my hutch. I'll give it to you when you're settled somewhere more permanent."

Anne smiled. "That would be great. Thanks for the gift, Mom. That was nice of you." A set of silver baby dishes must have cost her mother several hundred dollars. What had prompted her to buy it?

"So where does the child sleep?" Sarah asked, looking around. "With you?"

"Yes. I brought a portable crib."

"Where is she? I'd like to see my granddaughter."

Anne gestured with her chin toward the bedroom. "She's sleeping, Mom. It's not a good time."

"I know how to be quiet. For heaven's sake, Anne! You act like I've never been around a baby!" Sarah crossed the room on high heels that sounded like gunshots on the wood floors.

"Can you at least tiptoe?" Anne whispered, following her mother. "I just put her down a little while ago. She's not a great sleeper."

"Serves you right. You never slept, either."

Anne stood in the doorway and watched as Sarah bent over the portable crib, close enough that her exhaled breath ruffled Lucy's curls. Lucy slept on, oblivious, in her usual humpbacked pose.

"I always put her on her back, like the doctor said to, but she just flips over," Anne whispered.

"She's as stubborn as you are," Sarah whispered back. "I remember you sleeping in that exact turtle position. What am I smelling? Garlic?"

"Probably. I made pesto for lunch."

"Sounds like work. Did you have company?"

Her mother had probably seen the dishes in the drainer. "Yes. Hattie and her family," Anne said, suddenly defensive. She didn't want her mother to know that Sebastian had been here, too, or that he stopped by every day.

It had been eight days since her fall, but Sebastian still brought her food sometimes. Wine, too, despite the fact that she had ordered him to stop worrying about her. To prove she was fine, and to thank him for looking after her, she'd invited him to lunch today. To make things less awkward, she'd also invited Hattie—now back from her sister's wedding—as well as Hattie's husband and four children. They'd all hit it off, talking about books, politics, and the occasional movie, though Anne and Sebastian hadn't seen any movies recently.

At one point, Sebastian said, "We need to get out more," making Anne laugh and point to the baby. "I'm hardly in a position to go to the movies," she'd said, though she'd felt a little thrill at the word "we."

Not that Sebastian had meant anything by it. He avoided touching her and seldom looked her in the eye. He was always busy fixing things in the cottage: a loose baseboard, a lamp that didn't work, a cupboard with a missing hinge.

Sarah was saying something so odd that it made Anne wonder whether she'd misheard. "Mom, what did you just say?" she asked.

"That I shouldn't have had so many children. Seeing Lucy makes me remember how overwhelmed I was when you were born. But your father always wanted one more. Even after you, he wanted more. So stubborn!"

"Which of us wouldn't you have had, if you could turn back the clock?" Anne teased.

Her mother frowned. "You, I suppose."

Anne felt like someone had punched her in the throat. She went to the couch and sat down. "Gee, thanks."

Her mother followed and perched on the other end of the couch, where Elly had been sitting earlier tonight. Both Sarah and Elly were built like greyhounds. Their faces were all sharp angles, their hair was gold and straight, and they had broad mouths and tidy ears. They were elegant, royal-looking women. The difference was that Elly was quick to smile and laugh, while Sarah was always the first to judge.

"You look upset," Sarah said. "I'm sorry. But you did ask."

"I did," Anne said.

"I'm not saying I don't love you."

"Right. I know, Mom. It's fine." Anne wondered what she could do to make her mother leave.

"You're not listening to me." Sarah reached over to take one of Anne's hands.

"I *am* listening, Mom." Anne removed her hand and made a show of fiddling with the hairband on the table, slipping it onto her head and smoothing her hair behind her ears. "I'm just not sure I want to hear anything you have to say."

"I never hated you."

"Oh. I feel so much better now!"

Sarah waved a hand impatiently. "This is coming out all wrong. I need to tell you this in my own way. Stop asking questions."

"I only asked one."

Sarah took a deep breath, then said, "Look. The truth is, I married your father because I was dizzy with love. I gave up my singing career for him because Neil wasn't like any man I'd ever met. He was smart and funny and good-looking. He swept me off my feet."

How odd, Anne thought, that when Elly had been sitting there, she had talked about how crazy she'd felt about Hans. Maybe this was

the genetic curse of all Bradford women: they ripped their hearts out
of their chests and handed them over to men, trusting them to care for
them. Hadn't she done the same with Colin? And Laura with Jake?

Anne closed her eyes briefly, trying to picture her father's face. She
couldn't. But she could feel the scratch of his stubble on her cheek as
he bent down to kiss her good night and sometimes heard his deep,
rumbling voice in her head. *Night-night, Anna Banana. Don't let the
bedbugs bite.*

"Your father and I had a wonderful honeymoon in Florida, and then
we came back to the inn and started working so hard that we waited
five years to have Laura," Sarah was saying. "That was still an incredible
time for us. Your father was devoted to Laura. Well, she was just like
him. Athletic and so smart." She smiled. "Once, Neil thanked me for
giving him the son he always wanted."

Anne felt a prickle of sympathy for Laura, having to live up to *that*.
No wonder she'd spent all her time in horse barns.

"Then Elizabeth came along two years later," her mother continued. "By then things were even more difficult. We thought we might
be all right after Grandpa Bradford died, but his unfortunate habits
left your father and me even deeper in dept."

"Grandpa's gambling, you mean."

If her mother was surprised that Anne would come right out and
say this, she didn't show it. "Yes. That man loved betting on anything:
the horses at Suffolk Downs. The dogs at Wonderland. Poker. Your
father wanted to sell Folly Cove to cover Grandpa's debts, but I
wouldn't allow it. I just dug in. Luckily, Elizabeth was easy. Always
happy. And so pretty." Her mother smiled. "Talented, too. The best
singer of you all. So much like me!"

"And so modest, like you?"

Her mother didn't seem to hear this. "Even with our money troubles, Neil and I were still so in love. We had our family. He had his
daughter and I had mine. I thought we should stop there."

"But you didn't."

"I meant to." Sarah pursed her lips at Anne. "However, like you, I
didn't take the necessary precautions to prevent an accident." She jerked

a thumb over her shoulder toward the bedroom. "I wanted to get my tubes tied, but of course that would have been expensive. A major surgery. And your father refused to have a vasectomy. Like most men, he's a medical coward."

"Mom!" Anne held up a hand to stop her. "It doesn't seem right for you to say things about Dad when he's not here to defend himself. And please don't call Lucy an 'accident.' She's the best thing I've ever done in my life!"

"I'm only stating facts. Anyway, between you being such an active baby and how hard I was struggling to keep the inn going, I was exhausted. Flossie had to step in to help. Your aunt adored you. At the time I was glad. Now I don't know."

Anne was confused. Why was her mother telling her all this? Sarah was usually of the pressed-lips Yankee School of Communication. What had caused these confessional floodgates to open?

"What do you mean, you don't know if you're glad that Flossie adored me?" At least somebody did, Anne thought.

Sarah cocked her head at Anne. "The thing is, I never really felt like you were mine. You belonged to everyone but me: to your father, your aunt, your sisters. And then, well." She shrugged. "Your father started drinking a few years later and running around, so I kicked him out. That left it up to me to provide for this family. To keep everything going. Luckily, by then Laura was old enough to watch you whenever Flossie couldn't. You never needed me."

"Of course I did! You were still my mom," Anne said, her throat tight with resentment.

"I still *am* your mother!" Sarah said. "That's why I've decided to give you a gift, too."

"I don't need any gifts."

"Yes, you do. I want you to move out of this dingy cottage."

Anne laughed, startled. "And do what? Move in with you?"

"No, no. Of course not. I love you, but I've already told you I can't have a baby disrupting my routines. I'm too old for that. Sixty-five next month! Can you believe it? Of course, my friends say I hardly look older than you girls." Sarah smiled, no doubt hearing these imaginary friends. "Anyway, I found you the most darling little apartment. With an ocean view! That's my gift to you."

"I already have an ocean view." Anne pointed to the porch.

"Yes, but you can't stay here forever. It's going to be winter soon. These walls aren't insulated. Think of the baby." Her mother reached into the pocket of her blazer, pulled out a folded sheet of newspaper, and handed it to Anne.

It was a classified ad for an apartment in Rockport: ground floor, water view, small yard, near the train station. For an astonishing amount of money. Anne handed the paper back. "This looks nice, but I can't afford it."

"Don't worry about that. I'll pay your rent."

"Why would you do that? Flossie's letting me live here for free. Is it because you're ashamed of me? You can't stand having your wayward daughter on the property?"

"Why would you say that? Of course not!"

"I don't know, Mom. You made it pretty clear that I should tell people I'm getting divorced."

Sarah waved a hand. "That doesn't mean I'm ashamed of you. Only protecting your reputation."

"And the family's," Anne added.

"Of course."

"Well, either way, I can't take your money."

"Why not? I give your sisters money."

"You do?" This conversation was getting stranger by the minute.

"Of course. Who do you think helped Laura buy the stables and that house they're in? I pay for Kennedy's tuition, too. And I've been giving Elizabeth a little stipend to help her get established in her singing career."

What singing career? Anne nearly said, but that was beside the point. "Why would you give Laura money? She has a business. So does her husband."

Sarah shrugged. "Yes, but somehow they're still struggling. She asks me for help every now and then. I'm happy to do what I can."

Anne couldn't believe this. How could Laura bear to put her hand out for their mother's money? "What about Elly? Does she ask for help, too?"

Her mother shook her head. "I offered. I know what it's like to be a struggling artist."

And yet Sarah hadn't offered Anne a dime. She felt a coil of anger, hot in her belly.

Not that she would have taken her mother's money.

Sarah was explaining how she was prepared to give Anne first and last months' rent and a security deposit. "After that, I'll pay your rent for one year. By then you should be on your feet."

"But why, Mom?" Anne said. "I still don't understand. Why do you want me to move out, when I'm perfectly fine here? Anyway, I won't take your money."

Her mother laughed a bizarre little "he-he-he." "Why not? You'll have to eventually. When I go, Folly Cove will be yours. Yours and your sisters'. You can all live in splendor then. Meanwhile, it isn't right, you living off your aunt. Especially not in this dreadful little house!" She wrinkled her nose. "It smells damp. I'm sure there's mold. And mold isn't good for babies."

"Lucy and I were living in a rain forest in Puerto Rico, remember?" Anne handed the paper back. "We're used to damp. When I find a job, I'll move closer to wherever I'm working. Not before then."

Sarah brightened. "Then I'll *give* you a job! You can wait tables at the inn. Tend bar. Or work in the kitchen, if you'd rather."

It was tempting. Cooking at the inn might give her a foot in the door at other restaurants. "What about Rodrigo?"

"Rodrigo would be glad to have another pair of hands. Besides, he's always had a soft spot for you." Sarah crossed her legs and folded her arms. It was the posture of someone whose thoughts and emotions were at odds with what she was communicating in words.

But what was her mother conflicted about?

"Mom, are you doing this because of Aunt Flossie? I know you don't like her."

"I don't *dislike* her," Sarah said. "Though Flossie is a meddler. The sort who never learned the value of minding her own business. But no. That's not why. I'm doing it because life is too short for regrets."

Sarah got to her feet and walked over to her coat. She picked it up from the chair and swung it around her shoulders like a matador's cape. "If you change your mind about the apartment, my offer is open. I know what it means to be a single mother. I don't want you to struggle the way I did."

"I'll think about it. Thanks."

"Good. If you do insist on staying here, at least let me send in the painters. These walls are ghastly. And the paneling makes the cottage so dark."

"I love the paneling," Anne said. "And we can't paint it. This isn't our house."

"This house is more mine than Flossie's. Let me know when you're tired of pretending you're still living in some third-world country. And come to the inn. We'll talk to Rodrigo about what you can do in the kitchen. Good night."

Anne watched her mother from the window as she made her way back up the hill to the car. Sarah was hunched against the wind like an old woman, her long coat flapping around her thin legs. If this had been a fairy tale, she could imagine her mother being blown out to sea, the coat turning into an enormous pair of wings to carry her away.

She placed the palm of her hand on the window for a moment, wishing she could call her back and say the things her mother would never want to hear: *I love you. I need you. Please don't go.*

CHAPTER TEN

The morning after her visit with Anne, Sarah chose not to drive down to Flossie's house along the narrow winding road that led from the inn to the shore. Instead, she walked the path her girls always took, from the inn's back porch through her gardens and down the rocky trail to the beach.

She hadn't driven because she didn't want to alert Flossie to her arrival. Not because she wanted to surprise her sister-in-law—both of them were too old for surprises—but because her courage might fail her. She still hadn't found the right words to tell Flossie that Neil was dead.

Not that the right words existed.

Cars were parked along the road outside Flossie's house. She must be giving one of her classes. For decades, Flossie had taught what Sarah still called "New Age" classes, though she knew they were more acceptable now, even mainstream: yoga, meditation, and some sort of Sacred Drumming Circle, perish the thought. These classes had become so popular in recent years that people now, unbelievably, booked rooms at the inn around Flossie's weekend sessions.

Recognizing an opportunity, Sarah had proposed a marketing campaign to Flossie, linking a stay at the inn with meditation and yoga, all at a discount. "We could do retreats for women," she suggested. "Folly Cove weekends designed to help them find their inner goddesses or whatever it is you think they've lost."

Flossie had burst out laughing. "Good God, Sarah. Not on your life. I teach people who are far enough along in their journeys to find me. And why would I want more students? I have trouble keeping up with the ones I have." Then she'd narrowed her eyes. "Of course, I might be persuaded to reconsider if *you* join my classes. A little yoga would unbend that stiff spine of yours."

That, of course, was the end of that.

Now Sarah wrapped her mink coat more closely around her as she stood on the slight rise above Flossie's tall, narrow gray Victorian, wondering whether she should leave or wait for the class to finish. It wasn't cold here in the sun, but the sea breeze was steady, and she still felt chilled from the shock of the news about Neil's death.

Rhonda had walked her from the office back to the apartment after Sarah read the attorney's letter, where she'd brought her a brandy, then made her take a hot shower and tucked her into bed. "Want me to call Laura?" she'd asked as she hovered at Sarah's bedside. "Elly's staying there, right? They could come over. Anne, too. You should have your daughters by your side at a time like this, Mrs. Bradford."

"Absolutely not," Sarah had said. "No need to upset the girls. Not yet. Their father left us thirty years ago. I don't even know why I'm upset, frankly. We can wait to tell them. But thank you," she remembered to say, waving Rhonda off with a smile. "I'll be fine now."

She wasn't fine. But, as she'd admitted to Rhonda, Sarah couldn't understand why not. How was Neil being dead different from him being gone? Why did it feel as if the floor were tilting beneath her, or even the earth on its axis?

Perhaps it was because the news had opened a door to so many memories she'd shoved into various corners, labeling them as useless artifacts of a former life. Now Sarah felt as if she'd waded into a dark, disorganized closet of mothballed emotions and she was choking on the smell.

There was the first time she'd met Neil, for instance. He'd seemed like all the other too-young men who had ever flirted with Sarah when she performed in Boston or the Berkshires, New York or New Hampshire: slightly drunk, good-looking, sheltered. Drawn to her, no doubt, because she exuded sex and confidence in her jewel-tone dresses (bought secondhand and tailored by her own hand to hug her body), with her thick blond hair cascading down her shoulders. When she sang, sometimes Sarah would choose a man just like Neil and direct her voice at him. Audiences loved that sort of thing.

Sarah typically stayed away from these men: too inexperienced and financially insecure to be of interest to her. But Neil was different. Clever, educated, well mannered. And fun! Goodness, he could be fun, with his willingness to laugh at the world. Neil thought everyone should do exactly what they wanted, which made him both the best companion imaginable—and the least responsible.

He didn't introduce her to Flossie until three days before the wedding, when Neil took her aside, his dark eyes ablaze with excitement, and said, "My sister's coming to the wedding after all! I just found out she's arriving tonight. I'm so glad. Aren't you glad? Tell me you are!"

Neil was always excitable. But when it came to Flossie he was nearly out of his mind with adoration. "My sister's my best friend," he declared.

That put Sarah immediately on guard. She couldn't have her husband thinking Flossie was his best friend. Not if Sarah was going to be his wife. "I can't wait to meet her," she'd said sweetly, knowing she would have to be very clever around Flossie if she was going to succeed in a contest to secure Neil's affection.

Nothing, however, could have prepared her for Flossie's eccentricity. Flossie arrived at Folly Cove by taxi, having flown all night from France. She'd been living in some convent and was dressed in a nun's crimson robes, her head shaved, a ratty knitted brown shawl over one shoulder.

The Bradfords were obviously horrified by Flossie's appearance, especially Neil's father, who was always in a suit unless he was wearing tennis whites. Neil's mother took to her bed and said she wouldn't get up again, even for the wedding, unless Flossie saw sense and "put on something decent."

Nothing could have prepared Sarah, either, for the bond between Neil and his sister, forged through years of reading the same books; of traveling with their grandparents through Europe and India; and of going to the sorts of precious, single-sex private schools with their own dress codes and vocabularies. Sometimes it seemed as though they were speaking in an obscure dialect, Sarah had so much trouble following their conversation.

Flossie had pulled Sarah aside after their disastrous rehearsal dinner, where Sarah had to lie and say her parents were dead and she had no siblings. She'd led them to believe she'd grown up in Back Bay, the college-educated daughter of a wealthy older couple who had introduced her early to opera and the symphony, which was how she'd developed her love of music. Her friend Mabel had agreed to come and back her up; she'd played her role of debutante beautifully, despite the multiple glasses of whiskey she'd consumed while flirting with Neil's father.

Fortunately, the wedding was held in the era before Google. Lying was easier then.

"I want you to know that I only showed up for my brother," Flossie had told Sarah at the rehearsal dinner. She had changed into a plain pair of black slacks and a black cashmere pullover sweater (both belonging to Neil) with a scarf of her mother's. She still looked like a nun.

"I appreciate you coming," Sarah had said. "It means a great deal to Neil. And to me, of course. I was eager to meet you."

"I can tell," Flossie said, rolling her eyes. "Look, you don't have to like me. We're not going to play at being sisters or anything. I just wanted to lay eyes on you. Frankly, I don't hold much store in the institution of marriage, but you'd better make my brother happy. If you don't, you'll have me to answer to. I intend to return to France, but that won't stop me from coming back to make your life a living hell if you hurt him, understand?"

"I will be everything to your brother," Sarah had said, relieved to hear Flossie was leaving again.

"Nobody is ever *everything* to another person," Flossie had said. "All I expect from you is honesty and kindness."

Sarah had delivered both, in those early years. It was Neil who'd let everyone down.

Flossie returned from France around the time Elly was born. Nobody knew why. But even she couldn't stop Neil from leaving Folly Cove.

Thirty years ago, almost to the day, he had abandoned them.

Or, alternatively: thirty years ago, Sarah had thrown Neil out of the house.

Both things were true, depending on who was telling the story.

Neil had been drinking steadily since they'd gotten an offer to purchase the inn, unsolicited, from a developer. He'd always been a heavy drinker, but he was never mean or abusive. He favored beer with whiskey chasers, and the more of those he drank, the jollier he got.

Her husband's drinking hadn't worried Sarah at first. She'd grown up expecting men and bottles to go together. In her Irish neighborhood, which featured a dog track and a horse track and triple-decker apartment buildings that shuddered beneath the planes taking off from Logan airport, children routinely had to collect their fathers from the bars at suppertime.

Not that she'd ever known which one was her father. "He was a rotter," her mother told her. "That's all you need to know."

Sarah could handle a man who drank. She'd learned that as a child, coping with her mother's boyfriends, and, later, on the road with the Sweet Tones. Some member of the band always seemed to have had too much. The patrons, too.

For the first ten years of their marriage, Neil drank only after five o'clock and was sober and cheerful during the day. A "functional alcoholic," Flossie called him. Sarah was inclined to agree.

But when Neil saw she wouldn't budge and agree to sell the inn, he began drinking with abandon and turned on her.

"I won't stay on this cold rock a minute longer," he'd exploded their last night together. "Can't you see this place is killing me?"

"They'll tear the inn down if we sell it to a developer," Sarah had said. It was the same tired argument. "This is your home. Home to your sister and daughters. The Bradfords built this place! Doesn't your family's legacy mean anything to you?"

"I don't give a rat's ass about Folly Cove!" Neil bellowed, his handsome face bright red and angry. "This inn is a curse on the Bradfords. If we take this offer, we could pay off the debts and start over again. Buy a condo in Manhattan or a bungalow in Tampa!"

"You forget that we have children in school. Besides, I *want* to live here! And I am not a quitter!" Sarah had finally shouted back. She didn't say that it was the only home she'd ever known—he still didn't know that about her.

"But what about me?" Neil had pushed his face close enough so that she could smell despair like an extra scent on his skin. "I won't ever be happy again if I stay here!"

"My God. Listen to you! Don't be such a baby," she'd said. "What about the girls? Don't they matter to you?"

He'd waved a hand. "The girls would be fine anywhere. And Anne's not even mine."

This wasn't the first time Neil had implied that Sarah had cheated on him. He'd been suspicious of every man she'd been friendly with through the years. But it was the first time he'd said something so directly accusatory.

"Of course she's yours," Sarah had said, but even to her own ears it sounded improbable.

Neil's oldest high school pal, Garth, had started coming around the inn in the evenings after Elly was born. He was a widower, quiet and bookish, balding. Garth had taught Sarah to play Scrabble. She'd enjoyed his company, even more so because he was one of the few of Neil's friends who didn't make her feel stupid for not having been to college. (Neil, who was still under the illusion that she had a degree, always joked that Sarah must have slept through most of her classes, especially history.)

Garth seemed to enjoy teaching her; with his help, Sarah mastered the basics of bookkeeping and marketing. Many weekends, Neil drank in the inn's pub while Sarah and Garth played cards or Scrabble in the library, worked together on the accounts, or simply walked through the gardens.

Then, one night, Garth had leaned over to kiss Sarah when she'd excitedly played a seven-letter word at Scrabble. A congratulatory kiss, misinterpreted by Neil. He had immediately, drunkenly banished Garth from the inn with a solid left to the jaw, sending the other man sprawling onto the pavement in front of a group of astonished guests gathered for dinner.

Sarah hadn't ever been unfaithful. But shortly after that night she'd discovered she was pregnant with Anne, and Neil had become convinced the baby wasn't his.

During his final rampage before leaving, Neil also accused Sarah of not loving their youngest daughter. "I've seen you push Anne away. You don't make time for her because you can't stand the sight of your own mistake!" he'd shouted.

"Don't be an idiot," Sarah said. "I don't have time for Anne because I'm the one doing everything around here!"

"Everything?" Neil had yelled. "Who takes care of the girls? They're practically motherless! If Flossie and I weren't around, they'd have nobody. You work them like dogs. I can't believe you have them cleaning rooms. Laura's only ten!"

"We can't afford much help," Sarah had said. "It's only temporary."

"They're not meant to be charwomen. Laura and Elly are Bradfords!"

"So is Anne!" she'd said. "And that's why we have to keep the inn. This is who they are. And who I am now."

He'd stared at her then, dangerously quiet. "Oh, yes. You are a Bradford," he said. "You married me to become one. I can see that now."

"No," she said, but she couldn't quite meet his eyes. They'd never had this conversation, so dangerously close to the truth. "It's *you* I loved. *You* I married."

"I don't believe you." Neil stood up. "I'm leaving. You can choose: me or Folly Cove. You can't have both, Sarah. If you really love me, you'll come with me." He held out a hand and waited.

When she didn't take it, he'd nodded. "Fine. Tell people whatever you like. Say that I ran off. Or that you kicked me out because I'm a bum and a drunk. I don't care. I'm going."

Sarah knew better than to chase a man. She would wait for him to come back to her.

And she had waited, long after she thought she'd stopped.

Sarah felt her eyes sting and swiped at them with her fingers, careful with her mascara. There was no point in crying anymore. Her life would remain unchanged except for one thing: she was a widow. Truly alone.

A sudden movement on Flossie's porch startled her. Sarah stepped back beneath the low-hanging branches of a scrub pine as the front door opened.

Women began emerging onto the wraparound porch. Women of all shapes and ages, carrying yoga mats in bright colors, their voices muffled by the sound of the sea. Hatless, healthy-looking women with high color in their cheeks. Women with enough money to be doing yoga classes on a Tuesday morning.

Sarah had never understood women like these. For her, work was a frame; it gave her the parameters within which she made the rules and expected others to follow them. Work was her sanctuary and her safety net. Her identity, after she'd succeeded in shedding her old self so completely.

Beyond the house, pearly clouds were gathering along the horizon. The sea was nearly as gray as the air, the sand dun-colored. Flossie came outside to wave good-bye to the women from the porch. When the last of them had driven away, she turned with her arms folded to look across the ocean, her strong back to Sarah.

After a moment, though, Flossie called to her without turning around. "I know you're there, Sarah. You might as well come down here and say whatever you came to say."

Sarah approached warily, as if Flossie were a wild animal that might bolt. Flossie turned around as Sarah climbed the porch steps. She was dressed in those awful black yoga pants and a brown zip-up hoodie. With her short, spiked gray hair and enormous dark eyes, she reminded Sarah of the tiny saw-whet owl Neil had rescued one night after it flew into his car windshield.

He'd brought the owl to his sister. Flossie had fed it live crickets and mice in her bathroom for two weeks, then set the bird free. Now the owl lived in the pines above this house and occasionally still came down to visit Flossie when she sat out on the deck.

Sarah followed Flossie into the living room, where there were framed photographs on every surface and so much furniture that you needed to thread your way between chairs, hassocks, and tables. "Why don't you ever have a good clear-out?" she said. "I'm amazed your students don't fall over something and sue you."

"Part of what I teach them is balance. Physical and spiritual. Tea?" Flossie suggested, gesturing for Sarah to sit.

"No, thank you. I don't like your Chinese tea," Sarah grumbled. "You always make it too strong."

"You should learn to like it. Chinese tea is full of antioxidants."

"Yes, I can see what wonders it does for you." Sarah chose the only decent chair in the living room, a white wing back with carved legs.

This chair, a fine antique, was a Bradford heirloom. Flossie probably had tens of thousands of dollars in antiques and artwork in here. If she'd only sell some of these things and invest the money, she could buy decent clothes and a new car. Though of course Flossie insisted that she didn't need material goods.

"Well?" Flossie said. "What is it?" She perched on the worn tapestry couch across from Sarah. This looked like the place where Flossie ate, read, and perhaps even slept: the table and floor in front of the couch were strewn with dishes, newspapers, and books.

Despite the yoga class—or maybe because of it—Flossie looked tired and drawn. They were seated close enough together that Sarah could see the other woman's huge pores and the fine lines around her eyes and mouth. She barely suppressed an urge to remind Flossie that a little makeup went a long way at their age. On the other hand, women who wore no makeup risked less when they cried.

She did not want to see Neil's sister cry. But what choice did she have, since she was about to break her heart?

"I've had a letter from an attorney in Florida," Sarah began, then had to stop and clear her throat before adding, "It's about Neil."

Flossie's expression crumpled and she looked down at her own small, rough hands. "I see. When?"

"Yesterday." Sarah realized with a start that Flossie must already know what was coming. "Neil has died." She gentled her voice anyway. "I'm sorry."

Flossie nodded, still not looking up. "What did the attorney say?"

"Not much. Only that Neil died from liver cancer. From the drinking, I suppose. I don't know any details."

At least the attorney had spared her that much. Sarah didn't want to imagine Neil frail or in pain. She'd rather remember the way he'd looked with the girls, healthy and tan, running and laughing as if he were just one more child among them.

After a moment, when Flossie neither looked up nor spoke, Sarah said, "Are you all right?"

Flossie nodded again. "It's not exactly tragic for anyone to die at sixty-five, is it?"

"No, I suppose not," Sarah said, though she'd forgotten for the moment that Neil was ten years younger than she was.

Of everyone, Flossie was the only other person who knew this fact, because of circumstances beyond Sarah's control. To Flossie's credit, she had never divulged the truth about Sarah's age or her true background to Neil or the girls.

Flossie stood up and began moving around the room, aimlessly touching the furniture as if she'd been struck blind and had to feel her way. "I mean, we might think it's tragic, since he was younger than we are, but most people would not," she said. "They would say, 'He had a good long life.'"

"Well," Sarah said warily, "I'm not so sure about 'good.'"

"It was getting better," Flossie said.

"How on earth do you know that?" Sarah said crossly. "And how did you know Neil was dead? You did, right?"

"Yes." Flossie went to the far corner of the room and opened an oak cupboard big enough to hide any number of family skeletons. She reached onto the top shelf and brought down a Priority Mail box from the post office, then carried the box over to Sarah and set it on the coffee table in front of her.

Sarah felt her breath leave her in a great whoosh of air, as if someone had slammed something into her gut, as she read the black sticker on the box: CREMATED REMAINS. The return address on the box was Venice, Florida.

"It arrived late yesterday, but I haven't wanted to open it," Flossie said. "I wanted you to be with me." She sat down across from Sarah again, the box between them.

"Good of you," Sarah said dully. Why had Neil sent the box to his sister and not to her? Did he think she wouldn't want it? Or that she'd toss it into the ocean, unopened?

That thought was more tempting than she'd ever admit. Goddamn Neil.

"He wrote to me about a month ago," Flossie said gently, "saying he was thinking about coming back to Folly Cove, but then he was diagnosed and told he had only weeks left."

Neil had written to Flossie? A buzzing started in Sarah's ears, drowning out the sound of the surf. Her eyes swam. "Why did he tell you but not me?"

"I'm his sister."

"I'm his wife!" Sarah said, then pressed her lips tightly shut.

"Of course you are," Flossie said. "But you know it isn't the same. Neil and I felt unconditional love for each other, no matter how disappointed we were in each other from time to time. You kicked my brother out of his own house. I've been supporting him. Sending him money so he didn't always have to live on the street."

"You knew where he was?" Sarah asked, too astounded for a moment to be angry. "All this time?"

Flossie shook her head. "He always gave me a post-office box, and every time, the boxes were in different cities."

"It was his choice to live the way he did," Sarah said. "He abandoned us!" Mortified, Sarah felt her shoulders start to shake and pressed a fist to her mouth. "He could have come home," she said around it, the words muffled.

"Really?" Flossie clasped her hands in her lap. "You would have let him?"

Sarah nodded, though the truth was complicated. When Neil accused her of having another man's child, a hinged door had snapped shut on her heart. He should have known she would never break her marriage vows. They were sacred to her. If nothing else, the Bradford name was the one thing she'd ever owned that was worth keeping.

Not her maiden name, Brogan. Derived from the Irish for "shoe," for God's sake. *Shoe!*

She'd made up a stage name: Sarah Simmons. For years, she'd hidden herself successfully in plain sight of the Bradfords, until Flossie accidentally stumbled onto her secrets.

"We might have been happy, if he'd come back." Sarah shut her eyes, picturing Neil as he'd been: tall and vibrant, the girls clinging to him like monkeys. "We could have tried again."

"Perhaps," Flossie said, then stood up and went to the kitchen. She returned a moment later with a glass of water and a tumbler of brandy, set these on the table next to Sarah, then proceeded to read the papers Sarah had given her, nodding as she skimmed the will and Sarah sipped the brandy.

Flossie finished reading and neatly slid the papers back into the envelope. She handed the envelope back to Sarah and said, "I have something for you to read, too. Drink your brandy."

She waited until Sarah had obediently taken another sip, then stood up and went to the narrow table beneath the windows, retrieved a white business envelope, and gave it to her. Sarah's name was scrawled across the front in Neil's handwriting.

Sarah had to breathe carefully around a sharp pain beneath her rib cage. The brandy burned at the back of her throat. She swallowed hard to avoid retching. "Should I read it now?"

"Up to you."

Sarah couldn't walk home in this state. She couldn't imagine standing up, much less moving around the box on the table. The box that looked far too small to contain Neil.

She slit the envelope open.

Neil's handwriting was nearly illegible. He must have been extremely ill. She had to puzzle over several words.

My dear Sarah,

I hope this note finds you in good health. I expect if you're reading this, my sister has kept her word to me and I am gone now. I regret any pain or sadness you may feel over this fact, though I suspect that you will deal with this in your usual practical manner, moving forward

with one delicate but determined foot in front of the other, as you have
always done.

    First of all, I want to apologize properly, as I should have done years
ago, for accusing you of having an affair. I know Anne is my child. I knew
it then, really. I was just looking for an excuse to leave Folly Cove, and it's
always easier to leave someone behind in anger, is it not? I hope you'll
forgive me. I would have come home to apologize in person, but I would
rather have you remember me as I was, not as I am now. Just know that I
am sorry from the bottom of my heart. From every cell of my being.

"Oh." Sarah looked up at Flossie through blurred vision and took
another sip of brandy. "He says he's sorry."

"Yes," Flossie said. "He wrote to apologize to me about certain things,
too. He was trying to make amends. It was part of his AA membership,
to do that. To ask forgiveness."

Sarah pictured Neil as he used to often stand when he was talking
to her, tucking his hands into his pants pockets and rocking back and
forth on his heels. She remembered him asking her to dance that first
night she'd sung at the inn and doing exactly this motion. Neil rocked
on his heels whenever he was nervous.

She went back to the letter then.

    I won't bore you with details, but you should know that I am sober
now, and had the Fates not intervened and had their little joke, I
would have come home to ask if we could try again as man and wife. I
waited too long, I expect, for you to consider such a thing, but I like to
think we could have made a go of things.

    Once I dried out, my life did improve, though I'm not sure you
would have approved of it. I found work at Sharky's, a restaurant on
the beach in Venice, Florida, near the pier. I was humbled by the gen-
erosity of the owner, who, despite my lack of real work experience,
entrusted me to serve his customers. Some of the young couples re-
minded me of us on our honeymoon, you with your yellow hair in the
moonlight so long ago, teaching me the wonders of what it really means

to make love to a woman. God, remember the sand? Who ever thought it was a good idea to make love on a beach?

But I digress. You would have laughed, dear one, if you'd seen how I spent my last days before I grew too weak, sifting through the sand at Caspersen Beach for fossilized shark teeth. Remember our days doing that, how in the end you proved, once again, to be the more determined of the two of us? I have thought of us often, these last days, even as delusional as I am sometimes on the morphine, and I swear I could hear you singing to me from time to time.

In the end, though it was tempting to travel home to see you and the girls once more despite my precarious state, I chose to stay here to spare you the odious task of being caretaker for one more person, when you have had so many depending upon you already.

I have you to thank for saving Folly Cove and for keeping the Bradford name out of the ditch. I'm sure you've done a fine job with the girls as well. Please give them my love. However, it's very important to me that you tell them the truth now about your own history—all of it. My illness gave me plenty of time to spend on the computer, and I now know that my mother was right when she said you were an impostor. I don't care one whit about that. In fact, I rather admire you for it, and I always enjoyed buying your stories hook, line, and sinker, my dear. But I do believe the girls deserve to know, if only for their own medical histories and so forth.

It will be a difficult task, but please do this, Sarah. Not only to spare your own conscience, but as your last act as my wife, because I am asking you to do it. I will rest easier in the afterlife if I know everything is out in the open.

With all my love, Neil

Sarah folded the paper carefully and tucked it into the envelope, barely resisting the urge to shred it between her fingers. How dare he ask this of her?

"Well? What did he say?" Flossie asked, studying her with those wide owlish eyes. The sun had come out and was pouring through the front windows now, highlighting her gray hair so that it looked silver, nearly metallic, as if Flossie were wearing a helmet.

"Don't pretend you didn't read it." Sarah finished the brandy in two swallows.

Flossie didn't deny this, only said, "Neil's right. You need to tell the girls."

"No. And don't you do it, either." Sarah stood up, gathering her coat, thankful for the reservoir of anger stiffening her spine.

"They need to know the truth," Flossie said mildly. "Especially now that Neil's gone. I'll tell them if you won't."

"And if you do that, I will sell this house right out from under you," Sarah said. "The property is mine now. You saw the will."

"You wouldn't do that."

"Try me. Do you know how much shorefront property is worth on Cape Ann these days?" Sarah took Neil's note and folded it into her coat pocket. "I am sorry for your loss."

"And I'm sorry for yours."

"Thank you," Sarah said.

"When will you tell the girls that Neil is gone?"

"I'm not sure they need to know that, either," Sarah said. "Why bring them more pain?"

"What about a memorial service? Doesn't my brother deserve that, at least?" Flossie stood up suddenly, her cheeks flushed. She looked less like an owl now and more like a ninja in her black clothes, ready to leap over the coffee table.

"I'm not ready to think about that yet. Anyway, it's for me to tell the girls, not you. They're my daughters." Sarah nearly threw herself toward the front door. She'd pulled the door open when Flossie stopped her again.

"What about the ashes?" Flossie said. "Aren't you taking them with you?"

"You keep them," Sarah said without turning around. "Neil sent them to you. Obviously, he still didn't trust me."

Sarah felt the damp sting of tears on her face as she stumbled up the path toward the inn, wrapping the coat around her as the wind fingered its way beneath her clothes, chilling her to the bone.

CHAPTER ELEVEN

M onday, her mother called to invite Elly for late-morning coffee.
"We've hardly spent any time together," Sarah said. "I suppose
you and Laura have been busy."

Too busy for your own mother. That's what Sarah was implying. Elly
didn't rise to the bait. Instead, she simply said she'd be delighted to visit
this morning.

She rode Kennedy's bicycle to the inn around eleven o'clock. Kennedy was in school, Jake was at work, and Laura was mucking out
stalls, so Elly was glad of a distraction. She'd checked her e-mails and
jobs online and there was nothing new. Not even a text from Ryder.
Well, what did she expect? She'd made it clear that she wasn't expecting anything from him, and then she'd left for Massachusetts without
even calling him to say good-bye. She had only herself to blame for
feeling stupidly wistful about what might have been between them.

It didn't help her mood when Sarah pointedly raised the subject of
friends as Elly was buttering one of Rodrigo's fresh raspberry scones and
her mother was sipping black coffee. They were seated on the enclosed
sunporch on white wicker chairs, a hooked rug in jewel tones at their
feet, crystal vases of bright orange mums on the tables. Elly had been
determined to feel relaxed, at least, if not completely happy to be here, by
focusing on the warmth of the morning sun on her face and listening to
the faint rhythmic growl of surf beyond the lawn and garden.

She remembered those rare mornings when the inn was empty—usually off-season, like January or March—when she and her sisters were allowed to play out here. They'd lie on the floor, on these sunlit squares of brightly colored wool, and argue over Monopoly. Or they'd gather their dolls and make a complicated neighborhood where the Barbies were always getting dressed in different sparkly outfits and marrying the sexless Ken dolls. Oh, the hours they'd spent searching for those lost tiny plastic high heels!

As they got older, Laura would bring them out here to play hairdresser. Once, they'd horrified Sarah by braiding their hair into cornrows with beads from a kit Aunt Flossie had given them. She'd brought it back from one of her group yoga retreats to Jamaica.

"I did not raise you to be hippies or Rastafarians," Sarah had shouted. "Take those off at once and wash your hair!"

"You must miss your friends in Los Angeles," her mother said now. "Are you seeing anyone special?"

"No, not really." Elly pushed thoughts of Ryder aside. "It's a nice change, being here. I love hanging out with Laura and Anne. And Kennedy's a great kid."

"Your friends must miss you, too."

Elly pictured Frankie, her closest friend in Los Angeles, even though Frankie was fifty years old and a widow. Frankie lived below her in the apartment building and was one of the few besides Elly who ever sat outside on the narrow wrought-iron balconies overlooking the courtyard. They had met when Frankie called up from her balcony to ask if she could borrow a cup of sugar; Elly had responded by pouring a cup of sugar into a sandwich bag and lowering it down with a rope to Frankie's balcony below.

"I'm sure a few of them do," she told her mother. "But absence makes the heart grow fonder, right?"

"Except when it comes to your career, of course," Sarah said. "You can't ever let people in the industry forget your face. Or your beautiful voice! I learned that the hard way, when your father left us and I tried to resume my own singing career. I had been away too long. You've got to keep putting yourself out there if you're going to make it."

"I know." Elly glanced around the room, trying to find any other subject that wasn't her career. "I like the watercolors in here. They're new, right?"

Her mother didn't bother glancing around. "Yes. A local woman did them. I try to support the Rockport Art Association. Now, what about your friends here? Have you seen anyone?"

When Sarah mentioned her classmate Paige Martinson, saying Paige had gotten married at the inn recently and was now a high school guidance counselor in Rockport, Elly said she'd like to see her. She followed Sarah into her office to get Paige's contact information off the computer.

Sarah paused to greet a couple by their first names and asked about their stay. The man and woman were in their seventies, birders with their telltale floppy-brimmed hats cocked at rakish angles. The woman went on about red-bellied woodpeckers and bluebirds, then said, "And we saw an entire flock of harlequin ducks off Andrews Point! Can you believe it? That's a lifelong bird for me!"

"I'm so very glad the birds behaved themselves, Mandy," Sarah said, pressing Mandy's bony hand between her own, sounding so sincere that Elly had to smile.

"You're so good at that, Mom," Elly said, once they were closeted in Sarah's tiny office off the reception area.

"At what?" Sarah was scrolling through her computer's address files.

"At making people feel welcome."

"I'm glad when my guests are happy," Sarah said, glancing up at her in surprise. "It's not an act. When people are happy at Folly Cove, they return here with their children. And with their children's children. Ah," she said, looking at her computer again. "Found it."

She read Paige's cell phone number and e-mail to Elly off the computer and waited until Elly had put them in her phone, then said, "It's a shame you had to miss that gorgeous wedding. They were going to Italy for their honeymoon. Tuscany. Such a beautiful time of year to be there."

Her mother could sound so convincing about things she knew nothing about that for a minute Elly nearly asked her more about Italy, then remembered: Sarah had never been anywhere. Her mother, as far as Elly knew, had never left New England, other than for her Florida honeymoon.

Once, Elly had been hospitalized after a car accident while she was in college. She'd been on a ski trip to Vermont with friends and the car went off the road on a patch of black ice. Elly was in the front passenger seat; she'd spent a week hospitalized in Burlington. Her mother never came to see her.

"It's Christmas week at the inn," Sarah had explained at the time. "You know what that's like. But I can send you anything you need, darling. Just let me know what."

At the time Elly had accepted the situation. It was only when she overheard the nurses talking, saying, "That poor girl, all alone for the holidays," that she felt angry. She'd never said any of this to her mother, though. What would be the point?

"I'll be eager to hear what Paige says about her trip," Elly said. She didn't dare tell her mother that Paige hadn't invited her to the wedding. Her mother would be furious if she knew.

The lack of invitation was Elly's own fault. She and Paige had kept in touch until a couple of years ago, when Hans left her. Paige had reached out and e-mailed her that Christmas. Sent her a card. She'd even phoned a couple of times and left messages. Elly never answered, too sunk in her own solitary misery.

Sarah peered at Elly above the frames of her blue reading glasses. "Elizabeth, may I ask you a straightforward question, please?"

Elly had given up on asking her mother not to call her "Elizabeth." "Sure."

"As delighted as I am to have you here, I'd like to know your plans for the future," Sarah said. "The older I get, the more I realize how short life is. I'm sure you're losing ground on your career, being here so long. Unless, perhaps, you're planning to audition in New York?" Her mother's eyes sparkled suddenly. "I dreamed of being on Broadway when I was young."

"I don't want to be in New York, Mom." Elly took a deep breath, then added, "Actually, I've decided to bag the whole singing thing."

"Oh, no!" Sarah looked stricken and put a hand to her throat. "You mustn't give up your dream!"

"Mom, take it easy." Elly stared at her in alarm. "It's not the end of the world. I'm not that good. I'm not even sure it was my dream in the first place. I think it was more yours."

"What do you mean?" Sarah cried. "Of course it was your dream! You're the best singer in our family!" She stood up from her desk chair and reached for a photo album on the shelves behind her.

"Yes, in our family," Elly murmured. "But that's a pretty small sample size."

"I know quality talent. You are a brilliant singer." Her mother slapped the album onto the desk and started flipping pages until she reached a picture of Elly as a teenager, wearing a striped shirtwaist dress, a picnic basket dangling over one skinny arm.

Elly recognized the photograph: it was from the summer she'd been cast as the mayor's daughter in a community theater production of *The Music Man*. She was fifteen at the time. Sarah had grumbled about Elly not landing the part of Marian the Librarian, even though everyone, especially Elly, knew she was too young for that part.

"You stole the show in *The Music Man*!" her mother said. "And remember the Marblehead Arts contest your senior year of college? Everyone said you were the best talent they'd ever seen!"

"Still a small sample size, Mom." Elly gently closed the album. "Look, can't you just be happy for me? Be glad I've found work I like. And a place I enjoy living. I have a good life in Los Angeles." Though, even as she said this, Elly felt a flicker of doubt: she hated the smog. The traffic. The endless cycle of rejections. The power plays of producers and directors, the celebrities and their need for spotlight, Hollywood's constant pressure to age backward.

Her mother sagged against the desk chair. "How *can* I be glad when you're throwing away your future? I know you're older now. Too old to be called promising. But surely there's something you can do with your voice, rather than lie down and give up?"

"It wasn't my decision," Elly said, stung. "I didn't *give up* on singing. The Fates decided for me."

"No! I will not stand for that. You're much too young still for resignation to an ordinary life." Her mother's eyes were dry but red-rimmed. She looked her age, for once. Like a woman long past her prime instead of a woman in charge.

"I know you're disappointed, Mom, but that's how it is," Elly said. "I'm ordinary. Hurrah. I can stop beating myself up. Listen, I've got to go. I promised Laura that I'd pick Kennedy up from school."

"What do you mean? It's only noon. And we're having a conversation here."

It was more like having a scolding, Elly thought, but she kept her voice even. "I know, but Kennedy has an early-release day and an orthodontist appointment. I'll see you again soon, all right?"

Sarah nodded and let her go, dismissing her with a cheery wave, though her lips were trembling.

Elly felt like she was slinking out of the office, exuding a smoky trail of defeat behind her. She felt so suddenly despondent that she decided to text Paige. She needed to spend time with someone outside her family. Amazingly, Paige texted back immediately and said she'd love to meet up.

"Of course you can keep the car," Laura said two hours later, when Elly brought Kennedy back after a tortuously long orthodontist appointment. "I owe you for sitting around in the orthodontist's office while I was teaching. Besides, you deserve to have a little fun. Stay out as long as you like."

Laura wouldn't have been so generous if she'd known what Elly was planning: since she had the car and was alone, tonight was the perfect opportunity to stalk Jake at work and find out what secrets he was keeping. The more time Elly spent here, the more she was convinced that Jake was hiding something.

Paige was meeting her at three o'clock for a glass of wine. That gave Elly enough time to stop by Jake's office before meeting her.

Jake's receptionist greeted her with a smile. She was a pale, malnourished brunette in cowboy boots and dangling turquoise earrings, obviously some kind of wannabe Sundance catalog model. Not Jake's type, Elly thought with relief. She hoped to hell Laura was right and her husband was trustworthy. On the other hand, would that make Anne the one who was lying? Elly refused to believe that without proof.

The hygienist, who came out to call a patient while Elly was waiting for the receptionist to finish on the phone, was a more likely lover for Jake: a young, athletic-looking brunette whose skirt was several inches too short even for those legs. A Jennifer Lopez sort of skirt, the kind she was always tugging down on *American Idol*. No wonder J. Lo had upskirting Web sites devoted to her.

The receptionist—Kim, according to the name tag floating between her nonexistent breasts—hung up the phone and smiled. "Sorry to keep you waiting. How may I help you?"

Elly had her spiel ready: she was visiting from the West Coast and overdue for a checkup and cleaning. "I wondered if I can get one here." She hoped Jake wouldn't catch her. But if he did, she had a pat speech ready for that, too. She really did need a cleaning.

Kim consulted a calendar on her computer. "No problem. We'd be happy to fit you in. Did you have a date and time in mind?"

"Not really. Anytime in the next couple of weeks."

"All right. First available, then?"

"Wait. Is he good, this dentist?" Elly asked after poking her head around the corner to assure herself that the hall was empty. That distant whining sound of a drill assured her that Jake was busy.

"Oh, yes. The very best. He trained at Tufts. You can't get better than that."

"Good." Elly dropped her voice to a whisper. "I've had some rotten luck with dentists. You know the sort of thing I mean, Kim, don't you? Dentists who think they can do whatever they want with their hands while they've got you trapped in the chair?"

Kim's eyes—a bright, unnatural green from her contacts—widened. "I do know," she whispered back. "The same thing happened to me once with a doctor! But I can assure you that Dr. Williams is a gentleman. A family man. Well liked. Skilled, too. You won't feel any pain at all."

"He doesn't have a roving eye? Or hands? You're absolutely sure?" Elly said, leaning deeper into the window. Kim's fingertips were bloodred, like rose petals resting on her computer keyboard.

Kim looked uncomfortable. "Yes! Dr. Williams is a very sweet and caring man. You're completely safe here." She hurriedly began talking about available appointments.

"Nothing after six o'clock next Wednesday?" Elly interrupted.

"Oh, no. The office closes at five o'clock every night except Tuesdays and Thursdays, when we're open until six."

"Really? Only until six? And Dr. Williams never works on Wednesday nights?"

"No. He used to work late every night," Kim said with a touch of regret, "but now only Tuesday and Thursday evenings. We'll have to book you a few months' out if you need an evening appointment. Those fill up fast."

"Thank you. You've been super helpful." Elly smiled and extracted her body from the window. "I'll call once I've got my schedule sorted." She left then, aware of the receptionist's curious eyes like twin hot spots on her back.

Elly didn't care. She'd gotten what she wanted: evidence that Jake was up to something. Where was he going, those nights he wasn't working? Obviously, he was doing something that cost money, but what? Gambling? A drug addiction? A mistress?

Or had she been living in Hollywood so long that her imagination was running wild with soap opera plots? Maybe Jake really was the decent guy that Laura and his employees believed him to be, and his dental school loans and insurance were killer debts. Life was expensive, as Kennedy had pointed out.

But Kennedy, too, seemed overly anxious, relying on food for comfort instead of friends. What was worrying her? Body issues? Boys? Mean girls? Or did she know something about her father that she wasn't telling?

Paige was already at the Waterside Pub by the time Elly found a parking space along the Gloucester harbor. She'd chosen this place because they used to frequent it with stolen ID cards when they were teenagers. She needed a drink right now for the same reason she'd longed to drink back then: her family was driving her nuts.

Inside, Elly inhaled the comforting stink of fried food and stale beer. She smiled as she spotted Paige waving from a table near the rear of the dark, heavy-beamed room, causing several men at the bar to turn their heads and grin as they watched Elly walk across the room.

"Hey, good-lookin'. Sit right here," one guy said, patting the cracked red leatherette stool next to his. He wore a biker jacket with patches sewn over it and an American flag headband.

"Thanks, but no," Elly said.

Never mind the fact that these guys were parked in a dive bar at three o'clock in the afternoon; it was still gratifying to be noticed. Especially in the nondescript outfit she'd worn today: faded jeans with tall black boots and a black T-shirt beneath a long tan cardigan. In Southern California, Elly was just one more blonde, and not a young one, either. To most men there she was invisible.

At least she wasn't brunette. If you were over thirty-five and brunette in Hollywood, you might as well be dead.

Paige was dark-haired and had a pleasingly solid build. Her physique should have made Paige an asset in field hockey and lacrosse, both of which she'd played with Elly in high school, but Paige was too sweet. If a girl on the other team fell down, Paige stopped what she was doing to help her up.

Today Paige wore an orange knit dress that made her look like you could roll her down a hill. "Well, I have to confess, it took all my courage to see you, California Girl," Paige said after they'd embraced and sat down. "I knew you'd be all Hollywood and Vine, while I look like the Great Pumpkin in this outfit. But I haven't had time to catch up on laundry since the honeymoon. It was the only clean thing I had."

Elly grinned. She'd forgotten how breathless and excited Paige always sounded. "You look exactly like you," she said. "Adorbs as always."

It was true. And with Paige smiling at her from across the sticky pine table, Elly immediately felt happy—as well as acutely aware of how much she'd missed seeing people who'd known her all her life. "Let's see that ring he put on your finger, Missus," she said.

Paige thrust her hand across the table, giggling as Elly genuinely admired the antique setting—it had belonged to Paige's grandmother—and the simple solitaire diamond. It was classy, like everything about

Paige's family. An understated ring that screamed old North Shore money.

They shared a pizza and drank glasses of red wine infused with so much tannin that Elly's mouth puckered. Paige talked about her honeymoon in Italy and her new husband, John, a mechanical engineer with two children from a first marriage.

"He wasn't my mother's ideal candidate, as you can imagine," Paige said ruefully. "But the good part about waiting to be our age before getting married is that our moms get desperate enough to accept anyone with at least three working limbs, right?"

Elly laughed. "My mom's more desperate to have me sign a recording contract. She's not a big fan of marriage in general." She snagged another slice of pizza. "So how did you meet John?"

"At the school where I work. I hate to admit this, because it sounds so unprofessional, but I was his son's guidance counselor. I helped him and John work through the college application process and apply for scholarships."

"John must be a lot older, with a kid in college."

"Not really. Five years. You and I are getting up there, too, girlfriend." She reddened, then blurted, "I wanted to invite you to the wedding, Elly. But I thought you'd stopped wanting to be friends."

"Never!" Elly said. "But don't worry. I'm not offended. Just sorry I missed your big day."

Paige sat back in her chair, peering at Elly from beneath her dark brows. "So why did you go AWOL on me?"

Elly hesitated, then plunged. She and Paige had known each other too long for her to lie or make small talk. "I met this guy and thought I was in love. He went back to Europe suddenly and the breakup knocked me flat. It also left me with an STD. I was licking my wounds and feeling sorry for myself."

"Oh, crap, crap, *crap* guy," Paige said, screwing up her face.

"He *was* a crap guy," Elly admitted. "I can see that now. Don't know why I couldn't before."

Funny how telling Anne and Paige about Hans was slowly but surely leaching her memories of their power. Elly knew she could tell

Paige the rest, too—Paige would be sympathetic, if Elly wanted to confide her fears about infertility—but Anne was right. There was no point in worrying about that until she'd met a man who made her believe she could be as good a mother as her sisters were.

"Well. He'd better not try coming here, or I'll run him over with my car," Paige promised.

Elly laughed, then took Paige's hand and squeezed it. "I really am sorry I missed your wedding. Mom told me it was spectacular. You'll have to show me pictures."

Paige brightened. "I have a video link I can send you. But only watch it if you're bored out of your skull."

"I've got a better idea. I'm staying at Laura's. Bring John over there and we'll watch it together. I'd love to meet him. I'll buy a bottle of champagne and we'll toast your happy day."

"Sounds good. But why are you staying at Laura's and not with your mom? I was always so jealous of you, living at Folly Cove. Your inn always seemed like a movie set to me."

Elly wondered how to answer this and straightened in her chair. This was an effort; the table was sticky, probably from beer being steadily dripped onto its surface by Gloucester fisherman for three hundred years.

The truth was that she'd never even considered staying with her mother. "Mom doesn't exactly have space for guests."

"Really? I thought your mother lived in one wing of the inn."

Elly shook her head. "Not for a long time. You used to come to that part of the inn to see me. After Laura and I went to college, though, Mom moved into a two-bedroom apartment in one corner. Not even the back corner, since guests pay extra for ocean views. So she doesn't have a lot of room."

"Huh," Paige said, taking a thoughtful sip of wine. "I always imagined Sarah Bradford as lady of the manor in a dining room with a chandelier, eating off fine china, a butler at her elbow. Everything silent except for a ticking grandfather clock in one corner."

"Well, she does use real china and sterling silver," Elly said. "And she has nice antiques. Family heirlooms. But Mom lives modestly and likes her solitude. Anyway, Laura's the one who called to invite me, and Mom's kind of mad at me right now."

"Really? Why?"

"I quit singing."

"You quit completely?" Paige put a hand to her chest. "But why? You were so good!"

Elly shrugged. "I know. But there are lots of singers in the world. I'm nothing special, it turns out."

"I'm sorry," Paige said. "It's always such a shock, isn't it, to wake up and realize your life is as good as it's going to get?"

"God, I hope that's not true." Elly snorted. "Look at me: No job. No husband. Not even a boyfriend! I can only go up from here."

"You will," Paige said loyally. "You love California, right? So at least you've found the place you belong."

"And a career I like." Elly told Paige about her production design work.

"You're finding your way," Paige pronounced. "That's not easy. Especially not as an artist. Just keep following what you love. I always tell my students that sometimes you have to let go of the life you planned so you can make room for the life that's waiting for you."

Elly tried to imagine letting go of her L.A. life. What if, instead of returning to California, she stayed right here? What did she have in Los Angeles that she needed?

A few contacts. But she could network in Boston.

An apartment. But it was soulless and expensive.

Good weather! Except Los Angeles was smoggy, and in the back of her mind was the vague, thrumming anxiety that the city could catch fire, run out of water, or suffer a devastating earthquake any minute.

Then there was Ryder. But he was a pleasant, passing thing, she reminded herself, no matter how much his texts and occasional phone calls made her smile.

"There isn't much to keep me in California," she admitted.

Paige patted her hand. "I'm sure you'll figure it out. Meanwhile, just be glad to have this time with Laura and your mom. And with Anne, too. It's great that you're all together again."

"How did you hear Anne was back?" Elly turned the empty glass between her hands, wondering whether she dared to order more of this wretched wine. Better not. She was driving Laura's car, and she needed to be alert enough to follow Jake undetected when he left the office at five o'clock. "I didn't realize you were friends."

"We're not. I mean, I know Anne a little, because she was always hanging around and you were always trying to get her to leave us alone." Paige laughed. "That is, unless somebody else did something mean to her. Then you went all pit bull, protecting your baby sister. Remember bitchy Jade Killian? How you shoved her up against the cafeteria wall at school when she said something horrible about Anne's red hair?"

"Anne was a pest, but she was *my* pest," Elly said. "I'm glad you're seeing her. She needs friends. She's been having a rough time since the father of her baby went back to his wife."

"*What?* Anne had a *baby*? With a married man?" Paige's mouth opened wide in shock and failed to close.

"You didn't know?" Elly wished she could rewind the conversation and not spill Anne's secret, if it was one.

Paige shook her head. "I haven't actually *seen* Anne. I only knew she was home because of Sebastian. Remember him?"

"Sure. A hottie deluxe. We all had crushes on your big brother."

"Ew," Paige said. "Please don't say that. Gross."

Elly laughed. "Okay. So what about Sebastian?"

"He moved back here, too, about a year ago," Paige said. "He's renting a house on Halibut Point, somewhere along the road by the state park."

"Really? Last I heard, he was out saving the world."

"He still is. Sebastian was in Alaska for a while, working as a forester. Then he was working on sustainability agroforestry projects in Brazil. Now he's teaching at Harvard and doing a forestry research project on the North Shore. That's how he started spending time with your sister."

Elly remembered Laura's confession about her virtual romance. Not so virtual, if she was actually *seeing* Sebastian. "So he's spending time with Laura, and that's how he found out Anne is here?"

"No, no. Sebastian's hanging out with *Anne.*"

Elly opened her mouth, then closed it, processing this. "That's weird. Sebastian's so much older. I didn't even think they knew each other. Are you sure he's seeing Anne? Not Laura?"

Paige arched an eyebrow. "Yes! Seb told me he's been seeing Anne every day. Apparently, she got thrown off a horse in the woods because of my brother's stupid dog. Sebastian felt guilty about her getting hurt, so he's been helping her out. But he hasn't said one thing about a baby. Are you sure she's *got* a baby?"

"Ha-ha." Elly grinned. "Maybe your brother and my sister are playing house. Anne's staying at Aunt Flossie's cottage, free from Mom's prying eyes. That would be sweet if they got together."

"I doubt that will ever happen. Oh, not because of Anne," Paige added quickly, "but because of Sebastian." Her face contorted. Paige was obviously struggling to decide how much to say.

Elly waited, trying to read Paige's expression and remembering how she used to look after field hockey practice, sweaty, her ponytail high and tight. She and Paige would laugh as their lips—distorted and numb from the mouth guards they wore on the field—refused to make words properly, giving them strange speech impediments.

Funny how you could see a friend after such a long time and notice the way she'd aged, but then the changes gradually faded as you kept looking at her. It was as if all her past selves were still there, waiting to be revealed by memory.

Paige finally said, "Listen, I think you should tell Anne to be careful around Sebastian. My brother would hate me for telling you this, but he's been pretty depressed since his wife killed herself."

"Oh my God. I'm so sorry." Elly sat back in her chair, stunned. "When did this happen?"

"About eighteen months ago." Paige clasped her hands around her empty wineglass, causing Elly to signal the waiter to bring them another round. She'd swing through McDonald's for a coffee if she had to; this conversation definitely required more alcohol.

"I don't even know who Sebastian married," Elly said. "Did I ever meet her?"

"Probably not. You were in California by then, I think, and she

wasn't from around here," Paige said. "Her name was Jenny O'Don-
nell. Sebastian met her while they were both in the Peace Corps in El
Salvador. They got married there, actually, so they could avoid all the
fuss of a big wedding here. Sebastian's idea, I'm sure. You know how
my family does weddings."

"Like the Kennedys," Elly said. "Not that my mom's ever going to
complain about that."

She was rewarded by a slight smile. "Anyway," Paige went on, "I
flew to El Salvador with my parents and sisters for the wedding. Jenny
was pretty—that kind of tall, skinny brunette who always looks like
she should have a cigarette in one hand and a martini in the other—
and she and Sebastian had a lot in common: Ivy League, liberal politics,
Good Samaritan ideals."

"Sounds like a good match."

Paige nodded. "My parents were relieved because Jenny was the
'right' sort of girl. They were convinced the Peace Corps was just a
phase with Sebastian, that eventually he'd go into finance like my dad.
And I was just glad Jenny wasn't visibly unhinged. Sebastian had a
habit of collecting crazies and strays."

Paige paused while the waiter set down two more glasses of wine
and removed the empty glasses, then said, "Man, this is hard, telling
you this."

"Don't tell me if it's upsetting."

"I want to, though. It might be good for you to know this if Anne
starts getting close to Sebastian. You might have to warn her."

"About what?" Elly said, alarmed.

"That Sebastian might seem functional on the outside, but inside
he's a complete mess," Paige said. "When he and Jenny came back
from the Peace Corps, Sebastian went to grad school in forestry and
threw himself into research. He seemed happy. But Jenny was floundering. She couldn't find a job that made her happy and had trouble
making friends. She didn't even want to come to family dinners. Eventually, she stopped leaving their apartment at all."

"Anxiety?" Elly guessed.

"Yes," Paige said. "And depression. Jenny finally saw a psychiatrist, who put her on medication. After a while, she seemed better. Then she got pregnant and went off the drugs. Everything spiraled downhill fast after that."

"Why did she go off the meds? Because of her pregnancy?"

"No," Paige said. "As I understand it, the psychiatrist was in favor of her continuing the medication. But Jenny was one of those health zealots, always claiming she wanted to cleanse her body of toxins. Pretty soon, her anxiety came roaring back and was worse than ever. She stopped sleeping and started cutting herself."

"God. And the doctor couldn't do anything?"

"Nobody could. Jenny went haywire." Paige smiled slightly. "Sorry. That's a terrible word. And so inadequate to describe what happened to her. But it was like all of Jenny's circuits started firing at once. Her brain was on overdrive. She began having panic attacks and had to be taken to the ER a couple of times because she couldn't breathe. Finally, Sebastian got the call he'd been dreading: Jenny deliberately drove their car off a bridge. She was seven months pregnant."

Elly's eyes stung, imagining the woman at the wheel, the desperation this act must have taken, Sebastian's shock and grief. "Are they sure it wasn't an accident?"

"Oh yes. There was no reason for her to go off that road otherwise. Nothing wrong with her car or the bridge. And it was a dry night. The conclusion of the accident report was suicide." Paige swabbed at her eyes with a cocktail napkin. "I felt sorry for Jenny. And for her family. But I feel sorrier for Sebastian. He was so excited about being a dad! Now he'll never be the same. That's why you need to warn Anne."

Elly pictured Anne in her little cottage by the sea, lying on the floor to play with Lucy or holding the baby on one hip to watch the surf break on the rocky beach below. Anne was so alone. She might seek out Sebastian for comfort, just as he might be drawn to her. Was that a bad thing?

Life was difficult. And complicated. Maybe it was important to seek solace where you could find it and to give it generously when you could. Still, Paige was right: Anne should know Sebastian's history, if she didn't already, in case she was considering a relationship with him.

Especially since whatever Anne went through from now on would impact Lucy.

"I'll talk to Anne," Elly said. Then, desperate to cheer Paige up, she said, "Hey. Want to have some fun tonight?"

Paige gave her a suspicious look. "I'm married."

Elly laughed. "Not that kind of fun. I'm inviting you on a spy mission."

"Who are you spying on?"

"Laura's husband."

"What are you planning to do, a stakeout?"

"Exactly," Elly said. "I'm going to park near his office and follow him when he leaves work."

"Wow. Very double-oh seven! But why?"

"To see where he goes! Jake has been getting home late every night, like nine o'clock. But when I stopped by his office today, the receptionist told me they're only open two nights a week."

"Does Laura think Jake's having an affair? Is that why you're doing this?"

"She doesn't know I'm doing it." Elly bit her lip, wondering how much to tell Paige, then decided she'd say nothing about Jake and Anne or Laura's suspicions. That could only lead to more rumors. "Come with me."

Paige glanced at her watch. "Can't. Sorry. I'm holding a talk for parents about college financial aid tonight."

"A thrill a minute."

"Hey," Paige said with a laugh. "If I can figure out how other people pay for college, maybe I'll be able to do it for my own kids. That's enough thrills for me." She stood up and gathered her things. "Good luck. Though I don't know whether to hope you find something out about Jake or not. Marriage is a tricky business."

"Right. That's why sisters need to help sisters," Elly said.

Laura knocked on Kennedy's door after finishing her last lesson of the day. "Hey, how's your poor mouth since the orthodontist?" she called.

The door remained closed and there was no answer. Laura knocked again. She tried to respect her daughter's privacy, seldom entering the bedroom unless she was invited. Many of the other moms she knew disagreed with this.

"How will you ever know when they're in trouble if you don't snoop?" Meredith had asked at the last school fund-raiser. "I found condoms in Luke's bedside table! And a joint!" She'd sounded nearly triumphant.

But Laura had grown up with a mother who was militant about clean bedrooms. She and her sisters were expected to make their beds every morning and keep their rooms as tidy as the guest rooms in the inn, "just in case we ever need to rent out your rooms, too."

Her mother had tried to joke with them about this. At the same time, Sarah had made it clear that where they lived was a business, an income property. If there ever came a time when Sarah needed to use those rooms to make money, her daughters knew they'd better be prepared to make sacrifices. Their bedrooms did not belong to them: they belonged to the inn.

For this reason, Laura had always told her own daughter that her bedroom was a sanctuary, a room she could keep exactly how she pleased. Her private space.

"Kennedy?" she called again. "Are you in there?"

She nudged the door open with her knee. Kennedy wasn't in the room. She must be in the basement watching a movie.

It had been a while since Laura had stepped foot in her daughter's bedroom with the lights on; lately, whenever she stopped by to kiss Kennedy good night on her way up to bed, there would be no light other than the glow of Kennedy's iPod. Now Laura noticed that her daughter had gotten rid of her stuffed animals. When did that happen? Where were they?

Probably stuffed in the closet. She glanced around, noticing more changes: a red scarf draped over the bedside lamp. Tubes of lipstick on the dresser. A new pair of black leather motorcycle boots stood next to the desk.

Overnight, this had become a teenager's room.

Laura swallowed hard. Somehow, she'd missed her daughter's metamorphosis from chubby child to blossoming young woman.

She walked over to the bed and smelled something like incense as she got closer. Wait: it *was* incense, a stick of it jammed into a holder shaped like a Buddha. Patchouli! Oh God. Shades of Aunt Flossie. She was so ill equipped to be the mother of an adolescent.

Laura stretched out on the bed. Maybe she'd close her eyes just for a minute, then go downstairs and find her daughter, see what she felt like eating for dinner. She turned onto her side to face the wall, keeping the filthy cuffs of her jeans off the bed. She was still in her stable clothes. She'd taught four lessons this afternoon, then fed and watered the horses and brought them in for the night.

When she opened her eyes again, it was to the sound of someone singing. A beautiful voice and an old song she recognized: "I Got Rhythm."

She turned back over and watched in astonishment as Kennedy— her own Kennedy, in jeans and a T-shirt—tap-danced in front of the mirror, imitating a few of Gene Kelly's moves. The movie was playing on Kennedy's laptop, which she'd set up on the dresser. Kennedy's gentle, lilting alto was surprisingly pure in tone.

When had Kennedy started singing? And *dancing*? Who had taught her?

Elly, of course! They must have been watching the movie and practicing steps whenever they weren't shopping for her mother's birthday party. Now Laura remembered how Elly had hinted at something like this.

"Mom would love to see her daughters reunited onstage," she'd said at dinner a few nights ago.

"Count me out," Laura had said. "If I had to stand next to Anne, I'd probably end up spitting on her. And I don't sing. Not anymore."

Watching Kennedy, though, made Laura remember how it had felt when the three of them sang together. Their voices had blended so naturally that they were always harmonizing. She and her sisters sang while cleaning rooms at the inn, polishing silver, or doing any of the other millions of mindless tasks their mother assigned.

Their reward, sometimes, would be to have Sarah join them with her powerful alto and jazz licks. Her mother's voice was smoky and lusty; as she got older, Laura understood it was the sort of voice that would cause men to want to buy Sarah drinks and take her to bed.

Laura waited, forcing herself to lie still until Kennedy finished the song. "Hey," she said then. "That sounded really good. You have a lovely voice, honey. I don't think I've heard you sing since you were in elementary school. Remember that musical you did? *Annie?*"

Kennedy visibly winced. "I wanted to be Annie or any of the other orphan girls. Instead they made me play the orphanage lady. They said I was too big to be a girl. But I *was* a girl!" She turned around, plaiting her hair in a braid as she walked over to the bed and sat down. "I tried to quit before the show, but you wouldn't let me."

"Why did you want to quit? Because you didn't get the part you wanted?" Laura sat up and gently pushed Kennedy's hands down. She began doing her hair in a French braid.

"No. Because a boy said my boobs looked like balloons."

Laura inhaled sharply. So many things a mother didn't know: the hurts, the taunts, the times when your child hid in a bathroom and cried. "I'm sorry."

"Why are you apologizing? It wasn't your fault. That kid was a moron."

Laura was about to correct her, to tell her not to use the word "moron," then bit her lip and finished braiding Kennedy's hair instead. That boy *was* a moron. "So are you going to sing for Grandma at her birthday party?"

"I don't know. Maybe." Kennedy raised her head and felt the braid. Laura could see her daughter's smile in the mirror. "Elly says we all have to sing. Even you."

"Oh, no."

"Why not?"

"I haven't sung a note in more than twenty years!" Laura said. "My voice would sound like a rusty gate."

"So you'll have to practice. Come on. We could practice together," Kennedy said eagerly. "What songs do you know?"

"Not many, anymore," Laura said with a sigh. "Anyway, I should really start dinner."

Kennedy grabbed her hand. "Not until you sing! Please, Mom! I want to hear you. Elly says you always had a better voice than hers, even."

Laura laughed. "Elly is being kind. She's the one who had the best chance of a singing career."

"But she didn't make it," Kennedy said.

"Not yet. But she might still."

Kennedy shook her head. "She's too old, Mom."

Laura felt terrible for Elly suddenly. But she supposed everyone went through that sort of disappointment. The bigger the dream, the harder the fall.

For a while she'd thought she might as well die as keep living, after she lost that first baby, knowing she might have given up her dream of making it to the Olympics for nothing. If Jake hadn't been so tender with her, so compassionate after the miscarriage, she never would have pulled out of that depression. Because of his steadfast belief that she would find her way, Laura had the courage to eventually open the stables and teach riding lessons.

Laura wished Elly had a husband, or even a boyfriend who gave her that kind of unwavering love and support. But her sister seemed to have no interest in men, except for the guy she worked with in California and had talked to occasionally while Laura was within earshot. He made her laugh. Laura had seen his name come up on Elly's phone a few times: Ryder. That was it. But he hadn't called in a while.

"Ready to sing, Mom?" Kennedy was standing in front of her now, hands on her hips. "Come on. I'll do it with you."

"I don't know the words to anything," Laura said.

"You must. What songs did you sing when you were a kid?"

"I don't know. Nothing comes to mind." Laura stood up. "Come on. Let's go downstairs."

"No! We have to do this!" Kennedy grinned. "You're my prisoner until you sing your way free."

Laura sighed, but she felt the corners of her mouth twitch. "All right. Does it count if the song is dumb?"

"Any song," Kennedy said eagerly. "Maybe you can even teach it to me."

Laura laughed. "I doubt you'd want to know this one," she said, and started singing "What Shall We Do with the Drunken Sailor?"

To her surprise, Kennedy chimed in, singing several verses with her. Afterward, the two of them collapsed on the bed, breathless and laughing.

"Where did you learn that song?" Laura said. "It's so old. Did Elly teach it to you?"

"No. Anne sings it to her baby," Kennedy said, then slapped her hand over her mouth. "Oh, crap," she mumbled.

Laura reared up from the bed and grabbed Kennedy's wrist. "What did you say?"

Kennedy sat up next to her, blue eyes downcast. "Anne sings that song to her baby. That's how I learned it." She peered through her fringe of blond bangs, gauging Laura's reaction.

"Who said you could see Anne?" Laura demanded.

"You didn't say *not* to," Kennedy pointed out, suddenly chin-jutting and defiant.

"But you know how I feel about Anne," Laura said desperately, wondering now what she'd told Kennedy. She couldn't remember.

Kennedy shook her head. "I heard you tell Aunt Elly that you don't want Aunt Anne coming around here, but I don't know *why*," she said. "Why, Mom? What did she do?"

"It doesn't matter."

"It does to me! She's my *aunt*! And Lucy is my only *cousin*!" Kennedy stood up. She went across the room and sat on the white wicker rocking chair. The chair that used to hold stuffed animals and now held a sulky teenager. "Just because you're pissed off at her doesn't mean I have to be!"

Laura sighed. How had she gone, within minutes, from singing and dancing with her daughter to this shouting match?

"No," she said carefully. "You don't have to be angry at Anne. I was wrong to expect you to take sides."

Kennedy hunched forward over her knees, rocking a little in the chair, her eyes wild. "But you'll be mad at me if I keep seeing her."

"What do you mean, *keep* seeing her?" It took all of Laura's willpower to control her voice. "How many times have you been over there?" And how, she wondered, could she be so clueless about her own child's whereabouts?

Kennedy clenched her fists on top of her knees. "Three times. Just to see the baby, mostly."

Despite herself, Laura was curious. "What's she like?"

"The baby?" Kennedy was grinning now. "So cute, Mom! She has red hair like Aunt Anne's! And it's curly! And Lucy laughs at everything! Anne taught me how to give her a bottle, and I've changed her diaper twice!"

Laura couldn't help smiling, too. "I bet you're a wonderful cousin."

"You're really not mad at me for going over there?"

"No, honey, of course not. I just wish I'd known where you were."

"You were busy," Kennedy said. "You're always busy." Her face shut down again.

Laura reached for her. "Come over here, you."

Slowly, Kennedy uncurled from the chair and shuffled over to the bed, dragging her bare feet—blue toenail polish, another one of Elly's touches, probably—until she was standing in front of Laura. Laura pulled her down without warning and sat Kennedy on her lap, wrapping her arms around her.

"You still fit in my arms," Laura said, burying her face in her daughter's hair. "And I bet Lucy is nowhere near as cute as you were when you were a baby."

"Mom, you're being ridiculous," Kennedy said, but she slumped against Laura's shoulder, a warm solid bundle, half child, half woman.

CHAPTER TWELVE

E lly parked on the street as far from Jake's office as she could, while making sure she could still watch the door. A few minutes after five o'clock, she spotted Jake's receptionist, wearing a light-colored coat that billowed like a tent around her skinny legs, emerge with a green handbag big enough to carry a toaster. The woman climbed into a sporty Dodge and zipped out of the parking lot.

The next person out the door was the dental hygienist. She wore a red cape that made her look like a superhero and carried no handbag at all. Elly watched her closely as she waited in front of the building, half expecting Jake to come out and put his arms around her—she really was beautiful.

Instead, the hygienist was picked up by an older woman in a battered sedan. The poor thing must still live with her mother.

Elly had to wait ten more minutes for Jake. She nearly didn't recognize him. He'd ridden his bicycle to work—she had seen him leave home this morning, with his khaki pants cuffed by steel bracelets of some sort—but now he emerged from the office wearing what looked like a costume: a black motorcycle jacket and black jeans tucked into black boots. He carried a helmet under one arm that was definitely not a bicycle helmet.

Jake walked around to the back of the building. A minute later, he shot out of the alley on a red Suzuki motorcycle and made a rapid exit from the parking lot.

"What the hell, Jake?" she muttered as she pulled onto the street and followed.

Elly nearly lost track of him on the road, since she was working to stay a few car lengths behind. She was afraid Jake might recognize Laura's car if he spotted her in the rearview mirror. Plus, he was particularly adept at weaving between lanes of traffic. Her heart was hammering and she gripped the wheel so hard that her wrists ached.

He took the ramp to Route 128, but rather than head north toward Rockport, Jake took the southbound exit toward Boston. It was easier to keep him in sight on the highway. Elly followed at a steady distance, her eyes watering from focusing so steadily on her target. She was afraid to even blink.

Jake continued south to Route 60 in Medford. She took the exit ramp two cars behind him, nearly lost him in Medford center, then caught up on one of the side streets near Tufts University. For a minute, Elly felt silly for having been suspicious. Jake was probably visiting an old dental school buddy.

Then she remembered: Tufts Dental School was actually in Boston near the theater district, on the opposite side of the Charles River from Medford.

A few minutes later, Jake turned into the driveway of a three-decker blue house with porches on all three levels. The house was identical to most of the others on the street, aside from its bright color. It had a peeling white picket fence around a tangled garden that looked as if it had once been a labor of love but was now abandoned. Container pots of dead plants sat on the steps, interspersed with jack-o'-lanterns. The faces of the pumpkins had the usual triangle eyes and jagged teeth.

The only things on the porch were a swing and a bicycle. Paper ghosts and pumpkins decorated the first-floor windowpanes, low enough to have been put there by a child.

Elly parked across the street from the house. Jake turned the motorcycle off, dismounted it, and removed his helmet before climbing the stairs to the porch. He moved quickly, bouncing up the steps two at a time; he might have been a teenager, seen from this distance.

Jake turned the knob and entered the building without ringing any of the three bells lit yellow by the black metal mailboxes. She had no way of knowing which apartment he was entering. Either the door to the front entry wasn't locked or he had a key.

Elly glanced at her watch: five thirty. Laura, she knew, was expecting Jake home at his usual time, around nine. Until then, she'd be tending to her students and Kennedy, making dinner, doing laundry.

Laura would have food ready to put on the table when Jake arrived. She would wait to eat with him and would probably have a bottle of wine open and ready to pour. Maybe she would have poured herself a glass before Jake got home and sipped it while she was cooking. These were her sister's habits.

Now, knowing that Laura had no idea where her husband went after work made Elly so furious that she slammed the door shut when she got out of the car. She mounted the steps to the house in a fury and tried the front door. It was locked. So Jake had a key!

Either that, or whoever lived here had been watching for him and let him in.

Damn it. Elly leaned her forehead on the cold front door. Did she really want to know what was on the other side?

For her sister's sake, yes.

She rang the third-floor buzzer, then the second floor. No answer. When she rang the first-floor buzzer—she'd chosen that one last, because of the obvious evidence of a child living there—she was admitted almost immediately to a front hall papered in a wild Chinese print: men in robes flying kites, decorative bridges, and flocks of birds on a bright gold background.

Given her suspicions about Jake, she fully expected a woman to open the door. Instead, she was greeted by a man. Thirtysomething, narrowly built. He had a cartoon hero's jutting jaw and a shock of thick black hair that stood nearly straight up, as if he'd been tugging on it. He was the sort of man who looked like he would swagger when he walked. A *swashbuckler* was the odd word that came to Elly's mind.

Then the man smiled and two deep dimples appeared on either side of his mouth, causing her to smile back despite her foul mood. He was cute and had teeth like sugar cubes. Elly could imagine sucking on them.

"Oh, hey," he said easily, still grinning. "You're not the pizza delivery guy. Can I help you?"

"I'm looking for Jake."

The man's face went nearly as white as his teeth. "I'm sorry, who?"

"Jake," Elly said. "Jake Williams." She edged the toe of her boot toward the door in case he tried to close it. "Tell him Elly's here." She thought about adding, "His sister-in-law," but decided to let the guy wonder if she was Jake's wife.

The man glanced down at her boot, then back up at her face. He had beautiful eyes, dark and soft. His expressions were so transparent that it was easy for Elly to track his thoughts: he was thinking about denying that he knew Jake but then decided to concede without a fight.

He sighed heavily, and it was as if all the air went out of him. His shoulders rounded over his skinny chest. Now Elly recalculated his age as more like late twenties.

"I guess you'd better come in," he said.

"Pizza guy, pizza pie! Pizza guy, pizza pie!" a child cried from within the apartment. This chant was followed by a sharp screech that could have been made by a parrot.

A small boy ran into the room from the opposite side just as Elly entered from the front door. He was the source of the screeching.

The boy was a miniature of the handsome man. Dark hair, dark eyes, dimples. He even wore the same sort of outfit, a snug bright T-shirt and jeans. He was still shrieking. Elly covered her ears as the child ran smack into the man's legs, where he clung for dear life.

"I'm going to get you!" a man growled from the other room, and Jake came barreling after the toddler, hunched low in a monster pose, arms swinging heavily in front of him. He nearly ran into the other man, too, when he noticed Elly and almost failed to stop in time.

"Oh, Jesus," he said, still hunched over, peering up at her. He straightened slowly. "Oh, God, Elly. What are you doing here?" He worked his jaw, as if it were threatening to seize up. "Is everything all right at home? How did you find me?"

Both men and the boy stared at her, wide-eyed, as if Elly had suddenly beamed into their living room from outer space. Which she might as well have, because Elly could make no sense at all of what she was seeing. She could be in a parallel universe.

Was Jake here doing pro bono dentistry work? Was this man a cousin she didn't know about?

Then Jake touched the man's arm and she understood. Elly felt her mind go blank with shock. Her knees threatened to give out.

Jake stepped forward and took her arm, guiding her gently across the room to a couch strewn with tiny metal trucks. He brushed a few vehicles to the floor and sat her down.

"Is everything all right at home?" he repeated. "Are Laura and Kennedy okay?"

Elly wondered how to answer this as the little boy tugged at Jake's arm, begging, "Chase me, chase me!" How could Laura and Kennedy be okay? How would they ever be okay again, if this was the lie Jake had been living?

"They're fine," she said. "They don't know I'm here."

"Hey, Brad," the other man said. "Let's go outside and watch for the pizza guy!" He opened the front door again.

The little boy ran to him and took his hand. "Pizza guy, pizza pie!"

Jake stood up, still looking agitated. "Wait. His jacket," he said. "It's getting cold out."

"He'll be fine for a few minutes. We'll just be right out front," the man said over his shoulder to Jake, then closed the door behind him.

Elly glanced around the apartment. The furniture in the living room was inexpensive but comfortable: a faux leather couch and recliner, an artificial Oriental rug in bright orange and blue, framed prints on the walls.

In the next room, she could see a table laid with three red place mats. A crystal vase of fall flowers stood in its center, and the floor beneath the table was occupied by a complicated wooden train track looped around the table legs. Train cars were scattered beneath the table as if they'd tumbled off bridges.

"Brad's very into vehicles," Jake said, following her glance as he sat down beside her again. "I'm sure he's going to be an engineer or construction worker. My son's all boy." He said this last sentence wistfully, startling Elly into wakefulness again. It felt that way: as if she'd been dreaming and was only now returning to consciousness.

"Brad's your *son*?"

Jake nodded, a flicker of pride in his eyes. "We had a surrogate. I'm not the biological father, of course," he added quickly, seeing her expression. "I've just been helping Anthony raise him."

"And Anthony is?"

"You just met him," Jake said.

"We didn't actually meet."

"Ah. No. I guess you didn't. All right. Anthony and I, we're, he's," he said, and stopped to take a deep breath before finishing. "We're in love," he said finally. "Oh, Jesus, Elly. I can't imagine what you must think of me." Jake rubbed his hands on his black jeans vigorously, as if trying to warm them up, though the apartment was overheated. "Or maybe I can."

Surrogate mothers were expensive. Elly thought of Laura's consignment clothing, of her sister's determined efforts to keep the heat low to save money. Of Laura asking their mother for Kennedy's tuition money. "I don't think you should worry about what I think, Jake. You need to worry about Laura."

"She doesn't know about any of this."

"Obviously. But you have to tell her."

"I can't!" Jake's face was pinched. "I've tried, Elly. A *million* times, I've tried! But I can't do it. I can't hurt her!" His voice was desperate. "I'll lose everything! Kennedy would hate me. And what would she tell her friends at school?" He shook his head. "I know what that school's like."

Elly stared at him in disbelief. "But you can't keep up this charade. What about Laura?"

"Do you think she'd really want to know?" Jake's face was so drawn that the outline of his skull seemed to press outward from beneath the skin, as if at any moment his cheekbones might jut through the flesh. "What would Laura do if she and I split up? I know she loves me. Look at all we've built together. The house. Her business and mine. Kennedy! I can't give all of that up, Elly. I don't think Laura would want to, either. At least not until Kennedy goes to college. Anthony understands. He's willing to wait."

Elly wondered about this. Anthony had let her inside rather than keep her standing in the hall: maybe he'd wanted exactly this sort of confrontation to bring things to a head. He was a young man and still handsome. He and Jake had a child together.

Then she thought of Anne, and of Laura's suspicions. "What about Anne?" she asked. "What was all that about? Did anything really happen?"

Jake's lips had gone the same putty-white as his complexion. "Something. But not what you think."

"You don't know what I think. So tell me."

"I approached Anne. I did what she said."

"But why, Jake? When you're so obviously attracted to men?"

"I wasn't always attracted to men." He offered the ghost of a smile. "Or I didn't let myself know I was. With Anne, I was testing myself. Trying to manufacture something that wasn't there."

Elly still felt confused. Unbalanced. "Manufacture what, exactly?"

"Desire for a woman." He had calmed down now, his breathing more regular, though again he had to rub his hands on his jeans. "I met Anthony at that conference I went to in Las Vegas, the weekend Anne came to take care of the horses for Laura. He was a blackjack dealer in one of the casinos. I don't know if it's because I was so out of my element or what, but things got complicated. Fast."

"So you came home and decided to bait yourself with Anne, is that it?" Elly didn't want to understand, but somehow she did. She could see it all: Jake's dogged and hopeless determination to turn himself into something he was not—a straight man—as he had probably been trying to do all his life.

"Yes," he said. "Anne happened to be there. I needed to tempt myself with someone who wasn't my wife. Part of me still hoped, I guess, that it was marriage that had robbed me of desire. Not the fact that I wanted to be with a man instead of a woman."

Elly considered this. Jake had grown up in a conservative Catholic family. Played lacrosse in college, joined a fraternity. What torture it must have been to be gay yet afraid to explore his sexuality. He'd made himself miserable trying to do the right things for his family. As Laura had. What a sad mess.

"So what really happened?" she asked.

"I went into the guest room while Anne was asleep and pulled the covers down to look at her. I touched myself. But that's all that happened. I swear! I never meant for her to wake up." He pressed a hand to his face, covering his eyes for a moment, then dropped it. "I told Laura about it so she wouldn't know what I'd done with Anthony in Las Vegas or guess what I really was. *What I am.* It's the same reason I kissed Anne at that Christmas party. I wanted to tell Anne the truth. That's why I went looking for her at the pub. I was hoping she'd understand. Forgive me, maybe."

"That's pretty twisted, Jake."

"I know. I know. But I didn't want to be gay! I'd been with only one man and a couple of women in college. I wasn't sure of anything for years." Jake was talking fast now, his words slamming into one another. "I fell in love with Laura. With who she is! Laura's everything I've always admired in a person: brave and honest. Smart. True to herself."

"She is," Elly said.

"I thought I could control my feelings for men. When Laura got pregnant in college, I took that as a sign that I was on the right path. I always wanted to be a father. I thought, all right, I'm attracted to men sometimes, but I knew I could control my feelings. And I did, until Anthony."

"But Laura miscarried. Didn't you take that as a sign, too?"

Jake shook his head. "No. Anyway, I couldn't leave her. Laura was so down. She'd stopped riding competitively because of me. And I knew she'd be a wonderful wife and mother." He sat back against the couch, his eyes bright, his jaw clenched. "But I've been a shit husband."

He looked so pained that Elly wanted to comfort him. Jake was right: her sister loved him. Thought he was good and kind and hardworking. And he was, in most ways.

On the other hand, she wanted to kill Jake for lying. For hurting Laura. Even though Laura didn't know where he was right now, or where her husband had presumably been spending most of his evenings and probably some weekends, Laura was in pain. She already knew that Jake didn't love her in the way she needed to be loved.

That was not necessarily unforgivable. But it had to be remedied.

The door opened and Anthony appeared, holding a box of pizza. Brad was at his side, pink-cheeked and excited. "We got it, Daddy!" he yelled. "We got the pizza guy, pizza pie!" Then he ran straight into Jake's arms.

"What am I going to do?" Jake asked, raising his eyes to Elly above the little boy's head.

"What we're going to do right now is eat some pizza," Anthony said, hurrying over to set the box on the table in front of them. "Then we'll figure it all out together. Right, Elly?"

She sat stunned on the couch, all three of them looking at her now, and nodded.

Lucy went to sleep just after six. Anne settled on the couch to read her e-mail.

She'd had two responses from teaching jobs, but now that her mother had offered her a job in the kitchen, she wondered whether she should stay in Flossie's place and work here. That would make the most financial sense.

Flossie had made it clear that she'd be happy to watch Lucy if Anne wanted to work at the inn. This would give her a chance to try cooking full-time. Rodrigo could teach her a lot. And, frankly, any other option seemed too exhausting. Other jobs she'd found would require her to commute long distances or pay an astonishing amount of rent.

Then there was the daunting matter of day care. Anne didn't even know where to begin with that. She hated the idea. She wanted Lucy to be with family while she was still so small.

Her thoughts were interrupted by a knock on the door. She answered it and was surprised to see Sebastian. "You and your dog are off the hook," she'd told him as they'd said good-bye the last time she'd cooked for him. "I'm completely healed! No more guilt. No more stopping by with pity meals or wine, thank you."

She hadn't seen him since, and that was four days ago. Now Sebastian held a bottle of white wine in one hand and a bag from the local Chinese place in the other. "I hope I'm not intruding."

Anne smiled. "Are you kidding? Lucy fell asleep early, so I didn't bother cooking. I was about to forage for crackers."

He laughed. "This is only from the local place, but I think it can compete with crackers." Sebastian followed her into the living room and made himself at home in the galley kitchen, heating the food in the microwave and opening the wine while she took down a pair of plates and laid silverware on the counter.

Anne ate hungrily and asked what he'd been working on today. He was excited, Sebastian said, because he'd gotten permission from the city to continue the research he'd started in Dogtown for another year.

"You know Dogtown's haunted, right?" she said.

"Of course. Don't forget I grew up around here, too," he said.

"I was always spooked by that one story about James Merry," she said.

"Who?"

"That guy who raised a bull in Dogtown so he could wrestle it every year, until it eventually killed him in 1892 when he tried it the third year in a row."

"Not that you can blame the bull for that, I guess."

"Right. The guy was asking for it," Anne said. "The creepiest bit is that there's a rock with Merry's name and the date of his death-by-bull written in red paint to look like blood."

Suddenly they were both laughing so hard at the absurdity of the story that Anne had to put down her wine before she spilled it. "So why are you so excited to keep working here?" she asked. "I mean, you've traveled all over the world. Why stay in Massachusetts?"

"I realized that no matter how far away you go, sometimes you have to go home to figure things out," he said. "Besides, for a tree guy like me who's interested in the intersection between climate change and natural resources, Cape Ann has a fascinating history. Think about it: just twenty thousand years ago, New England was covered by a huge glacier. Then the glacier melted and exposed all sorts of rocks and boulders in this area."

They discussed the history, then, of people who'd been landing on Cape Ann for eleven thousand years, starting with the Vikings and the

French. "They were followed by John Smith and the European settlers who fished and farmed and cut lumber," Sebastian said.

Then came the granite quarries, he added: paving stones made from Cape Ann granite were used in New York, Boston, and other cities. He grinned. "Obviously, I could talk history all night. Sorry. But the point is, you and I are just the tiniest blip in our history. Working in Dogtown reminds me of that every day."

"That certainly puts our petty problems in perspective," Anne said. When Sebastian fell silent and started poking at the food on his plate, she nudged him with her elbow. "Why are you really here tonight? You look like you have something on your mind."

Sebastian ran a hand through his auburn hair, streaked with lighter copper strands from spending so much time outdoors. "I do. My sister Paige saw Elly today."

"Really? That's good. Elly hasn't seen any of her old friends. She's feeling a little lost, I think," Anne said. "I haven't been much good to her because I can't go out at night. Also, she's doing all this shopping for Mom's birthday celebration, which is turning into a circus. Elly thinks we're all going to sing and dance to songs from *An American in Paris* because that movie was made the year Mom was born."

Sebastian was looking at her with one eyebrow raised, obviously waiting for her to finish. "I'm babbling. Sorry," she said. "What does Paige seeing Elly have to do with you coming here tonight?"

"Paige told Elly that I've been seeing you."

Immediately, Anne wanted to lodge protests: he was coming around to check on her, no other reason. By the way Sebastian cleared his throat and then hurriedly stood up to scrape the plates, though, Anne knew he had more to say.

God. She hoped this wouldn't turn into a conversation about Jake. What if Laura had told Paige the same awful story, and Paige had repeated it to her brother? Sebastian had witnessed that horrible confrontation with Jake and Laura in the bar. What if he believed Laura's version of things?

Now he suggested they move to the couch. "I always feel like I'm on an interrogation stool here at the counter," he said, pointing to the low-hanging light.

She'd never noticed it before, but Sebastian was much taller than she was. So tall that when she sat on the couch, Anne curled her legs beneath her to avoid touching him, because his body seemed to fill the room.

How did they have sex in that car? They were almost twenty years younger then, of course. More flexible. Sebastian probably had no idea he was her first lover.

Thoughts of that night flooded Anne's memory, unbidden, causing her face to burn so hot that she put her palm to one cheek to cool it.

"You okay?" Sebastian drew his dark brows into a frown.

"I'm fine. Just nervous. You're acting very strange," Anne said, though she supposed he could say the same of her.

"Sorry. I don't mean to act strange. Sometimes I can't help it."

"Join the club," Anne said, and tried to smile, but felt her lower lip quiver and bit it instead.

Sebastian watched her mouth as he said carefully, "Paige didn't know you had a baby. She was surprised to hear that from Elly."

This was unexpected. "Why didn't Paige know? You never told her?"

He shook his head. "I figured that was your business."

"Does Paige mind that you and I are starting to be friends?"

He smiled. "No. I think she's glad, actually."

"Oh. That's a relief." Anne felt her shoulders relax a little.

Sebastian leaned forward and clasped his hands around his knees, his hair falling over his eyes. "Paige wants me to tell you about my wife. I'm just struggling to find the right way to start."

"There's no need," she said. "I mean, talk, if you want. Otherwise, it's okay if you never tell me."

"My sister's right. I need to tell you," he said.

Sebastian began hesitantly at first, the words coming two or three sentences at a time, with long pauses as he felt his way through his history with Jenny: how they'd met in El Salvador, where he'd fallen ill with typhoid fever and nearly died. Might have, if Jenny hadn't cared for him. His decision that theirs was a partnership where each could make the other a better person and the world a better place.

"I'm speaking in clichés—I know," he said. "But we were young and unbelievably idealistic."

When they returned to the States, Jenny had trouble adjusting, he continued. Depression took root. She wore the same clothes day after day. Dishes piled up in the sink until Sebastian came home from work to clean the house and see that she ate something. She saw one therapist after another, and was institutionalized for a few weeks after they'd been married five years. Medication seemed to help.

Then, when Jenny got pregnant, she stopped taking the pills, he said, because she was afraid of hurting the baby. "I'd come home from work and she'd be curled on the bed, as if she were literally trying to hold herself together," he said.

"The poor thing," Anne said. "It sounds like she was in hell. You, too." She felt tension in her own shoulders, watching him.

"Yes," he said. "'Hell.' That's the right word for it."

Once, when Jenny was about seven months pregnant, Sebastian arrived home to find her on the kitchen floor, a carving knife in one hand. She'd made several cuts along her wrists, though nothing deep. "At that point I called 911," he said. "She hated me for that, but I was terrified."

The EMTs convinced Jenny to check herself into the psych ward of the local hospital, but it was a pointless exercise, Sebastian said. "Jenny managed to check herself out and disappear."

When he fell silent, staring across the room with a bleak expression, Anne finally touched his hand. It was cool, rough from his work outdoors. "Where did she go?"

He shrugged. "I still don't know. She came back three days later, wearing the same clothes she'd had on when she left. She was probably on the street somewhere."

That night, Sebastian had talked to Paige on the phone. They'd discussed having Jenny committed; he was worried not only for her safety, but for the baby's. Jenny, who never left the house, took his car keys after they went to bed and drove off.

"She left me a note. I found it when I woke up and she wasn't in bed with me."

"What did it say?" Anne was nearly holding her breath. The tension was unbearable.

"That I shouldn't worry." He shook his head. "As if that were even possible. But the note said Jenny planned to visit her parents for a couple of days. If they agreed with me, she promised to check herself into another psych facility. And, God help me, I chose to believe her. I went back to sleep, figuring I'd call her parents in the morning and check on her."

"You were able to sleep?" Anne was shocked. Then again, who could predict how you'd act during an event that extreme?

He nodded. "I was wiped out. Mentally and physically exhausted. An hour or so later, I got the call from the ER."

Jenny had driven up to New Hampshire along Route 1, and had apparently aimed the wheels of her Toyota straight for the railing while crossing a bridge she must have crossed a thousand times before, Sebastian said. She was going ninety miles an hour. According to the police report, it had been deliberate.

"I might as well have killed her myself," he said.

"Don't say that. It wasn't your fault!" Anne said. "You did everything you could to take care of her."

"No," he said. "I should have gone after her that night. Called the cops. Something!"

"But if you'd tried driving when you were that tired, it might have been you going off the road!"

Sebastian turned to her, his hazel eyes the color of damp bark. "No. Any way I look at it, it was my fault, Anne. Jenny knew that the only reason I didn't leave her was because she was pregnant."

Jenny must have overheard him talking to Paige on the phone about having her committed, he added.

"I thought Jenny was asleep. But she was probably listening from the top of the stairs when I told my sister that I didn't think I could go on being responsible for Jenny's life. My wife killed herself because she knew I'd lost faith in her. In us."

"Oh, Sebastian," Anne said softly. "Don't you see? You had no choice but to demand that she get help. You couldn't have trusted her around the baby otherwise. Or had any sort of marriage."

He looked at her, his eyes bloodshot. "Thank you for saying that, but you're being too kind."

"I'm not," she said. "I'm just sorry you went through all this. You must have felt so alone."

Sebastian was rocking a little next to her on the couch, still bent forward, his elbows on his knees. "What I felt was useless," he said.

Anne touched him again. His arm first, then his back. The heat of Sebastian's skin through his flannel shirt was like an electric charge on her palm, but she kept her hand there.

"Listen," she said fiercely. "Every single thing you did for Jenny and your child, you did out of love. But sometimes loving people isn't enough to save them. They have to save themselves." She wrapped one arm around him and rocked with him, her hip and thigh pressed against his.

"You see why my sister said I needed to tell you," Sebastian said, breaking free of her embrace. He went to the counter, where he poured them each more wine.

"No," she said. "Not really. But it's good you did. You've been carrying all this around for a very long time. It's time you shared it."

He nodded, then pushed his hair out of his eyes with an impatient gesture that by now was familiar to Anne. "I went to therapy for a while. That helped until it didn't. I told a few friends. But you know what's helped the most? Being alone in the woods, doing my work. When I'm outside, I feel more insignificant, somehow. I don't know why that makes me feel better, but it does."

Anne smiled. "I know what you mean. That's why I sit outside on the porch with Lucy or walk with her as often as I can. I feel unimportant in the scope of things when I'm in the woods or near the ocean. Less weighed down by my own stupid little problems."

"You haven't ever told me about Lucy's father." Sebastian was still leaning against the kitchen counter. "Did you meet him in Puerto Rico?"

She nodded, missing the warmth of Sebastian on the couch beside her and wishing she knew how to ask him to sit beside her again. "We were living together when I got pregnant. I thought he was getting divorced. Turns out, he had other ideas."

"Must be nice to be here around family after going through that."

"Yes." Anne wasn't going to get into the ridiculous thing between herself and Laura, or tell him about her mother's odd behavior toward her and Lucy.

Sebastian crossed the room and knelt before her on the braided rug. "I'm glad," he said. "And I'm glad to be spending time with you. I can't lie, though: it's hard sometimes, being around you and Lucy. Painful. I'm afraid I'll never get to experience that sort of bond with a child. At the same time, watching you makes me dare to believe it might be possible someday."

"Good." She said nothing more. She didn't need to: it was as if Sebastian had suddenly invited her inside his thoughts and heart. As if he'd unbuttoned his flannel shirt and drawn her against him. Anne couldn't stop feeling the heat of his skin through that soft fabric against her palm even now, even though she wasn't touching him anymore.

She thought about reaching for him but kept her hands clasped in her lap. It wasn't a good idea. Sebastian was too wounded. So was she.

But sometimes your bad ideas are the ones you feel most compelled to follow through on anyway, she thought, as Sebastian regarded her a moment longer with those changeable hazel eyes, now warmed through with gold, before leaning in slowly to kiss her.

He smelled of wine and pine trees, of seaweed and damp leaves. She gasped in surprise at the warmth of his lips. Then his hands were on her breasts, her breasts so full that he groaned.

Anne leaned forward, wanting to press her breasts into his hands and longing to feel more of him against her. Sebastian caught her as she nearly fell against him.

He lowered her to the rug beside him, then rolled on top of her and kissed her hair, her face, unbuttoning her shirt as she undid his. Then their chests were bare, pressed together, and she thought she'd never been warmer, or more alive, than this.

CHAPTER THIRTEEN

Nine o'clock came and went without Jake or Elly returning home. Laura texted both of them at about nine thirty and received apologies from each.

Jake's text read, *Something came up. Be there soon.*

Elly's was more surprising: *Decided to stay with Paige.*

What about my car? Laura texted Elly back.

I'll get it back to you early, she replied.

Laura didn't really need the car—Kennedy was in a car pool, so she had a ride to school, and anyway, Jake's car was here—but she was disappointed to be spending the evening alone. She had been looking forward to talking to Jake and Elly about Kennedy.

It had been a wonderful afternoon and evening. She'd made dinner with Kennedy and they'd sung in the kitchen to songs on the radio, sometimes making up the words and laughing. Laura couldn't believe how quickly it came back to her: the sheer joy in the art of making noise, the easy harmonizing. At long last, she had found something she and Kennedy could enjoy together. She owed that to her sister.

By eleven o'clock, Jake still hadn't turned up and Laura was drunk. She'd had only one measly glass of wine while eating dinner with Kennedy. But after Kennedy went to bed, Laura turned on a recorded dance competition and finished the bottle of wine, weeping at one contemporary dance number performed by a crippled veteran.

Oh, the courage of people! The beauty of the arts! And now her own daughter, a dancer and a singer!

The house phone rang on the table next to her. For a minute Laura thought the sound was coming from the TV. Nobody ever called this phone except her mother, occasionally, and yet Jake insisted on keeping a landline despite the expense.

She picked up the receiver, which felt absurdly huge and awkward compared to her iPhone. "Hello?"

"Elly? It's Ryder."

"Ryder!" Laura said happily.

"You're not Elly," he said suspiciously.

"No, this is Laura. Her sister." Laura held the phone close to her cheek, remembering what it had been like to talk to her friends on the phone at the inn when she was young. Her mother allowed them to use the phone in the reception area—the only phone in the place—but made a fuss if they tied up the line.

"You could cost me a booking!" she'd yell.

Finally, Sarah had bought an egg timer to keep next to the phone. They were supposed to flip it over the minute they picked up the receiver.

"My mother was a bitch," Laura said, opening her eyes.

"What?" Ryder said.

"A *royal* bitch," Laura confided, giggling. "We were like her three little Cinderellas. All of us might as well have been her stepdaughters. Scrub, scrub, scrub. All the live long day!"

"Laura, am I calling at a bad time? It must be late there."

"Not too late for my sister and husband! They're still out on the town!'" Laura declared, waving an arm at the television, muted now. The contestant who'd been kicked off the show, some large-breasted celebrity chef, was crying her eyes out.

Well, it was time for her to go. Everyone had a time to go. And that chef had danced like two people in a mule costume. This made Laura giggle again.

"Elly and your husband are out together?" Ryder sounded startled.

"No, no, no. Elly is with her friend Paige. You know Paige? No, of course not. That's a Paige from a different book, ha-ha-ha! From way back in *high school*! You're Elly's friend from California! Hey, why aren't you calling her cell phone?"

"She's not picking up. I Googled you."

"Oh." That was odd. Elly always answered her phone. But Laura felt pleased that Ryder had bothered tracking down this number. Elly deserved to have a man in pursuit. In *hot* pursuit: he sounded hot! Every woman needed that. "Maybe she's asleep," Laura suggested. "Or her phone is dead. I don't think she knew she was spending the night with Paige. Her charger's probably here."

"Okay," Ryder said. "Well. Thanks. I'll try her tomorrow. Nice talking to you."

"Wait!" Laura yelled.

There was a pause, then Ryder said, "Yes?"

He had such a nice voice, Laura thought wistfully. Deep. She imagined a business suit, gray, over an open-necked white shirt. A blond guy who surfed in his spare time.

No, no. Surfers were Anne's thing. Elly went for bad boys. "Are you a bad boy, Ryder?" Laura said conversationally.

He laughed. "Not usually."

Ryder's laugh was lovely, too. Slow and warm. Laura closed her eyes, letting herself bathe in the sound. "You should come visit," she said.

"Visit there?"

"Sure!" Laura forced her eyes open. The dance show was over and the gloomy news was on. With the sound off, the anchorwoman looked two-dimensional, too skinny in that blue sleeveless dress. "Ryder, you're in television, right?"

"I'm a cameraman, actually. Mostly for music videos and commercials."

"But you're in the business!" Laura waved a hand in the air. That felt good, so she did it again. "Tell me. Why do newswomen always have to go sleeveless, but the men get to wear suits? Those poor girls must be freezing to death."

He laughed. "Blame it on Michelle Obama and her toned arms."

"Oh." Laura continued waving her hand, covering and uncovering the sleeveless girl child on the television screen with the slow arc of her fingers.

"I would like to see New England," Ryder was saying.

"You've never been?"

"Nope. Never been farther east than Idaho."

Laura's eyes drifted closed again. "And what was that like, Idaho?" She tried to draw the word out the way Ryder did. Like honey.

"So beautiful, it brings you to your knees."

"I bet." Laura sighed. "Well, Massachusetts isn't Idaho. But Cape Ann isn't bad. You should visit while Elly's here." She sat up straight, seized by a brilliant idea. "Hey! You know how to run a camera, right?"

"I'm a cameraman. Yes. That's me." Ryder sounded very solemn now. Perhaps he knew Laura was about to say something of the utmost importance.

"My mother's birthday is in three weeks!" she said. "You should come and film it! It's a very important birthday. Sixty-five years old, but she doesn't look a day over sixty-nine!"

"What?"

"Joke, ha-ha!" Laura said, laughing so hard that tears sprang from her eyes. "But I'm not joking when I say we need a good cameraman to capture the event on film. Could you do that? We would pay you, of course."

"You wouldn't have to pay me," Ryder said. "I'd like to be there."

"Great! You'll stay with us, of course."

She gave him the date of her mother's birthday before hanging up the phone. Another problem solved. She took care of everything, didn't she?

She'd fallen asleep on the couch by the time Jake showed up. Laura smiled at him, then arranged her face in a scowl when she saw the clock beneath the TV. Nearly midnight!

"Where the hell have you been, Jake?" she demanded, then immediately regretted her tone. She sounded like one of those TV housewives, and not even a wife from one of those clever Netflix shows.

"I'm sorry," Jake said.

"Forget the apologies! I need an exclamation!" Laura licked her lips, then corrected herself. "I mean an explanation!"

"Are you drunk, honey?" Jake approached the couch, but stopped several feet away.

"No," she said, hauling herself up the rest of the way. She was at a disadvantage with him standing over her. "Not anymore. What about you? Are *you* drunk? I hope so. That's the only possible reason for you being out this late, unless you had a goddamn accident." Her hand flew to her throat at the thought, but Jake looked fine.

He sighed. And then her fit, sensible, hardworking husband collapsed. Literally: as if someone had suddenly snipped the strings holding him upright, Jake's body puddled onto the floor. Then he turned onto his side and drew his knees to his chest, clutching them.

"Laura," he moaned. "Oh God, Laura, what are we going to *do*?"

Alert now, and frightened besides, Laura rushed around the coffee table to drop onto the floor beside him. She rubbed his shoulders. "What's wrong? Are you ill? Do you have a fever? Are you having a heart attack?"

"No, no, no," Jake moaned.

"Jake, stop it! You're scaring me!" Laura rested her palm on his forehead. He was warm but not hot.

"No, no," Jake went on. "Oh God, no. I can't do this. I just can't!"

Laura couldn't tell if he was moaning in distress or actually weeping. She stopped just short of slapping him. Wasn't that what you were supposed to do when someone got hysterical?

"Look at me!" she demanded. "I need to see your face."

When he finally turned her way, Jake's eyes were dry but red-rimmed, as if he'd been trying to force himself to cry but failing. His mouth was chapped and his nose was, too. Maybe he had a cold.

"Jake," Laura said, fully sober now. "What is going on?"

"Our life is over. Over!" he moaned. "And it's all my fault. I'm so sorry, Laura. God, I'm sorry."

She sat back on her heels. "Don't be melodramatic," she snapped. "What happened? Did you have a bad day at work?"

"Bad day at work?" Jake echoed.

"Yes."

He started laughing, softly at first, then frantically, ha-ha-ha-ha, like one of those terrifying clowns who chased you with a fake chain saw at the Topsfield Fair's haunted mansion. "Oh, God. A *bad day at work*! If only! Somebody suing me for a faulty bridge! A root canal gone horribly wrong! Laura, I would give everything we own if that's what this was about."

Laura sank back down onto the carpet, curling her legs under her. "Well, I wouldn't. I love everything we have," she declared. "You and Kennedy. Our house. The stables. So, no, I would not give it all away for this to be about a bad day at work. You're talking nonsense, Jake. I wish you'd have some coffee and snap out of this." She got to her feet. "You wait here. I'll make coffee."

"No. I don't need coffee." His voice was sharper now. "Look, I'm sorry."

"Stop saying that."

"I can't. And I'll probably say it a hundred more times tonight. Maybe every day of my life." Jake scrubbed at his face with both hands and stood up, swaying a little. "And you don't even know why, do you, Laura? You don't have a clue." He shook his head, his tone forlorn now. "Not a damn clue."

She faced him, speechless for a moment. What was it with these mood swings? Jake was always even-tempered. The man everyone trusted to be gentle. Careful about everything he did.

Except about Anne. Oh, Jesus. Let this not be about Anne.

"So clue me in," she said.

He read her expression. "This has nothing to do with Anne or any other woman, if that's what you're thinking."

"Yes, I was," she said, folding her arms. "Can you blame me?"

"No. You know as well as I do that our marriage is over. You've known it for a while, haven't you?"

Laura went to the couch and sank down onto it. The cushions were still warm from where she'd been sitting during those innocent hours when she'd been watching television and having her wine, waiting for her husband to come home. "Don't be ridiculous. I don't know any such thing. Whatever's wrong with our marriage, we can fix it."

"No," he said, "we can't. I'm sorry." Jake came around the coffee table to sit on the couch with her, a careful distance away. Beyond slapping distance.

"Why not?" she said, folding her hands on her lap.

"Because I'm gay."

She heard the words, but they made no sense. Laura smiled at him. "That's ridiculous. How can you be *gay*? We've known each other twenty years!"

He was silent, looking at her.

She had no choice but to reconsider his statement in their quiet house, with her husband looking at her. Waiting for her to understand.

College. Lacrosse. Parties. The pregnancy and his proposal. The miscarriage: Jake had been so sweet and tender, had insisted they get married anyway.

But before that: Laura had known something was wrong. That their tepid, infrequent lovemaking was nothing like what most of her friends shared with their boyfriends in college or even after college.

Jake was a gentleman, she'd told the few friends she ever discussed sex with openly. "He respects my needs."

Jake wasn't going to push himself on her, she explained. He always waited for her invitation to make love.

Laura knew nothing about sex before Jake. She'd saved herself for the man she planned to marry. She had rationalized that different people had different levels of passion.

But she had also known for a long time that passion was missing in her life. Now she knew why. How could she have been so blind?

"Oh God, Jake." Laura covered her face in her hands, breathing into her palms as if they were a paper bag because she felt dizzy and sick. "How long have you known?"

"A while now."

"How long?" she demanded, dropping her hands.

He sighed. "In college I thought I was bisexual. You know. I experimented a little. Then I met you and fell in love. I wanted to spend my life with you. I still love you. I still want that!"

"Don't," she said, her voice hoarse with the effort of holding in tears. "Please don't."

"But it's true!" he said. "I love your warmth, your kindness, your ability to solve problems, your family. *You*, Laura! I love you and our life with Kennedy. I've stayed in our marriage because I never wanted to hurt either of you. You're everything to me. You're my family!"

"Why tell me all this now? What big revelation have you had?" She stared at him, noting the blue shadow of his beard coming in, the fatigue in his eyes. "You've met someone."

To her horror, he nodded.

"When?"

"It doesn't matter when."

"It does to me!"

"Three years ago. I met him at that conference in Las Vegas," he said, and told the story of Anthony.

And then, because Laura insisted on asking for details she'd regret knowing later, Jake told her how he'd been finding time to spend with Anthony in the last few years, about their house in Medford. About their son.

Their *son*! Laura really did think she might be sick then. Jake sank cross-legged onto the floor in front of her, clasping his hands. In this position, she could be sick all over him. Good.

"Anthony picks up most of the expenses, but he's still in college, trying to finish his degree," Jake said. "So money . . ."

She interrupted him. "I don't want to hear about money. What about Anne?"

He shrugged. "There was never anything between Anne and me."

"Are you saying she was telling the truth all this time? That you made me mistrust my sister *for no reason*? I chose sides, Jake. And I chose *you*!"

"I'm sorry. I hate myself for that. But yes. Anne was telling the truth."

Laura clenched her hands into fists and imagined pummeling her husband's chest. Boxing his ears, whatever that meant. Doing permanent damage to his handsome betrayer's face. She imagined setting fire to him and rolling him into the rug, saving his life, but only after he was howling in pain, the way she was silently howling now.

She thought of something else then and shuddered. "Have you been tested?"

"Yes. You're fine. *We're* fine. And he and I have always used protection."

"Oh God," she moaned, leaning far enough forward to bite the edge of the pillow in her lap. Otherwise, she might have gone after her husband, biting and scratching until there was blood. "How could you do this, Jake? *How?*"

"I couldn't *not*," he said. "It's who I am, Laura."

And there it was: Jake was finally telling her the truth, the complete truth, for perhaps the first time in their lives, ruining everything.

Working with Rodrigo in the kitchen was surprisingly natural. Anne felt at home amid the rapid staccato of chopping blades and spoons ringing on metal pots, the steam rising, the shelves of spices and bins of freshly trimmed herbs.

Maybe she was at ease because she'd been playing here since she was a child. If Flossie couldn't watch her, Sarah sometimes handed her off to Rodrigo. "Here," she'd say, "help sift the flour," or "Stand on this stool and stir the gravy. Tell Rodrigo when it thickens."

Anne might arrange the salads, too, or she garnished the plates and soups. The inn served three meals a day, seven days a week. Breakfast was typically a buffet with an omelet station, but for lunch and dinner, there were choices of two chowders and two soups, several salads, at least a half dozen standard entrées, and the specials.

On one side of the dining room's swinging doors was the kitchen, with its frenzied dance of preparations. On the other side was the tranquil dining room, with a fire lit for chilly days and nights and fresh flowers on the tables in every season. Only china plates and sterling-silver place settings were used, and the glasses were of such thin crystal that to Anne, as a child, they'd seemed to be made of rounded sheets of ice.

At the start of every meal, Rodrigo would watch the customers anxiously, waiting for some sign that his dishes were going to be enjoyed, not just experienced. Anne did that, too: while she was cooking in Puerto Rico, she realized she could read her customers' microexpressions even before they'd finished tasting something.

During her childhood, Rodrigo was a noisy, temperamental young man who could be boundlessly entertaining, with his stories of his vast, extended Brazilian family, or he could cut you with a look. Now he was probably in his midsixties, portly and quiet, a dignified man whose dark hair was threaded with silver. Put him in a suit and he could be an attorney.

Despite his Brazilian background, Rodrigo turned out classic New England meals—lobster, rack of lamb, prime rib—as well as certain recipes unique to the Folly Cove Inn, like a creamy Alfredo pasta dish with chicken, spinach, and artichokes.

As executive chef, Rodrigo supervised those cooking beneath him. The staff included Doris, a wiry, bird-beaked woman in her forties. She'd recently been promoted to sous chef after the last guy left to cook at a hotel in Danvers, she told Anne as she showed her around.

"Rodrigo is extremely invested in the smallest details of what we do," Doris warned her, "like the quality of parsley used as a garnish on the potatoes and whether someone's lamb is medium rare as requested. So if you see something out of whack, speak up."

Anne thought she'd start out as a prep cook, maybe chopping things for salads, but instead Rodrigo talked to her about what she'd been doing in Puerto Rico, then made her a line cook. The pace and duties suited her, especially since she was working alongside both the vegetable cook and the pastry chef.

The other Folly Cove cooks were men younger than she was, probably in their late twenties. They had met at the local vocational school, and Rodrigo had asked them to come in on Monday with Anne so they could work the kinks out of a few new recipes.

Anne's shift was from eleven to eight, with a long enough break in midafternoon that she could walk back to the cottage and nurse Lucy. Flossie pronounced the baby "good as gold" when Anne returned at eight o'clock Monday night and nursed Lucy once more before putting her down for the night.

Flossie seemed to be in no hurry to leave. She shared the dinner of mashed potatoes, roast chicken, and squash that Anne had brought back, and they opened a bottle of chardonnay.

"I can't thank you enough for watching Lucy," Anne said as the wine warmed her throat and loosened her shoulders. She massaged her neck. "I'll find a sitter by the weekend."

Flossie waved a hand. "No need. Let me watch the brat. Lucy's welcome in my drumming classes, and I'm only teaching one yoga class this weekend. My students won't mind if Lucy joins us. I can set her playpen up in the studio." She grinned. "I'll have that baby doing her downward dogs and chanting 'om' before you know it."

They talked about Rodrigo and the kitchen staff then. Anne could hear the sea sighing below the cottage and imagined it, black and sparking beneath the full moon, frothing white along the shore.

She remembered another moonlit autumn night when she was sixteen and brokenhearted over some boy. Bereft, too, because Elly had recently left for college. She'd come here to Flossie for comfort, as she usually did.

Flossie had encouraged Anne to talk about the boy, even to cry a little. Then she'd led Anne down to the beach. They'd stood barefoot in the cold damp sand of Folly Cove, gazing out at the angry-looking charcoal water and the gleaming white path cast across it by the moon.

Suddenly, a trio of humpback whales crested directly below the moon, making Anne gasp. "Did you see that, Aunt Flossie? Did you?" She'd hopped up and down on the sand, her broken heart forgotten.

Flossie had laughed and told Anne she often saw whales feeding off Jeffrey's Ledge. She began sharing facts about whales then, some of which Anne still remembered: how the blue whale was bigger than any dinosaur, its heart the size of a car and loud enough to be heard two miles away. How beluga whales could imitate human speech, and humpback whales learned songs from one another.

"What I want you to remember, Anne," Flossie had said as they'd walked back to the cottage that night, "is that you are but one small creature in an infinite universe of wonders. Open your eyes to the marvels around you, and you will always keep the small things in perspective. Even love is a small thing, compared to what's all around us."

Now, watching Flossie get up from the stool and wash her plate, then stand it carefully in the dish drainer next to the sink, Anne felt a rush of love for her. She suddenly wanted to buy her a gift.

"When's your birthday?" she asked as Flossie picked up her coat, preparing to leave.

Flossie smiled. In the dim light of the cottage, the smile made her look like a druid who could happily dwell in a tree trunk. "I don't believe in birthdays," she said. "No point in celebrating the day you were born. Time is an artificial human construct. Every day should be a celebration of life."

"Oh, come on," Anne said. "Just tell me."

"No." Flossie put on her jacket, still smiling.

"Why not?"

"Because if I tell you, you'll do something silly, like throw me a party. Nobody needs to make a fuss over me. Save your energy to fete your mother."

Anne looked at her curiously, still remembering that night on the beach when she was sixteen. "Were you ever in love?" she asked.

"Of course. We all fall in love."

"Were you in love with lots of people? Or just once?"

"I've been in love many times. I expect I'll fall in love again while I'm still on the green side of the sod." Flossie adjusted her jacket collar.

"Okay, but who was your first true love?"

"You don't want to hear all that nonsense," Flossie said.

"I do!"

Flossie sighed and came back over to the couch. "All right. I'll humor you." She sat down and unbuttoned her coat. "He was British. I met him in France, where we were both studying at the same monastery. France has a great tradition of training Westerners in Tibetan Buddhism," she added, "largely due to the influence of Alexandra David-Néel."

"Who?"

Flossie gave her a pitying look. "You really ought to read more, dear," she said mildly. "David-Néel was a French explorer, a feminist and spiritualist who visited Tibet when it was still closed to foreigners. She wrote about thirty books and greatly influenced beat writers like Jack Kerouac and Ginsberg. You've heard of them, presumably?"

Anne made a face. "I did graduate from college."

"Yes, well, see that your education doesn't stop there."

Again, Flossie's rebuke was mild, but Anne knew she meant it. "Fine. Back to the love of your life," she said. "What was his name?"

"Clark." Flossie said his name softly. "He was older than I was and had already been married and divorced. He'd traveled all over the world working odd jobs. A bit of a gypsy." She smiled. "A devilishly handsome man, especially attractive to a plain girl like me."

"You've never been plain!" Anne protested.

"Yes, well, I've never been beautiful, either. Not like your mother or you girls," Flossie said. "At any rate, I thought I'd met my soul mate. We studied together at the monastery, and for a while we traveled together. We went to Thailand, where I taught English, and to Nepal and Bali. In between, we'd return to the monastery, where Clark was eventually put in charge of the gardens as the monastery expanded and accepted more religious scholars. Not all of them wanted to be monks or nuns, of course. Some were simply studying Buddhism to practice it in their own lives. I helped teach some of the beginning classes and worked in the kitchen." She smiled. "Imagine! Me in a kitchen! A wonder I didn't poison anyone."

"Flossie, what happened with Clark?" Anne pressed, eager to hear the rest of the story.

"He was trying to decide whether to stay at the monastery full-time right around the time I got the call from Neil, begging me to come home for his wedding." Flossie spread her hands and studied them, as if her own journey might be revealed there, mapped across her calloused palms. "Of course I came home. I wasn't about to miss my own brother's wedding." She swallowed hard, not lifting her eyes from her hands. "Shortly after I returned to France, Clark had made up his mind."

Anne put her hand over one of Flossie's. "He became a monk?"

Flossie looked up and nodded. "I didn't blame him, of course. It was the right path. Clark never belonged in the real world."

"Don't you ever wonder what would have happened if you'd stayed in France?"

"Water under the bridge," Flossie said, waving that thought away. "I left the monastery soon after that, traveled on my own for a while, teaching English here and there and trying to find where I belonged. I came back to Folly Cove to help when Elly was born, and then you came along. You girls were my reward. I've been lucky enough to fall in love a few times since returning. Nothing serious, but enough to keep me entertained. I have a good life." She grinned, then squeezed Anne's hand and stood up, buttoning her coat again.

Anne walked her to the door, where Flossie kissed her cheek good night, and then, to Anne's surprise, embraced her. "Are you okay?" Anne said, rubbing her aunt's narrow back.

Flossie pulled away again and nodded, her cheeks flushed, her gray hair crested high. "Look, I need to speak with you and your sisters all together," she said. "Can the three of you come see me the day after tomorrow? I need to tell you something important."

"Can't you tell me now?"

"I'm afraid not." Flossie pulled on her black woolen cap. "We need to have a family meeting. I've already spoken with Laura and Elly. They said they can come midmorning, maybe ten o'clock. Is that all right with you?"

"Yes, I think so. That should give me enough time to feed and dress the little beast." Anne kissed her aunt's soft cheek again and noticed she was trembling. Yet the cottage was warm and Flossie had on her jacket.

"Can't you at least give me a hint?" Anne asked, a stone of worry heavy in her chest.

"No, dear, I'm afraid not. Now, good night. Sleep well."

To her shock, Flossie turned away abruptly, but not fast enough to hide the tears sliding down her cheeks before closing the door behind her.

CHAPTER FOURTEEN

"Try to eat. A little nosh, at least. You need to keep up your strength," Gil said. "Grief burns a lot of calories. I should know."

"Stop bullying me." Sarah put down her fork. "I said I don't have an appetite. Yet you insisted on going out to lunch. You and Rhonda. Impossible, both of you." She balled up her napkin and set it on top of her plate so the waiter would have no choice but to remove it.

Gil only laughed. "Oy vey. You could singe a fellow's scalp with that glare." He patted the top of his balding head between the ring of graying curls. "Seriously. Is it on fire?"

She refused to be amused. Sarah smoothed her skirt and looked away.

It had been six days since she'd received the letter from Neil's attorney. Flossie hadn't told the girls yet, but she was threatening to do it tomorrow if Sarah didn't.

"I said I'd give you a week to keep this news to yourself," Flossie said when they ran into each other by chance in the dining room this morning. "Time's almost up. I've invited the girls to my house tomorrow at ten o'clock. I will break the news to them then, if you haven't, and I'll deliver their father's ashes. There ought to be a memorial service. The girls need closure."

"They've forgotten all about him," Sarah had argued in a furious whisper. "Why dredge up all that old stuff and break their hearts? And if anyone has a memorial service, it should be me! I was Neil's wife! That's the proper thing."

"Then take the ashes," Flossie said, adding firmly, "Before tomorrow, you need to tell the girls about Neil, and about everything else, too. I can't keep this to myself any longer, and your children deserve to know." Then she walked away, the little tyrant.

A few minutes later, Rhonda had brought Gil into Sarah's office. She'd told him about Neil, of course, and Gil had arrived carrying a bouquet of lilies and his condolences. He had invited Sarah to "step out for a little while and forget your sorrows." She'd been so rattled by Flossie's threat that she'd consented.

But there was no escape from her memories. Just now, for instance, as Sarah turned determinedly away from Gil and looked outside, she could see the sea heaving itself relentlessly against the rocks below the window. He'd brought her to a restaurant on Rocky Neck. On the opposite side of the cove was the city of Gloucester, its skyline a mix of steeples, old brick mills, boxy warehouses, and Victorians: every shape imaginable and all in bright colors, like a child's jigsaw puzzle.

Rocky Neck was home to one of the country's oldest working artists' colonies. Sarah often sent tourists here so they could shop in the galleries but seldom came here herself. When did she ever have time to play tourist?

Families walked along the shore below them, scurrying like crabs among the rocks as they filled their plastic buckets like every generation before them. An endless stream of humanity had been arriving in New England from Europe to hunt for sea treasures since the fifteenth century, and the indigenous people were here doing the same hundreds of years before that. Yet who remembered any of the ordinary people, their joys and struggles? Who would remember her or her daughters?

Sarah watched a group of small children in bright jackets poking around in the tide pools with sticks, and thought about how, when her own girls were small, it was always Flossie who took them to the beach after Neil left, so Sarah could work.

"I've been a terrible mother," she said.

Gil chewed quietly—by the looks of him, he wasn't the sort of man to give up on a meal—waiting for evidence of this. When she didn't provide any, he said, "Yet somehow your daughters grew up and made lives of their own."

"You don't know anything about them."

"You forget I have a mole at the inn."

"Rhonda?"

He nodded. "Rhonda has told me all about your daughters. From what I hear, they don't seem to be raving mad. At least not outwardly." Gil had finished everything on his plate—broiled salmon with vegetables and salad, the meal of a man who had been told by his doctor to watch his blood sugar—and put down his fork. "If I'm remembering correctly, your girls also aren't homeless or drug addicts or even car thieves. All three work and live independently. In my book, they're wildly successful. So that makes you a good mother by default."

"No," Sarah said. "It only means they thrived despite my neglect. After Neil left, all I did was work."

"You provided a roof over their heads and put clothes on their backs," Gil said. "So you were never a balabosta—so what? Stop beating yourself up. You taught your girls to work for a living. *Mazel tov!* That's more important these days than knowing how to clean a house." He removed the napkin from her plate and gestured at the food. "Three bites. That's all I ask."

Sarah made a dismissive noise, but somehow his words had calmed her. She obediently forked three bites of salad into her mouth and then more, too, as Gil told her about his own brother, who had killed himself at the age of twenty. "Bipolar," Gil said, "back in the days when the doctors didn't know about such things."

Sarah eyed him suspiciously. Was there any way this man could have heard about her own problems all those years ago?

"I'm very sorry," she said. "That must have been terrible."

Gil waved a hand. "It was. Still, every day I'm grateful my own sons didn't inherit whatever genes drove my brother to his grave."

And that mention of his own sons, of course, compelled Sarah to ask about Gil's children, which led her to eat the rest of her salad and a dinner roll, too, while he told her that one was an engineer in Providence while the other boy was earning a master's degree in biochemistry at Boston University.

He'd seen more of them after their mother died, Gil said, "Probably because they're afraid I'll off myself and don't want to live with the guilt. But I think I've convinced them now that I'm okay."

"And are you really?" she asked.

"Of course not."

Sarah smiled, and Gil smiled back, though his dark eyes were solemn and his mouth turned down a little at the corners, like an actor forced to perform a part he hadn't perfected yet. "I'm not okay, either," she said, "but I can't figure out why. You deserve to mourn your wife. You lived with her, took care of her. I haven't even seen Neil for thirty years. What do I have to be sad about?"

"You're sad because somebody who was dear to you, a man who knew you back when you were young and beautiful and probably hopeful, too, is no longer among us," Gil said at once, then added, "Though you're still beautiful."

Sarah laughed. "Just when I was starting to think I could trust you, you say something ridiculous," she said, but she was unreasonably flattered. She couldn't remember the last time a man had said anything about her appearance. "I think you're right, that I miss knowing Neil was in the world more than his presence. I'm sad about him being gone because he was a good man, really, and because I know this news will hit my daughters hard," she said. "But I'm angry, too, because Neil never came back to apologize, or to let me apologize even, or to see what I'd done at the inn. In a way, I'd taken a dare. My husband left partly because he didn't think the Folly Cove Inn would succeed."

"More's the pity that he didn't return, then," Gil said. "You've done a wonderful job."

"Yes, but somehow it seems less of an achievement because Neil never saw me prove him wrong," Sarah said, and then her throat tightened up and she felt as if all the salad she'd just consumed was knotted in her stomach, a ball of green fiber pressing against her diaphragm.

"Excuse me," she said, and hurriedly stood up and went to the ladies' room, where she held her wrists under cold water and couldn't look at herself in the mirror, knowing what she'd see: an old woman hunched with grief.

When she emerged again, Gil was waiting in the hallway outside the restrooms, her coat and purse over one arm. He helped her into the coat but insisted on carrying her purse to the car, where he opened the door for her and waited for her to sit and do up her seat belt. Then he took a blanket from the backseat and laid it over her legs, tucking it in tenderly around her thighs.

"Are you all right?" he said.

"I will be. I think I'm still in shock."

"Of course you are. And I have to say the aftershocks will keep coming," Gil said. "My wife has been gone for a year, but I keep being reminded whenever it's the first time I do something without her that we used to do together."

Sarah stared at his hands fussing around her lap—brown as wood, veined, yet somehow still strong and capable, with their broad palms and sturdy fingers—and had the oddly comforting sensation that she'd been here before with him, doing exactly this, as if she'd come home to him after a long journey.

Then Sarah inhaled sharply and shook her head. She was an old woman with an old woman's delusions. "Thank you for understanding," she said. "Please, let's go back to my apartment."

"As you wish," he said, and drove slowly back to the inn, talking amiably about nothing.

Gil insisted on walking her into the apartment, still carrying her purse over one arm and yet somehow looking like a man who could hold his own in a bar brawl, with his stocky build and slightly bowed legs.

"Coffee or tea?" he said, moving straight to the kitchen as if he were coming home, too.

Sarah dropped onto the couch and pulled off her boots, curled her feet beneath her. "Tea," she said, and rested her head against the back of the sofa.

When she felt his weight on the couch beside her, she opened her eyes and saw that Gil had made two mugs of tea and put them on a tray with cream, sugar, and a packet of graham crackers, her guilty pleasure since she was a child and it was all her mother could ever get for the food stamps at the corner market.

"My girls don't know about their father," she said.

Gil picked up one of the mugs and blew on its surface, then said, "What don't they know? That he's dead?"

"Yes. Or that we were still in touch occasionally. I wanted them to forget him because I didn't want them wishing for a father they couldn't have."

"It sounds like you were protecting them."

"You have a way of putting things that makes me sound nearly saintly." Sarah considered the other mug, then picked it up. Not to drink the tea, but to hold something warm in her hands.

"My therapist calls it 'reframing.' Are you planning to tell them he's gone?" Gil asked. There was no judgment in his voice.

"I don't want to. I'm afraid they'll take it hard. My girls are so emotional. So full of love and longing. Strange, when I'm the opposite."

"Really? Are you?"

"Yes," Sarah said. "I figured out a long time ago how to compartmentalize my emotions and stop longing for anything. It was easier. My childhood was difficult, though my daughters don't know that about me, either."

She stopped talking then because she'd sloshed some of the tea onto her wrist. She winced, but welcomed the heat as a sharp reminder that she was telling this man things she'd kept for decades from her own family.

"I apologize," she said. "I'm not usually one for confessions. Something about you must bring it out in me."

"Then I'm honored," Gil said. "And for the record? I happen to think it's not always such a good thing for our children to know everything about us. Parents deserve privacy, too."

"That sounds like a bumper sticker."

"Good idea. I'll have to patent it." He reached for a graham cracker and crunched it shamelessly between his teeth, spilling crumbs down the front of his blue sweater. "So will you tell them?"

"If I don't, my husband's sister, Flossie—she lives in that house on the beach below the inn—intends to do it for me. She'll tell them everything, she says."

"Everything? You mean about you, too?"

"Yes."

"That doesn't seem right." Gil sounded indignant.

"No. But there's not much I can do about it." Sarah leaned her head back against the couch and closed her eyes again. She had started to shiver. Perhaps she was coming down with something.

"You're cold," Gil said. "Let me get you a blanket."

"I think I'm just exhausted from worrying about what my daughters will think when they find out I'm an impostor. Half the things I've told them have been lies. They're going to hate me."

"You should lie down if you're exhausted, *bubbeleh*."

"That would be the logical thing," she agreed, but Sarah was too exhausted to move.

After a few minutes, she felt Gil stand up and remove the tea things as he said, "You know, we're all impostors in our own lives, if only because we walk around on two legs like we're not animals," he said. "Your daughters might hate you for a while. So what? It's the privilege of the young to hate the mistakes of the old. Then they get old and find out what's what."

Sarah smiled, still with her eyes closed. "You're an optimist."

"A realist," he said. "An ex-optimist who's made a mistake or two himself."

She'd thought Gil was about to say good-bye and let himself out of the apartment, but then he was back, sliding his arms beneath her.

Her eyes flew open. "What the hell do you think you're doing?"

"Taking you to bed," Gil said. He laughed at her expression. "No, not like that."

"You can't carry me there. That's ridiculous."

"Indulge me," he said.

To her amazement, Gil picked her up easily and carried her down the hallway, where he toed open the bedroom door—closed, as always, because she left the heat off in this room—and said, "It's like a friggin' icebox in here," then lay her on the bed.

"What can I say? I'm a Yankee."

"Yeah, a Yankee. Not an Eskimo." Gil flipped the eiderdown quilt over her from one side, then added the afghan from the foot of the bed, tucking everything around her until she felt positively swaddled. After that he stretched out beside her.

"Don't get any ideas," Sarah said, though the heat of his solid body was instantly and immeasurably comforting.

"No worries about that. I don't take my clothes off unless it's at least eighty degrees," he said.

Sarah laughed and closed her eyes, forgetting, if only for a moment, who she was and what had happened, and all the troubles that might lie before her.

Anne spent most of the day working with the pastry chef, Sue, who was round, pale, and sweet unless you crossed her with an opinion of your own. She watched Anne make the oatmeal raisin cookies that her mother always kept in the reception area, several dozen of them.

Once Sue was satisfied with that effort, she put her hands on her hips and said, "Well, what's next? The bread?"

She walked Anne through the inn's bread dough recipes—sourdough and French bread today—and then, when the loaves were rising, asked her opinion about desserts. Anne suggested a cake she'd experimented with in Puerto Rico: a chocolate brown sugar butter cake.

"I could use a spiced pumpkin frosting since it's fall," she added.

Sue clapped her fat hands together in a puff of flour. "Terrific suggestion," she said, and left Anne alone after that.

Anne checked her phone. Thankfully, the recipe—culled from a magazine some tourist had left at the bar in Luquillo—was still in her notes. The beauty of this recipe was that she could partially freeze the cake layers to make them easier to fill and frost, so she was less apt to make mistakes in finishing it off.

She decided to triple the recipe, given that the restaurant had been full every night she'd been here, and began searching for ingredients: brown and white sugars, eggs, unsweetened cocoa, flour, baking powder, salt, baking soda, sour cream, and chocolate syrup. Everything was here. There were even cans of pumpkin puree and white chocolate bars for the cream cheese frosting. Maybe she'd add pecans as well.

Three hours later, she was finished. The cakes were the best she'd ever made. Anne asked Rodrigo to taste a sliver of one to be sure, and his brown eyes gleamed with pleasure.

At two o'clock, she was done for the day, plus she had tomorrow off. A good thing, since her arms and hands ached from the dough and her back was tired.

At home, she made soup from a leftover chicken she'd roasted the night before, adding whatever veggies she could find in the fridge, then put Lucy in the backpack and hiked through Halibut Point. She invited Flossie to come with her on the walk, and to share the soup as well, but her aunt shook her head and seemed subdued.

"Just tired," she answered when Anne asked if anything was wrong. "I'll see you tomorrow with your sisters, though, right? Around ten o'clock?"

"Sure," Anne said, though she'd forgotten all about that mysterious meeting. "I wish you'd just tell me now what it's about."

"No. The three of you ought to be together," Flossie said firmly, but her eyes held none of their usual mischief.

Maybe the baby was wearing her out. Lucy was enough to wear anyone out, Anne thought crossly some hours later, as she tried eating soup with one hand while keeping Lucy from screaming. She must be teething: yes, there was a bud, a shimmer of white, the gum inflamed around it, poor thing.

Anne finished her dinner and was about to consider taking another walk with the baby to see if that would soothe her when someone knocked at the door. Sebastian!

No, it couldn't be. Sebastian was out of town for three days, at a conference in Washington, D.C. They'd had their one night together—she was flooded with desire every time she remembered how they'd started making love on the floor of the cottage, on this small rug, until he'd gathered her in his arms and carried her to bed, her bra pushed up over her breasts and her panties halfway down her thighs because they'd been in too much of a hurry to undress properly.

Then there was the baby: finally they'd slid the crib out of the bedroom because Anne felt too self-conscious to make love with Lucy in the room. Mercifully, for once Lucy had stayed asleep.

He'd had to leave for Washington the next day. It worried her that she hadn't heard anything from him, especially knowing how vulnerable he was, now that he'd told her about his wife.

And about his unborn child. Oh God. To lose a baby.

Anne kissed Lucy's head as she opened the front door. As tired as she was, she was grateful to have her baby right here in her arms.

To her shock, it was Laura who stood on the porch outside, looking miserable. Her face was leached of color and her eyes were a flat cement gray. She wore an oversize sweatshirt and stained jeans, and her hair was unwashed. She had aged ten years since the last time Anne saw her.

"My God, what is it? Is everything all right?" Anne asked over Lucy's shrieks.

"Not here, apparently," Laura said, eyeing the baby. "What's going on with the kid?"

"Teething, I think."

Laura placed a gentle hand on Lucy's forehead. Then she worked her fingers into the baby's open mouth and felt the gums. "Yup. Let me in and I'll help."

"You're already in," Anne grumbled, but stepped aside.

Her sister went straight to the galley kitchen, stomping in her usual way even without boots. She pulled open the drawer with the potholders, pulled one out, and ran it under cold water. Laura stuck the potholder in the freezer for a moment, then returned and handed it to Lucy, who seemed to understand that she should jam it into her mouth.

The silence in the house was absolute except for the steady rhythm of the waves against the beach below and the ticking yellow kitchen clock, which, with Laura standing here, sounded like a bomb about to go off.

"I should have thought of that," Anne said. "The books always say to keep washcloths in the freezer for them to suck on to numb the gums."

"Frozen bagels," Laura said. "That's what I used for Kennedy. They last forever."

All Anne's long-dormant fantasies about having her sisters around when she had her first baby resurfaced momentarily. In college, whenever she'd fantasized about getting married and having a family of her own, she'd imagined she and her sisters would share maternity clothes and recipes and help each other through teething and tantrums. Their children would play at the Folly Cove beach every summer, knowing each other as family.

If she had stayed here and had a baby, Laura could have taught her to be a good mother, just as Laura had taught her how to tie her shoes and write her name when Anne was a child.

If Laura didn't hate her, that was.

"Thanks. I'll buy bagels next time I shop." Anne kept her eyes fastened on her sister's face, but Laura's expression was still flat. What had she come to accuse her of now?

Kennedy, she decided. Laura's daughter had visited several times. Well, she might as well come clean and get this showdown started.

"Kennedy's great with the baby," she said. "I suppose you've found out she's been coming around here to help out. Lucy loves her."

"I know. It's fine."

"It is?" Anne went to the couch and sat down. She wasn't sure whether to be relieved or not when Laura followed her, still with Lucy in her arms.

It was all like a dream, really, seeing Laura hold Lucy, but Anne couldn't decide whether the dream was good or bad.

"Yes," Laura said. "Though I was pissed off at first when Kennedy told me. You could have asked me first."

"How?" Anne demanded. "I was afraid you might slap me again!"

"I know. I'm sorry." Laura inhaled so sharply that Lucy looked up at her, grinning. Laura smiled back, but her lips were trembling. "Sorry. I'm a mess. You'd better take her." She passed the baby back to Anne. "You're probably wondering why I'm here."

"Oh, no. This all feels very normal," Anne said.

Lucy immediately started wriggling, so Anne stood her up on the couch. Lucy bounced on the cushions, shrieking.

"Jesus. I've forgotten how loud babies can be," Laura said, raising her voice above the noise. "Anyway, look. I came to apologize."

About freakin' time, Anne thought. "Why now?"

"Jake told me the truth." Laura started crying, but it was almost like she was standing under a faucet: water was running down her cheeks without any other outward sign of her weeping. "He told me a lot of things, actually."

"Like what?" Anne asked, thinking this day couldn't get any stranger. But it did. Laura said, "Jake's gay."

"What?" Anne's tone caused the baby to stop jumping and stare at her. Anne made a funny face while keeping her eyes on her sister.

"Yes," Laura said, sniffing hard. "He told me last night."

Anne stared at her, too shocked to speak, as her sister got up and went to the paper towel rack. When Laura pulled, several towels came unraveled. She took them all, fluttering the paper like a scarf beside her as she sat back down on the couch. She blew her nose on one end. "Apparently he's in love with another man. They have a son."

Anne didn't ask about the mechanics of that. She was already too confused and grief-stricken, looking at Laura's ravaged face and slumped shoulders. "Why did he go through that whole charade with me, then?"

"To see if he could get it up for women who aren't me, apparently."

"If he couldn't do that for you, I don't see how he could for anyone," Anne said.

Laura sniffed again. "Thanks for that."

"Have you told Kennedy?"

"No. Jake and I decided to tell her together next weekend. That will give us time to calm down and figure out what to say. Kennedy went to school this morning, and then she's spending the night with a new friend. I canceled my lessons for the afternoon. I just couldn't cope."

Anne wondered whether it would come as a surprise to Kennedy that her father was gay. She couldn't remember much of what her own parents had actually said during their various shouting matches, but the substance was clear enough: Dad thought their mother was playing around, and Mom said he was a lazy drunk.

"I'm so sorry, Laura," she said.

Laura shook her head. "I'm the one who should be apologizing. If I'd been using my head, I would have realized something was horribly wrong with my marriage. I mean, I guess I did know that, on some level, but I was too scared to dig deep enough to figure out what was really going on."

Anne thought about Colin, about his "business" trips to New York and his late-night phone calls. "It's not always easy to see the truth when you love someone," she said. "But it will be all right. You and Jake both love Kennedy. You'll work out a way to tell her, and you'll both be there for her. You followed the path you thought you were on, as Flossie would say. You got married and had a wonderful daughter. Your path just didn't lead where you thought it would."

"Thanks, sweetie." Laura smiled and held out her arms. "Here. Give that baby back to me."

CHAPTER FIFTEEN

Finding Colin was simple. Elly Googled his name and it popped up immediately. He'd been blogging about his still-unfinished novel, of course. Building his freakin' platform. She felt a zing of satisfaction and searched for the address under his wife's name, figuring if Wifey was the one paying the bills, she'd be the one whose address and phone number were listed in the white pages online.

Bingo: Writer Guy and Wifey lived in Brooklyn, just four hours away.

Elly was using her laptop in the kitchen. The empty house loomed around her. Not even Kennedy was home. She wondered if Jake had told Laura the truth last night. Guilt pricked at the back of her neck: if he had, it would be Elly's fault when the marriage fell apart.

Whatever happened, Elly hoped Jake would keep his promise and not tell Laura that Elly had forced him to come out.

"It'll go better with Laura if you tell her everything yourself," Elly had decided last night, as she, Jake, and Anthony tried to pretend they were hungry enough to eat pizza. "If Laura thinks you're doing this on your own, she'll be more inclined to believe you have her best interests at heart."

Once Elly finished the search for Colin's address on her computer, she called Anne to tell her, and was shocked to hear Laura's voice in the background. "Laura's at your place?"

"Yes. Elly, something awful has happened."

"I'll be right there," Elly said, after almost slipping up and saying, "I know."

At the cottage, she could see from Laura's haunted expression that the conversation with Jake had happened, but she continued to pretend she didn't know anything. She'd have to wait for Laura to confide in her.

Laura was holding Lucy, who was sucking on a dish towel. "What did you do, dip the towel in vodka to keep the kid quiet?" Elly asked.

Laura laughed. A thin sound, but genuine enough. "No. It's frozen so she can gum it to death. She's got jaws like a pit bull."

"You okay?" Elly asked softly. "You don't look okay."

"I think the answer's no, but I'm numb right now," Laura said. She told Elly about Jake while Anne carried Lucy into the other room to change her diaper and put her in pajamas.

"I still can't believe I was so stupid. And so blind!" Laura concluded.

"You were trying to make your marriage work," Elly said. "Jake genuinely loves you. I think that's probably what made it so hard for him to tell you." She stopped herself before she could slip up and say anything about following Jake and seeing his other life. His other family! "Does Anne know?"

Laura nodded. "I've apologized to her, of course."

"Good. And I've got just the adventure to take your mind off Jake," Elly said. "Anne! Get in here! I found Colin. Laura and I are going to help you get the child support he owes you." She showed them the map on her phone and explained her plan.

"But we can't just drive to his house in New York." Anne's face looked pinched, the freckles standing out across her nose. "Barbara will be there!"

Elly shrugged. "So? It's not like your existence will be a news flash to her. And it's time you got some financial support. Colin owes you that much."

"No," Anne said. "He didn't even *want* a baby."

"Did you plan to get pregnant?" Laura asked.

"No! It was an accident. We took a chance." Anne shot Laura a look. "For the record? You were right about the whole 'don't-date-married-guys' thing."

"Thank you. Though, for the record? I'm a bigger screw-up than you are. Remember that anytime I give you advice."

Laura paced the room, looking fierce now. Of them all, Laura was the one who had inherited their mother's ruthless determination. She would be fine without Jake, Elly decided with relief. "Come on," she said. "Let's hit the road."

"Elly's right, Anne," Laura said. "You made a mistake, but so did he. Legally, you're both financially responsible for raising Lucy. You need to make him help you."

"But Colin doesn't want anything to do with her! Or with me." Anne looked like she might cry. "He made that clear from the beginning."

"Then he should also have made it clear to his penis that no babies were to be made," Laura said.

Elly laughed. "Yes, Colin absolutely should have given that penis of his a good, stern talking to!"

Anne stared at them, and then suddenly she was laughing, too, hard enough that she had to clutch her side. "Stop!"

Elly wiped her eyes. She'd forgotten what it was like to laugh with her sisters. Nobody else could transport her to this euphoric, drunken state of mirth. "Let's go," she said. "If we leave now, we can be in Brooklyn by eight. I know they're home because I called them."

Anne stood up straight. "You did *not*."

"I did. Barbara answered the phone. I told her I was selling magazine subscriptions, and she said I ought to be careful, because they were on a no-call list. I thanked her and promised not to call again."

"Crafty," Laura said. "But they could still go out to dinner or a movie or something. That's a long drive to make if nobody's home."

"Oh, they'll be there," Elly said. "It's a weekday. Even if they go to the movies, I'm betting it would be an early show."

Then, without any more discussion, the three of them were putting on their jackets and heading for Laura's car, as if they took sisterly road trips every day of their lives.

Lucy settled easily into the rhythm of the ride and fell asleep within ten minutes. Elly glanced at Anne in the rearview mirror, and was relieved to see that her little sister looked less tense now, her eyes drifting shut, too.

Beside her, Laura was sitting rigidly upright, staring out the windshield as if it were her job to mentally steer the car through traffic.

"You're going to be okay," Elly said softly.

Laura didn't turn her head to look at her. "I know. In a weird way, I think I'm relieved that there's an actual reason my marriage imploded. A reason that has nothing to do with me."

Elly nodded and patted her sister's hand on the seat.

Anne had to stop and nurse Lucy by the time they reached the last rest stop on the turnpike before Connecticut. They piled out of the car and ordered cheeseburgers and fries that tasted of fish and old oil. They ate while Anne fed the baby, munching their way through the awfulness.

"It's like you get halfway through one of these burgers and you wonder what the hell you're eating and hate yourself," Laura said.

"But you finish it anyway," Elly said. "It's like a pact with the devil: no cheeseburger shall be left half-eaten."

"Rodrigo would have a fit if he saw us," Anne said.

Laura gave her a curious look as they headed back out to the parking lot. "Are you happy cooking? Do you like it better than teaching?"

"So far," Anne said. "And I think I can make enough money working part-time in the evenings so I can spend the days with Lucy."

"I'm wowed you and Laura are both such good moms," Elly said. "You give me hope." They were back in the car by then. "I mean, we didn't have much of a role model, right? Mom wasn't exactly Mother Teresa."

"More like Miss Hannigan," Laura agreed with a laugh.

"Who?" Anne asked.

"You know: the woman who runs the orphanage in the musical *Annie*," Elly said, and broke into song: "'Little girls, little girls . . .'"

Laura joined in. "'Everywhere I turn I can see them!'"

Anne was laughing. "Oh, man. Poor Mom. Remember how we used to sneak into her closet and play dress-up with her evening gowns? And that time I drew a sunset on the porch floor with her lipsticks?"

"'Poor Mom'? You need your head examined," Laura said. "God. All those chores. Bathroom after bathroom. Making beds. Peeling potatoes. She was a slave driver!"

"Well, Dad wasn't around, so she was probably panicked all the time about money," Anne said.

Elly rolled her eyes at Anne in the rearview mirror. "Still. She could have given us a hug once in a while. Would it have killed her? I see you two kiss your daughters every day and remember how we had none of that. We probably have whatever Romanian orphans all have."

"Attachment disorder," Laura said. "I think Mom has an attachment disorder. Which is really weird, since she grew up with rich parents in a tony part of Boston."

"Still, we turned out all right," Anne said.

"Speak for yourself," Elly and Laura said in nearly perfect unison, and then all three of them were laughing hard enough that Lucy woke up and threatened to cry again until Anne popped a piece of frozen bagel in her mouth, courtesy of one of the sympathetic workers behind the counter at the Dunkin' Donuts where they'd bought coffee.

Colin's house was on an upscale, narrow street of brownstones. Elly decided it was the sort of neighborhood where nannies would cluster at the park they'd passed before turning onto his street. Colin probably chatted them up before starting his arduous day of blogging at the coffee shop.

Elly was beginning to wonder if any man could be trusted. Look how their father had walked out on them. How Hans, Colin, and Jake had all kept secrets from the Bradford sisters. Not small secrets, either. *Crap, crap, crap men,* as her friend Paige had said.

Well, she was officially done with love and trust and all that, Elly concluded as the three of them mounted the front steps of Colin's brownstone, the baby in Anne's arms. From now on she planned to model her life on Flossie's: she would live a productive life in the company of women.

They stood back as Anne rang the bell. A woman who Elly assumed must be Barbara opened the door. She wore a short satin robe over plaid pajama pants. If she'd been a man, Elly would have called that garment a smoking jacket. Her hair was gray and cut too short; it made her ears stand out. They were slightly pointed at the tips.

Anne surprised Elly by speaking up first. "Hi, Barbara," she said. "Remember me?" She pushed into the hallway past the other woman.

Elly and Laura followed and stood behind her. The house smelled like laundry detergent and cats.

Barbara stared at the baby first, working her mouth into some unidentifiable shape. No sound emerged for a moment. Then she said, "Wait here. I'll get Colin."

"Thank you," Anne said, sweet as a Girl Scout with an order form for cookies.

Colin appeared moments later. He was wearing plaid pajama pants and a robe similar to Barbara's. Maybe Barbara shopped in bulk. He had the same curly gray hair and broad face as his wife, though on him the features were rugged and handsome.

Elly could see what Anne had found attractive about him: Colin exuded a sexy warmth even as he tried to stare them down.

"What are you doing here, Anne?" Colin demanded after a moment of openmouthed shock had passed. "How did you find me?"

"Nice way to greet the mother of your child," Laura snapped.

Elly gave Laura an admiring look.

Colin held up his hands, as if they had him at gunpoint. "What do you want, Anne?" he said. "It's over between us. I made that very clear in Puerto Rico."

"She wants child support, you loser." Elly edged forward so that she was standing next to Anne instead of behind her. "You forgot that little detail when you scampered back to Brooklyn and your surprisingly understanding wifey. I'm sure it was just an oversight."

"I can hear you!" Barbara called from another room.

"Good!" Elly yelled back.

"You're not helping," Anne said, turning around to glare at her sisters. "Go back to the car. I can handle this."

"No." Laura stepped forward, too, so that she and Elly were flanking their little sister. "We're staying right here until your needs are met."

"Jesus," Colin said. "What is this, your personal army?"

"Sort of," Anne said. "Meet my sisters."

Colin kept his eyes on Anne. "Look, we had an understanding," he said. "You wanted a baby. I didn't! You said you could take care of the child on your own, so I let you have things your way."

"But things are different now!" Anne said. "I thought we'd be together in Puerto Rico. You never said you'd leave me! But you did, and then I lost my job. I put all my money down on our apartment, so I had nothing left. I was supporting you because you told me you were getting *divorced*!"

Elly hoped like hell Barbara was still listening with those pointy terrier ears.

Colin's shoulders sagged. Elly wondered how old he was. Fifty? He was at that age when some men hold their youthful shapes and faces, while others fall apart. Colin had probably been handsome all his life, the kind of good-looking that would draw people to him, especially women, and let him command a room. A stage, even. He'd probably held on to his looks through the affair with Anne, but he was definitely falling apart now. He should have stayed in Puerto Rico.

"I don't know what I can do," Colin said, spreading his hands. "I don't have anything to spare."

"Oh, for Christ's sake, Colin," Barbara said, coming up behind him. "Give the girl some money so she'll go away. We can put our lawyer in touch with her in the morning." She pushed in front of Colin and stood squarely in front of Anne.

Lucy, appropriately, began to cry at the sight of her. "Tell your sisters to wait in the car and I'll write you a check," Barbara told Anne, raising her voice over Lucy's howls.

"We're not going anywhere until she has that money in her hand," Laura said.

Barbara tried glaring, but at three to one, and with a crying baby besides, it was no contest.

She finally shook her head, disappeared into another room, and reappeared with a checkbook. She wrote a check to Anne and handed her a business card.

"Here," Barbara said. "This is our attorney. Please contact us only through him in the future. And get that baby a DNA test. You're going to need proof if you insist on blackmailing my husband."

"How am I blackmailing him?" Anne demanded. "I'm just asking him to help support his own child, even if he never sees her again." She looked at Colin, who had retreated into the darkened hallway, using Barbara as his shield.

"I'd rather have you see Lucy than not, Colin," Anne said softly, as if gentling her voice might lure him out of the dark like a recalcitrant horse. "Wouldn't you like some contact with her, at least?"

"That's absolutely out of the question," Barbara said. "And if you show up here again, any of you, I'll sue you for harassment."

"Blah, blah, blah," Anne said in a singsong voice, causing Laura and Elly to giggle. "Come on, girls. We're done here. I'm sure we've kept these poor people up way past their bedtime." She turned around and pushed past Laura and Elly through the front door, leading the way back to the car.

Elly let Laura go ahead of her, then couldn't resist turning around to give Colin a little shove on the shoulder. "I bet you're a crap writer," she said. "I can't wait to read your novel and tweet my reviews."

Outside, Anne collapsed against the car. "That cowardly *jerk*," she said. "I can't believe he wouldn't even hold the baby. He hardly even *looked* at Lucy!"

"You're better off without him," Laura said gently.

"Yes," Elly said. "And at least now you'll have an easier time financially."

"I don't want his money!" Anne said, pressing one hand to her eyes while jiggling Lucy on her hip. Lucy's face was solemn as she grabbed on to Anne's red curls; she looked like she might cry, too.

"That money is for Lucy, not for you," Laura said. "Colin helped bring her into this world. You shouldn't have to do everything on your own."

"But I *wanted* to do it on my own," Anne said, shifting Lucy to the other hip when she started grabbing for Laura's silver necklace.

Laura took off her necklace and dangled it for the baby, who babbled happily as it swung in front of her. "We're Bradford women," she said. "We can all do things on our own when we need to, thanks to Mom. But Elly's right. We might be better off if we learn to ask for help sometimes."

Lucy finally caught hold of the necklace. The curve of her cheek and snub nose were so like Anne's when she was little that Elly had a sudden, visceral memory of carrying her little sister. Elly was only two years older, but she used to carry Anne on her hip or piggyback all over Folly Cove.

She remembered, too, how she and Anne used to hide under the sunporch with Laura, the three of them risking spiders and snakes to avoid their shouting parents. They kept a tea set and some stuffed animals under the porch, along with blankets to sit on or to wrap themselves in like magic cloaks as they played and listened to the distant surf. The sound of the ocean still reassured Elly. It was a sign that the rhythms of the world would stay the same, no matter what their parents did.

She had helped raise Anne, just as Laura had helped raise her. Now Kennedy and Lucy had all three of them. Lucky girls.

"Hand that baby over before we get back on the road," Elly said. "I haven't even held her yet."

Anne smiled. "She's all yours. Here."

Elly took the warm, solid little body. Lucy stared at her, wrinkling her tiny forehead as she tried to decide whether this new face was friend or foe. Elly held her close and started singing softly about drunken sailors.

Lucy grinned, and the four of them did a victory dance around the car, with Laura and Anne singing along with Elly, their voices as sweet in harmony now as they ever were.

Elly hoped Colin was watching them through the window, and that even if Barbara made him draw the curtains, he would do so with regret.

Flossie telephoned her early in the evening. Gil had slept beside her for a couple of hours, and then he had awakened her with a light kiss on the cheek and said he'd better go home before he got any ideas.

Sarah had rubbed her cheek afterward, suddenly minding the wrinkly leafy feel of her own skin less, now that it was warm from sleep and tingly where Gil kissed her.

"What?" she said into the phone, recognizing Flossie's number.

"I was just wondering if you've changed your mind," Flossie said.

"Of course I haven't."

She heard her sister-in-law's heavy sigh. "My God, you're a stubborn cow."

"Pot. Kettle. Black."

Flossie snorted. "You're indulging in some very passive-aggressive behavior. This is beneath you, Sarah."

"You're the one being aggressive," Sarah said. "You're blackmailing me, and I don't like it."

"Blackmailing you?" Flossie sounded genuinely surprised. "How is that possible, when you hold all the cards? You're my brother's widow. Folly Cove is yours now. You've already threatened me with kicking my keister to the curb if I tell the girls about Neil. I'd call that blackmail."

"Except you don't believe I'd do it."

"I can't control what you do," Flossie said. "I can only control what I do, and I can only do what I think is right."

"You're such a bitch," Sarah said, and would have been pleased with herself if her voice, already frayed from all the damn talking she'd done with Gil, hadn't snapped as she burst into tears.

"Sarah, are you all right?" Flossie said.

"I'm perfectly fine." Sarah hated the concern in her sister-in-law's voice. It was a painful reminder of the times Flossie had cared for her so many years ago. "Of course you must do what you think is right, Flossie. So long as you know that I'll be the one facing the consequences." She hung up the phone and covered her face.

What would she do if Flossie told the girls about her past? About all her lies?

Flossie had discovered everything about her many years ago, shortly after Neil left: Sarah's real name, where and when she was born. Flossie had even tracked down her sister!

"You sure had me fooled," Flossie had said once the secrets were out. "I really thought my brother was dating some rebel debutante.

Turns out, you were a townie putting on airs. A girl who grew up behind the King Arthur's Strip Joint and Motel. My mother was right. She always thought there was something fishy about you not bringing any of your people to your wedding. You said your parents were dead. And you never even told us about your sister!"

"Little Joanie," was all Sarah could think to say then, because of course in her mind Joanie was as she'd been the last time Sarah saw her at nineteen, still pretty, though worn down by that awful man. "She's alive?"

"Oh, yes," Flossie told her. "A widow with five children. But from the looks of her house, she's doing fine. A shame you never kept in touch."

How could she tell Flossie what her childhood had been like? Sarah had never told anyone.

"I'm not going to hold any of this against you," Flossie had said all those years ago. "Your secrets aren't mine to reveal. But you will need to tell your kids someday."

That day had apparently come.

Sarah was still sitting in bed. She pulled the cashmere blanket up around her shoulders, then turned off the lamps, as if sitting in the dark would somehow conceal everything Flossie was threatening to bring into the light.

She picked up the phone and thought about calling her back. But what could she possibly say to change Flossie's mind? She pressed the phone hard enough to her face that she could feel her cheekbone. So frighteningly easy to imagine the skull beneath the flesh, at her age.

She glanced toward the window, but it was dark.

She thought about getting up and going to the dining room for dinner. But then she might see Betty or Rhonda, and she couldn't face either of them and all of their questions. They were like her daughters, only worse, because she paid them to like her.

Maybe she should leave the inn. Not just for the evening, but go away for a couple of days while Flossie detonated a bomb in her family. But where would she go? She wasn't exactly flooded with invitations.

Some years ago, she'd written her own obituary, thinking she might send it to the newspaper to have it on file. In the end she hadn't sent it. There was nothing there of merit. What did she have to show for being alive so many years?

Her apartment, with nobody in it but herself. Daughters who were too busy for her. The inn that her children would sell the minute she was in the grave. Developers would build on this land eventually. All trace of her, and of the Bradfords, would vanish.

Sarah became aware suddenly that it was raining, the sound like a crowd of people tapping on her windows. She felt agitated enough to get up, finally, and pace the room.

A bath. A bath always fixed her moods.

She went into her en suite bathroom—classic black-and-white tiles, soothing seafoam green walls, luxuriously soft white Turkish cotton towels, all chosen by her own hand to provide instant comfort, though now these details seemed silly in the face of everything else— and started running water into her sunken whirlpool tub. Then she added her favorite rose-scented bubble bath.

Sarah made the water as hot as she could stand it. This wasn't good for her skin. But she didn't care: she had grown up in an apartment where there was never any hot water for bathing, so when she moved into this smaller suite in the inn, she had specifically asked the architect to design a bathroom around this tub, which could easily seat two, and always allowed herself as much hot water as she liked.

She sank deep into the water, letting it rise up to her shoulders, then up to her chin, clearing a space in the bubbles for her head. The water was close enough to her nose that her exhalations made it ripple outward, causing satisfying mountains of bubbles to rise around her face.

She could slide her head beneath the water and stay there. She would not be missed. Either the inn would go on without her, or it would not. Maybe Laura would move here with Jake and manage the place. Or Flossie could turn Folly Cove into a Buddhist retreat.

Perish the thought. If she did that, Sarah would find a way to haunt her from the grave.

Oh, why worry? What was left for her to do? She had accomplished her goal of saving the inn, of keeping the Bradford name alive, but that seemed to be of little importance to anyone but herself, especially now that Neil was gone. Laura wouldn't stay here. She'd probably join Elizabeth in Los Angeles or, God forbid, follow Anne somewhere foreign and cheap.

Sarah held her breath and sank beneath the water.

"Sarah? You in here?"

Sarah's head was underwater, but she could hear Flossie's voice calling; her sister-in-law had always been a strident woman. No ability to modulate her voice whatsoever.

Well, let her keep calling. Sarah didn't have to respond.

Suddenly, she remembered that she'd forgotten to lock the apartment door after Gil left. Sarah slid upright against the back of the tub and pulled the washcloth off the rack to cover her breasts. "Go away, Flossie!"

As always, commanding her sister-in-law to do something had exactly the opposite effect. Flossie let herself into the living room— Sarah knew this by the rattle of china in the upright antique corner hutch in her living room—and noisily charged through the apartment.

"I just wanted to make sure you're all right." Flossie peered her wizened monkey face around the door, then stepped into the bathroom. "Jesus, it's like a sauna in here. I've never understood the need some people have to practically boil their bathwater."

"Get out," Sarah said.

Flossie perched on the toilet, hands on her knees. "Nice tub. I didn't realize you'd put in a whirlpool. Looks like there's room enough for two."

"Not when I'm in here."

Flossie laughed. "Can you imagine what the girls would say if one of them stopped by to check on you and found us bathing together? They'd be the ones having strokes."

Sarah had to smile at that. "Except my girls don't give a damn about me."

"It's difficult for me to imagine a pity party smelling this good."

Sarah flicked bubbles off her fingers onto Flossie's black vest. "You're crashing the party. Leave if you don't like it."

"Your daughters love you, Sarah, but they don't really know you.

I've come to beg you one more time to let them see you for who you really are. They deserve that. So do you."

Sarah's hair was wet now and her shoulders felt chilled. She slipped deeper into the water and rearranged the washcloth to cover her breasts. Not that it mattered. She supposed Flossie's saggy old dugs weren't any perkier than hers. "My past is my own. I'd rather keep it that way."

Finally, Flossie said, "You're afraid your daughters won't love you if they know the truth."

"They won't! Not once they know I've lied."

"We all lie, Sarah. That's part of what makes us so interesting as a species: we communicate with language, and sometimes that language is compromised by our fears. That means relationships are always challenging. When you were institutionalized, I saw your medical records." Flossie turned her palms up. "They told your story. And seeing the truth didn't make me hate you."

"It made you pity me! That's even worse!" God, how Sarah wished she could drown herself right now. How tedious this all was. How tedious, and how painful, to look at Flossie and see that she was right.

"I didn't pity you, exactly," Flossie said slowly, frowning. "But I did feel sorry that you were treated so badly by your mother. Anyway, your childhood is part of who you are, and it's part of who your daughters are. They need to know where they came from."

"Why? So they can suddenly doubt themselves?" Sarah spit back. "So they can think of themselves as the grandchildren of a woman who whored herself for booze and very nearly whored her own daughters, and as the children of a mother who didn't know how to love them because she was too *busy* trying to keep the wolves from the door?"

"Yes," Flossie said. "All of that."

"If you tell them everything, you'll destroy them."

Flossie shook her head. "I know your daughters. They're strong women, Sarah. Maybe they'll be angry for a while, but they'll forgive you. If you let them." She leaned forward, her narrow face pink and shiny from the heat of the water. "I don't care about your real name or where you grew up. They won't, either. But they *will* care if you never tell them the truth and they find out. Come to my house tomorrow at ten o'clock. All three of them will be there. I'll tell them about Neil, and then I'll tell them about you."

The water, which had been so soothing, so hot and perfumed, now made Sarah feel like she was choking, lying in it and thinking about her hospitalizations, about how Flossie must have dug around in her things to find her birth certificate for the hospital and had then made calls and discovered Joanie and everything there was to know about Sarah's medical history: broken bones. Bacterial infections. Bruises. Burns. Her injuries served as a record of her mother's mental illness and of her own neglect and abuse. Her shame.

Flossie said softly, "Trust me, Sarah. You need to do this."

"No, I don't. Because I don't want my children looking at me with pity the way you are now." Sarah pulled the washcloth up to her chin. She wanted to cover her face with it.

"You're mistaking pity for compassion," Flossie said.

"I don't think so."

"Sarah, do you think our childhood was really better than yours? Financially we were better off, but our father drank and gambled. Our mother essentially medicated herself into oblivion with pills—that was easy to do in those days—and ignored us. That's why Neil and I were so close."

"You were lucky, having each other."

"You had a sister."

Sarah sighed. "I did. But she and I had different fathers and different childhoods. I looked out for Joanie when I could, but we were never close. That's why it used to kill me, when Laura and Elly and Anne were so close. Like their own little tribe. I felt left out of their magic circle."

"Your girls love you," Flossie said. "You just can't see it. And one of the best things you've done in your life is have three daughters who will look out for each other after you and I are long gone."

Sarah smiled a little. "I like the thought of that."

"Good." Flossie put her fingers in the bathwater. "It's almost my temperature now."

Sarah turned the hot water back on, using her foot to work the lever. "Good-bye, Flossie. It's time for you to go. I can't even pretend to do this anymore."

"Do what?"

"Pretend that I can tolerate your interference in my life."

Flossie stood up. "You're making a mistake. I want only the best for you."

"You have a funny way of showing it. Now get out."

Sarah waited until she heard her sister-in-law retreat through the hallway and shut the apartment door behind her. Then she held on to the tub railing and slowly eased herself up out of the water, shivering as the cold air hit her.

She blinked with shock, staring at her crystal jar of cotton balls and tubes of makeup and wooden hairbrush as if they belonged to another woman, things so unfamiliar to her now that Sarah could almost believe she'd been dreaming, only to wake the way you do, sometimes, feeling unmoored and alone. The rest of the night stretched out before her like a dark wood, terrible and cold, with no clear path through it, only the stirrings of her own fragile heart to guide her.

CHAPTER SIXTEEN

It was going to be a clear day, Anne thought, but right now morning mist lay across the calm green sea like gauze. Laura and Elly had driven to her house about nine thirty, after Laura finished getting Kennedy off to school and did her barn chores.

They'd had coffee and muffins—Anne made her favorite, banana nut muffins with chocolate chips, which Rodrigo still refused to see as appropriate for the inn—and now the three of them were walking up to Flossie's house for what Elly called "The Be-All, End-All Mysterious Buddhist Meeting with the She Yoda."

Elly led the way, her long legs carrying her across the rocky cove effortlessly, her blond hair bound in a messy bun, but with tendrils escaping across the collar of her blue jacket like some sort of sea creature.

Despite her shorter legs, Laura had no trouble keeping up with Elly. She still wore her jeans and riding boots; probably walking with Elly was easy for her because she was so accustomed to leading horses. Laura looked like she was finally sleeping better, though she'd confided over their coffee that this was the night she and Jake planned to tell Kennedy about their separation. She was worried about that.

Anne's struggle to keep up with her sisters brought back her memories of their childhood games, when she was the one calling, "Wait for me!" She was breathing hard from the exertion.

Of course she had a handicap. Lucy rode on her hip, and Anne would swear the baby was a pound heavier than yesterday. She should have put Lucy in the backpack, but that was often difficult, now that Lucy had decided she hated the thing.

"It's like trying to stuff a cat in a bread box," Elly had said this morning. She'd offered to hold Lucy's arms down to keep them from flailing, but in the end Anne decided to leave the backpack at home and carry her.

"Huh," Elly said. "If you were our mother, you'd put her in a straitjacket to make her behave."

Now, watching Elly hike freely, Anne thought about how having a baby had separated her forever from Colin, and for that matter, from anyone who hadn't experienced motherhood. She was bound to Lucy in a way she'd never expected, her baby's cries piercing her heart and causing her breasts to tingle. Her past inclination to take risks on surfboards and horses, on bicycles and in cars, with men and with jobs, was dampened now by her need to keep her child safe. She also knew she wouldn't have it any other way.

They reached the bottom of Flossie's steps and halted in silent mutual agreement. "Really, what do you suppose is so important that Aunt Flossie has to tell us all together?" Elly said, looking up at Flossie's sea glass and driftwood mobile tinkling in the wind.

"Maybe she's going to join another convent." Laura glanced at Anne. "You could live here this winter if she does. It would be a lot warmer than the cottage."

"Or maybe she's in love and running away with him," Elly said. "I saw some guy coming out of her house the other morning when I was visiting Mom."

"Probably a yoga student," Laura said.

"Not unless Flossie's in the habit of kissing her students after practice," Elly said.

"I don't think Flossie would run off even if she was in love," Anne said. "She doesn't let love dictate her life the way we do ours. Anyway, she seems happy living alone."

"That's what I'm going to be like," Elly declared. "Solitary and content."

Laura and Anne hooted, which caused Flossie to appear on the porch above them. "Well, look what the tide brought in. Come inside before that baby catches cold. It's raw out."

Anne was the last one to enter the house. She handed Lucy to Flossie, who immediately put her head down so Lucy could grab at her short gray hair, giggling.

As Anne took her boots off on the porch to spare Flossie's floors, she wondered when her aunt had started to worry about babies and cold weather. She could remember Flossie taking her down to the beach with her sisters even in snowstorms. Anne had loved it. There was something magical about the gray flannel clouds, the icy wet jewels on their faces, the waves thundering against the rocks while they built snowmen on the beach. They ornamented the snowmen with seashell buttons, necklaces of seaweed, and driftwood arms.

Once, she and her sisters had made a snow mermaid. Anne had cried when she melted; she'd loved seeing their mermaid lying on her voluptuous side, facing the open sea.

Flossie had passed the baby to Laura, who was dangling measuring spoons in front of her while Flossie made tea. Anne perched on a kitchen stool and glanced around at the crowded kitchen, interested, as always, in how other people cooked.

Copper pots and iron frying pans hung from hooks on a pegboard. Jars of spices, dried beans, and pasta were neatly arrayed on metal shelves, and a block of good knives stood next to the sink. Everything here was basic but functional, even the outdated gas stove and small white fridge.

It was the sort of kitchen you could cook in all your life and not miss anything, Anne thought with pleasure. There was nothing here like the unnecessary things some people were swayed to buy, like one-step corn kernelers, egg separators, pepper corers, or strawberry hullers.

"Let's go into the living room, shall we?" Flossie said, sounding suddenly formal now that they were holding their tea. "We'll be more comfortable there."

When they were all settled—the three sisters in a row on the couch, Lucy on a quilt on the floor, lying on her back with fingers in her mouth, looking at the odd sight of them all above her—Flossie sat on the white armchair, closed her eyes, and took several deep, steadying breaths.

Flossie wore her usual workout clothes. Her face, despite its deep lines, was elegant and carved looking, Anne thought, the cheekbones prominent. It was easy to believe that men still found her compelling and sought out her company. Perhaps the fact that she preferred to live alone made her even more attractive to them.

As she continued her deep breathing, Flossie's chest rose and fell, her jaw gradually relaxed, and the lines in her face eased a little. Anne half expected her to start chanting.

They waited silently for several minutes. Even Lucy was quiet. Anne was afraid to look at her sisters, because she knew they'd start laughing from nerves. She could see Elly's knee jiggling from the corner of her eye and put a hand on it to make her stop.

Finally Flossie opened her eyes. To Anne's shock, they glistened with tears. "I have some sad news to share," she began.

Anne felt her heart pounding and folded her hands, clammy from nerves. Was Flossie ill?

No. She wouldn't say that was "sad" news. Self-pity wasn't her aunt's style.

Flossie shifted her weight and pulled an envelope out of the pocket of her hooded black sweatshirt, then slid a letter out of the envelope and said, "I had hoped your mother would tell you this herself, or might join us here this morning. Since she has chosen to absent herself, the responsibility falls to me. Girls, your father has passed."

"What are you saying?" This was Laura, sounding querulous with shock. "Dad's *dead*?" She looked at the others. "Is this *new* news? I thought he probably died a long time ago, to be honest."

"Me, too. How did you hear this, Aunt Flossie?" Elly said.

Flossie held up a hand to stop them. "I will tell you everything," she said, "but I need to do it in my own way. Please remember this is my brother we're discussing here. My little brother." The tears that had been shining in her eyes were sliding down her cheeks, making her skin glisten, too. She pulled a tissue out of the box beside her and patted her face. "As your mother may have told you, Neil wrote to both of us from time to time," she said then.

"Of course she didn't tell us," Elly said. "Mom never tells us anything."

"Why didn't *you* tell us?" Laura demanded.

"Well, our correspondence was very sporadic," Flossie said. "Please don't be too hard on your mother. Or on me. We really had no way of contacting your father. He lived on the street a good deal of the time."

"Where was he?" Anne said.

"Different places, I think, but Florida at the end of his life. He'd finally gotten himself straightened out."

"After only thirty years," Laura said. "Gosh. Quite the overachiever."

"This isn't the time to say harsh things," Flossie admonished gently.

"Don't get me wrong. I loved Dad," Laura said. "He was so supportive of me, and so much fun. I think that's why it just about killed me when he left us. So I'm not really sure how I feel right now."

Flossie nodded. "Of course. And I don't blame you for being hurt. Neil never should have abandoned you girls the way he did, no matter how he felt about Folly Cove or your mother."

"So why did he?" Elly said.

"Your father was an alcoholic," Flossie said. "He wasn't in his right mind half the time. He was also riddled by guilt, especially when he was sober. He tried to stay in touch with you girls, sending you letters and cards and the occasional gift. But then he stopped after a few years. Not to excuse his behavior, but I think it was easier for him to divorce himself completely from you, because it was so painful for him to think about how he let you down."

"What do you mean? He never tried to stay in touch," Laura said. "I sure never got any cards or gifts from Dad. Did you guys?"

Anne and Elly both shook their heads. "Mom probably kept them from us," Elly said. "That would be like her."

Then Anne remembered. "The dolls!" she said. "Remember those dolls we got the first Christmas after Dad left? They weren't from Santa or Mom. There wasn't any tag on them at all."

"The 'my twin lookalike' dolls!" Laura exclaimed. "I'd forgotten all about those."

"Yours had red hair, Anne, and mine was blond," Elly said.

They'd discovered those dolls under the tree one Christmas, with no tags on the boxes. Even then Anne had known they were far more expensive than any gifts their mother or Flossie ever bought them. She'd been young enough to believe it was Santa's doing; she'd cried when Laura said only babies believed in Santa.

She and her sisters had immediately started arguing about which doll was prettiest. It was a few hours before they noticed that Anne's doll had the wrong eye color. She was crushed. But it made sense, if her father was the one who'd sent them, that he'd make a mistake like that.

"So Dad gave up on us," Laura said. "Figures. He's a man."

"Now you sound like me," Elly warned.

"Well, Bradford women don't exactly have a great track record with men," Laura said with a sniff. "We're born fools for love."

Anne was watching Flossie, who was staring at the letter in her hands. The letter had been folded and refolded so many times that it had multiple creases. "Is that a letter from Dad?"

Flossie nodded. "He wanted to come home, in the end. But then he was diagnosed with liver cancer. He didn't want to show up and be a burden to me or your mother."

"Yeah, because he knew Mom was pissed at him. She would probably have run him over with her car," Laura said.

"I don't know about that," Flossie said. "Your parents still loved each other. I know you find that hard to believe, but it's true." She looked at them, one at a time, to emphasize her point. "Now let me read this to you. It's from your father. He wanted me to do this."

"Can't we read it ourselves?" Anne asked. She didn't want to cause Flossie more pain.

Flossie shook her head. "Neil wanted it done this way. He loved you all equally, and he felt I should deliver this to you all at the same time."

"He could have written us separate letters," Laura grumbled, but Flossie silenced her with a look.

Then Flossie began reading:

My dear girls,

You have grown up without me. That is both a cause for sorrow, because of how much I missed, and a reason to celebrate, because I'm sure you were better off with me gone. I had hoped not to go to my grave without seeing you again, but the Fates, as always, have a way of playing tricks on us pitiful humans. If your aunt is reading this letter to you, it means my clock has run out.

I am sure you are angry with me for leaving. That's a good thing. Anger gives us strength. You were raised by your mother, so I'm certain you've all become very strong, independent women. But please don't let anger interfere with your ability to love, because love is the greatest gift of all.

I want you to know that I've followed you from afar, at least online, whenever I have been able and well. In a perfect world, I could congratulate you myself for all of your accomplishments. In this very imperfect life of mine, I must settle for saying I am honored to have had any small part in putting the three of you on this planet to follow your passions. I hope you will celebrate your accomplishments, keep taking risks, and continue to follow your hearts.

Know that I am always with you in spirit and watching out for you from wherever this new path takes me.

With all my love,
Dad

"Jesus, Dad," Laura said, sniffing. "When did you get so maudlin?"

"Dying has a way of doing that to you," Flossie said, and tucked the letter back into its envelope.

Then she stood up and went to the hall closet, opened the door, and took a box off the shelf above the coatrack. Lucy started fussing, so Anne picked her up and held her so she could see what was going on.

Flossie carried the box back to the coffee table and set it carefully in front of them. Then she stepped back as if something might jump out of it.

It was an ordinary white Priority Mail Express box, the flat-rate kind available for free from any post office. Flossie's address was scrawled on the front; the return address was Venice, Florida. It was an ordinary box in every way, except for several black strips of tape declaring CREMATED REMAINS in capital white letters.

Anne felt like doubling over from the shock. "Is that Dad?" she whispered. "Is he actually *in* there?" A bubble of hysterical laughter threatened to escape.

"Dad, come on outta there," Elly said, also whispering. When her sisters glared at her, she said, "Sorry."

"Seems like a waste of money to send it Express Mail," Laura said. "It's not like he's going anywhere. How long have you had him in that closet, Flossie?"

All three of them started giggling. Flossie joined in, and even Lucy's mouth was open wide in a grin.

Then, at nearly the same instant, the four women were weeping, shoulders shuddering, and Lucy sat in shocked silence, clinging to Anne's sweater.

"I'm so sorry, Flossie," Anne said finally. "It's just such a shock."

"Of course it is." Flossie's voice was brisk. "And you hardly knew your father." She hesitated, then added, "There are things you don't know about your mother, either. And, although she disagrees with this idea, I believe you should know the truth about her, because the truth concerns you, too."

"Shouldn't Mom be the one to tell us all this?" Laura said.

"Yeah, but you know she won't," Elly said. "Go on, Flossie."

Laura stood up and began moving around the room, agitated. "I don't know if this is such a good idea. I don't know if I can take any more surprises today." She glanced at the box on the table. "Aren't we even going to open that box and see if Dad's really in there?"

"He's in there," Flossie said. "Sit down, Laura. Just for a few more minutes. Then we'll open the box if you like."

"I don't like anything about this day," Laura grumbled. "I feel like I've fallen into a nest of bees." But she sat as directed.

Elly leaned over and buzzed in her ear until Laura shoved her away.

"So what do you mean, you need to tell us the truth about Mom?" Anne said, speaking over her sisters.

"Well, I suppose the first thing you ought to know is that your mother's childhood was very different from what she led you to believe," Flossie said. "She didn't grow up wealthy. She never had two parents. She didn't even grow up in Back Bay."

"What?" Laura said. "Where is she from, then?"

"Everett," Flossie said.

"Everett?" Elly asked. "You mean, *Everett Everett*, like down by the airport?"

"Yes," Flossie said.

"Wow," Elly said. "So who were her parents?"

"She never really knew her father," Flossie said. "She was raised by a single mother, very poor, in an apartment. She also isn't turning sixty-five. She's turning seventy-five."

Laura frowned. "But that would make her thirty-five when I was born. And almost ten years older than Dad! Did he even know?"

"I don't think so," Flossie said. "But I don't think he would have cared. She was beautiful at any age. Still is," she added softly. "And you mustn't be too hard on her. Your mother was fighting for her survival."

"But how do you know all this?" Anne said. "Why would Mom tell you but not Dad? Or us?"

"I had my suspicions when I first met your mother that she wasn't who she said she was," Flossie said. "And then, years later, Sarah mentioned a sister when you had your appendix out, Laura. Your mother was nearly hysterical when you went to the hospital in an ambulance, because she remembered her sister nearly dying of an infection in the hospital after a surgery. So I got in touch with a friend of mine, a DA in Essex County. He helped me look into her background. Her mother was still alive when she married your father, but she's gone now. Her sister is still alive, though. She lives in Revere. Her name is Joan."

"We have another aunt, living just half an hour away?" Elly asked, her voice squeaking with surprise. She shook her head. "God. Mom's a total impostor. I don't understand any of this! Why was she lying all this time?"

"She was ashamed," Flossie said. "She didn't want anyone to know where she came from, because she was trying to bury her past. Believe me, she had reason to: it was an unhappy childhood in every way. Then, when she met your father, the thing your mother wanted more than anything was to be accepted as a Bradford. My parents never would have condoned the marriage if they'd known her real background." She gave a short laugh. "Me, either, though I'm ashamed now to admit that."

"That must be why the inn meant so much to Mom, right? More than it ever did to Dad," Anne said slowly. "It was something stable."

"That's a pretty generous outlook," Elly said. "The other way to look at things is that she's a liar and a cheat."

Flossie clapped her hands on her thighs and stood up. "Well, that's probably enough news for one day. I'm sorry. There is a lot you girls will need to think about, and I'm sure you'll have more questions. I really was hoping your mother would join us for this conversation, but in any case, I'm glad you know some of this. Now, how about a walk on the beach to clear our heads?"

"Wait," Anne said. "We haven't opened the box."

"Do you really want to do that right now?" Laura demanded. "God, there's probably an urn in there, packaged in Bubble Wrap and packing tape or something horrible."

"Yeah," Elly added in a mutter, "and we all know the ashes in that box could be from anybody. Or *anything*! Somebody's dog, even. They probably sweep the ashes up together in the crematorium."

"Stop it, Elly," Anne said, casting a worried glance at Flossie.

Elly ignored her. "The bigger question is, what are we going to do with his ashes once we open that box?"

Oddly, Flossie was smiling a little, her eyes damp again. "I know the answer to that. Neil asked me to have you scatter his ashes here on the beach at Folly Cove. In his letter to me, he said he finally realized that, no matter how many years and miles separated him from the inn, this is still his home."

"Well, we can't do that right now," Laura snapped. "Not without Mom. And there ought to be a service."

"I didn't mean *now*, dope," Elly said. "God, Laura! Don't you ever get tired of being so responsible and literal?"

"Shut up," Laura said. "Don't you ever get tired of being so irresponsible and bitchy?"

"Girls," Flossie snapped. "Let's walk down to the beach. You can take your time to decide about a service for your father. I'll keep his ashes until then, all right?"

Still grumbling, Elly and Laura led the way down the path to the beach, followed by Flossie, dressed in a black wool watch cap pulled low over her dark eyes and a black pea coat. She looked like a miniature Navy SEAL. Anne followed them with Lucy, thinking of her father bringing them down to this very beach, even on days when the wind whipped the waves into a frenzy and the tips of their ears and noses turned instantly numb.

Her father had helped Anne and her sisters find enough sea glass at Folly Cove to fill a jar shaped like a heart.

He had once helped them make mouse costumes after taking them to see *The Nutcracker* in Boston.

Dad taught her to ride a bike, running beside her so she wouldn't fall. Anne had been astonished, when she was six, that her father could run so fast. Could outrun a bicycle and catch her when she wobbled and started to tip over, bike and all!

And, in the mornings, if Anne came into the bathroom while he was shaving, he'd lift her up onto the sink counter so they could make beards and horns with the shaving cream.

Daddy used to make her laugh so hard, she'd get the hiccups.

He'd loved her. He'd loved them all.

Flossie turned around, saw that she was weeping, and took Anne's arm as they descended the porch steps behind the others. "Are you all right?" she said.

"I think so," Anne said. "What about you? Are you okay?"

Flossie turned her head away, looking out to sea. "I feel lost. And terribly sad. My brother and I loved each other and fought with each other the same way you and your sisters do. It's a great gaping hole now, knowing he's gone, even though I hadn't seen him in years."

"I know what you mean." Anne tucked her arm into Flossie's and they stood there for a moment, watching her sisters pick their way down the rocky path to the beach, Laura's short hair feathering dark, Elly's blond head tipped back as she laughed.

It was cold but sunny. The water was so blue that the rest of the landscape looked bleached of color. A white tugboat churned in the distance and a cloud of sandpipers rose from the water, then settled back onto the beach. The tide was out, leaving ridges of sand and mud, endless patterns upon patterns on the gold crescent beach.

She had come to this beach countless times with her father and sisters. Moments like this one had already passed. She was lucky to have had those times, and to be here again.

Anne looked down at the baby in her arms. Lucy was leaning outward, captivated by the sparkling water, reaching as if she could grasp the dancing waves. Anne vowed to remember this exact moment, with the warmth of her child in her arms as the sea stretched before them, an ocean of miracles, the shadow of her father beside her.

Back at the house, Laura slipped a pair of boots on over her jeans and walked down to the stable, pulling her jacket collar up against the breeze. It was midafternoon and the sun was already starting its descent. Autumn was winding its inexorable way toward winter.

She didn't know how to feel about anything at the moment: not the change of season, her father's death, or Flossie's revelations about her mother, though she was perhaps the least surprised by those. Kennedy had said something to her once about her mother's birthday, saying it wasn't really the one they were celebrating, but Laura had ignored this and said, "Well, the point of a birthday is to celebrate a person, not an age, and Grandma has asked us to celebrate this special day in her honor. We need to respect her and do that."

What complete bunk. *Respect* her mother? How could she when she didn't even *know* her?

At the moment, all Laura felt was numb. It wasn't an unpleasant sensation, especially in the face of what she had to do tonight, which was to tell her daughter that her own parents' marriage was a lie, just like so many other things in Laura's life.

A couple of boarders were exercising their horses in the ring, making use of it before Laura started teaching. She had only two lessons today. Both were late in the afternoon, thankfully, so she could concentrate on doing ordinary, solitary tasks like bringing hay down from the loft and filling water buckets right now, rather than have to speak with anyone.

She hoped the barn would work its usual magic on her raw mood and give her strength for what was to come tonight with Jake and Kennedy. Meanwhile, she would push aside all thoughts of her own parents until tomorrow. What could she do about any of it now?

Laura greeted the boarders, breathing in the pleasurable smells of hay, sweet molasses Omolene, and horse, rolling her shoulders a little. Maybe she should take a ride, too. The weather would probably clear soon, judging from the fast-moving clouds, and Kennedy wouldn't be home until shortly before dinner, because Sandra was picking her up from school to take her to their house. Mysteriously, Kennedy had developed a friendship with Melanie, proving once again that a teen girl's mind is a mysterious thing.

Only when Laura wandered into the barn did she see the stranger seated on the bench just inside the stable doors.

"Hello, Laura," he said.

She stopped so suddenly that she breathed in a plume of sawdust kicked up by her boots. The man was in shadow, yet even in silhouette he was instantly recognizable to her, because she'd studied his photographs online so closely.

"Tom!" She put a hand to her mouth, her heart drumming hard. "What are you doing here?"

"The silence was killing me. I had to see you. I know this probably sounds silly, but I was worried about you when you cut things off like that." He regarded her for another moment, then smiled. "You look good. I'm glad."

"You, too," Laura said, amazed she could form words when her mouth felt like it did in Jake's dentist chair, when the hygienist stuck that rubber tube in her mouth and sucked everything dry.

And how could he say that? How *could* she look good, after the morning she'd had?

She banished those thoughts and focused on Tom. He looked nothing like the boy she'd known in high school. He'd grown from a skinny kid with lousy skin into a substantial man. Not fat, but tall and solid. He could have been a lumberjack or farmer, with his sturdy build and the way he seemed so at ease in a barn, surrounded by horses hanging their heads over the stall doors or passing them in the aisle, as one horse and rider did just then.

He was attractive, Laura decided: compelling to look at in the way a man is when he's confident. He looked vaguely British, in his wax jacket and corduroy trousers. The look suited him.

"I'm sorry," Tom said as the silence lengthened. "Maybe this wasn't a good idea. I don't want to intrude or make things awkward for you. I really did just stop by to make sure you're okay."

"You aren't making things awkward!" Laura realized from the heat in her face that she was probably blushing, and not prettily, either. Probably more like she'd been lifting weights. "Nobody's here."

Tom glanced past her through the barn doors, where they could hear the riders talking as the third horse entered the ring.

Laura laughed. "I mean, nobody in my family. Kennedy's with a friend."

"Your daughter." Tom smiled. "She looks a lot like you."

From Facebook, Laura realized, Tom knew a lot about her life. At least about those things she chose to share. She posted victories and celebrations. Not the burned dinners or shouting matches over laundry strewn about Kennedy's floor; not her worries over money or her resentment toward her mother; not the middle-of-the-day naps Laura took when she sometimes felt she couldn't go on.

Tom knew only the profile she'd chosen to present to the world. He had no idea that Jake had left her, that she'd just heard about her father's death, or that her mother had been lying to her all her life.

"Well. Guess I should be going," he said.

At that Laura realized she'd said nothing to indicate how happy she was to see him; he must think she was unhinged.

She was, a little. But she was also glad: Tom was here, and he was real. He cared enough to make the effort to find her even after those silly photos, and she didn't need to worry about what he thought about the way she looked. She'd shown him everything already. As in, *everything*.

This fact probably should have made her want to run and hide. Instead, as Laura met Tom's warm gaze—his face was as lined as her own—she suddenly relaxed. She smiled, and he smiled back. It was as easy as that.

"Why don't we go inside and I'll make some coffee?" she said. "Do you have time? I have a lot to tell you."

Tom's smile widened into a grin. Now she remembered the boy he'd been, circling his bicycle around hers, talking excitedly about math and chemistry. The sort of boy who was curious to know everything about the world and what it was made of, down to the most basic elements.

"For you? I have all the time in the world," he said, and followed her up to the house.

CHAPTER SEVENTEEN

Elly had seen Sarah in a fury many times before. Cut to childhood: a broom thrown at her once, when she'd failed to sweep beneath the kitchen counters; a sharp twist of the arm when Elly defied her mother and tried to sneak out to meet a boy at fourteen; sharp words when she'd eaten apples meant for a pie.

Now Sarah was shouting at her, though really she was angry that Flossie had told them everything. "It wasn't her place to share my history with my children!" she repeated. "I should have been the one to tell you!"

Elly waited her out for a while, letting her wind down, then finally put a hand up to stop her. "Chill, Mom." She was getting angry, too; she was too old to take this abuse. "Flossie told us because she knew you wouldn't. Don't you think we deserved to be told that Dad was dead, at least? And those lies about your background! Were they really necessary? Did you really think any of us would *care* that you didn't grow up rich? Or that you never finished college?"

"The Bradfords would have cared! You girls can't understand what it was like." Sarah's face was pink with rage. She was pacing in her office and—for the first time ever, perhaps—seemingly unaware that there were guests in the reception area, a family of four that looked ready to bolt as they witnessed the scene.

Elly rose from the chair in front of Sarah's desk and closed the office door after a friendly wave at the family group and at Rhonda, who looked as jumpy as a gerbil behind the reception desk. Sarah never yelled while she was working. Her commands were always made professionally and quietly, with an undercurrent of steel.

"Try me. What was it like?" Elly turned back to her mother, who was still pacing.

When her mother didn't answer, Elly said, "Okay. Never mind the Bradfords. Let's start with something easy. How about your age? Why did you lie about it? I can't believe you're seventy-five! You don't look it at all," she added, hoping to calm her mother with a compliment.

Sarah glanced at her, then away. Finally she went to stand in front of the windows with her back to Elly. "I work hard not to look my age."

That much was true. Sarah's face was heavily made-up this morning, her complexion smoothed by foundation, her eyes neatly outlined in navy blue, the lashes thick and black. But she was so pale beneath the makeup, she looked waxy. Like a corpse made up for an open-casket funeral. If the corpse was a showgirl.

"Sit down, Mom," Elly said gently. "I'm sorry I upset you. Let me get you some water."

Sarah waved a hand. "I don't want any damn water." She sank into her office chair, gripping the handles like the chair itself might take off and start flying around the room with her in it. "Jesus Christ. Damn it all to hell."

Her mother never swore and didn't let them get away with it, either. Elly had to press her lips together because her first impulse was to laugh, hearing these words coming out of her mother's delicate mouth, painted its customary rose pink. "Mom, start at the beginning. Come on. Please? At least tell me why you lied about your age."

Sarah's eyes flickered across Elly's face and beyond, to the closed doors behind her. She had recovered enough from her tantrum to sound exasperated. "Your father was barely twenty-one years old when I met him. A baby! And I was thirty. Nearly thirty-one. His parents had enough problems accepting me into the family as it was. Even though I fabricated a background I knew they couldn't refuse, they considered me an unsuitable match for Neil because I was an entertainer. The

Bradfords went to Harvard. They went into banking or the law. They rode horses and played golf. But they were never entertainers. So there was that strike against me already. Now, what do you think they would've said if they'd known their golden boy was going to marry a woman who might be too old to give them any little Bradfords? Remember, having children after thirty back in those days was simply not done. Unless you were Catholic and couldn't help it, of course."

"Still, it seems unfair to Dad."

"Oh, for heaven's sake, why?" Sarah asked. "I was every bit as sexy and beautiful at thirty as most women his age. More so, because I had the confidence they lacked! And your father was legally an adult when we got married. It wasn't like he got a bum deal. I gave him children. And then he didn't want you in the end, anyway, did he?"

Of course her mother wouldn't miss an opportunity to rub *that* in, Elly noted. "What about the rest of it? Did you actually grow up in some crap apartment in Everett?"

Her mother turned away. "Yes. But you can't let anyone know any of this, Elly. I mean it. The reputation of this inn rests on me being the person I am today, not who I was too many years ago to count. Please." She turned back to face Elly, her blue eyes wide and brimming over. "I beg you. Hate me if you want. But I had my reasons. Now please go. Leave me in peace."

Elly sighed. "I don't hate you, Mom. But it'll take a while for us to adjust to everything. And you have to start being honest with us from now on, okay? I mean, do you really have a sister?"

Her mother nodded, but she pressed her lips tightly together, as if terrified something else might escape.

"Well, tell me about her. Is she older or younger? All Flossie told us is her name."

"Joanie," Sarah whispered. "She's five years younger than I am. I haven't seen her in almost fifty years. She was a sweet little thing."

"Wow. Do you want to see her again before you die?" Elly hated to put it like that, but having just seen her father literally in a box, the possibility of losing her mother seemed far more imminent.

Sarah looked startled. "No, I don't think so. What would be the point?"

"I don't know," Elly admitted. "Just to find out how she's doing, I guess. What about your birthday? The invitations have all gone out. They say you're turning sixty-five. You've just blatantly lied to about a hundred people. Never mind to your own family. Doesn't that seem just the tiniest bit wrong to you?"

"Like I said, I had my reasons for everything. What are you planning to do, Elizabeth?" she demanded. "You can't possibly change the invitations. They're already in the mail!"

"The one thing I won't do is lie for you," Elly said. "You got yourself into this mess, Mom. You'll have to figure a way out of it. Just know that the more you lie, the less we'll ever trust you. Is that really what you want?"

"I don't know what I want," her mother said, "except for all of you to quit badgering me."

"Fine. I'm done," Elly said, and left before she could say anything she would truly regret, aware of Rhonda's curious eyes on her back as she heard the office door shut behind her.

Outside, the sun was a bright, merciless eye. The landscape lit up around her, oranges and golds and reds. Elly blinked and walked back slowly to Laura's house with her head down. Just when it seemed like her family couldn't get any more dysfunctional, there was a whole new level of crazy.

She didn't notice the man sitting on Laura's front steps until he stood up. Then she recognized the ponytail and broad shoulders, the pierced ear.

"Oh my God," Elly said. "Ryder! What are you doing here?"

He looked confused. "Your sister invited me," he said. "Laura thought I should come film your mother's birthday party. Didn't she tell you?"

"No," Elly said. She went up to him tentatively and touched the collar of his leather jacket.

Ryder wrapped his arms around her, smelling as he always did: of lemon and salt, making her imagine him either drinking shots of tequila or shaving. Once, she'd seen him do both at the same time. "You okay? What's going on?" he said.

"Can you please just tell me I'm normal?"

Ryder kissed the top of her head. "Sorry, babe. If you were normal, I probably wouldn't be here."

Somehow, having Tom in her kitchen made Laura lose track not only of time but of her life: of the strange, surreal news about her father's death; of her mother's falsehoods; and even of Jake and the pain of knowing their marriage was a sham.

"As devastated as you are, though, isn't it still better to know the truth?" Tom said after she told him about Jake.

She had to admit that it was, though the financial practicalities of a divorce terrified her.

Well, if she had to sell this house, she would. She was determined to separate her life from Jake's as quickly as possible, and she was going to do it without her mother's help. In fact, if there was any way to avoid even *telling* her mother what was happening, she would. She wouldn't feel bad about shutting her mother out of her life, either. Not after all the lying her mother had done.

"I don't want to tell her, because I don't want my mother meddling or criticizing," she told Tom. "She lost the right to give me advice when she lost my trust. Besides, I know she'd want me to stay with Jake."

"Why?" Tom asked.

"She's not a huge fan of divorce, obviously. My father was missing for thirty years, and she still calls herself Mrs. Bradford."

Laura felt reassured by Tom's presence, by his easy acceptance of the things she told him, just as she had been when they were teenagers. He listened intently and spoke little, other than to reassure her that Kennedy might be more resilient than Laura believed.

"She has a lot of support in her life, between you and her aunts," Tom said. "Anyway, she might already suspect something. Teenagers have pretty powerful radars when it comes to the adults in their lives. Kids pluck things out of the air. It's the nature of humans to be observant so we can survive."

Then one of Laura's boarders had come up to the house and knocked on the door, letting her know that her four o'clock lesson had arrived.

"My God. I completely lost track of time," Laura said, pulling her boots back on.

"In a good way, I hope." Tom stood up, too, watching as she zipped her jacket and ran a hand through her short hair.

Laura felt shy, suddenly, remembering the photos she'd texted him. "I'm glad you found me," she said. "I'm just sorry it's such a crazy time. Jake and I haven't even officially separated yet. I'm not ready for much."

A slow smile spread across Tom's face as he returned Laura's gaze, and she couldn't help but smile back.

"Are you open to the possibility, though?" he asked.

"The possibility of what?"

He crossed the room to take her in his arms. "The possibility of us," he said, kissing her so deeply that she thought her knees might buckle.

When Laura came up for air, she smiled again. "I don't know," she said. "Do that again so I can think about it."

The four o'clock lesson went quickly, though Laura had to keep reminding herself of where she was and what she should be doing. So did her five o'clock lesson with Blythe, who was nineteen years old and Laura's most advanced student.

Star was calmer with Blythe astride him than with anyone else. Laura folded her arms and moved around the center of the ring with the stopwatch, timing Blythe and Star over the cavallettis. She'd set the basic jumps at four feet and was happy to see Star clear them smoothly, not even a hoof tick.

She called them back to the center of the ring and gave Blythe a few pointers on form, then waved them off. Blythe would untack Star and groom him; she had started helping Laura out in the afternoons in exchange for extra lessons.

Finally, after the horses had been brought in from the pasture and fed, Laura walked back to the house, thinking again about Tom and about the strange events of the afternoon.

She felt her stomach clench as she raced through dinner preparations, anticipating the conversation she and Jake were going to have with Kennedy. Omelets were the obvious choice. She was too tired and frazzled to make anything requiring more thought.

She was grating cheese when Kennedy arrived, dropping her back-pack to the kitchen floor and announcing she wasn't hungry, because she'd gone to Melanie's house after school and her freezer "has pretty much an entire Costco store in it."

"I still want you to eat something," Laura said. "I'm guessing there weren't a lot of vegetables involved."

"Mom," Kennedy moaned, flopping down on the chair next to her backpack. "Don't make me eat. Please, please, please don't make me. I will explode!"

"Well, all right. Sit with us anyway."

Laura glanced at her. Kennedy had done something different with her hair. There was a blue streak along one side and it was pinned up in back. She was also wearing a sweater Laura didn't recognize, some-thing black-and-white striped that made her look like a mime.

"Fine. I'm sitting." Kennedy took out her phone.

"How was it at Melanie's?" Laura asked.

"Good." Kennedy was slouched over her phone, smiling as she tapped something into it. "How's your day been?"

The sight of her daughter, still innocent of what was to come, was nearly Laura's undoing. She hastily turned back to the counter and started chopping spinach so hard the blade left grooves in the cutting board. "Fine."

By the sudden heat Laura felt on the back of her neck, she knew Kennedy had looked up from her phone to watch her. "What's wrong, Mom? You're, like, *murdering* that spinach."

"Nothing. Can you set the table, please?"

"Why are we eating so early?"

"Your dad's coming home early."

"Really? Why?"

"No reason."

"Where's Aunt Elly?"

"She's having dinner with Anne tonight."

Laura held her face carefully in check, hoping nothing would betray her emotional state, which was somewhere between volcanic and sinkhole. She told Kennedy about seeing Anne and the baby today at Flossie's, but decided to wait and tell her about Neil's death later. Kennedy had never even known her grandfather, and right now wasn't the time for more drama. There was plenty coming.

"So now that you and Anne are good again, can I hang out with them whenever I want?" Kennedy was bouncing in the chair with excitement.

"Sure, as long as you ask Anne first." Laura glanced at the clock. Jake would be here any minute. She felt like something was holding her forehead stretched tight, like Botox gone wrong. "So tell me more about your time with Melanie. Did you have fun? Is she nicer than you thought?"

"She's okay, I guess. But, oh my God, Mom, you would *not* believe her house!"

Kennedy started detailing the wonders of Sandra's home: the couch with its recliners and cup holders built in, the indoor lap pool, Melanie's room with its canopy bed and her own projector television. "It's so cool. Like she lives in a mall!"

"Wow, that's really something," Laura said, struggling to banish all judgment from her voice.

"I know, right?" Kennedy said. "But it's okay. Melanie's still jealous because I have horses and the beach. Since we're friends, it's like we have a city house and a country house."

"Sure," Laura said. "Great."

The omelets were in the oven now and she was making English muffins. Laura finally allowed herself to pour a glass of wine. It was only as she took the first sip that she remembered drinking the night Ryder called. She'd forgotten to tell Elly about inviting him. Her mind was slipping. Wasn't he supposed to arrive today? Maybe Elly had met up with him and taken him to Anne's.

Jake arrived as she was buttering the muffins, his voice too hearty from the hallway. "Hey, where are my beautiful girls?" he called.

"In here, Dad!" Kennedy said. "You won't believe where I went after school! Try to guess!"

"Let's see." Jake came into the room and hugged Kennedy. "Spain? Senegal? Timbuktu?"

"Daddy!" Kennedy laughed and pulled away. "I was at Melanie's! It was super fun!"

Jake met Laura's eyes. He looked as exhausted as she felt, his brown eyes dull and bloodshot. "I bet," he said. "Tell me all about it."

They sat down to dinner. Laura kept her fork moving and continued to swallow bits of food as she watched her daughter talking, still a child who believed everything would always be this way, the three of them a happy family that sat down to eat dinner together nearly every day.

Laura closed her eyes. *Remember this*, she thought. *At least you gave your daughter this for a little while.*

At the cottage, Anne put Lucy down for a nap after leaving Flossie's, then carried the baby monitor with her down to the dock, shivering in the cold, to think about everything her aunt had told them.

Her father was dead. Anne studied the water, the steady folding of the waves and the light mist rising as they crested, and realized that what she felt—besides the pure grief brought on by his letter so filled with regret—was a sense of relief. She no longer had to wonder where her father was. She could stop wondering if he'd ever return. There was pain in that, yes, but peace, too.

Her mother was another story. Why had Sarah felt so compelled to pretend she was something she wasn't? Anne understood her mother's motivation on a certain level—Sarah was in survival mode, no doubt, as she searched for a way out of her difficult life—but she felt angry at her and, more than that, cheated. She had no father now, and not even the mother she'd thought she had. She knew it didn't make sense to be angrier at her mother than her father—at least her mother had stuck around and provided for them, educated them, and raised them to be independent. Yet she was, for whatever inexplicable reason. Anne chewed her lip in frustration as she mulled all of this over.

By the metallic scent in the air, she could tell rain was coming. Maybe sleet. The cottage would be cold tonight. Her mother was right about the lack of insulation; the wind fingered easily through the old walls of the tiny house. She'd have to find another place to live by winter. But she'd be damned if she asked her mother for help. Sarah didn't deserve to be part of Anne's life or Lucy's, either, until she'd explained herself better.

Anne's cell phone rang as she continued looking out at the water, watching a cormorant diving for fish, its sleek black neck long and snakelike as the bird emerged from the waves. It was Sebastian, saying he was back from Washington and wanted to see her.

"I can bring takeout," he suggested.

Anne smiled at the sound of his voice and arched her back as a warmth spread between her shoulder blades, as if he'd placed his hand there. "No, let me cook," she said. "You've been on the road for days. I'm sure you're tired of eating out. I'll throw something quick together."

After Lucy's nap, Anne borrowed Flossie's car and drove to the store. Carrying the baby in the backpack, she bought fresh spinach, arborio rice, and chicken breasts.

She put the baby to bed early—for once, Lucy was cooperative—and started sautéing chicken breasts to go with the spinach risotto she'd made first. They'd have it with a salad on the side and a loaf of French bread she'd baked from the extra dough Sue had given her to bring home from the inn's kitchen. Everything was ready by the time Sebastian arrived with a bottle of cabernet around seven o'clock.

Anne had turned the electric baseboards on—the only source of heat in the cottage—but they still had to wear their sweaters as they ate. After dinner, she made a pot of tea with dried mint from Flossie's herb garden.

Sebastian built a fire in the woodstove while she brewed the tea. The cottage warmed quickly. They shed their sweaters and talked easily. Sebastian had gone to Washington to present a paper at a forestry conference. He told her a little about the research he'd based his paper on—before returning to Massachusetts, he'd been studying the effects of shading and warming on the leaf growth and shoot densities of alpine shrubs in the White Mountains—then asked about Anne's first days in the Folly Cove kitchen.

"So you like it?" he said after she told him a little about what she'd been doing.

"I do," she answered. "I love cooking. I always have. There's an art to creating food that's as beautiful to look at as it is delicious." She gestured at the half loaf of crusty bread still on the table. "That bread is so simple, just yeast and flour and salt. Yet with a few touches—maybe you add some fresh rosemary and oregano, or salt the crust—you end up with something unique. I never get tired of tasting food in restaurants and imagining what I'd do differently. I love breaking the rules, even if whatever I make fails a few times before I find flavors that work together. Experimenting with food makes me happy."

She stopped, her throat tightening, as she remembered something: her mother teaching her to poach an egg. *Something so simple but so easy to do wrong,* Sarah had said, standing beside Anne, who was on a stool in the kitchen, watching and waiting with a slotted spoon.

Her mother had taught her so much. Yet part of what she'd taught Anne was never to trust anyone.

Sebastian smiled at her, oblivious to the change in her mood. He looked tired—he'd just flown into Boston that afternoon, then had driven home to walk the dog before coming here. Mack lay at their feet, occasionally casting hopeful looks toward the table and thumping his tail when Anne gave him a bit of chicken.

"That's great that you're happy," he said. "I was worried you might resent having to work at the inn, after everything you've told me."

Anne shook her head. "No. When I was little, the inn's kitchen was the place I felt most at home. It was like this magical giant's house to me. There were all of these huge glass jars of flour and sugar, and long stainless-steel counters too tall for me to reach, with these enormous pots hanging above them or stacked on the shelves underneath."

It was like watching magicians at work, she thought: Rodrigo and the staff transforming raw ingredients into beautiful food, the waiters moving in and out of the kitchen like dancers, balancing plates on their arms.

"The pots on the bottom shelves were so huge," she explained to Sebastian. "Big enough for me to turn them into furniture. I pretended they were tables and chairs. Rodrigo never minded having me in the kitchen. He'd set me up in a corner out of the way. So many delicious smells! And so many complicated sounds and rhythms going on above my head! Almost like being at the symphony. I knew my mother wouldn't bother yelling at me, because she was busy conducting it all. She hardly noticed I was there."

Anne stopped herself from saying more, aware suddenly that her mother's lack of attention had never seemed important to her in the past—she always had her sisters and Flossie—until she'd had her own daughter. Now the idea of her mother being too busy for her stung.

She forced herself to smile at Sebastian, who'd been watching her face as she talked. She was probably talking too much.

Nerves. Anne was anxious, wondering why he hadn't touched her since arriving, other than a brief kiss on the cheek when he greeted her. Meanwhile, her entire body felt like it was electrified whenever she turned toward him. She longed to feel his hands on her thighs and hips, pulling her against him. But Sebastian remained reserved, apart.

"Sorry," she said. "You're so quiet. You must be tired."

"It's not that. I mean, yes, I'm tired. But I'm trying to work out what to say to you."

Her stomach felt suddenly leaden. "About what?"

"A few things. It's complicated." He got up and took their mugs to the kitchen counter, where he filled the sink with hot water and started washing the dishes. Anne didn't mind this. She understood that Sebastian was the sort of person who had to be in motion to think; she was the same way, her mind always calmer and more focused when she was doing tasks with her hands.

They cleaned the kitchen together, Sebastian's back to her as he scrubbed the dishes and pots after she'd scraped them and put the food away. He told her more about Washington and about an exhibit he'd seen at the Smithsonian.

Sebastian was wearing business clothes of a sort she'd never seen him wear: gray wool trousers and a striped, collared shirt. No tie. He must have taken the tie off on his way over, or maybe on the plane. Imagining this gesture, his competent fingers untangling the knot of his tie, made Anne want to unbutton her shirt right now while his back was turned. She imagined untucking his shirt and lifting it, pressing her bare breasts against his warm back.

She took a damp paper towel and moved to the other side of the counter, wiping bread crumbs into her hand from where she'd sliced the loaf. "My aunt told us today that our father is dead," she said before realizing the words were there, ready to be hurled into the air.

Sebastian spun around to face her across the counter. "My God, Anne. I'm so sorry. That must have been a shock. Was it? How do you feel? I know you haven't heard from him in a long time."

"Thirty years." She shrugged. "I don't really know what I feel. A little helpless, maybe. I hardly remember him. It was weird, having Flossie tell us instead of Mom. She has his ashes. Did you know you can mail cremated remains in a post-office box? They even have a special sticker they put on it. Black, of course."

"Oh, man," he said, and came around the counter to embrace her, resting his head on her chin. "I really am sorry. How did he die? Where was he?"

"Cancer. He'd been living in Florida. Apparently, Mom and Flossie both heard from him once in a while. They just never bothered to tell us. Weird, huh?" Anne felt her breath catch in her throat: another betrayal. And by Flossie, of all people.

"They were trying to protect you, I'm sure," Sebastian said. "Come on. Sit down. You poor thing. I'm so sorry," he repeated.

They carried their mugs to the couch. Anne set hers on the table, and noticed that Sebastian's shirt was damp from the sink. She turned on the couch to face him, pulling her knees up to her chest as a barrier between them. Not to keep him away from her, but to make it more difficult for her to reach over and lay a hand where the damp shirt adhered to his skin.

"The thing is, I never really understood why Dad left," Anne said. "I mean, I know he and my mom fought a lot—I have some memories of that—but I never really knew why. Or why Flossie stayed here with us, when she and Mom never really got along, either."

"She probably stayed to take care of you," Sebastian said.

"Mom could have hired nannies for that."

"Not while she was hospitalized."

He said this as if he were reminding Anne of a fact, but she knew nothing about this. "When was my mom in the hospital?"

"She was hospitalized several times after your father left," he said. "I remember, because my grandmother and Flossie were friends. My grandmother used to bring me here when I was a kid to help Flossie take care of you girls. I think my grandmother also helped out at the inn from time to time." He smiled at Anne. "You were little, still in elementary school. I'd already gone off to middle school and thought you were a royal pain."

Anne laughed, then bit her lip, thinking back. "I don't remember you coming to the house. Or anything about that time, really. Why was Mom hospitalized?" She imagined everything from cancer to a hysterectomy, but not the answer Sebastian gave.

"She had several nervous breakdowns," he said. "Three that I remember. She was in and out of McLean Hospital for several years."

McLean was a psychiatric hospital outside of Boston. "My God. I never knew any of that. I just remember her going away sometimes."

"I'm sure that was by design. Your mother wouldn't have wanted anyone to know. Maybe not even her own people."

"What people? Mom's parents died before she married my father, and she didn't have siblings," Anne said, then caught herself: she was repeating her mother's lies. "No, I take that back. Flossie just told us Mom has a sister, and her mother was still alive when Mom married Dad, though we never met our grandmother."

Sebastian nodded. "I remember my grandmother saying, 'That poor woman, cut off from her real family.' I was impressed at the time because my own grandmother was tough as an old boot. She never felt sorry for anyone. In any case, Flossie kept the inn going and took care of you whenever your mother wasn't well."

"God. How horrible for Mom. I still can't believe Dad could leave her flat like that. Never mind his own children," she said, aware of the bitterness lacing her words.

"Your father might not have survived if he'd stayed here," Sebastian said gently. "I don't excuse his behavior. But after living with my wife, I know it's possible for mental illness to make people do all sorts of things. Your father was an alcoholic. He probably had to remove himself from places and people that triggered his drinking."

Anne looked at him, her face hot with shame. "You knew?"

He shrugged. "Most people in town did."

Anne thought of her mother, of the strength it must have taken to keep going. "I'm surprised Flossie didn't tell us any of that."

"Perhaps she was only telling you the things she thought might impact you directly." He glanced at his watch. "I should probably go. It's getting late and you've had an emotional day. I really am sorry about your dad."

"Don't go. Please." Anne unwound her arms and legs and leaned over to touch his knee. "Why don't you spend the night?"

He didn't exactly flinch, but his eyes were wary. "It's probably not a good idea."

She removed her hand. "I take it you're regretting our night together."

Sebastian's eyes were dark with pain, all of the gold light rinsed out of them. "Of course not," he said softly.

"Then what? You felt ambushed," she guessed. "The same way you felt ambushed by me in high school."

"What are you talking about?"

"You don't remember?" Anne laughed. "Boy, that's the perfect end to a hideous day. Here I've been worrying about it pretty much since it happened, and you haven't given that night a thought. You don't even remember!"

"Anne, what are you talking about?"

"Your sister's graduation party and the way I stalked you, then practically threw myself into your car!"

"I wasn't aware of you stalking me."

"Of course you weren't!" Anne lowered her voice because of Lucy. "I don't remember meeting you when I was little. The first time I remember seeing you was at Paige's party. I watched you all night. Biding my time. I'd chosen you, you see."

"Chosen me for what?" Now he sounded really confused.

Anne willed him to put his arms around her and tell her that she hadn't made yet another mistake, becoming involved with him. You'd think she'd learn to be more cautious. But maybe having a father who left you and a mother who was never truthful only taught you that pain was the natural course of love.

"I wanted you to be my first lover," she said. "That's why I chose you."

"You're kidding."

"No." Anne stood up and went to the counter, flicked off an imaginary crumb, then moved the jug of dried hydrangeas to the center again. "I was a virgin and didn't want to stay that way. You seemed like the perfect choice, because you were older and about to go away and see the world."

"Why was that a good thing? Me going away?"

She turned around. Sebastian was sitting straight up on the couch, his hands on the knees of his gray trousers like a man at a bus stop. "Because I didn't want any complications, just like you don't want them now," she said. "And I don't blame you. Love is for fools."

Oh God. She'd said the one word she'd been determined not to say: *love.*

Sebastian stood up and came over to her. "Anne. Stop this. You're nobody's fool."

"You should go," she said. "It really is getting late."

"I'm not going anywhere until I explain," he said.

For a minute she felt a flutter of hope. Maybe Sebastian would take her in his arms and kiss her as he had before, warm her with his breath and hands.

No. He was pointing to the couch and politely asking her to sit down. Once she had, he sat on the coffee table facing her.

"I can't believe you think I don't remember the night of Paige's party," he began. "It was like a dream. You were so beautiful. So honest and open. I was sick to death of girls I'd met in college. All those games. I thought about you every day for months after I left. I wanted to get in touch with you, but I knew it was foolish: you were only sixteen and I was already in college, ready to go abroad. I knew it wouldn't work. You needed time to finish high school and grow up." He rubbed his face with one hand, bringing color to his cheeks. "I had no idea I was an experiment for you, but I'm flattered that you chose me for your first time."

"You are?" Anne felt her shoulders relax a little. "I was afraid you'd feel used or something."

At that Sebastian laughed, and it made her realize he hadn't laughed since his arrival for dinner. "I assure you, that never crossed my mind," he said. "I just felt lucky as hell."

They smiled at each other for a moment, and then Sebastian grew serious again. "But having said all that, I'm not ready for you, Anne."

"What do you mean?'"

"Exactly that. I was in a terrible marriage. A very painful one. I haven't recovered from how Jenny," he began, and took a deep breath. "From how Jenny chose to end her life, and our baby's. When I look at you and Lucy, like I told you before, it gives me hope. You're a wonderful mother. Everything a mother should be. But I'm not ready to be a father."

"I wasn't asking you to be," Anne said, hurt making her sound sharper than she'd intended. "Making love doesn't mean we're going to get married. Sex doesn't catapult you into fatherhood. Believe me," she added bitterly, "Colin taught me that well enough. You and I are just getting to know each other. I don't even know if I'm staying at Folly Cove."

"I understand all that," he said. "But being with you does mean being with Lucy, too. It's a package deal, right? And I'm not equipped to be around a baby. I can't even bring myself to hold her."

Anne thought about this and realized she hadn't seen him touch Lucy, other than the day she'd fallen off the horse and Sebastian had been the one to put Lucy in her crib. "Why not?"

"Isn't it obvious? I'm afraid," he said. "My wife killed herself and our child. I wasn't able to protect them. I feel cursed. I know that's not logical, but there it is. So, as much as I care about you, I don't think it's wise for us to continue seeing each other." He stood up. "I hope you understand."

"I don't," she said. "I think you're being a jerk and a coward." She stood up, too, anger making her back and knees feel stiff. "But since that's the case, you're right. You should leave. I had a father like you. A quitter! And the father of my child isn't any better. I don't need a man in my life who quits the minute he's afraid. We're all afraid, Sebastian. But some of us stick it out anyway."

He pulled on his jacket. "We could be friends," he said. "We could take things slowly."

"No," Anne said. "We've gone too deep for us to take things slowly now. But I wish you luck and a happy life. I really do."

Sebastian walked through the door, head down. Somehow she prevented herself from slamming it shut behind him.

Her phone rang on the counter. Laura's number was on the screen. Anne grabbed it, ready to rant and weep. "Hey."

Anne had expected her sister to recognize from her tone that something was wrong. To ask. Instead, Laura was the one sobbing. "You have to come to the hospital."

"Why? What happened?" Anne asked, clutching the phone so hard to her face that she bit the inside of her cheek and tasted blood.

"It's Mom! She fell. They think she had a stroke. They're doing tests now. I'm here and so is Elly. Hurry, Anne!"

"I'll be there as soon as I can."

Anne hung up and ran out the door. Sebastian was just backing out of the driveway. "Wait!" she shouted. "I need you to take me to the hospital!" she said once he'd rolled down the window.

"What's going on?"

"My mom's had a fall, maybe a stroke." Then she remembered the baby. "Shit. Lucy. I don't have a car seat. It's still in Flossie's car."

"Take my car," Sebastian said. "I'll stay with the baby."

Anne nodded, mute with gratitude, and ran inside to grab her jacket and boots.

CHAPTER EIGHTEEN

Sarah was lying in a dim room, but this wasn't her bed. Not her sheets and pillows. These were rough and smelled of bleach. She would never allow these linens on her bed! Or on any of the beds at the inn.

She tried to turn over, but something restrained her. As if her wrists were tied. There was a beeping sound, loud beside her. As if a truck were backing into the bed.

She panicked. She was in a hospital!

Her eyes flew open. Sarah saw the hospital bed, the white blanket on her body. But she couldn't be back at McLean! Not again! She'd done everything they'd asked! The therapy, the medications!

She reached up with her free hand to touch her scalp and was relieved not to feel any sticky spots. The last time at McLean there had been electric shock therapy. They'd put her under for that. She'd wake up not remembering anything, but she'd have telltale spots where they used the gel to make the electrodes adhere to her scalp.

"You won't feel any pain," the doctor had assured her. "You'll sleep like a baby. And you'll wake up feeling so much better. We've made a great deal of progress in this area of mental health."

Some progress. Still the white gowns, the shuffling patients medicated until their eyeballs rolled around in their heads.

Three times she'd been hospitalized. The ECT treatments came last. They had worked, somewhat, to help her overcome the crippling anxiety, the depression. But Sarah was determined never to return. So far she hadn't.

So where was she now? A hospital, yes, obviously. But this place felt different. Busier. And nobody was moaning or screaming or muttering.

Sarah forced herself to breathe slowly and evenly. She tried to sit up. Instantly, she felt a restraining hand on her arm. She tried to shake it off.

"Easy, Mom. Let me fix the bed."

Elizabeth was here! Then this must not be the terrible past but the beautiful present. Thank God.

Elly, she reminded herself. *She doesn't like the name you gave her. How could she know you named her for that choral director in high school, the one teacher who ever thought you'd amount to something? God bless Elizabeth Murphy.*

There was her daughter's lovely face, hovering above her own. The eyes wide and clear and blue, the blond hair a smooth curtain. Sarah tried to smile, but something felt wrong with her mouth. She felt one side go up but not the other, as if it were stitched in place.

And Elly looked all wrong, too. There were lines around her eyes. The cobwebs of age.

Her daughter was a woman now, with a life of her own, Sarah remembered. Older like the rest of them. How was it possible that all three of her daughters were this old and this unhappy? Disappointed with their lives, even with so many options at their fingertips? Options she'd never had.

Disappointment was like an epidemic among today's young women. If you could have it all, maybe you were never satisfied with any of it. Tragic.

Sarah winced at a sudden pain in her neck. She remembered everything now: today, and the days that came before it. Maybe this was it, the death she'd thought was coming. Never enough time in a life.

The weeks and months and years had flipped by so fast that she could still remember dancing the very first time with Neil, the two of them swaying cheek to cheek to "Summertime," and then "I've Got the

World on a String," his male scent of starched shirts and spicy after-shave. She could recall those moments with her husband as if they'd been last night, even as she was massaging her arthritic hands. Hands so thin now, the veins showed through the loose skin like blue twine.

Goddamn Neil. The nerve of him, to die.

Elly looked worried, but she was still angry with her, too. Sarah could see that in her daughter's eyes: the flinty gray beneath the blue. Elly's anger felt physically painful, like the sharp pricks of a Swiss Army knife.

Yes, that's what Elly would be, if she were a weapon: something small with multiple blades. Sneaky and quick.

"Death by a thousand cuts." Wasn't that what the Chinese did for punishment, once upon a time? *Lingchi*. Neil had taught her that word. Neil, who read everything. Who had gone off and seen the world without her. Then died before he could come home again. Had to be shipped home in an ordinary little box, manhandled by incompetent postal carriers.

Well, whose fault was that? She thought this, but was aware of tears. Of a dark hollow space beneath her rib cage. Her chest heaved. So unpleasant, grief. It left a bad taste in her mouth and an anvil press-ing down on her heart.

Laura was here, too, approaching the bed to peer down at her. She would never be a small and sneaky knife. Laura's misery and anger turned her into something blunt and hard, a war hammer or a mace. Sarah could imagine her eldest daughter wielding a weapon on horse-back. Fearless. Determined. Steadfast. Furious.

Laura had certainly been furious last night, when Sarah had called and asked her to come to the inn. "Why didn't you dial 911, if you could get to the phone?" Laura had shouted when she'd arrived and found Sarah on the floor. "Why did you call me instead? What if it's too late?" Yelling at her. Red in the face. Terrified and angry.

Sarah had passed out again before she could explain the shame, the need to avoid hospitals at all costs. She'd held her head high, always, even knowing people talked about her hospitalizations. How unstable she was.

"Her husband left and took her mind with him," she'd heard a woman say once as she passed.

But Sarah had shown them. She was a rock, as solid as the granite around Folly Cove.

Now she remembered the phone call that had sent her tumbling down the back staircase. Flossie. Saying she didn't care if Sarah kicked her out of the house. Off the property. She was sorry, but she had told the girls everything.

"It was time," Flossie had said. "You should have been there to do it yourself. This foolishness has gone on long enough, Sarah. You don't want these lies hanging over your head forever. It was one thing to lie to your husband, but these are your daughters."

Sarah had been upstairs, checking on a room that Betty said had a mold issue. She was on her way back down to the office when Flossie called. She had started shouting at her husband's sister the way she used to shout at Neil toward the end. She'd finally thrown her phone down the stairs. How tremendously powerful that anger felt, as if she could hurl the phone through the walls!

Then a moment of confusion as Sarah's vision blurred and her face tingled. She'd chalked that up to being angry, too. But her balance was off, and as she began her descent she slipped and lost her footing.

She'd fallen all the way down the back staircase. There was nobody to hear her cry out. Rhonda, Betty, Rodrigo, and the rest of the kitchen staff had gone home for the night. She didn't even know if Anne had been cooking for the dinner shift.

Anne. What sort of weapon would she be, if she were angry?

Anne was her strongest daughter. The one who had never needed her. She would be something nuclear. Poof, and you were nothing to her. Vaporized. Ash.

Laura's face had floated out of view and Elly was speaking. "Mom? Mom, can you hear me? Do you need something? Should I call the nurse?"

Sarah moved her lips. Or thought she did. Hoped. She wanted to ask for water, but no sound emerged.

"Nurse!" Elly called.

. . .

"I feel like absolute crap," Elly said, cradling her chin in her hands, elbows balanced on her knees. "You know what my last words to Mom were yesterday?" She dropped her hands from her face. "'Don't expect me to help you,' or something like that. It's probably my fault she had a stroke and fell down the stairs."

Elly looked at her sisters, who looked back at her with expressions smoothed blank by shock. The three of them were in the waiting area while the nurse examined their mother. They'd already spent two hours in the ER, where Sarah had undergone a series of tests, including an MRI, and where several times they'd had to tell the nurses to stop shouting at her.

"Just because she has white hair, that doesn't mean our mom's deaf, for Christ's sake!" Elly had yelled at them. "She can hear you fine!"

Still, they'd had to correct the paperwork to give the nurses their mother's real birth date. Oddly, the nurses didn't seem all that surprised.

"You'd be amazed how many people lie," one chatty RN told them.

"Elly, your mother had an ischemic stroke," Ryder said now. "No way was this your fault, babe. Her fall was an unlucky accident, that's all."

She and her sisters swiveled their heads to look at him. Elly had nearly forgotten he was there. Ryder was sitting apart from them, off in a corner. He looked so out of place that he seemed to have come from another country, or maybe even a different dimension, with his long blond hair, his earring, his leather jacket and blue jeans.

"He's right," Laura said. Elly could tell by the look she gave Ryder that Laura was surprised he was here, too, even though she was the one who'd invited him. "Nothing anybody said or did caused this."

"I don't know about that." Anne was curled up against Laura on the short orange plastic sofa, some sort of cooking sauce splattered on her off-white sweater.

"What do you mean?" Laura demanded.

"Maybe the stroke was caused by stress. Like, by Mom knowing Aunt Flossie told us everything. Everything except the fact that Mom was hospitalized before. Three times, at least."

"What?" Elly and Laura said in unison, loudly enough that Ryder sat up straighter.

Anne nodded. Her red hair was bright beneath the fluorescent lighting, streaked with gold highlights. "I found out Mom suffered from depression and spent time at McLean's. You don't remember that?"

"No," Laura said, "and I was a lot older than you. If that really happened, Mom and Flossie must have been pretty crafty to keep it from us."

"Do you ever remember Mom being gone?" Anne asked. "Because I definitely do."

Laura frowned. "A few times, sure. Flossie stayed with us when Mom went to a hotel conference once. I think she was gone about a week. Oh, and Flossie stayed with us another time, too, when Mom had to go away and take care of a sick cousin or something. I remember that because Mom missed my sixth-grade graduation."

Anne lifted an eyebrow. "There you go. Flossie must have been covering for her."

"I don't get it, though," Elly said. "Why didn't Flossie tell us that while she was spilling the rest of it? Maybe it's not true, Anne. Mental breakdowns? Does that sound like Mom?" She looked from one sister to the other, but saw only doubt on their faces.

"Where's Flossie now?" Laura said. "Did either of you call her?"

Elly hadn't. Neither had Anne. That was probably better, Elly thought. "Let's not call her yet," she said. "If she's the reason Mom got so worked up, it won't do her any good if Flossie shows up here. What about Lucy?" She turned to Anne. "Where is she?"

Anne's cheeks turned pink. "I left her with Sebastian. He was at my house having dinner."

"Oooh," Laura and Elly chorused.

"Really!" she protested. "I'd like it to be different, believe me, but it's not."

Elly reached over to pat her hand. "Give it time."

Ryder stood up and stretched. All three sisters turned to stare at him, Elly inhaling sharply as Ryder's shirt rode up, revealing his strong tanned stomach above his jeans.

They hadn't made love yet—Elly had spent the afternoon showing

him the area, hiking around Halibut Point and having coffee on Bearskin Neck at a café overlooking the water. He'd made her see Cape
Ann with a Californian's eyes, marveling at the small wooden houses
with their picket fences, the rocky coves, the birch trees and pines, the
vibrant colors of the leaves, and the Gloucester fisherman's statue—
which Ryder claimed he recognized from the boxes of frozen fish
sticks his mother used to serve.

She'd been intending to take him to bed right after dinner, after
making polite conversation with Laura, who she guessed would still be
reeling from having told Kennedy that she and Jake were separating.
But Jake was still at the house with Kennedy and said Laura had gotten a call from Sarah. Everything had moved fast from there; Ryder
had driven her to the hospital in his rental car.

"I'm going to find the cafeteria," Ryder said now. "Anybody else
want something?"

They asked for soup and coffee, offered him money. He refused it
and left.

"So what's up with that guy, Elly?" Anne gestured at the door after
Ryder was gone. "He looks like Leonardo DiCaprio on steroids. Like,
if I were a bear, I'd totally wrestle him."

Laura snorted.

"Don't you dare laugh," Elly warned her, then turned to Anne.
"Laura invited Ryder to film Mom's birthday party. He's a cameraman
I know from Los Angeles. A friend, that's all."

Just then the nurse poked her head in the door. "Your mother's
awake and wants to see you girls." She was the oldest nurse they'd seen
yet, but her eyes were a lively green. "What a lucky mom, having three
daughters. Please try not to tire her out, though."

Their mother looked like a porcelain doll. That was Elly's first
thought as they crowded back into the hospital room.

Sarah was a tinier version of herself. Her blue eyes were enormous
in her narrow face. Without makeup, her eyebrows were gray, nearly
nonexistent. Her eyes were lashless, her lips pale and chapped. She
looked nearly flat beneath the white hospital blankets.

"How are you feeling?" Elly asked.

"Like a million bucks." Sarah's speech was only slightly slurred.

Elly was relieved that her mother could speak—the doctor had told them it was a minor stroke and that no surgery was necessary, just medication to dissolve the clot. The drug was being administered now through an IV. She'd also been afraid the stroke might impact her mother's facial expressions, but other than a slight droopiness to one side of her mouth, there wasn't much sign that anything was wrong.

"I'm sorry we argued, Mom. I really am." Elly touched her mother's hand and was reassured to feel how warm it was.

Her mother went to wave the hand at her, then remembered the IV and put it down. "Don't be ridiculous. I was in a snit over nothing. Here I am, alive, with all of my girls. Who gives a hoot if I'm sixty-five or seventy-five?"

"That's the spirit, Mom," Laura muttered. "Just keep lying while you're dyin'."

Elly jabbed Laura in the ribs.

Sarah peered over Laura's shoulder. "Where's Jake? I thought he'd be here."

"Home with Kennedy," Elly said quickly, so Laura wouldn't have to lie. Though, for all she knew, that was the truth.

"And the baby? With Flossie, I suppose," Sarah said. "Flossie's hogging that baby. I do hope you'll bring her to the inn, Anne. At least for a little visit."

"I will," Anne promised. "How long does the doctor say you have to stay here?"

"Just two days, and then I go to rehab. Maybe a week in all." Her mother's mouth opened and shut, as if she were exercising her jaw. "Oh no. My God. The Sanderson wedding is the weekend after next! More than a hundred guests. I forgot all about it!" She jerked her head around on the pillow, agitated.

"Don't worry, Mom," Anne said. "We'll take care of it."

"Right," Laura said. "We'll all pitch in."

"But you have your business to run, Laura." Sarah's voice was querulous. "And don't you have a horse show coming up?"

Elly was astonished that her mother could remember so many details after what she'd been through. "It's fine, Mom," she said. "We'll all work together."

"Me, too," Ryder said from the doorway.

"Good Lord, who brought the Viking?" Sarah asked.

Elly laughed. "I did," she said, glancing at Ryder, who grinned back. "This is Ryder. My friend from California."

Sarah lifted her head to look at him again. "Well done." She dropped her head back again.

"You should just plan on resting, Mom," said Anne.

"I will if you take care of that wedding," Sarah said. "Everything you need is in the blue folder on my desk. Rhonda can help you find it." She closed her eyes.

For a moment nobody said anything. Elly looked at her sisters and they looked back at her, all of them waiting for something to happen next.

"You're dismissed," Sarah said, opening one eye. "Go! Don't just stand there with your mouths hanging open. I'm not going to die yet."

To Laura's shock, Kennedy claimed that she had already known about Jake.

"But how?" Laura demanded, disbelieving.

She and Kennedy were sitting on the living room sofa the night after Sarah's stroke, sharing a bowl of popcorn. Before getting the call from her mother, she and Jake had told Kennedy during dinner that her father was moving out. It was a stilted conversation with Jake doing most of the talking. They hadn't told her about Anthony specifically. Only that Jake had been struggling for a while, and that it was time for him to "come out of the closet," as he'd put it, making awkward air quotes with his fingers.

"We hope you know this isn't your fault, and that we both love you very much," Jake had added.

Kennedy had rolled her eyes, looking so much like her grandmother when she did it that Laura had thought, *Atta girl*.

"No duh," Kennedy had said. "You're *gay*, Dad. I get that it's nothing to do with me. How would it be? Can I go upstairs now?"

Jake had wept during the conversation, but Laura had felt numb and surprisingly removed. She'd managed to find him a box of Kleenex. Let him go back to Anthony for comfort. She'd been about to send him on his way when her mother had called. She'd had to ask Jake to stay until she got home from the hospital, and was surprised to find that it was a comfort to have him there to hold her when she returned and told him about her mother.

Kennedy had gone to school as usual today. They'd had dinner separately—Laura had gone to the hospital to see her mother—and now she'd lured Kennedy downstairs with popcorn, hot chocolate, and the promise of watching *Singin' in the Rain* again and teaching her a few more steps. Party plans for her mother were apparently still on. This afternoon the nurses had assured them that Sarah would go to rehab for a few days, but she'd be home soon.

"Seriously," Laura said to her daughter now, taking another hand-ful of popcorn. "How did you know Dad was gay?"

"You don't want to know."

Laura considered this. Kennedy was probably right. "Tell me anyway."

Kennedy picked up her hot chocolate and studied the whipped cream, then dipped her finger into it and licked it. "From Dad's porn," she said finally.

"What?" Laura nearly choked on her popcorn.

"On the computer," Kennedy said. "I used his desktop a few times for a project. And, you know, there it was. Gay porn."

"Kennedy Sarah Williams," Laura said, "don't you dare lie to me. There has to be more to the story than that! Dad wouldn't just leave a porn site open on his computer."

Kennedy gave a world-weary sigh. "Yeah, see, there's this thing with Google, where you type in a search term and it starts filling in the letters. You know about that?"

"Of course."

Kennedy shrugged. "Okay. So, I was on Dad's computer, looking stuff up about reproduction for our biology unit. I typed in 'penis,' and all these sites with pictures popped up."

"Oh. I see." It felt like a wad of cotton was stuck in Laura's throat, choking her as she tried to mentally block the images her daughter must have seen on Jake's computer.

"It wasn't S and M or anything," Kennedy reassured her.

"Oh. Good." Laura put her head in her hands.

"But it was guy-on-guy stuff. You know. Men kissing naked. Penises everywhere."

"Stop! Enough!" Laura kept her face covered for another moment, trying not to see "stuff," much less "penises everywhere."

"Sorry. You asked." Kennedy slurped more of her hot chocolate.

When Laura was finally able to look at her daughter again, she said, "So from that you decided Dad must be gay."

"Well, not right away. First I thought maybe the same thing happened to him that happened to me, right? That he'd landed in those sites accidentally. But I tried it again a few times and the same thing happened. On his desktop *and* on his laptop. Dad never erases his search history," Kennedy added. "*Always* erase your search history if you don't want anybody tracking where you've been online."

Laura managed a smile, while at the same time worrying about what online activity her own daughter might be hiding. "Thanks for the advice. But why didn't you tell me? Or ask Dad about it?"

"I tried, but Dad denied it. He said it was an accident. And I didn't want to tell you, because, well. I just didn't." Kennedy shifted in her seat and glanced at the television screen, though nothing was playing.

"Because you were trying to protect me. And maybe a little part of you didn't want it to be true."

Kennedy nodded, turning back to Laura, her blue eyes bright with tears. "I'm sorry I didn't tell you. What if Dad's been sleeping around and you get a disease or something? It would be all my fault! What if you get AIDS and *die*?" She was sobbing now.

"Oh, honey." Laura reached over and gathered her daughter into her arms. "Is that what you've been worrying about? Don't! Dad is not sleeping around. I promise. And I've been tested. I'm absolutely fine. So is he."

Kennedy sniffed and wiped her eyes on her sweater sleeve. "What are we going to do without him, Mom? I hate Dad! But I already miss him, and he's only been gone like an hour!"

Laura moved over and put her arm around her daughter, resting her cheek on top of Kennedy's soft blond hair. She thought of Neil leaving them, of how hurt she'd been that he was no longer at her horse shows and how angry she was that she had to step in and help her mother with the inn and her younger sisters. She was only beginning to realize how furious she'd been with her father.

She still was, though less so. Now she thought about Neil being an alcoholic and struggling to survive both his own addiction and his guilt, and how, at the end, he'd wanted to come home and hadn't been able to do it after all. She was saddened by that thought, even though Laura knew she would have met his return with mixed emotions.

"The thing about families is that they're very, very complicated," Laura said. "We think we know our parents, but there will always be some parts of their lives that we can't know, because they're the adults and we're the children. I feel like that about my own mom and dad."

She pulled Kennedy a little closer, reveling in the solid warmth of her. "You're going to feel angry with Dad for a while. But he still loves you, and I'm sure he misses you already, too. You can see Dad anytime you want. And right now we're going to watch *Singin' in the Rain* and practice our dance moves. Okay?"

"Okay." Kennedy sniffed. "FYI, nobody says 'dance moves' anymore, Mom."

"Oh. Good thing I have you to keep me current."

CHAPTER NINETEEN

"I like a woman who plays hard to get, but you really didn't have to go to all this trouble and hide from me in a hospital," Gil said. "Phone tag would've been sufficient."

Sarah snorted. Ordinarily, she would be horrified to have a man pay her a visit while she was recuperating, but Laura had brought her pretty blue robe with the white satin piping. The blue brought out her eyes, and the sleeves were long enough to cover the terrible sight of her aging arms without being a nuisance. "Don't flatter yourself," she told Gil.

"Oh, don't worry. I know you've probably got a dozen suitors," he said, "but I enjoy a challenge. Here. These are for you. Where would you like them?"

He had brought eighteen pink long-stemmed roses arranged in a vase with salal and ivy. Must have set him back a hundred dollars easy, Sarah thought, but she waved them away. "Over on the windowsill with the others is fine."

She had received several arrangements in the two days they'd kept her in the hospital, though she wasn't about to admit to Gil that they were all from her daughters, except that fat monstrosity of a cactus dish garden from her sister-in-law.

The note Flossie had attached to the cactus dish was the usual metaphor-laden message, something about the cactus representing endurance, hers and Sarah's, and their ability to stand the test of time.

Then the Zen clincher: "We cannot forgive others until we forgive ourselves, and we cannot do that until we look at our own failures and see them as lessons learned."

Anne had brought the cactus to the hospital. Flossie hadn't been in to see her yet, making Sarah wonder whether Flossie still believed Sarah's threat to kick her off the property. She hoped not.

"What is it?" Gil said, startling her. She'd forgotten he was here.

"Oh, nothing."

"Your secrets are safe with me. Who else can you tell, if not a nearly perfect stranger?" He leaned forward and touched her arm, his face serious. His eyebrows were still dark even though his hair was going white in places, making him look serious when she knew he probably meant only half of everything he said, just like her. "Come on, *bubbe*, tell me," he said.

She looked at him suspiciously. "Doesn't that mean 'grandmother?'"

Gil sat back and laughed. "You got me there. I guess that's not exactly the kind of hot talk a woman wants to hear."

Sarah moved up a little against her pillows, primly tucking the white blanket and sheet snugly around her waist. "I am in a hospital, in case you hadn't noticed. Your timing for hot talk leaves a little to be desired."

"I'll work on that. So tell me, Sarah." Gil wasn't grinning anymore. "What's got you so down?"

Oh, what the hell, Sarah thought. "I'm a liar, and I've been caught with my pants down around my knees."

He stared at her for a minute, his brown eyes round as marbles, and then Gil let loose with a real belly laugh, causing one of the nurses—the real crabby one, Mrs. Finich—to smile when she walked past the door.

Gil wiped his eyes. "You want to confess them to me? I'll hear you out if it'll make you feel better. And I promise you that whatever lies you've told, they're not so bad."

"Don't be so sure."

"Try me."

And so Sarah told him everything, about her little sister and the chilly apartment near the airport, about sleeping in a parked car and how her mother couldn't keep a job because of the drinking.

"You think I like being on welfare? Do you?" her mother would scream whenever Sarah asked why she didn't get a job so they could pay the bills.

Her mother traded the welfare stamps for a pint every week, Sarah told Gil. "She thought I didn't know this, but of course I had to grow up sharp, observing every little thing she did. It was a matter of self-preservation."

Her poor sister, Joanie, had never been sharp. Had simply said, "Yes, Ma," to anything their mother said or did. Joanie had married that old fart when she was just seventeen so their mother would have a roof over her head.

Even when Sarah told her the truth, Joanie hadn't believed the marriage was a setup, one their own mother had dreamed up to get them out of that dump. Ma had pushed the man at Sarah first, but when Sarah wouldn't let him up her skirt, there was Joanie, younger and even more innocent.

"Joanie was as blond and pretty as I was," Sarah told Gil, "but as dumb as a post and soft as soap."

When Sarah tried to warn Joanie about their mother's plan to move in with them after the wedding, Joanie had said, "You're just jealous because I'm the one who got a husband first. And a house of my own! And what do you have, Sarah? Nothing at all!"

"I told my sister she didn't have to marry that toad," Sarah said, "but she wouldn't listen. She was afraid our ma would go hungry if she didn't do it."

Not long after that, Joanie was pregnant. "She had five kids before her husband finally died," Sarah said. "God, the picture of that horrible man lying on top of my pretty little sister still turns my stomach."

She looked away from Gil, pretending to catch her breath when really it was the tears she was trying to catch. All this time, she'd been missing her sister, she realized. Had felt bad for leaving her.

"I still feel guilty," she said.

"Why?"

"Because it should have been me! I was the oldest. If I'd married the guy, Joanie would've been spared. She always tried hard in school. Maybe she would have even made it to community college."

Gil reached over and took her hand, stroked the back of it with his thumb. "You need to let that go," he said. "You were a kid when all that happened. A kid trying to survive."

"Maybe. But it gets worse, see. I tried to forget about everything so hard, I never even told my own family," Sarah said. "My husband, my girls? They didn't know any of this. Not because I was ashamed of Joanie, but because I felt so bad that I wasn't strong enough to help her. I ran away. Just like Neil."

"Did your sister's life turn out okay?"

"I don't know. I think so. She's a widow with five kids. Flossie says she lives in a nice house."

"Good. And do you forgive Neil for leaving you?" Gil asked.

Sarah sniffed and nodded. "He couldn't help it."

"Right. So now you have to forgive yourself," Gil said. "I want you to remember yourself as that scared little girl. You can help her by saying, 'It's okay, honey. You did the best you could, and things turned out fine.' Can you say that for me?"

"Don't be stupid," Sarah said, feeling cross and scared, too.

"Say it," Gil urged. "Come on. I know you can do it."

Sarah closed her eyes. "I can't."

"You can. Repeat after me: 'It's okay, honey. You did the best you could, and things turned out fine.'"

Slowly, he said the words again, halting after each phrase until Sarah repeated it after him.

When she opened her eyes again, Gil was smiling at her with a light in his eyes that looked suspiciously like love.

"God, you're a sentimental jerk," she said.

"I am what I am," he said. "Lucky for you."

When they told Sarah she was being moved from the hospital to the rehab center after two days, she'd been horrified all over again by the idea.

"I need to be back at work!" she complained to that bossy child doctor with the square black glasses that made him look like a cartoon character. He'd suggested that she attend the chair yoga session in the PT room, too, and she'd been livid. Yoga was for people like Flossie. People who had time to lie on their backs with their legs in the air.

Ultimately, though, rehab was a pleasant surprise. The PT was adorable, a young man just out of college with dimples. The food was tolerable, and she was able to catch up on Fox News in her sunny private room, where she didn't have some commie roommate moaning at her to change the channel.

Flossie finally showed up on her third day in rehab. For once, the woman was in something other than yoga pants, but Sarah wasn't sure the wide gray wool trousers and oversize white wool sweater paired well with red Chinese slippers. She looked like a knitted sock monkey.

"You look like you'll live," Flossie pronounced, handing Sarah a strangely shaped gift. Wrapped in newspaper, of course, because Flossie was the queen of recycling. "How are you feeling?"

"Like somebody cut my puppet strings." Sarah dangled one arm. "I'm still too weak on one side to pick up my applesauce spoon."

"Well. You never did like applesauce."

"True enough." Sarah opened the newspaper and discovered a handmade driftwood frame—Flossie had been making these for years—and, inside it, a photograph of Sarah and Joanie. Sarah was six and Joanie was in her arms, a chubby baby in a white sundress that matched Sarah's. Both of them had bows in their hair.

Sarah's eyes filled. "Where did you ever dig up this artifact?"

"I had to ransack your bedroom closet." Flossie pointed to a small suitcase near the door that Sarah hadn't noticed her carrying. "Ostensibly, I was gathering your coming-home outfit."

"Thank you," Sarah said, setting the picture down gently on the bedside table with its box of scratchy tissues and plastic cup. Why did hospitals and rehab centers insist on buying the same things people did for preschools?

"So, are you tossing me out on my ear?" Flossie crossed one short leg over the other, knocking her foot into the side of the bed. "Have you put my house up for sale?"

"You know better," Sarah said.

Flossie nodded once, sharply. "How are the girls?"

"They're like scared little rabbits. Not one of them has said a thing to me about any of it since my fall."

"They're worried about you, Sarah," Flossie said. "Every mother should be so lucky."

"And every sister." Sarah reached out to touch Flossie's hand. "You've always known how to take care of me and my girls. Thank you."

Flossie nodded. "It'll be good to have you back."

They finally discharged her two days after Flossie's visit. "All set, Miss Sarah? Last day, dear! You must be so glad to be going home."

It was her favorite aide, Monique, that little brunette with the very white smile and an engagement ring with a diamond bigger than a tooth. Some doctor had snapped her up, most likely. Good for her.

"Ready when you are," Sarah said. "My daughter should be here any time now."

"She's just outside in reception," Monique said. "Your granddaughter, too. She looks just like you!"

Heavens, Sarah thought. If Monique saw a resemblance between herself and Kennedy, she'd better sign up for double sessions of Pilates next week.

But Kennedy looked different. Her new hairstyle was very becoming, cut above the shoulders and with a new slant to the bangs. She actually looked like she had a neck. She wore black leggings under a bright green tunic with birds on it, and chunky boots.

Not Sarah's idea of high fashion, but she knew girls wore these sorts of outfits now, playing hippie because the hippies were dead. Thank the Lord.

"Hello, Kennedy," Sarah said, smiling from her wheelchair, which of course wasn't the least bit necessary, but the hospital insisted on it.

"They'll give you a wheelchair so you don't fall and sue their hind ends," Flossie had warned her. "Don't freak out about it. Just enjoy the ride."

"How do you feel?" Laura was asking. She looked thinner, too, but other than that, no change: she was dressed as if she'd come straight from the barn, and smelled of horses and hay.

Laura must have seen her noticing this, because she said, "Sorry, I just came from mucking stalls. They said I had to be here by ten o'clock. But they've taken forever on the paperwork. I bet you're hungry, Mom. It's nearly noon."

"Not very, no." Sarah tipped her head up to smile. "Thank you for taking time out of your busy day to fetch me."

There. In the hospital, Sarah had had plenty of time to think, even with her daughters visiting her, sometimes one at a time, or occasionally all three arriving together like a gaggle of geese, honking their laughter down the hall so that the noise reached the room before they did. And during this strange thinking time, Sarah had decided she must find ways to be kinder and more grateful, especially to her daughters. Flossie would be gone one day and she would need to rely on them.

Laura looked surprised. "Of course, Mom. I'm happy to do it. Elly and Anne would have come, too, but they're busy at the inn, getting ready for the Sanderson wedding tomorrow."

"And Jake? I imagine he must be busy at work," Sarah said. Really, you'd think her daughter's husband would have come to see her at least once, after everything she'd done for his family.

Laura seemed not to have heard the question. And no wonder, with Kennedy bouncing on the balls of her feet like she was on a pogo stick. "Can I push the wheelchair? Can I?"

Monique laughed. "Sure. So long as I have hold of one handle with you. That way we'll make sure we don't dump your grandma out on the street by mistake."

The rehab center was located next to the hospital and only twenty-five minutes from home. Laura drove like a little old man in a hat. Sarah had to keep telling her to speed up.

"I'm going the speed limit, Mom," Laura snapped finally. "I can't afford a ticket."

Sarah felt her own back go rigid. When would Laura finally get a grip on their family finances?

But she wouldn't say a thing. Sarah reminded herself of her vow to be nicer to her daughters. "How's Jake?" she asked. "Still working long hours? I was surprised he didn't stop by the hospital." All right, that was a small criticism. But only an implied one, and not of Laura!

The car jerked to one side of the road. "Sorry, Mom. Pothole," Laura said.

Sarah eyed her suspiciously. Her daughter's hands—which could be pretty, if she'd do something about those raggedy nails of hers—were white on the steering wheel. The sight of them made Sarah's jaw clench.

In the backseat, Kennedy had fallen blessedly silent. But that, too, was reason to be suspicious.

"Laura," Sarah said. "What aren't you telling me? Is something wrong at the inn? Are Elly and Anne handling the wedding all right?"

"They're doing a great job. Everything is fine at the inn." Laura was breathing noisily, like one of those circus fire eaters.

"Then what's going on?" Sarah asked.

"Nothing, Mom. Just so glad you're coming home." Laura's hands were still firmly on the wheel.

They were passing through Rockport Center. The road to Bearskin Neck was eerily deserted. Hardly any traffic now that leaf season was nearly over. Christmas shoppers wouldn't be out until Thanksgiving.

"You can tell me," Sarah urged. "Is it money? Do you need more?"

"No." Laura's head was cocked at a funny angle.

"Is it Jake?" Sarah said. "Did the two of you have a fight?"

Her daughter jerked the wheel again and shouted, "Goddamn it, Mom! Leave me the hell alone! I'm trying to fucking *drive!*"

"Mom!" Kennedy yelled from the backseat. "Don't yell at Grandma! She just had a *stroke!* What if she has a *heart attack?* Just *tell* her, okay?"

Laura pulled the car over onto the shoulder and threw it into park so fast that the car jerked to a stop.

Not much room, on this narrow road. Sarah cast an uneasy glance over her shoulder. Still no other cars. Was her daughter having a breakdown? Oh, Lord, not that. Anything but that. She knew Laura had her dark days. But let it not be the way it was for her.

Please let my daughters cope with life better than I did, she found herself praying. To whom, she did not know. Certainly not to that fat Buddha of Flossie's.

Laura was hunched over the steering wheel, gasping like a dying trout. Her shoulders were shaking. Sarah put a tentative hand on her arm. Laura shrugged it off angrily.

Finally Sarah turned around and raised an eyebrow at Kennedy. "Maybe you'd better tell me what's going on."

Kennedy's eyes were wide, bright blue, and very worried. Sarah flashed to her sister's face. That's who Kennedy looked like: Sarah's own little sister, Joanie. Whom she hadn't seen since God knows when. Joanie would be an old woman now.

But Sarah knew Joanie must remember, as she did, the worst day of their lives. Joanie was so terrified when they couldn't wake Mom on the couch that she was shrieking nonsense words. Mom had a bruise on her forehead and blood on her ear. The pill bottle was on the floor. Sarah had to bundle Joanie up and send her to the neighbors before the cops came.

"Sorry for your trouble," the officers kept saying. As if they knew anything about the sort of black, seeping swamp of misery that could invade a person's every pore. That Sarah herself had to push back after Neil left her, when she was alone with these children and so much work and the whole world seemed to dim around her.

Please, God, whoever you are, don't let that happen to Laura. To any of my girls. I will not stand for it.

Sarah felt her eyes fill with tears. She undid her seat belt and got out of the car, causing Kennedy to yelp in distress. Sarah walked around the car, opened the driver's side door, and firmly pushed Laura over into the passenger seat.

"Good girl," she said when Laura put on her seat belt as Sarah climbed behind the wheel. The car was still running.

Sarah eased the car back onto the road toward the inn. She wouldn't take them home. She would take them to her apartment at Folly Cove, where she would ask someone from the inn's kitchen to bring them tea and a meal. Rodrigo's cooking could raise the dead.

Which is what Laura looked like, her face gray and puckered as she tried and failed, tried and failed to stop crying. "I didn't think this would happen," she said. "I'm so sorry, Mom."

Sarah kept her mouth shut. Kennedy said, "Mom, tell her. Grandma needs to know."

Sarah waited some more.

Finally Laura gulped hard and said, "Jake and I have separated."

Sarah felt her stomach lurch. "What has he done?"

Laura was silent beside her, staring out the window.

"Damn it, Laura. What has that man done to you? Whatever it is, I will fix it. I will pay whatever needs to be paid to fix it. You cannot give up on your marriage."

"It's over, Mom. I'm sorry. There's nothing even you can do to fix this."

They had arrived at the inn. Sarah pulled up to the door and put the car into park, throwing the gearshift so hard that the car shuddered as if it, too, were tired of this whole dramatic business of being alive.

"I don't think I can accept that," Sarah said. "I will not have that man cause you pain."

Laura turned to look at her then, the strangest little smile on her face. "I don't think you have any choice, Mom. Neither do I."

Sarah watched out of the corner of her eye as her granddaughter's hand, small and white, reached over the seat to touch her mother's shoulder. Then she felt Kennedy's other hand touch her own shoulder. Patting it gently.

So rarely was she touched that Sarah nearly wept from the tender, surprising warmth of it.

CHAPTER TWENTY

By nine o'clock the following Saturday night, the Sanderson wedding reception was in full swing in the Folly Cove dining room. Elly led her mother into the pub, where it was quieter. "Now, that's what I call a real 'man's man,'" Sarah whispered, gesturing with her chin. "So handsome. I could look at him all day."

Elly had to smile a little. "Glad you're feeling more like yourself again, Mom."

She followed her mother's gaze to Ryder and Sebastian, who were deep in conversation at the bar. The two had met at the wedding reception, where Sebastian was a guest—he seemed to know everyone—and Ryder had been helping the videographer. Now Ryder was assisting the bartender; they hadn't counted on so many wedding guests surging toward the pub.

Meanwhile, Anne had spent the evening in the kitchen with Rodrigo, and Laura had double-checked the rooms as Rhonda worked the front desk. That left Elly to look out for Sarah.

"Come on," Elly had argued with her sisters, dreading the idea of an entire evening spent with her mother. "There must be some other job I can do. I don't have your civil veneer. I really am afraid I'll go off on her for all the crap she pulled on us."

"No," Laura had said sternly. "We can't let Mom tire herself out, and you're her favorite. She's more likely to do whatever you say."

"I'm not her favorite anymore," Elly said. "I'm not a singer and I say what I think. Anne should do it."

Anne put up both hands. "Don't look at me. Remember, Mom told me I'm the child she never should have had. I'm also the wayward single mom. Besides, I should be in the kitchen helping out."

"Yeah, and Mom's too used to me being her little slave because I've been getting handouts from her for years," Laura had argued. "She doesn't listen to a word I say. It *has* to be you, Elly." Then she and Anne had high-fived each other.

Now it was more than halfway through the night, and so far everything had gone smoothly. Elly watched Ryder with Sebastian, their heads close together across the bar: one light, one dark. Ryder was broader through the shoulders but nearly as tall as Sebastian.

Earlier tonight, he'd told Elly admiringly that "Sebastian knows the name of every damn plant in New England." He'd met Sebastian that morning in Dogtown to grab some sunrise shots and planned to go there with him again. "Unbelievable light here, man. So different from California."

Currently, Sebastian was studying a copse of deep woods made up of hemlock, white pine, and cedar that an MIT professor named Frederick Norton began planting in the 1930s, Ryder added. "Wrap your mind around that, right? This dude planted an entire forest, and it's already hundreds of feet tall!"

Elly couldn't wrap her mind around it. She also couldn't believe she was sleeping with a guy who used words like "dude."

"Are you even listening to me, Elizabeth?" Her mother was urgently tapping her arm. "Who is that good-looking man over there?"

Elly glanced at her worriedly. Why didn't she recognize Sebastian? She was relieved to see that her mother's color was good. Sarah was wearing a vibrant blue suit that brought out her eyes and a diamond brooch shaped like a bird.

"I am listening, Mom. That's Sebastian Martinson. Paige's older brother. You know him."

"No, no. Not him. Of course I know Sebastian! I meant the *other* man. Your Viking friend from California. It's *his* name I can't remember."

"Oh," Elly said, surprised. She'd been sure her mother would write Ryder off as a drifter or worse, because of his ragged appearance and long hair. Not to mention the earring. "That's Ryder."

Had her mother really called Ryder a "man's man"? And "handsome"? Elly grinned. Ryder would be thrilled if he knew.

Ryder must have won her mother's heart when he'd bowed low in greeting her when he'd arrived to work the bar tonight and kissed her hand. *Kissed her hand.*

"Mom's not going to knight you for that or anything," Elly had teased him. "You're laying it on a little thick."

"What?" he'd asked innocently, lips twitching. "I thought that's how things were done in proper New England. But what do we lowly Californians know?"

She'd punched his arm. Now, though, she watched Ryder talking animatedly to Sebastian at the bar and was pleased that he was here. She felt a slow heat spread through her body as she thought about every small thing they'd done together in bed. Of every small thing that she wanted him to do to her next. Of his hands. His hips. His . . .

"And does your Viking have a last name, too?"

Elly flinched. Mom was going to love this one. "Argenziano."

But all Sarah said was, "Goodness. That's a mouthful. You'll have to think hard about whether to take his name when you marry."

"Mom, we're not getting married. I told you. Ryder's just a friend."

"That's certainly not how it looks to me. But what do I know? I'm an old woman. Much, much older than I appear, as you very well know." She gave Elly a sly look, then rose abruptly from the chair where Elly had parked her with a glass of seltzer. "Excuse me, dear. I see someone I absolutely must say hello to."

Elly watched in astonishment as her mother patted her hair and then sashayed—yes, that was the right word for it—over to the bar. Who was she going to see?

There were the Sanderson brothers, making a lot of noise at the bar. And in the far corner was a wedding guest, a paunchy guy in his forties, flirting loudly with Laura. Did her mother mean him? Elly wondered, even as she admired how attractive her sister looked tonight.

Laura's hair was back to a rich chestnut after Elly had practically dragged her out to a salon yesterday, and she looked sexy but classy in a snug black dress with a sweetheart neckline that Elly had found in a vintage shop last week.

But Sarah ignored the Sandersons and Laura, too. Instead, she headed straight into the arms of a short, balding guy standing near the pub entrance. He embraced her, grinning, then pulled away to look at Sarah. He said something that made her laugh.

Elly had no idea who he was. Since they were in the pub, the guy could have just stopped in for a drink. And was that Rhonda from the front desk, coming over to stand with the man and her mother?

Yes, it was Rhonda. She waved at Elly from across the room and made a gesture at their mother and the man, indicating that Elly should join them. Elly smiled and waved back, but went to the opposite side of the pub to talk with Ryder and Sebastian. From here, she could keep an eye on her mother without being intrusive.

Elly still didn't know how she felt about any of the things she'd learned about her parents recently. She had to give Sarah credit for doing her best to keep the inn going and give them a home. But it was hard to love someone who never removed her shiny suit of armor to reveal the soft flesh underneath.

And Dad. She wasn't sure how she felt about him, either. They hadn't yet talked about a memorial service, As far as Elly knew, the box of his ashes was still being stored in Aunt Flossie's closet with her yoga mats.

Despite his weakness for alcohol, her father had given Elly childhood memories that still comprised some of the happiest moments of her life: hiking in Dogtown, building incredibly intricate beach sculptures out of found objects, riding bikes into Rockport for ice cream and teaching her tricks. Elly could still do wheelies and bunny hops on a bike because of Dad, which had made Ryder nearly fall over laughing when she showed him these stunts on Kennedy's bike the other day.

Elly had given up thinking about her father years ago. But the knowledge that he was truly gone made her feel old even now, in her snug and sparkly silver dress with all of her silver bracelets and long earrings. Losing a parent was like losing one more layer between you and whatever lay beyond, which in Elly's mind felt like emptiness.

"Hey, you all right?" Ryder had come out from behind the bar. He slipped an arm around her shoulders. "You're shivering. Want my jacket?"

"No. I'm okay. Just thinking about my dad."

He kissed the top of her head. "It'll keep hitting you, sweetie. That's what grief does."

Like Ryder would know, she thought bitterly. His parents were both alive and well and still schoolteachers in northern California.

"Who's that guy walking with your mom?"

"Walking?" Elly blinked away her tears and looked around frantically. If she lost Mom, her sisters would have her head.

Sure enough, her mother was sauntering out the door on the short guy's arm, leaning her head in his direction and giggling like a prom queen.

"She can't leave on her own," Elly said, and started after them.

"Wait." Ryder put his hand on her arm. "She's not exactly on her own, right? I think you should let her go."

Elly tried to wriggle free of his grasp. "No. She's my responsibility. I don't want Mom having another stroke!"

Ryder's expression was sympathetic, but he held on to her. "She's not going to have another stroke just because she's with someone who isn't you, Elly."

"But I don't even know who he is!"

Ryder sighed and released her. "All right. Calm down. Let's follow at a discreet distance."

Elly nodded and waited for Ryder to ask the bartender if he could handle things on his own. When the man nodded, they left the pub, tracking her mother and her companion. Her mother's pale hair was like a flame in the dark. The cold air bit into Elly's bare shoulders and she started shivering harder; Ryder took off his jacket, and this time she put it on, welcoming the warmth of it and the smell of him around her.

"You don't know who your mom's with?" Ryder said, whispering though they were a good distance away.

"No idea. But Rhonda seems to know him."

"So he's a regular at the inn, maybe?"

"Could be," Elly said.

She relaxed a little as her mother and the stranger approached the door to her mother's apartment on the far side of the inn. Probably Sarah hadn't wanted to admit to Elly that she was tired, so she'd asked this man to walk her back.

Then, to her astonishment, instead of saying good-bye at the door, the man followed her mother inside!

"They're probably just having a nightcap," Ryder said, but he was grinning as he put an arm around her and pulled her close.

"I'm giving them ten minutes, and then I'm knocking on the door," Elly said, gritting her teeth against the cold.

"Yeah, and they'd better have both feet on the floor," Ryder said.

Reluctantly, she laughed and pressed her face against his shirt to warm her nose. The shirt had shocked her: it was striped and had a collar. She was used to seeing Ryder in T-shirts.

They were quiet for a few minutes. Elly realized that the two of them had started swaying a little, dancing to the distant strains of the wedding music, their bodies close enough that she could feel his shirt buttons and hip bones. Ryder's hands were locked behind her waist.

She turned her head and saw gulls roosting on the garage roof in front of the inn, like small white ghosts in the dark. "I guess my mom's a widow now, officially. That's such a weird thought. Think you'll ever get married?"

"I haven't ruled it out." He pulled her a little closer. "I mean, what's the alternative? Live alone? Avoid the ordinariness of making dinner every night?"

"It's so crazy, though, to think we're expected to choose one person and be happy forever," Elly said.

"I never knew you were such a romantic," he teased.

"No, I mean it. It's crazy to think that way, isn't it? The whole idea of marriage is insane. I wonder what would have happened if my dad had stayed here instead of taking off. Probably they would have gotten divorced, because Mom was always so disappointed in him. Maybe he knew that, and that's partly why he left. Really, why do we even bother falling in love? It never lasts."

"I don't know." Ryder's voice was thoughtful. "Humans can't seem to help falling in love. We give our hearts. Our whole selves. We can say all we want about how cool it is to have so many hookup options, to swipe people we like on Tinder or whatever. We can have sex without commitments or children or, sometimes, even without kindness. Is that really better than trying to stick it out and grow old with somebody?"

"I don't know." Elly laughed uncertainly. "Probably."

Ryder leaned back a little to look at her. "Do you really think that? I don't. I think we're all searching for the same thing: that one person we think we can't live without. And, if we find that person, the next thing we want is a family, because otherwise life can get pretty damn lonely. Look at you, now that you've come back. I can see how you are with your sisters. You're feeling whole now, because you're with people who've known you all your life. Maybe it's pointless for us to fight against that bonding urge, Elly. Maybe we should just go with it. Couple up and make a family."

He was right about her sisters, how it felt to be with them again: whole. But Elly's throat constricted as she imagined having to tell Ryder about Hans and her surgery, about the very real possibility that she might never be able to have children.

She pulled out of his embrace, shivering as she stood alone in the cold night air. "What are you saying, Ryder? That you feel that way about *us*? Or are you talking philosophy here about the whole human race?"

She saw the gleam of his teeth as Ryder smiled. Above them, the night sky was black except for a few pinpricks of light from the stars and a fingernail of moon.

"Both, I guess," he answered. "Elly, why did you invite me here?"

"I didn't," she said quickly. "My sister Laura did. And she was drunk. Otherwise, you wouldn't be here. I didn't plan on any of this. I didn't think you and I should be together."

Ryder was silent long enough that she could hear one of the gulls on the roof chortling. She imagined the bird laughing at the silly humans below. *All this discussion about whether to mate, when they should just get on with things and lay their eggs.*

"So you're saying that if it had been up to you, you never would have invited me to come," he said at last, "and that we shouldn't be together."

"Right."

"Okay," he said. "Fine. Well. That clears things up. I'd better get back to the pub." He turned sharply away and started walking fast toward the bar.

"Ryder, wait!" Elly called, but his long strides had carried him too far across the lawn for him to hear her. Either that, or he was choosing to ignore her. Probably for the best, she told herself, since she had no idea what she'd say to Ryder anyway.

Then he was gone, the pub door opening to cast a square of yellow light on the grass and shutting again, leaving her alone in the cold and silent dark.

Laura had allowed herself to text Kennedy exactly once yesterday from the inn, while she was helping Rhonda navigate guest check-ins for the Sanderson wedding.

Several couples had complained about the noise from the bar and wanted to be moved, but the inn was full. Laura had provided noise-canceling fans and a 10 percent discount on the rooms. This had thrilled the guests, especially when Laura had called a friend with a restaurant in town and convinced her to give the couples a twenty-five percent discount on lunch after they checked out today.

Laura was afraid her mother would be angered by these decisions. Instead, Sarah had smiled at her and said, "You show great business sense, dear."

That vote of confidence gave Laura the courage to text her daughter, who was staying at Jake's house in Medford for the first time that weekend, despite images of Kennedy having dinner with her husband and this unknown man, Anthony, and their little boy.

You okay? she'd texted.

Fine. Quit worrying! Kennedy had replied. Laura could almost picture her daughter rolling her eyes as she thumbed the words.

Now it was the next morning. Laura knocked decisively on Elly's door after feeding the horses and turning them out, even though it wasn't quite nine. "Hey, I'm treating myself to breakfast at the Pancake House in Rowley. Do you and Ryder want to come?"

"No." Elly's voice was muffled, as if she were lying with her head under a pillow. "Ryder's out with Sebastian, roaming the woods or whatever. I'm sleeping in. Headache."

"All right," Laura called back. "Feel better."

In the car, she hesitated at the top of the driveway, then turned in the direction of the inn. Maybe Anne would come with her. The baby wasn't old enough for pancakes, but Laura had vivid memories of too-long Sunday mornings alone with Kennedy when she was small, when Jake would be out biking.

Or spending time with someone else.

No, she absolutely would not let herself think like that. Jake said Anthony was the first. She had to believe that if she was going to stay sane. Anyway, what did it matter now?

Anne was up and dressed; she'd already had breakfast and been out for a walk. Her auburn curls were tangled, as if she'd been tugging sweaters on and off all morning.

"Let me grab my coat," she said at once when Laura invited her out.

"But you've already eaten. Are you sure?"

"Anything to get out of this house," Anne said. "It's cold in here and Lucy's fussy."

As Laura stood there, watching the baby make heroic efforts to roll from one side to the other on a blanket laid out on the floor, she realized that Anne was right: the cottage was freezing. Laura could smell the damp in here. She imagined streams of water running down the shingled walls, turning the wood green and slimy.

Anne had dressed the baby in a footed sleeper and a sweater; Lucy was probably warm. She looked happy enough, fat as a puppy. Still, Laura picked her up and held her close.

The baby grinned and tried to grab her hoop earrings with a little screech of delight. Laura took her earrings off and then burrowed her face in the baby's neck just to smell that familiar intoxicating cocktail of scents: baby shampoo, powder, milk.

"She's a little monkey," Laura said when Anne returned. "Just like you were."

Anne smiled, wrapping a scarf around her neck. "Do you actually remember me being a baby?"

"Remember you?" Laura laughed. "I couldn't get rid of you! I was always in charge of watching you. You clung to me like a barnacle. Even in elementary school, you used to run after me if our classes passed each other in the hall. You'd grab on to my leg, and the teachers had to pry you off me."

"God. You must have been mortified."

"Naturally. I was a very cool kid," Laura said as Anne buckled Lucy into her car seat.

"You were," Anne agreed. "I always thought you were a goddess."

"You did not."

"Seriously!" Anne said. "I was in awe of everything you did."

"You shouldn't have been. I wasn't a very good big sister."

"What do you mean? Laura, you were great to me," Anne said. "Especially when Dad took off. Remember how you told me the next day? You helped Elly and me make a fort under the dining room table while Mom was upstairs, and you told me to get my favorite toys and bring them under there, because what you had to say might make me sad. You told Elly the same thing. She and I knew everything would be all right as long as you were still there, telling us what to do." She laughed. "You were so bossy."

"And jealous," Laura said with a sigh. "Especially of you."

"Of me? Why? Elly was the beautiful one."

"Yes, but you were the one everyone wanted to spoil," Laura said. "I'd get so angry whenever Flossie let you off the hook for something."

"I don't blame you." Anne patted Laura's thigh. "Mom always gave you too much responsibility."

Laura nodded. "So what do you think Mom's going to do, now that Dad's dead?"

"Maybe she'll get married again."

"God, really? I can't imagine her with anyone."

"You didn't see her flirting with that guy at the pub? She left with him. Elly followed them to Mom's apartment, and he went inside with her!"

"No!"

"Yes!" Anne insisted. "Elly said she gave them ten minutes, and then she knocked on the door to check on them, but Mom wouldn't let her in!"

"Do we know who he is?"

"Yes. Elly asked Rhonda when she got back to the pub. Apparently he's Rhonda's uncle. He and Mom have had a few dates."

"So not a serial killer, presumably."

"Probably not. Anyway, I called Mom this morning to see how she was feeling, and she sounded fine." Anne hesitated, then added, "There was music playing in the background. Some kind of jazz singer. At nine in the morning!"

"Oh, Jesus. Spare me the life where Mom's a hot single."

Surprisingly, there was no wait at the Pancake House, even though they'd arrived at the post-church crunch time. Both of them ordered pancakes, eggs, and home fries. She and Laura talked about the wedding and the various kitchen crises that cropped up during the reception.

"You handled it all very well," Laura said. "Everyone I talked to was pleased with the food."

"Rodrigo handled it. He's my hero," Anne said. "That guy is unbelievably organized, and he hardly ever yells, which gives everyone this incredible sense of calm and confidence."

"So do you think you'll stay?"

"I don't know," Anne said, frowning as Lucy started whining. She handed her some sort of tiny rag doll that Laura suspected Flossie must have made. It looked vaguely Buddhist: plump and beatific. Lucy managed to push it into her mouth, sucking with such intensity that both women laughed.

"Look, I've had an idea," Laura said. "I don't think you should keep living in that cottage for the winter, and I know you don't want to move in with Mom. What would you think about living with me for a while?"

Anne's eyes were shining, silver-blue with surprise, and her cheeks had gone pink. "Are you serious?"

Laura shrugged. "Why not? I could use the company. You'd be doing me a favor. And Kennedy would love having her cousin around. We could try it for the winter and see how it goes. I mean, the worst that happens is that we'll hate each other, right? And we already know we can survive that."

"I never hated you! Did you really hate me?"

Laura thought about this. "If you'd asked me even a few weeks ago, I might have said yes. But when Flossie called and said you were missing that time you rode General, and I saw you all bloody and beat-up in the car after you fell off, I was worried sick. So, no. Not really. I was just scared about losing Jake. But it turns out I'd already lost him a long time ago."

"I am sorry, Laura. About ever causing you to doubt me."

"I know you are. And I'm even sorrier for doubting you." Laura glanced at Lucy, who was peacefully teething on the spoon and watching everyone in the restaurant. The baby was the object of much admiration, with her wide blue eyes and red curls; people stopped by to comment on her looks, or on how good she was being, and Lucy always smiled up at them.

So happy and trusting, just as Anne had been. Anne grew up expecting people to love her, because everyone did. Meanwhile, Laura had been old enough to observe their mother's unhappiness and anger; their father's abrupt departure; their mother's leaving them for days or even weeks at a time and Flossie stepping in, short-tempered and harried.

"You know, when you told us Mom suffered mental breakdowns, I said I didn't remember any of that," Laura said. "But I actually do."

"Really? More than her just going away, you mean?"

Laura nodded. The noise in the restaurant, she knew, would prevent anyone from eavesdropping on the conversation. "When I was at school, sometimes I'd come home and find Mom screaming at you and Elly. I'd feed you and put you to bed so Mom could go back to work at the inn. And there were lots of nights when I heard her sobbing in her bedroom. Sometimes she didn't even notice if Elly had a nightmare or you walked in your sleep."

"Poor you, Laura. You must have felt like you had the weight of the world on your shoulders," Anne said, touching her hand. "I'm sorry."

"Don't be. Going through stuff like that as kids is what makes us who we are as adults, right?" Laura smiled. "Or maybe that's just my rationale, now that I'm putting Kennedy through a divorce. But I do feel sorry for Mom. She must have felt so isolated, if she deliberately cut ties with her own family and then found herself without a husband. It's like she was stuck on her own little island of misery."

"An island of her own making," Anne reminded her.

They paid the bill and went out to the car. Waiting for traffic to pass so she could pull out of the parking lot, Laura said, "So will you think about living with me?"

Anne turned to her and smiled. "I've already thought about it. The answer's yes."

Sometime after eleven, Elly finally forced herself out of bed. Laura was still gone. It was raining. Not hard, just a light, uncertain patter on the windows that made the glass ripple green.

After an hour of television and too much coffee, she went out to the garage, looking for something to help her calm down. Finally she climbed onto Kennedy's mountain bike and pedaled down the road into Dogtown in search of Ryder and Sebastian. She had to see Ryder and explain that she hadn't meant things the way they'd sounded last night. She was glad he had cared enough about her to come here. He needed to know that before he left, even if they couldn't have a future together.

Over the next hour, Elly rode deeper into the woods, following the rutted trails that crisscrossed through Dogtown. Even this late in the season, the branches had enough leaves to make visibility difficult. The leaves had mostly turned russet and brown.

She rode as fast as she could, pedaling hard. The problem was that she couldn't remember where Sebastian was working. She'd just have to cover as many trails as she could.

If she didn't find Ryder here, she'd have to hurry back to Laura's to catch him. She had noticed this morning that his bag was neatly packed and that he'd slept downstairs on the sofa in the den. He must have come into the guest room they'd been sharing to get his things while she was asleep.

Ryder had been upset enough last night that he'd stayed on at the pub when Elly said she was going back to Laura's. "I don't understand," she'd said. "Why are you so angry? I was just telling you the truth about Laura being the one to invite you here, and you already knew that."

Ryder had sighed. "Elly, if you don't understand, it's probably better if I don't explain it." Then he had turned away and started talking with a man standing next to him.

He was so infuriating. Of course she never would have invited him to New England! Why would she? They weren't a *thing*. They had never been *official*. He wasn't her *boyfriend*. They were colleagues in a fluid industry and just happened to hit it off in bed. That was no basis for a relationship.

And yet the thought of Ryder leaving now, before her mother's birthday party next weekend, made Elly feel slightly insane. She wanted to see him, if only to argue her points about men and women and the fallibility of marriage. To make him keep the promise he'd made (to Laura, she reminded herself) to record this important birthday for her mother.

This important *fake* birthday. God. It was no wonder she didn't trust anyone, when even her own mother lied to her.

She jolted over logs and stones, once biting her tongue and swallowing blood. She had to push hard to ride the bike through thick tufts of yellow grass that were like hands grabbing at the wheels. After an hour or so, she was tired, and the icy November wind began to cut sharply through her jacket. By now it was raining harder. The narrow strips of sky between the trees looked gray-green. Every bush and tree shed water on her, until she was soaked. The light had turned a brooding gray and the trails were thick smears of mud with treacherous rocks. She fell off the bike once and went headfirst into a bramblebush, twisting her wrist.

Elly checked her phone after another series of switchbacks and realized now nearly two hours had passed. She was shivering from the cold and damp, and she was completely lost in Dogtown.

Her father had warned them about this any time he'd brought them here. Dogtown was a maze littered with rocks, signs of previous ice floes that had pushed and scraped boulders across the earth before melting and dumping them in heaps, as if some giant baby had been playing with stones and then left them in random piles.

Elly stopped the bike and straddled it on a small rise, trying to get her bearings. She saw none of the famous landmarks: not the gigantic terminal moraine, piled high with thousands of huge boulders. Not Peter's Pulpit, the enormous rock that sat at the turn in Commons Road. Not the Whale's Jaw, a boulder that once resembled a whale rising with its mouth open toward the sky but had since fallen into two ungainly pieces, its jaw broken in a way that made Elly cry when she'd seen it for the first time, imagining it as part of a real creature.

She couldn't be near the Babson Boulder Trail by the reservoir because she didn't see any of the marked cellar holes from the original inhabitants. All she knew for sure was that she was in the woods on a single-track trail. Because the sky was overcast and visibility was poor, Elly couldn't even tell which direction she was facing. She should have stuck to the wider paths and cart roads.

It was too cold to stand here with her teeth chattering. Elly climbed back on the bike and continued riding. Surely she'd eventually see something familiar, or even reach the outskirts of Dogtown, if she continued in a reasonably straight line. The important thing was to keep moving and stay warm.

Elly tried to take her mind off her rising panic by remembering some of the stories her father had told her about this place. Many of them were about women who didn't fit in anywhere.

Just like me, she thought dully.

There were the witches of Dogtown, like Tammy Younger and Luce George, who claimed they could cast spells. And there was Easter Carter, a spinster nurse who owned the only two-story house here. Easter practically lived on boiled cabbage and had a boarder, a former slave who dressed like a man and went by the name of John Wood-man, who earned money building stone walls.

Maybe that woman had built some of the stone walls right here along this rutted trail, Elly thought, still scanning the area for familiar landmarks.

Who else? Becky Rich, of course. She made brews from native berries and told fortunes from coffee grounds. Elly and her sisters used to love picking berries here. They'd mash them up and mix them with ground leaves and water, pretending they were making special potions, whenever their father brought them here and told them to play while he read a book.

Her father would know where she was, Elly thought. He could have rescued her. But he was gone, and that thought made her weep, the tears mixing with the rain on her face. *Daddy.*

God, it was cold. Elly couldn't even feel her toes. The numbness made her think of the last resident of Dogtown, Black Neil, another freed slave. He slaughtered hogs for money and lived in a cellar hole until 1830, when the town sent the constable into Dogtown to get him out of there because his feet were frostbitten.

Elly stopped the bike to catch her breath, listening to an animal crashing through the underbrush. Even squirrels sounded as big as wolves here, she reminded herself; the only predators in these woods were the coyotes, and they didn't typically attack humans. Still, she was frightened, her lungs burning, her thighs liquid from the exertion.

The crooked tree trunks around her seemed to rise in human form, twisted and angry, their arms reaching for her. Elly was starting to really panic now; she blinked hard to turn the trees back into themselves, but even then their roots looked like twisted feet and their knots looked like eyes.

The woods were growing darker rapidly, an afternoon mist rolling in to cloak the tree branches with thick white scarves. Another animal crashed through the trees nearby and she jumped, then saw the flash of a deer's white tail. She hoped nothing was chasing it. She got on her bike and pedaled again, tears streaming down her face, mixing with the rain.

Just then Elly spotted two slight, hunched figures moving toward her through the pale curtain of rain. She went very still, squinting as the shapes began to take on details. One wore a bright yellow hooded raincoat, dark pants, and a red brimmed hat; the colors burned like a flame against the gray and russet landscape. The other was all in black.

"Daddy," she whispered, the tears of relief starting until she remembered again that Neil was dead. Her father would never show her these woods again. She put her hands to her face and cried into them, weeping for the loss of him and for all her childhood and those times with her sisters that were gone for good.

"Elly? There you are. We were worried, child."

Elly dropped her hands in astonishment. Flossie stood before her in a black rain suit and knee-high boots. "Laura and Anne came to my house to see if you were with me," she said. "They were worried about you."

"They called me, too." Sarah, wearing a remarkably un-Sarah-like rain outfit of bright colors, stood next to Flossie. Even more remarkably, she was smiling, her blue eyes soft on Elly's face. "I'm glad you're all right," she said briskly. "What on earth were you thinking, riding a bicycle into Dogtown in this horrible weather? You should have more sense than that. Come, now. Let us take you back to Laura's."

Elly set the bike gently on the ground and stood there, closing her eyes as she felt her mother and Flossie steady her, one on each side, their murmuring voices steady as the rain.

CHAPTER TWENTY-ONE

The weather had turned so suddenly cold that Laura insisted Anne bring Lucy over to her house for the night. "We'll get things sorted and move you out of the cottage next weekend," she'd said, "but I don't like the idea of you two shivering in your sleep over there."

Anne was glad to be at Laura's, not only because of the bitter temperature, but because of the immense surprise of seeing her mother and Flossie arrive with a dripping and half-frozen Elly, whom they had managed to find in Dogtown.

"What even made you think to look there?" Anne said to Flossie.

"Just call it an old woman's intuition," Flossie said, gesturing at Sarah. "That old woman, not me. She thinks Elly has taken the news about your dad's death especially hard, and that's where he always took the three of you."

Anne rooted around in Laura's cupboards and fridge and made a rich vegetable stew with barley, adding herb dumplings to stretch the recipe for all of them. Flossie went out to her car and brought in a couple of bottles of Spanish red wine—a gift from one of her admirers, she said coyly—and they feasted. When Sarah yawned, Flossie fussed over her, then helped her back into the startling yellow rain jacket before driving her back to the inn.

Anne was tired, too. She put Lucy to sleep in the portable crib in the office, where she would be staying on the pull-out couch, shoving aside

Jake's desk to make room for it—good riddance, she thought—then considered going to bed, too. But it was still early, so she carried the baby monitor downstairs.

Laura and Elly were seated on the leather sofa in the living room. They'd opened another bottle of wine and held glasses in their hands, the wine a rich cherry color in the light cast by the table lamps.

When Anne came in, her sisters moved their feet and patted the middle cushion. She sat between them, then slid onto the floor, taking a cushion with her so that she could sit on it and face them. Laura poured her a glass of wine and handed it to her.

Elly looked ill. Her eyes were bloodshot and her California tan was gone; even her lips were pale. She and Laura were discussing their mother's birthday party preparations for next weekend and what songs the three of them ought to rehearse with Kennedy, but Elly was barely able to keep up her end of the conversation. She sounded drugged.

"Do you think you caught a cold, being in Dogtown?" Anne finally asked. "Your voice doesn't even sound like yours."

"You can't catch a cold from the cold," Elly said, sniffing. "That's a myth. You have to be exposed to a virus."

Laura glanced at Elly. "She sounds like that because she's been crying. Ryder seems to have disappeared."

"What do you mean?" Anne looked at Elly. "Wait, he's not actually *gone, gone*, is he? I thought he was staying here until Mom's party."

Elly tucked her hair behind her ears and shrugged. "We had a fight. He left."

"Are you sure?" Anne asked. "Maybe he just missed dinner."

"No," Elly said. "His stuff is gone, too."

"But why?" Anne asked. "What did you fight about?"

"She told Ryder that I'm the only reason he's here," Laura said. "I was really drunk when I invited him," she added. "I didn't mean to do it."

Anne laughed, then stopped when she saw Elly's stony expression. "What's the big deal? I'm sure Ryder doesn't care why he was invited, as long as he gets to be with you, Elly. And he wouldn't take off without saying anything." *That would be more like Colin,* she thought.

"Tell her the rest." Laura nudged her foot against Elly's thigh. "Tell Anne what you said to Ryder at the wedding reception."

Elly set her wineglass down on the table hard enough that Anne was afraid the stem might snap. "I told him that if it had been up to me, I wouldn't have invited him at all. That I never intended for us to be together."

"Ouch," Anne said, wincing.

Elly nodded. "I got lost in Dogtown because I was looking for him. I thought Ryder was with Sebastian, and I wanted to apologize before he left. He'd already packed up his stuff, so I knew that's what he was going to do. Ryder must have come here and gotten his things while I was out."

"He's definitely gone for good. He sent me a text saying thanks for everything," Laura added. "The thing is, I thought maybe Ryder got a job or something and had to fly back to California before Mom's birthday party."

"He would have loved that dumb party," Elly said mournfully. "All the singing and dancing. The dramatics."

"Mom's or ours?" Laura teased.

Nobody laughed. Anne gazed into her half-full wineglass, frowning. "What if Ryder didn't really leave?"

"He took his bag," Laura reminded her.

"Okay, but if he made a return flight for *after* Mom's party, Ryder probably wouldn't want to pay to have the ticket changed. He could be staying somewhere else, figuring he'll spend the week touring Boston or something. Maybe he's hoping Elly will go after him."

"No. Ryder's not that manipulative," Elly said. "And he's not that hard up for cash. He wouldn't care if he had to pay extra to change his ticket."

"But maybe Anne's right, and Ryder doesn't want to give up on you completely," Laura said excitedly. "I've seen how he can't take his eyes off you."

"Stop. That sounds stalkerish," Elly said. "Anyway, none of this matters. It's probably better if he leaves. I mean, what would I say? 'Oh, wait, I just remembered that I *did* mean to invite you here'? That would be lying. I'm not Mom," she reminded them.

"Well, you could say you didn't realize how much you wanted to be with him until he showed up." Laura sounded impatient now. "That's true, right? Look at you! I've never seen you so distraught. You really care about this guy, Elly."

"Laura's right," Anne said. "You went to Dogtown by yourself in the rain, and on a *mountain* bike, all because you were so desperate to find Ryder. What does that tell you about your feelings?"

Elly sighed and sank deeper into the couch. "Still, it doesn't matter how I feel about him! No way can we be together."

"Why not?" Anne asked.

"Because the other reason Ryder took off is because we were talking about families," Elly said. "He believes people might as well couple up and reproduce, because that's what humans are meant to do. And I don't even know if I can have kids. He'd walk away if he knew that."

"No," Laura said, "you only *think* that's what he'd do. That's different from having had an actual, honest conversation with him about your relationship and whether he wants kids." She tossed back the rest of her wine, then added, "I sound so wise, don't I? I'm obviously the poster child for honesty in a marriage."

Elly smiled. "You're doing a great job now."

Laura waved her away. "Hey, I just had a thought. What about Sebastian? Ryder said he wanted to go to Dogtown with him again. What if he did that today, then went back to Sebastian's house? We should call Sebastian. And by 'we,' you know who I mean." She looked pointedly at Anne.

"Oh no." Anne put her hands up. "Not a good idea. Sebastian works hard. He might be asleep."

"It's only eight o'clock," Laura protested. "Last I checked, we're not asleep, and look at the day we had."

"Plus," Anne said, "Sebastian has made it pretty clear he doesn't want anything to do with me."

"That's too bad," Elly said.

Laura said, "Okay, but you need to call him for Elly, not for you! Look. Just get Sebastian on the phone and ask if you can speak to Ryder. Be casual. It doesn't have to be all cloak and dagger. Just tell him we're concerned because we're going to need another videographer for Mom's party if Ryder decided to go back to California. You don't have to whine."

"I wouldn't *whine* at him!" Anne protested. "I know why he doesn't want to see me."

"Whatever the reason, I'm sure it's temporary," Laura said.

Anne shook her head. "I don't know about that. He's pretty messed up."

"Why?" Laura looked curious now.

Anne glanced at Elly. "You didn't tell her about his wife?"

"Oh my God," Laura said. "Sebastian has a *wife*? Seriously? What's *wrong* with you, Anne?"

"It's okay. She's dead," Elly said.

Laura's mouth opened, then closed. Finally she said, "I'm so sorry. How awful for him."

"She was pregnant," Elly added. "Killed herself."

"Jesus!" Laura said. Now she looked at Anne and shook her head. "Well, you always did like the hot needy ones."

"Shut *up*, Laura!" Anne folded her arms. "Let's not even go there with what men we choose. I could say a few things to you on that subject."

"Stop!" Elly said. "Everyone in this room has lousy taste in men, okay? The Bradford women are genetically predisposed to be bum magnets. But, Anne, please. Call Sebastian," she pleaded. "For me. Could you? I'm dying. If Ryder's still here, I have to see him."

"Oh, all right. Since you're terminal," Anne said.

"Bring the phone in here!" Laura and Elly chorused as she left the room.

"No way!" she said.

Anne locked herself in the downstairs bathroom and turned her back to the mirror to avoid seeing her pale, freckled face as she dialed Sebastian.

"Hello?"

His voice sounded deeper on the phone. "Sebastian?" she said.

"No. It's Ryder. Hello, Anne."

"How did you know?" she began, then remembered that Sebastian had put her number into his phone. Some sort of picture probably popped up with it. "Wait. Why are you answering Sebastian's phone?"

"He's asleep."

"Oh," she said. "I'm sorry. I thought I was calling early enough."

"That would be hard to do. He's been in bed since about seven."

"Is he drunk?"

"No. Just feeling down."

Anne put a hand to her heart. "I'm sorry. So you guys must be at his house."

"Yeah. We were in Dogtown, but when the rain started, we hiked back here. I had my cameras, and Sebastian said it was too wet to work anyway."

"Are you sure he's okay?"

"Yeah. I checked on him a little while ago." When Anne was silent for a moment, Ryder added, "I know what's going on with you. He told me."

"Oh," she said.

"It isn't you."

"Thank you for saying that, but listen. I was actually calling Sebastian to find you."

"Oh." Ryder sounded surprised.

"I mean, I wanted to talk to him, too, of course. But I wasn't sure he'd speak to me."

"He definitely wants to talk to you," Ryder said. "Don't give up on him, Anne."

"I'm not going anywhere," she said. "I'm moving in with Laura. Will you tell him that for me?"

"Sure. So why were you calling me?"

"Elly's really upset about how things ended with you guys."

"They didn't end," Ryder said. "They never began, according to her."

"I don't think that's true," Anne said. "Anyway, she wants to talk to you."

"She said that?"

"Yes," Anne said. "Can you come back to Laura's?"

"No," Ryder said. "I don't want to crowd her."

It was a standoff, Anne realized: Ryder needed Elly to come to him. "She looked all over Dogtown for you today," Anne said. "She got lost in the rain. If our mom and aunt hadn't found her, she'd probably still be out there."

"Your mother was in Dogtown? Really? No offense, but that's pretty hard to picture. She must be feeling better."

"Apparently she seems to have forgotten she should take it easy. But that's Mom."

"Good for her."

This was off topic. She had to fix things for Elly. "Listen, what if I bring Elly over to Sebastian's house so she can talk to you? Would that be okay? I won't even come inside. She can text me when you guys are done talking. Do you want to see her?"

"Only if that's what she wants," Ryder said.

Fifteen minutes later, she and Elly were pulling up in front of Sebastian's house. Anne hadn't been here before; because of the baby, Sebastian had always come to the Houseboat. But there were only five houses on the road, and she spotted Sebastian's Jeep parked in the driveway of the third house down, a small white eighteenth-century Cape.

"You sure Ryder wants to see me? He *said* that?" Elly was clasping and unclasping her hands in her lap. She'd brushed her hair and put on a little makeup; the effect of that was to make her look even paler, almost ethereal in the dark car.

"Yes! He practically begged me to bring you." Anne smiled at her. Elly and Ryder wouldn't care how their meeting came about once they saw each other. "Go inside now, before Lucy wakes up and makes Laura mad."

Elly laughed and leaned over to hug her. "I'll text you when we're finished talking."

Anne grinned back. "No, you won't. You'll be busy doing other things."

She was still smiling as she pulled out of the driveway, even as she glanced in the rearview mirror and wished she were going inside Sebastian's house, too.

Ryder opened the door and stepped aside. Elly was careful not to let her shoulder brush against his.

It was a mistake to ever get involved with him, she thought, remembering their easy banter at work. She'd ruined their friendship forever.

"Hey," he said. "Thanks for coming over."

"No problem." Elly deliberately kept her tone light, thinking maybe *that's* what it took for a Bradford woman to make things work out with a man: the willpower to never scratch beneath the surface of relationships. Nothing ruined a good time like commitment, right?

She had lived alone since college and enjoyed it. Yet a part of her had to acknowledge that it would be difficult now to return to her silent apartment in California, to the absence of sounds she'd started to take for granted: voices in the kitchen, muffled footsteps overhead, other people's showers and laughter. The sounds of a family.

"Come sit down," Ryder said. "I made a fire."

He led her into the living room. It was furnished with odds and ends, clearly a rental. A laptop staked a claim on a heavy oak desk by the windows. It was the sort of desk that Charles Dickens might have used, with a rolltop open to reveal shelves with tiny compartments. Forestry journals and textbooks created a paper city around the desk chair.

"Sebastian works constantly," Ryder said, following her gaze. "You must know about his wife. I think he's trying to put himself into a coma."

"Yes. So sad." Elly sat on the couch facing the fireplace, a predictably squashy piece of furniture with a tatty floral slipcover.

The room was painted a deep bronze, and the lower half was paneled in a rich dark wood. Ryder pulled the desk chair across the room so he could face her, his back to the fireplace. Between the dark color of the room and the way he was backlit by flames, his face was shadowed, his expression inscrutable. In silhouette, Ryder's strong features appeared to be exaggerated, as if some artist had drawn him here with quick, broad strokes.

She smiled. "You fit right into this old New England house. Nathaniel Hawthorne would be proud."

"Right," he said, drawling the word the way he did. "Let me just get my pipe and my Bible." He leaned closer, resting his elbows on his knees. "Elly, what happened? It's like we were talking and everything was okay with us. Then suddenly it wasn't."

"I don't really know," she said. "I wasn't trying to drive you away." That, at least, was honest.

"Really? Because it sure sounded like that."

Elly took a deep breath and let it out again. "No. I didn't invite you here. That's true. But once you arrived, I loved being with you. Then I got scared."

"Scared of me?"

"No. Scared *for* you. Because you were talking about a future with me."

"Fine. I get it. You don't see a future with me. It's okay. I never meant to push you." Ryder stood up, went to poke at the fire. "Glad we got that out of the way so we can be friends." The logs caught and flames rose again, dancing orange and hot.

Elly bit her lip, fighting the urge to go to him, to draw him over to the couch and pull him down on top of her. "I think we're way past friends."

He returned to the desk chair, but she shook her head. "Come over to the couch, Ryder. Please."

"I don't think it's a good idea. Not if we aren't going to . . ."

"I just need to see your face when I tell you something else. That's all."

Ryder complied, slowly moving around to the sofa, using his knee to push the coffee table out of the way. Elly felt her chest constrict when the firelight revealed the deep creases of unhappiness around his mouth and eyes.

"What I'm going to tell you isn't going to be easy for me to say," she said softly, "and it'll probably be rough for you to hear. But I want you to understand why I panicked the other night."

She told him then, about Hans, about everything from the heady start of the love affair to his abrupt departure, her diagnosis and surgery, her potential infertility.

Ryder was quiet as she talked, other than an occasional murmur. Once, he reached over and rested his hand on hers for a moment, then drew it away.

"When you were talking about families that night at the wedding reception, I know you were probably speaking in general terms, not about us specifically," Elly said. "But I also understood that you might want kids, and I probably can't give them to you."

"I wasn't talking in general terms." Ryder reached for her hand again.

She let him take it. Wanted him to, although once he was rubbing his thumb over her palm, she wanted to pull away again. It was as if he were pressing the bruises on her heart.

"Oh," she said. "Well, then it's good I told you."

"Yes," he said. "But none of that changes how I feel about you."

Ryder moved closer to her on the couch and put an arm around her. His shirt was warm from the fire; his body was even warmer beneath it. She wanted to lean in to him, to inhale wood smoke and that particular Ryder scent, something spicy.

"It should, though," she said, staring at the fire. "If you think you want a family, you should quit seeing me now, while you're ahead."

"Wait." He pulled away to look at her. "Is this the old 'it's not you, it's me' speech?"

"No!" Elly said. "I just don't want you holding on to any unrealistic expectations about us."

In the firelight, with his skin tinged gold and the bright streaks in his hair, Ryder looked as though he could have stepped out of the fire, like a man molded out of light. Elly had never wanted to kiss anyone as much as she wanted to kiss him right now. She realized she was holding her breath, and let it out slowly.

One of the logs smoldering on the grate fell suddenly, startling them both. Ryder turned toward her again and took both of her hands in his. "If, by 'unrealistic expectations,' you mean that we'll make love more often than we fight, take cool vacations even when we're broke, argue about where we want to live, and think about whether we want kids and how to have them, then sure. Yes! I have some damn unrealistic expectations about us. I hope you do, too."

He leaned forward to kiss her, and then it was like she was made of fire, too.

CHAPTER TWENTY-TWO

They spent the next week preparing for their mother's birthday
party. With Anne living here now, it was easy for Laura to gather
her sisters in her living room to work out the choreography for two of
the songs from *An American in Paris*, and it helped take her mind off
Jake's absence.

Anne, the most athletic and limber of them, took the Gene Kelly
part in "I Got Rhythm." She was still a surprisingly good tapper—her
childhood dance lessons hadn't been forgotten.

Laura agreed to help them sing, but she refused to dance. Elly, though,
was still a decent tapper, Laura thought. Elly and Anne choreographed
the trickier bits to make them simpler while Laura provided cheerleading
from the sidelines.

Somehow Elly and Kennedy had managed to find a white duck-
billed cap, linen trousers, and white sweater for Anne to wear in "I Got
Rhythm." Kennedy would be dressed as a French schoolgirl with her
hair in braids. They'd even found wide-lapel suit jackets from the
1950s for Kennedy, Elly, and Anne to wear when they sang "'S Wonderful" and some old French posters to use as a background.

Anne had enlisted Kennedy's help in finding the perfect recipe for
an Eiffel Tower cake. This involved Anne baking chocolate sheet cakes
and cutting them into squares of decreasing sizes that could be layered

on top of one another into a tower shape; the layers would be stacked on top of thin layers of buttercream frosting.

"Since the real Eiffel Tower is gray," Anne said excitedly, "I'll make a gray fondant with a silvery buttercream to cover the entire cake. We can roll a brick pattern into it. I'll make a cylinder for the top, too."

Meanwhile, throughout the week they were also taking turns visiting Sarah to make sure she was resting enough and eating well.

"It's weird, but she actually seems happy," Elly reported to Laura after her turn on Monday. "And Flossie's been over there a lot."

"Yes, and that guy she's seeing, Gil, seems to be spending time with her, too," Anne told them all after visiting Sarah on Tuesday afternoon following her shift in the kitchen. "He and Flossie were both having tea with her when I finished in the kitchen. And Flossie had brought Lucy over to see Mom."

They were seated around Laura's kitchen table for dinner. Only Kennedy was missing; she'd joined the chorus at school, to Laura's delight, and was staying late most nights to rehearse for their holiday concert.

"So maybe Flossie did the right thing, telling us everything," Laura said, setting a pot of chili on the table. "Mom's been hiding from us, in a way, all these years, and now it's like she's out of the closet. Like Jake," she added with a laugh that she hoped didn't sound too bitter.

"Or it could be that having a stroke was a little mortality wake-up call," Ryder interjected. "Your mom is appreciating everything now."

"Do you think she's ready to talk about a memorial service for Dad?" Anne asked.

"I don't know," Elly said. "When I mentioned it to her yesterday, she bit my head off. I think she's afraid of it, truthfully. She might not be emotionally ready yet to say a final good-bye."

"But why?" Laura said. "What does she care? She has obviously moved on."

"Maybe she has," Elly said. "Or maybe she's just pretending. I still wouldn't put anything past her."

"I'll ask her," Laura said. "I'm going down there tomorrow."

She phoned her mother first thing in the morning, as soon as she was finished turning the horses out and cleaning stalls, to say she was coming.

"Oh, really, that's not necessary," Sarah said. "I'm sure you have a lot on your plate now, dear, with the separation. I wouldn't want to add to your burden."

"Mom, it's fine," Laura argued. "It's not like Jake helped me much around here anyway."

She nearly added that her life was actually easier and happier without Jake in some ways, especially with her sisters around, but refrained. She still hadn't told her mother the real reason behind their separation and wasn't sure how she'd find the courage to admit to her mother that Jake was gay.

"What about the birthday party?" she asked. "Are you still feeling up for it?"

"Sure," Sarah said with unexpected nonchalance. "Nothing to worry about there. It will all go fine with you three girls in charge."

This was strange to hear, Laura thought as she hung up the phone and pulled on her jacket. It wasn't like Sarah to relinquish control of anything. Certainly not of her own birthday party, which, in years past, she'd obsessed about planning for weeks.

There had been a rainstorm the night before. Now the morning glistened clear and bright, but there was wreckage everywhere: tree limbs and leaves, bits of bark. Even a few roof shingles had blown onto the lawn during the storm, Laura noticed. A wonder she didn't hear any of that last night.

The thought of facing the impending winter on her own—clearing snow, keeping the furnace going, having lessons cancel when the roads were impassable—made Laura feel anxious.

But you're not alone, she reminded herself: Anne would be with her. And Kennedy. Tom, too, maybe.

She passed a stand of phragmites. The reeds were tall and yellow this time of year, with thick tufts at the tops. As children, she and her sisters had called them "lion tails" and had tried bringing them into the inn, to their mother's horror. She smiled and texted a photo of them to Tom at his office.

He'd been so sweet, coming around for lunch twice but respecting her wish not to take their relationship anywhere yet. She wanted to give Kennedy more time to adjust to going between her house and Jake's before introducing her to Tom.

"It's too soon for anything more," Laura had said as she walked Tom to his car after lunch yesterday. "I'm sorry. I hope you're not disappointed."

"It's fine," he said, then grinned and waggled his eyebrows. "I'm happy to wait. Just seeing those photos of you was enough to steam up my glasses and keep me going for years."

The inn was quiet, but Rhonda stood sentry at the desk in her customary crisp blouse and skirt. "I just wanted to say hi to my mother," Laura said, tugging her fleece down around her hips and suddenly aware that she smelled strongly of barn.

"She's in her apartment," Rhonda said. "Don't tire her out before her big party!"

Rhonda, Betty, and the rest of the staff at Folly Cove had rallied around Sarah since her stroke. They were her family, too, Laura thought.

"Thanks for looking after her, Rhonda," Laura said with a smile.

Her mother's apartment was accessible from inside the inn, but instead of following the long hallway to the north wing, Laura went back outside and around to the apartment's outside door. Her mother always preferred visitors to come in that way.

This end of the inn was shaded by birch trees in summer, a thick grove of them. Now, with the leaves gone, the birches gleamed white against the deep blue sky, like pale arms swimming through space. Laura remembered how she and her sisters had peeled the bark away from the birches, pretending they were Indian maidens as they inked secret messages to each other.

Odd how those fleeting memories of childhood were resurfacing with increasing frequency, now that Anne and Elly were here, as if the physical presence of her sisters gave Laura's mind permission to open doors long closed. Surprisingly, many of those doors opened onto happy times.

Her mother's door was unlocked when she tried it, so Laura called, "It's me, Mom," and walked into the living room.

Her mother was lying on the couch, her white hair thick and loose around her shoulders. She wore a gold satin dressing gown and, beneath it, white pajamas and white fur mules. She had the satisfied, sleepy expression of a cat purring in the sun.

"Wow," Laura said. "You look good, Mom." She glanced around the room and saw the rumpled bed through the doorway to her mother's bedroom. She quickly looked away again, wondering if her mother had actually entertained Rhonda's uncle here for more than just tea. She suspected the answer was yes.

Sarah's lips twitched at Laura's expression. "I *should* look good. Everyone has been taking such good care of me."

"I'm glad." Laura was surprised by the surge of anger traveling up her spine and making it impossible for her to sit down. Where did that spring from? She'd been working so hard to let go of her anger— toward Jake and her father, and toward her mother, too. But it was definitely still there.

She paced the room. "It was scary, seeing you in the hospital like that." She stopped and looked at her mother. "But not as scary as some of the things Flossie told us."

Sarah looked up at her, blinking hard. "You sound very angry, Laura."

"I am! How could I not be?" Laura unclenched her hands when she realized she was holding them in fists at her sides and tried to take a deeper breath. "There's so much you hid from us! You never told us where you were from. Or that you had a sister! And you never told us that you'd been in touch with Dad, even when we asked you where he was. You even let us believe he could be dead!"

"And now he is," Sarah said quietly, and began weeping, her narrow shoulders folding forward.

"Oh, Mom." Laura tried to cling to her fury, but the sight of her mother—so frail, hunched like that, her ankles impossibly thin, the knob of her spine clearly visible now with her head bent like that— made her own throat tighten. Her mother was an old woman. An old woman who had done some stupid things.

An old woman who was the only mother she'd ever have.

"Come on, don't cry, Mom," she said, and sank to the couch then, nudging her mother's feet over so she had room to sit.

"How can you expect me not to cry when you're *yelling* at me like that?" Her mother lifted her face. The mascara trailed down it in black threads.

This was so similar to something Kennedy might say to her that Laura nearly laughed. "I'm sorry, Mom. Come on. Wipe your eyes."

She reached over and pulled a tissue out of the box on the end table. Maybe this was the way life worked, Laura thought: your mother raised you, and then it was your turn to take care of her. As simple as that.

Her mother took the tissue and dabbed at her eyes. "I'm a sight, I bet."

"No. You look like you've been crying, that's all. But you're still you."

"Oh. Great." Sarah balled up the tissue and stuffed it into her pocket, sniffing.

"So what is it? Were you really crying because I yelled at you? Or were you crying over Dad?"

"Both, I guess, but more over him. We made such a mess of things, he and I. But you know what makes me the maddest?"

Laura shook her head.

"All this time when I thought I was so independent, I was actually waiting for Neil to come home, and I didn't even know it until now."

"Because you loved him so much?"

Her mother shrugged. "I suppose there was love. But, more than that, I wanted to show him he was wrong, you know? I was waiting for the day your father would walk back into the Folly Cove Inn and say, 'Wow. She did it. This joint is a palace.' I wanted him to eat his words, all those horrible things he said about how I would fail because the inn was a curse on the Bradfords."

Laura smiled. "He would have. This place is beautiful. And you did it all yourself."

"With your help, of course. All you girls. I couldn't have done it without the three of you."

"It might have been easier without us kids around."

"Different. But not necessarily easier. Of course, I'm the one who screwed things up, too. I know that. But I still couldn't figure a way out of it all."

"What do you mean?"

Her mother sighed and finally lifted her gaze from the floor, slowly turning her head toward Laura. It was unnerving, like watching a doll come to life. "It's true what Flossie told you girls. I lied to your father and his family about everything: my own family, my education, my history with men. Do you know that your father actually thought I was a virgin?"

Laura had to laugh. "You're kidding."

Sarah looked offended. "It wasn't so far-fetched. There were more virgins back in those days. And remember that he thought I was ten years younger. It was plausible. That's the thing I've discovered about lying: you've got to keep the untruths as plausible as the truth."

"I'll remember that," Laura said, rolling her eyes.

"That's why Jake fooled us for so long, you know," Sarah said suddenly, sitting up a little straighter. "He made every lie he told seem possible: the dental school loans, the insurance costs, his office overhead. That's why we never guessed what he was really up to. I should have known he was gay. Such a pretty dresser and all."

Laura covered her face briefly with one hand. "So you know."

"I figured it out." Her mother gave her a sharp glance. "You weren't going to tell me, I know. But I've had time to think about it, since you told me about the separation. What he did to you is unforgivable. But I suppose you'll have to be civil to him for Kennedy's sake. That's the way divorce is done these days. I just hope you have a good lawyer."

"We haven't actually made it to the legal part yet. We're still talking."

"Well, believe me, having a lawyer sooner is better than later," Sarah said. "I'll set you up. I know somebody."

"Okay. Thank you." Laura looked at her curiously. "So are you ready to have a memorial service for Dad? Elly wants to do it before she goes back to California."

"She's going back?"

Laura nodded. "But Ryder says if they try it out there for another year and she wants to come east after that, he'll move with her."

Sarah's face broke into a smile. "The Viking. I'm glad she held on to that one."

"Yes, I like him, too." She patted her mother's foot. "So what about a service?"

"You fix it. I'll show up. Whenever you want. So long as it's after my party."

"Good." Laura started to stand up, but her mother reached over and encircled her wrist with bony fingers.

"Wait," she said. "About the lies, there are a couple of other things I want to tell you. My biggest regrets of all."

"Okay. I'm listening." Laura felt herself tense up again.

"First off, I'm sorry I never told you about my struggles." Sarah looked away, swallowing hard, her pale forehead gleaming in the morning sunlight, her delicate profile sharp.

"Your struggles?" Laura had no idea what her mother meant.

"My depression, or my breakdowns or whatever." She shrugged a little. "I've had to fight the blues all my life. Singing helped, but medication helped more." She turned to look at Laura again, her gaze very direct now. "I worry you might have those same lows I had. You know what I'm talking about?"

Laura clasped her hands on her jeans and nodded. "I do."

"I don't want you to suffer like I did. There's help for that sort of thing. There's no shame in asking for it." Her mother's voice was fierce now. "Your aunt Flossie, believe it or not, with all her love of nature and no makeup, and anti this and anti that, she's the one who helped me decide it was okay to take the pills when we found what worked. So now I'm telling you. If you need help, ask me, and I'll see that you get it. I'm not kidding here."

Stunned, Laura reached for her mother's hand again, needing to touch her, to convey all the gratitude she felt but couldn't say. "Okay."

Sarah nodded, her voice brisk again. "Good."

"What's your other regret? You said you had two."

"More than that. So much more. But the biggest regret is that I lied about my sister," Sarah said softly. "Joanie. I wish I'd kept in touch with her." There was a note of longing in her mother's voice that Laura had never heard before.

"You do? Why?"

"Oh, for all sorts of reasons," Sarah said. "I wish I'd seen Joanie grow up. I haven't seen her since she was nineteen. Now she's a mother and a widow. Probably a grandmother, too. And I wish I'd helped her. I couldn't have done much for her financially—she married a wealthy man—but Joanie was sweet and always thought the best of people. I watch you girls and wonder now what it would have been like, having a sister all my life."

"At least you have Flossie," Laura said, not knowing any other way to comfort her. It was true: losing a sister would be terrible. It would be like losing a part of yourself.

"Yes. Flossie's a pain in my side, but she's *my* pain." Sarah smiled and gripped Laura's hand harder. Her fingers were cool and slim, but strong. "Most of all, I wish I could have been as good to my little sister as you've been to yours," she said.

"Oh, Mom," Laura said.

The two of them sat together on the couch in silence then, watching the birch trees beyond the window sway in the wind.

Sarah had provided entertainment for many parties, both as a singer and as the owner of the Folly Cove Inn, with her daughters as a trio. But from the moment her birthday party began she was astonished at their talent.

Such a credit to her, the guests said.

"Oh, well, your birthday comes only once a year, and my girls insisted on going all out for this party!" Sarah said, smiling graciously at each and every one of the wonderful people at her party.

Only that nosy art association president, Rose, had commented on her age. "Sixty-five, imagine that!" she'd said. "Did you ever think you'd get this old, back when you were their age?" She nodded toward Sarah's daughters, who were, thankfully, out of earshot.

Sarah laughed and lowered her voice, pretending to be conspiratorial. "What can you do? Age is just a number. You're as young as you feel. How young do *you* feel, Rose? You don't look a day over sixty! You must take marvelous care of your skin."

Elly had transformed the dining room into a Paris bistro, with

cafés overlooking a street! Anne did a marvelous job singing and dancing to "I Got Rhythm" with Kennedy, and all the girls got together
and did "'S Wonderful." How cute they looked in those oversize suits!
Elly's voice, especially, was as clear and perfectly pitched as ever. Sarah
clapped her hands delightedly after each song.

Dinner, too, was a treat. Roast lamb with mint sauce, mashed potatoes, green beans. All her favorites, and perfectly prepared. And the
cake! Anne had baked it herself: a cake in the shape of the Eiffel Tower!
Everyone cheered when the cake was brought out on a wheeled cart, as
well they should. Her daughter was a master pastry chef!

Sarah made a wish—she'd never tell what it was—and blew out the
candles. The effort left her exhausted, but the applause was worth it.
Then she ate her piece and a few bites of Gil's, too. The girls had looked
surprised to see him—he wasn't on the original invitations mailed out,
of course, because they'd done that before Sarah had known she
wanted him to be included—but she'd gotten around that by saying he
was Rhonda's "plus one."

Even Flossie behaved herself. She wore a clean pair of black trousers and a white blouse, with a green tweedy sort of vest that made her
look like a leprechaun.

The band started after dinner. The lead singer was a friend of Rhonda's, and someone—Elly? Laura?—must have told them to play Sarah's
old jazz favorites. Sarah tapped her foot as she watched Laura slip onto
the dance floor with her new man, whose name Sarah had already forgotten. They seemed well matched. He wasn't tall or especially handsome, but there was something solid and reassuring about him, and he
made Laura smile.

Then Gil asked her to dance. Sarah very nearly said no, because
who would think a man built like this one could be anything but bull-
ish around a dance floor, as he was in life?

Besides, they were playing "I've Got the World on a String," her
absolute favorite song, and the first song she'd ever danced to with
Neil. It would break her heart to dance to it with someone else.

It all came back to Sarah then, how Neil had taken her in his arms
and moved her around the floor of this very dining room as smoothly

as if they'd been dancing together all their lives, even though it was the first time they'd met. She'd sung this song to him from the stage after he'd helped her untangle a microphone cord, and he'd asked the band to play it again, just the instrumental, so he could sing it with her while they danced.

Suddenly, Sarah's eyes were brimming with tears, and she didn't have a tissue. She didn't even know where her purse was!

Now she was in a panic, thinking of her makeup and of how awful it would be to snivel at her own wonderful party. The girls would be upset if she looked unhappy. She didn't want to do that to them, not after all the trouble they'd gone to for her lately.

No, not just lately. Ever since they were children, her daughters had tried hard to please her. It was her turn to try to please them, for once.

So she smiled up at Gil, who had produced a handkerchief for her. Sarah wiped her eyes and said, "I think I'd like to dance after all," and he led her away.

Everyone gathered around the dance floor to watch them, applauding as if she and Gil were young and in love, with their whole lives ahead of them. Sarah sang a little of the tune, making Gil say, "You sing like an angel," and helping her remember that, with music, she could always say what she felt, even when the words failed her.

CHAPTER TWENTY-THREE

"Can you *promise* I won't die on the trail?"

"Jesus, Elly." Laura laughed. "Nobody has died riding with me yet."

"Yeah, and riding General is like riding a *sofa*!" Anne said. "Right, Laura?" She and Laura started laughing.

"Hey. Know what's more annoying than an insider horse joke?" Elly said. "Listening to you two howl like hyenas on crack."

This just made Laura and Anne laugh harder. Elly finally started laughing, too, as she waited for Laura to finish bridling and saddling her horse, trying not to mind that it was big and black, like some fire-breathing devil beast.

Laura led the horse over to the mounting block and helped Elly onto its back. Getting on a horse was harder than it looked, Elly discovered. She launched herself too vigorously into the saddle and probably would have slid right off the other side if Laura hadn't grabbed her calf.

"Easy there, cowgirl," Laura said. "Put your feet in the stirrups. Don't let go of the pommel and you'll be fine."

"What's a pommel?" Elly looked around. The only other time she'd ever been on a horse was at a California dude ranch—a director's mis-conceived idea of a team-bonding exercise for the production company—and that saddle was like a horse recliner, high up in front and back, so there was plenty to hang on to. This saddle was English—she knew that much—and nearly flat.

"The pommel is the front of the saddle," Anne said.

"Oh." Elly tucked one entire hand under there. No way was she letting go.

This whole Sunday-morning riding expedition was not her idea. She was exhausted after their mother's birthday party last night and would have happily spent the day sprawled on Laura's sofa in front of the fireplace, watching baby Lucy chew on the Sunday paper and maybe dragging Ryder back to bed if the house emptied out. But she was flying back to California next Sunday with him, and this was the last day all of them were free, since Laura and Anne were working during the week and they were planning to scatter Dad's ashes on Saturday.

Two of the production gigs she'd been pursuing by phone had led to interviews with producers; one was for a TV spot, and the other was for a music video with a new talent from Australia. Ryder had convinced Elly to check them out. He had also assured her that he would consider moving to New England if she wanted to do that instead of staying in L.A.

"Why on earth would you want to do that?" Elly had asked, astounded.

"You've got a lot more water in Massachusetts than in California," Ryder answered. "And a lot more sisters. Plus, no earthquakes or fires."

"We have blizzards. You're forgetting about snow."

"I'd like snow, I think," he'd said. "You could teach me how to make a snow angel. Or an igloo. And I'm sure I could find work around Boston. It could be a good move for us, right?"

"Yeah, sure," she said. "Let's see how enthusiastic you feel about Massachusetts after I bring you home for Christmas and you get to experience the wonder of having to tunnel through six feet of snow in your sneakers."

Finally, Laura got Elly settled on General and instructed her about the reins. This seemed pretty easy: all she had to do was pull the rein on the right and the horse turned that way. Ditto on the left. Easier than driving a car.

They set off down the road, walking the horses single file along the shoulder since Route 127 was only two lanes. Elly didn't really need to steer the horse at all, since General plodded along with his nose practically buried in the tail of Anne's horse.

Anne was riding one of the boarders, a mare with the mysterious name of Cadno. The name meant "Fox" in Welsh, Laura said, which made sense, given the horse's shiny rust color. Laura's horse, Star, was a pretty mahogany color; his coat gleamed like polished wood. But Elly was glad she wasn't riding him. That horse pranced like he was on springs.

Elly had never bothered to learn to ride; she was too entranced by voice and dance lessons. Anne rode for a while, but she had never trained like Laura, and preferred riding the trails. Elly had once seen her little sister sitting backward on a horse. Another time, Anne had stood right up on a horse's bare back as it trotted around a ring.

Now Elly tried to imitate Anne's relaxed seat in the saddle. Though, unlike Anne, who didn't bother with stirrups despite Laura's admonishments, Elly kept her feet jammed in the metal rings.

As they rode, they discussed the party—all of them agreed it had gone better than they'd hoped and that Mom seemed happy—and talked about the sweet weirdness of watching Sarah dance with Gil toward the end of the night.

"God, they were like one of those old couples you see in Viagra ads on TV," Laura said. "I mean, that guy couldn't take his eyes off her!"

"Please do *not* put that image in my head," Elly said. She turned around to look at Laura, resting her hand on General's wide black rump. This horse really *was* like riding a sofa. A rocking sofa. Somebody should invent that.

"Yeah, and when I dropped Lucy off at Flossie's this morning, she told me Gil spent last night with Mom," Anne added.

"Wow," Elly said as they turned down the main trail leading to the tip of Halibut Point. (She'd refused on principle to ride in Dogtown, even with her sister-guards.) "You don't think this is some kind of sympathy screw? I mean, since Mom had a stroke and she's a widow, and his wife's dead, it's like the perfect Lifetime movie, right? Or a Nicholas Sparks novel for seniors."

"A sympathy screw? Elly, ick!" Anne groaned.

"And who would be the one granting it, anyway?" Laura demanded.

"It's got to be Mom," Elly said. "She feels sorry for him because he's a widower. Guys don't know what to do when their wives leave them or die."

"Or maybe Gil feels sorry for *her*, because she had such a crap childhood and then her husband took off and died before coming home," Anne said.

"Well, either way, they're perfect for each other," Laura pronounced.

"What about Saturday? Do you think she'll actually come when we scatter Dad's ashes?" Elly asked.

"She told me she will," Laura said. "Flossie says she'll help make sure Mom's there. I mean, it's kind of strange that we're not having a memorial service for him until summer, but I'm guessing Dad would rather have us spread his ashes now than leave him in the closet until then."

They all laughed. Elly let her back relax a little more but kept a firm grip on the reins as they circled around to the far side of the Babson Farm Quarry, with its piano-sized chunks of granite piled here and there.

From there they passed the fire tower, then continued down a trail toward the water. The vegetation here consisted mostly of marsh grass and shrubs. Elly tried to remember the names their father had taught them—catbrier, shadbush, arrowwood, and bayberry—and wished she could remember which was which.

It was a clear day, but colder than the previous week. The wind here was fierce now that they were out from the shelter of the trees. Sea spray slammed against the rocks below and they had to shout to be heard. They stopped the horses for a few minutes to watch the birds feeding close to shore, mostly grebes and loons.

Elly told them about her job prospects in L.A., but of course all they wanted to hear about was Ryder. That made her start teasing Laura about Tom. Elly wanted to ask Anne about Sebastian—he'd be able to name these stupid bushes, for sure—but she didn't dare. She hadn't seen Sebastian at their mother's birthday party, even though Paige came with her husband.

Last night, when Elly and Ryder were getting ready for bed, she'd asked him why Sebastian hadn't come, but he'd only shrugged. "I don't know," he said. "I thought he would. We talked about it. But the guy's a cipher. Maybe your sister's better off without him."

Anne had either been too busy at the party to notice Sebastian's absence, or else she was resigned to the fact that he wasn't into her. Either way, Ryder was probably right.

"Hey, Elly," Laura called from behind her. "Ready to put the pedal to the metal?"

"Are you kidding? No way!" Elly patted her horse's neck. "General and I are happy poking along. We'll watch, if you two want to go crazy and race around."

"It doesn't work that way with horses," Laura said. "They're pack animals. If we let our horses run, General's going to want to come along."

"Come on, Elly!" Anne said. "It'll be fun. And what can happen if you're between us? It's not like General can go anywhere."

"Wait," Elly said. "Let me think about this: no."

They continued badgering her as they rode along Ipswich Bay, where it was clear enough to see the Isles of Shoals off the coast of New Hampshire and even Mount Agamenticus in Maine. Finally, as they turned away from the water along the path leading to Gott Avenue, Elly caved.

"Just for a minute, though. And if you hear screaming, put on the brakes."

"Got it," Laura said. "Go on, Anne. I'll stay behind her and make sure she doesn't fall off."

"Gee, thanks," Elly said. "I feel so confident now, knowing you'll be galloping behind me. I'll be in the perfect place to get trampled."

Anne laughed. "Relax, Elly. Laura's horse won't trample you. Horses hate getting their hooves messy. And you're going to love this!" Suddenly she was off, urging her horse forward by leaning forward and squeezing her legs against its sides.

General seemed as startled as Elly: he reared his head up in surprise at the sight of Anne dashing away. And then, before Elly could imitate what Anne was doing with her posture and legs, the black horse was running flat out beneath her.

Elly laughed as the wind made her eyes tear. It was an incredible sensation. The horse's gait was so smooth that it felt like they were floating over the rocky trail. So this was why her sisters loved to ride.

"Holy hell, this is great!" she yelled back to Laura. Or at least she thought Laura was back there: she could hear nothing over General's hooves thundering beneath her.

They were gaining on Anne's horse. Then General thrust his head down, and no amount of pulling on the reins slowed his powerful gallop, even though Elly was yelling at him in no uncertain terms, "Whoa! Halt! Stop!" It was like the reins were attached to a concrete pylon.

"Oh, shit, I think he's got the bit between his teeth!" she heard Laura shout behind her.

"What does that even *mean*?" Elly shrieked as General put on another burst of speed, sailing past Anne's horse on the narrow trail.

"He's running away with her," she heard Anne yell as she passed. "He's probably headed back to the barn!"

Well, Elly thought, if that was the case, all she had to do was hang on. Surely General would stop once he reached his stall and grain bin. She didn't have to turn him toward the stable: the horse definitely knew the way. She kept hold of the reins simply so they wouldn't dangle, absurdly worried that he might get his legs caught in them and fall.

They burst out of the trail and onto Gott Avenue, still a dirt road here, but wide enough that Elly didn't have to worry about being wiped off against a tree. She kept her body low against the horse's neck, afraid of throwing him off-balance. There must be a reason jockeys did this, she reasoned, just as she looked up and spotted a Jeep headed their way.

Elly heard Anne yell, "Car!"

Then both sisters were pulling up on their horses alongside her, essentially blocking General in and moving him over to the side of the road as the Jeep jerked to a stop. Anne leaned over and grabbed the black horse's reins.

"Jesus. What are you idiots *doing*?" Sebastian yelled as he climbed out of the Jeep.

"We're okay," Laura called back. "Elly just got a little overexcited with having her own horse and all. She decided to race us back to the barn."

Elly would have glared, but she felt so weak from delayed fright that she found herself sliding off the horse. Regrettably, she forgot to remove both feet from the stirrups before dismounting. The horse was too damn tall. She was left with one foot in the stirrup and the other not quite touching the ground.

"Ow, ow!" she yelped. "Doing the splits here, Sebastian. Help!"

Now Laura and Anne were laughing their hyena howls again, but Elly didn't care. All she could feel was grateful once Sebastian released her foot from the stirrup and caught her as her legs gave way.

Elly turned around to face her sisters. "I am never, ever going to ride with you two maniacs again."

Then she limped away, leaving Sebastian holding the reins, getting as far as the Jeep before she collapsed against it.

Sebastian drove Elly back to the barn. Anne led General, meek as a mouse now, sandwiched tightly between her horse and Laura's.

"You're awfully quiet," Laura said. "Is it because we saw Sebastian, or because we almost killed our sister?"

Anne smiled. "Both," she said. "Though it was worth it, seeing that dismount at the end."

"Talk to him," she said gently. "He needs to know how you feel."

"How can I tell him that when I don't even *know* how I feel?" Anne said.

"Oh, I think you do."

They reached the driveway to Laura's house a few minutes later. Anne didn't know whether to be relieved or exasperated to see that Sebastian's Jeep was already gone. "He must have dumped Elly off like a sack of laundry," she said. "He was probably scared to see me."

"Yeah, well, you're a scary woman," Laura said, looking at her over General's back. Her eyes were shadowed by her velvet riding helmet, but Anne could see that she was smiling. "Go to him, Anne," she said. "What's the worst that can happen? You get hurt?"

"Yes!" Anne said.

"Look, it's time you learned something from your big sister, since you never listened to me when we were kids," Laura said. "Don't make the same mistake I did. Don't wait around for something good to happen. Go after what you want. Tell Sebastian exactly how you feel and what you need. Then listen to him. If things don't work out after that, at least it won't be because the two of you were keeping secrets."

Anne considered this as she helped Laura untack and groom the horses. She thought about it some more as she took her time in the shower and then dressed in her favorite jeans and a soft blue sweater Laura had given her from a pile of Kennedy's castoffs.

Finally she called Aunt Flossie to see if she could keep Lucy a little longer, then asked Laura if she could borrow the car.

Laura waved her off with a grin. "Atta girl. Go get him!"

Elly, who had just finished nursing her sore limbs in a hot bath, said, "We expect a full report when you get back!"

Anne half expected Sebastian's Jeep to be gone when she arrived at his house, but it was parked in front. Mack was on the lawn; he barked when he saw her, then wagged his tail and trotted over to greet her. Mack leaned against her legs and wriggled with pleasure as Anne rubbed his ears.

"If only your owner were as easy to please as you are, I'd be all set," she said.

"I might be, if you rubbed my ears like that."

Anne looked up and saw that Sebastian had come down the front stairs. He wore jeans and a black sweater that made his hair look copper in the sunlight.

"Who are you kidding?" she said. "You're too skittish. You'd run away."

He smiled, but his hazel eyes were shadowed and solemn. "Is Elly okay? I had to help her into the house."

"Seems like you're always rescuing one of the Bradford women," Anne said lightly. "I guess Laura will be next."

Sebastian laughed. "I doubt it. The Bradford women hardly ever need rescuing," he said. "Especially when the three of you are together. Or should I say five, counting your mom and Flossie?"

"I think Flossie probably counts for two," Anne said.

"Agreed."

"I was coming from your house when you saw me before," Sebastian said. "I felt bad about not going to your mother's party. I wanted to apologize."

"You could have called."

"I wanted to see you," he said, then corrected himself. "I *needed* to see you, Anne."

There was a brief silence. Anne could hear the dog panting. Mack grinned his doggy grin as he turned his head from Sebastian to her and back again, until they both had to laugh.

"I think my dog is trying to figure out whether you're coming inside," Sebastian said.

"Am I?" Anne stopped patting the dog but still had trouble meeting Sebastian's eyes.

The problem was that when she looked at him, she wanted to know everything: how he'd ripped one knee of his jeans, where he'd bought the leather watch he wore on his left wrist, whether that scar on his ear meant he'd once had it pierced.

And, most of all, how he would respond if she were to walk up to him right now and press her body against his.

"It's kind of a mess," Sebastian was saying. "The house."

"It's a nice house," Anne protested absurdly. How did she know it was nice? Only because it was Sebastian's. "I mean, it's nice on the outside. And I don't care if it's a mess. I live with Lucy, remember. Living with a baby means living with mess."

He laughed. "Then come in," he said, and led her up the porch steps, where he held the door open for her to go inside first.

Or she *would* have entered first, if Mack hadn't forced his way past her legs, his tail thudding so hard that Anne felt it knock against her knees as she lost her balance.

Sebastian caught her before she hit the doorjamb, wrapping his arm around her waist from behind. And then he went very, very still, with Anne's hips pressed against him, the wind sighing in the pines behind them.

"Is this your idea of inviting me in?" Anne said finally.

"I think it is," Sebastian said.

Then he turned her around and kissed her. His kiss was brief but warm. Then Sebastian sighed as Anne leaned against him, reaching up to put her arms around his neck.

She kissed him next. Anne leaned so far forward that she fell off the step, trusting him to catch her, feeling nearly suspended in air as her body met his and they were caught together in this one moment in space and time where all that came before simply didn't matter. They were here now.

Before they walked down to the beach, Flossie insisted on being the one to open the box of remains. "It's addressed to me," she said when Sarah argued that she was Neil's wife. "You can't open another person's mail, Sarah. That's against the law."

"Since when have *you* cared about laws?" Sarah said. "You teach yoga without a license. You should be arrested for encouraging people to meditate instead of being useful." But she'd stepped aside with the girls while Flossie took a letter opener shaped like a mermaid and began sawing at the tape like she was carving ham.

Finally Flossie got the box open. And then there was plastic and Bubble Wrap to deal with, a lot of it, and suddenly ashes were rising in a black plume because Flossie had cut through the plastic, too.

Everyone stepped back as if the box might detonate here in Flossie's cluttered living room, which in some ways would have been a mercy to the planet, Sarah thought, given the absurd amount of junk in here.

"Why didn't Neil think to use an urn, at least?" Sarah fretted, so she wouldn't have to say the obvious: nothing inside that box looked like her husband.

"Well, it's not like Dad packaged himself up for mailing," Laura said, and then she and her sisters looked at each other and started that laugh-crying thing the three of them had been doing since they arrived.

"Mom!" Kennedy said. "Get a grip!"

Finally Sarah and Flossie agreed, after some discussion and a little more arguing, to carry the box down to Folly Cove as it was. Flossie handed the box to Sarah, but when she felt how heavy it was, she handed it back. She'd never make it down to the beach if she had to lug her husband.

She was the only one who'd truly dressed appropriately for the occasion, in a black lace dress she'd ordered online. It was a Diane von Furstenberg, fitted, with a zipper down the back and a scalloped hem. Classy. And besides, Diane was a woman Sarah had long admired for marrying that prince and deciding to start her own business. Now, *that* was a role model.

But the shoes were a mistake, sling-backs that slid on the rocks as if the soles were made of ice. She finally waited until her daughters, Flossie, and even Kennedy with the baby were all walking in front of her, Laura carrying Neil's remains now at the head of the line. Then Sarah took off the shoes and carried them.

Not that the others were in any position to judge her attire. They'd agreed that Neil would want this to be informal, just family, and that they'd do things more properly for the memorial service in June. Flossie had worn probably her best yoga clothes, the ones that weren't so faded. Laura and Kennedy were in jeans and jackets.

Anne was dressed in her kitchen uniform, those checked pants so loose they looked like pajama bottoms. Her blue jacket set off her red hair so it flamed against the sky, the curls everywhere, reminding Sarah of how Neil had looked on the beach, always hatless and happy.

Only Elly had dressed the way a Bradford girl should, in a short black skirt that showed off her legs and tall black boots over her tights, with a fitted green jacket and striped scarf.

But there was nobody to see them anyway, down here at Folly Cove in November on the gold beach. So Sarah set her shoes down on one of the big flat rocks and dug her toes into the sand.

She had never learned to swim. The reason she always sent Neil down to the beach with her daughters was one she'd never told them: because it terrified Sarah to see her little girls in the maw of this great growling beast of water, their pale limbs tossed this way and that, their sleek little seal heads bobbing and disappearing until Sarah was numb with fright as she watched them with their father in the waves.

Maybe she would tell them this one day. Her girls should know that their mother had held herself watchfully apart sometimes not because she didn't care, but because she loved them with a tenderness that felt like fury and wanted to protect them and provide for them in ways nobody had ever done for her, as if she could spread some kind of force field of love that would shield them from all the hurts in the world.

Laura was opening the box now, and the girls began lifting handfuls of Neil to the wind. They let their father's ashes mix with the green surf, serious at first, and then laughing as the ashes swirled around them like black smoke, these three women who were so different and so much a part of her that Sarah felt her heart would break and mend and break again as she watched her daughters lose themselves in this moment, with the vast and beautiful sea flinging itself at their feet.

ACKNOWLEDGMENTS

I am fortunate to have the support of so many generous people, especially my husband, Dan. He makes me believe in myself as a writer, even during times when I drop my head onto the desk in despair. He also keeps producing meals so wonderful that I feel rewarded at the end of the day, no matter how my writing has gone.

My mother turned me into a reader inspired to write. She read constantly and across a wide variety of genres while I was growing up, and never tried to censor what I read. Mom is still my first and most important critic, because I value her honesty and insights. She's also an ace navigator when I'm researching a setting.

My children are the reason I live and breathe—Drew, Blaise, Taylor, Maya, and Aidan—and their boundless enthusiasm for my work helps keep me going. So do their own adventures, which they're so generous about sharing with me.

My wonderful extended family—all of you Cooksons, Boyles, Schneiders, and Robinsons—include the best cheerleaders any writer could ever have.

Susanna Einstein, my agent, deserves my deepest gratitude for her sharp editing eye, witty insights, and a cheerful willingness to entertain any book projects I suggest—even the insane ones. I am so blessed to have found her.

At Penguin Random House, I want to thank my dear friend and editor, Tracy Bernstein, who astonishes me every day for more reasons than I can list here. When Tracy took a leave, editor Katherine Pelz kindly stepped in to usher this manuscript into its final stages—I am indebted to her as well. Many thanks also to the entire Berkley/New American Library team, especially Claire Zion and Frank Walgren.

In addition to my in-house publicist, Caitlin Valenziano, I have Rachel Tarlow Gul of Over the River Public Relations to thank for helping me reach readers. And I am lucky to count many brilliant women in my community of writers. First and foremost: Emily Ferrara, who helped me explore Rockport, bought me a writing retreat for my birthday, and contributed her wonderful poem to the book. Susan Straight, Maddie Dawson, and Toby Neal also provided their friendship and support as they tirelessly critiqued drafts of this novel and kept me company on writing retreats.

Other writers and editors have been gracious with their support. Special thanks to Karma Brown, Elisabeth Elo, Amy Sue Nathan, and Sonja Yoerg, as well as to the Tall Poppy Writers, the Girlfriends' Book Club, and the booksellers and readers who support authors everywhere.

FOLLY COVE

HOLLY ROBINSON

A CONVERSATION WITH HOLLY ROBINSON

Q. Folly Cove *revolves around broken families and secrets that shatter relationships. Many of your other novels feature families that are anything but mainstream and happy, too. Why is that?*

A. Most novelists write fiction that springs from our own experiences. After my parents divorced, my father married another woman; he then left her and remarried my mom. I was also divorced from my first husband, but he and I stayed friends. My second marriage blended my two children with my husband's two, and then we had another son together. Writing fiction allows me to explore complicated family constructs. I hope my books help others learn that it's possible to find peace, love, and happiness in a family, even if the relationships continue changing shape in surprising ways.

Q. Like most of your previous books, Folly Cove *is set on the North Shore of Massachusetts. What do you find so compelling about this setting?*

A. I must have been a New England sea captain in a former life. The moment I drove north of Boston, it felt like coming home. There is a rich sense of history here, because people began to settle this part of the country in the 1600s. You can see that history in the antique houses and old mills, and in the moss-covered stone walls threading through the woods. I love the area around Folly Cove—a real place near Rockport—because of the granite quarries. I look at the giant blocks of granite lying around these quarries and marvel at the enormous effort it must have taken to cut them up and ship them down to Salem and Boston. Dogtown is full of mystery, too, with its ancient foundations and tales of women living on their own with just dogs for company.

Q. *In* Folly Cove, *you've created two strong-willed women in their seventies—Sarah and Flossie—who, despite their differences, are almost like sisters. They also seem to have robust working lives and intimate relationships with men. It's unusual to find women this age in novels. What prompted you to write about them?*

A. My mom. She is funny, wise, and very elegant besides—and she's in her eighties. I spend a lot of time with her and occasionally do things with her friends. These women are amazing storytellers and have fascinating experiences to share. I think there should be more older characters in fiction. Besides, I believe in second chances, especially when it comes to love and friendship, which both Sarah and Flossie get here.

Q. *Why did you choose to tell the book from four points of view?*

A. Ha! If I had known how hard it was going to be, I would have cut myself off at two! Originally, I was going to tell the story just from Anne's point of view. Her voice came to me first. Then her sisters kept demanding to be in the book, and I thought the conflicts between them would make for a tense, compelling read. I had reached the three-quarter mark in writing the novel when suddenly Sarah's voice started clamoring in my head. I had to start over from the very beginning of the book, but it was a good choice in the end, because it allows us to know more about why Sarah made the choices she did in raising her daughters.

Q. What's your approach to writing novels? Do you craft a synopsis first, or just write the story and see how it develops?

A. I do both. I often write a synopsis first—some of the most challenging writing I ever do, because it takes so much thinking and planning, and the writing is awful. Then, as I write the manuscript, the plot morphs as the characters start taking over. That's a more instinctive process. Sometimes it feels like you're strapped to the top of a locomotive, and other times it feels like you're pickaxing your way up an icy mountain.

Q. Has it gotten easier for you to write a novel, now that you've written so many?

A. Oh, how I wish! Sadly, writing novels is like having children: just because your labor is harder with one child than another, it's no guarantee that this child will be more special.

QUESTIONS FOR DISCUSSION

1. Why do you think Laura believed her husband, Jake, when he told her Anne tried to seduce him? What would you do if your husband said that about your own sister?

2. The sisters all have different relationships with their mother, Sarah, yet each of them feels like she's a disappointment to her. Do you think Sarah loved her daughters equally? Is it even possible to love your children equally?

3. Laura stayed with Jake for many years despite the fact that he didn't seem to desire her physically. What kept her in the marriage? Should she have left him sooner?

4. Were you disappointed by the resolution with Neil, or do you think it was better that the novel ended this way?

5. Two of the sisters, Anne and Elly, have lived away from home, while the third sister, Laura, stayed. How did leaving Folly Cove change Anne and Elly? Do you think it's important to live away from the place where you grew up? Why or why not?

6. Why do you think Flossie stayed on at Folly Cove despite the tensions between her and Sarah? How would you describe the relationship between these two women?

7. If you had to predict what these characters will be doing five years after the novel ends, what would you say?

Photo by Meg Manion

Holly Robinson is the author of the novels *Chance Harbor*, *Haven Lake*, *Beach Plum Island*, *The Wishing Hill*, *Sleeping Tigers*, and a memoir, *The Gerbil Farmer's Daughter*. She is an NPR commentator and a journalist whose work appears in publications such as the Huffington Post, *More*, *Parents*, *Publishers Weekly*, and *Redbook*.